New Friends and Hidden Spies

The Modern Warlock Series, Book Two

Stone Keye

Dragon Tech Media

Dragon Tech Media
Saint Gabriel, LA

Cover Design by Steven Novak
ISBN: 978-1-7348585-0-1
First Edition: April 2020

DEDICATION

To Moose,

My truck-riding, snack-sharing, frisbee-playing companion who has been a great source of inspiration.

OTHER BOOKS BY STONE KEYE

The Modern Warlock, The Lion and The Hidden Master, Book One

The Modern Warlock, The Dragon and The Lost King, Book Three

The Modern Warlock, Book Four (mid 2021)

Death's Arbiter (Early 2021)

Looking for more information? Visit www.StoneKeyeBooks.net to get latest information on all of my books.

Chapter One

Jason took a deep breath to clear his mind. He had hoped that upon his return, things would be quiet. Home for only a few minutes and already an issue to deal with. Hopefully, this would turn out to be nothing, but it seemed that wherever he went, trouble followed. You would think that there should be a rule that says, after killing multiple people that wanted to kill you, you receive an automatic six months of quiet. He'd never been that lucky.

"Do you want some back-up?" Guilford asked.

"No, I think I got this. But if things go bad, feel free to join in. But leave the hat, I think it might get in the way." Jason smirked. When Jason first met Guilford, he was wearing a hat that looked like a cross between a leather cowboy hat and a Santa cap.

"As for the things that are trying to break in, don't worry, they aren't dangerous. As for my hat, it goes everywhere with me," Guilford said with a wink.

Jason gave his girlfriend Catie a quick kiss. She had been his rock when his life had fallen apart. He met her when one of his friends had convinced him to have a drink at a bar. Jason didn't want to go, preferring to hide at home, but eventually relented. It wasn't long after they arrived at the bar that he spotted Catie walking in with her friends. He couldn't take his eyes off of her and watched her all night. He loved the way she tossed her long sandy-blonde hair and she had curves he longed to explore. He wanted to go talk to her, but his courage failed him. At the end of the night, she walked over to him.

"I have been waiting all night for you to come over and talk to me," Catie stated putting her hands on her hips.

Jason tried to respond but only came out with, "I, uh, like your shoes."

Jason's friend slapped his forehead in disbelief.

"Well, thanks, I guess. Anything else you like about me?" Catie asked, almost laughing.

Finally, Jason's courage came back to him. "You mean, besides your beautiful eyes and a smile that stops my heart?" Jason replied, then blushed after realizing what he had just said.

Catie paused. "Much better. My name is Catie by the way," she said, and Jason could feel his face turning a neon red. "Here's my number. After the shoes comment, I want a steak dinner at a nice restaurant." She started to walk away then turned back. "Oh, and yes, Saturday night would be perfect."

They had been together ever since.

Shaking his head, Jason pulled himself back to the present and walked out the back door. Looking at the time on his phone, it was close to noon. When he left the Castle a few minutes prior, it was around eight in the morning. He noted the time differential for future reference. Stepping onto his back porch, he paused to enjoy the warm sun. It was a nice day for late winter. A bark came from behind and Bull ran up.

"Thanks for coming, bud," Jason said, glad to spend some quiet time with his dog. Bull was a Labrador-mix, big, black, and with a heart of gold. Bull was also a Laciter, a magical race sworn to protect earth and its realm. Normally, Bull used his dog form but when needed, he would revert to his Laciter form that looked like a huge wolf-like creature.

Jason could have Stepped to where the intruders were, but whatever was trying to get through his property's protective barrier, wasn't making any progress and he needed time to clear his head. The barrier was the first spell he had ever cast, and it would need to be replaced with something stronger. But dealing with the would-be intruders was his first priority. He suspected that Guilford had sent the intruders to test Jason. Exactly what the test was, he didn't know.

The would-be invaders were on the far side of his property, which meant cutting through his woods. He loved spending time there and walking through them would be good for his soul.

Without really thinking about it, Jason camouflaged his warlock uniform to look like jeans and a t-shirt. He really did like his uniform but didn't think it would fit in with his neighborhood. His nosy neighbor would be all over the gossip channel if she saw him in it.

Bull bounded about and kept bringing him sticks to play fetch. Jason added a little magic to give his throws some extra distance. With Bull being a magical creature, he responded by putting on a burst of speed. Returning the sticks in seconds, ready for the next throw. If anyone was watching, it would be a problem trying to explain Bull's speed. Jason had detected no one nearby but kept an eye out.

Jason slowed his pace as he entered his woods. Despite the locals believing the area haunted, he always loved his walks there. Now the woods felt different. It still felt welcoming and peaceful, but with his senses up he detected magic throughout the area. In some ways the rumors were true, there was magic in this place, a lot of it.

Bull stopped and barked. *They know you are here. Be nice!* Bull said.

Jason stopped and gave Bull a confused look. He then watched as an orb appeared. It was bright white and quickly broke into several smaller orbs that spun around and then reassembled back into one. It did this several times before the orb rushed toward him. Instinctively he put up his shield to block whatever was coming at him. Even with his shield he could feel the emotions emanating from whatever now spun around him. Joy, love, and happiness to name just a few gushed from the entity.

Jason. Family, the orb said.

Bull looked at him and nodded. Jason lowered his shield and the orb split into multiple, smaller orbs. The orbs slowly approached.

Connect, the orbs said.

Jason slowly opened his senses and waited for the orbs to connect. The orbs slammed into his mental wall and instinctively he pushed back. It didn't feel like he was being attacked. It felt more like rambunctious puppies wanting attention.

Go slow, Jason warned.

The orbs stopped; a single orb reached out to connect with him. Even with just the single orb, a huge amount of emotions and information flooded over him. He took slow, deep breaths to regulate the flow and keep the connection from overwhelming him. Finally, he managed to control the incoming flood and started to understand what it was trying to tell him.

The information came in the form of emotions and images. From what he could guess, the orbs were multiple magical beings that lived in the forest and had been waiting for the day to talk with him. Jason watched as images of the would-be attackers appeared. He could feel the orb trying to tell him that the attackers were really friends. There was more it wanted to say but he needed to learn how to communicate with it better.

"Well, I guess we need to invite our new friends in, but just in case, I will need to confirm they mean no harm."

Happiness flowed from the orbs, then they reassembled into one orb and led Jason to where the attackers were. He promptly followed.

As he approached the intruders, he camouflaged himself so he could have a little time to assess them without them seeing him. There were four of them, each about five-foot-tall. They were using some sort of spell to make them look human. Using his magic, he looked past their spell, finding the intruders were anything but human. The fingers on their hands looked more like short claws and their eyes were bright gray. The most noticeable feature was their heads. They were larger than a humans, with what looked like ram's horns embedded in their skulls. Sensing nothing that could be considered dangerous he dropped his camouflage and walked over to greet them.

They were so engrossed in their efforts to get past his property's barrier, they failed to notice him walk right up to them. As he approached, he could hear them arguing with each other about the best way to get past the barrier. He waited a full minute for them to notice him but when they didn't, he decided he had waited long enough.

"Gentleman, is there something I can help you with?" Each stopped what they were doing and looked at him.

"Are you a warlock?" one asked.

"Of course he is, just look at the uniform," another said.

"Just because he is wearing a warlock outfit doesn't necessarily make him a warlock," the first replied.

"How many times have you seen someone wearing a warlock uniform that wasn't a warlock?" the other countered.

The argument went on for a minute and was quickly leading to a fight. The two started pawing the ground, making deep growling noises. Jason decided he couldn't afford for them to draw attention from his neighbors.

"Yes, actually, I am a Senior and am studying to be a Master someday. Who and what are you and why are you here?" Jason asked.

This caused the four to stop their bickering, so Jason continued. "To be clear, from my perspective I have found four intruders trying to break into my property. If I don't get answers soon you will see what a Senior can do to his enemies."

After Guilford's comment about them, Jason didn't believe these four creatures were dangerous, but he hoped his threat would help them concentrate.

One of the creatures stepped forward. With a hint of gray hair and his wrinkled face, he looked older than the rest. Jason guessed he was their leader.

"My name is difficult to pronounce in your language so I will go by Kraskat. It is nice to meet you." The creature tried to extend his hand to shake, only to bounce it off the property barrier.

Jason scanned the creatures one more time, finding them harmless. He did detect a wand on Kraskat, but it looked weak, nothing he couldn't handle. He also sensed that Guilford was monitoring the situation. Bull barked his approval and wagged his tail. It seemed that all signs deemed these entities were safe to allow in. Jason stepped outside of the barrier and shook Kraskat's hand.

"Nice to meet you Kraskat, my name is Senior Jason Canin." He turned to the next one to introduce himself.

"Senior Canin, it is an honor to meet you. My name is Bill," after learning that the name of the first creature was Kraskat this caught Jason off guard. But before he could ask about it, they started their arguing again.

"Bill? Your name is not Bill, it's not even close," Kraskat exploded, looking incredulous.

"My name can be Bill. Kraskat isn't close to your real name either. At least Bill will fit in here better than yours."

The four started arguing, it was clear that this was typical behavior for them. When the pawing at the ground started again, Jason decided this needed to stop.

"If you want your name to be Bill, then I will call you Bill. But you four must stop your arguing before it draws attention. As it is, we are pushing our luck and we need to get moving. Please follow me."

He lowered the house barrier allowing the four to enter.

Kraskat continued, "Let me introduce my other two friends..." but before he could say their names the two interjected.

"Popov. Nice to meet you," one said extending his hand.

"Butterfly. Also nice to meet you," the other said.

Kraskat shook his head, "Butterfly? That is a bug not a name."

"Well, I like it and it will be my name." Butterfly stomped his foot.

"It is very nice to meet both of you. Butterfly is a rather unusual name but if that is what you want to be called, so be it," Jason said.

He paused, deciding that his faulty property barrier needed to be fixed now. He concentrated then cast a spell to replace the flawed barrier. What now appeared was much stronger and less detectable. While he was replacing the barrier, Bull properly introduced himself to the four, currently getting his butt scratched by Bill.

With Kraskat, Bill, Popov, and Butterfly in tow, they walked back through the forest. The orbs he had encountered before were there to greet them and flew around them madly. The four new guests could also see them and kept saying "nice to meet you" as the presence flew around them.

As they approached the house, they saw Guilford walking toward them.

Kraskat smiled when he spotted him. "Look, it's Master Guilford."

Guilford welcomed them, giving each a warm hug. He greeted them using a language that sounded very guttural, chatting with each a bit.

Finally, Guilford looked up at Jason. "Jason, sorry. I should have told you that I knew them, but I wanted to see how you would handle the situation. Nice job, but I'm surprised that you didn't know their language."

Jason agreed. "It would've been helpful, but after the second attempt on my life, emphasis on non-human languages was dropped."

Guilford's smile disappeared. "You and I need to catch up very soon."

"Agreed, but first I want to know why I have four visitors and how you know them."

"Let's go inside and discuss." Guilford gestured to the house

Jason led everyone into the house, his family now in the kitchen. Catie stood and took a step back. His son John and daughter Kira both smiled and moved toward the visitors to greet them. John let out a quiet, "awesome" and Jason wondered if his kids could see past the visitor's magic.

Guilford made quick introductions.

"Butterfly? What a wonderful name," Catie exclaimed, relaxing when they were introduced. This caused Butterfly to hug her. Kraskat put his head in his hands and sighed.

"Are you hungry? Can we make you something to eat?" Catie asked. Jason really wanted to get to why these four were here but knew this would have to wait. Catie was in full hostess mode and would not be distracted.

"We tried these things called pancakes; they are most wonderful. Have you heard of them?" Kraskat asked peering around the kitchen.

"You are in luck. Jason makes some of the best you will ever have. Grab a seat while he whips some up," Catie said.

Jason wanted to argue but a look from Catie made it clear there was no arguing. He went with the next best plan which was to shut up and start cooking.

Realizing he was also hungry, he went into full chef mode. Jason enjoyed cooking and whipped up pancakes, bacon, fruits, and a few other items he loved. For warlocks, one of the prices of using magic was that it burned calories. Being a warlock meant Jason was almost perpetually hungry.

Jason put the food out and everyone dug in. While Jason had an enormous appetite, his guests gave him a run for his money. Jason made a couple more batches of pancakes and by the time everyone finished, the food was gone. Running out of patience, he felt it was time his guests told him everything.

"Now that we are all full, can I get a little information on why you are here?" He received a look from Catie telling him he was being rude, but he felt that his guests' arrival was probably not a good sign.

Kraskat began. "Jason is right, you deserve to know why we are here. But let me tell you a little about us, our people are called Ramscians and we live in another realm. It is much different than here on earth. We live in harmony with our planet and everything we do is judged on how it promotes our people and protects our planet."

"That's very cool," John said. "I wish we had more of that here."

John was Jason's oldest and a high-school senior. John stood as tall as Jason with blonde hair and a runner's build. John's hair always looked like it needed sheared. He could go to a barber and two days later look like it had never been cut.

"Agreed," Jason said.

"As for how we got here. We were hunting, not far from our home, when we found someone who looked like a wizard performing magic. Whatever he was doing destroyed everything near him. We tried to stop him. I rammed him as hard as I could with the others right behind me. This caused some sort of explosion and we found ourselves in your realm with the wizard. He was dead and when we saw other wizards appear, I picked up his wand and we ran off. That was about two weeks ago."

Kraskat pulled out the wand that Jason had detected and handed it to him. Jason took it, turning it over in his hands. During Jason's training an employee of the Castle tried to kill him with a similar wand. The wand was an unusual hybrid, with a metal warlock handle and the rest was wood from a wizard's wand. He could feel a little power coming from it but either it had been depleted in the explosion or it was just a weak wand. The magic in the wood tried to struggle against his control, but the warlock part of the wand was definitely in control. He experimented by using it to levitate a chair off the ground. This needed more investigation later.

"I've seen a wand like this before." He wanted to add, "and this is not good." But thought it best if he kept that part to himself. He handed the wand to Guilford.

"I have been a warlock for a long time, and I have never seen anything quite like this. Where have you seen one before?" Guilford frowned as he turned the wand over in his hand.

Jason didn't want to frighten his family by relating the entire story, but he wasn't going to be able to just brush this off.

"Master Jenkins was not happy that you gave me my grandfather's wand," Jason said. He watched as Guilford nodded and lowered his head.

Catie looked up. "Who is Master Jenkins?"

"A master warlock that tried to have me killed several times," Jason replied. "He wanted my wand, and he recruited some minions to help him get it. He gave them a wand like this to kill me, but they all failed. We hoped that he had only created a few, but it looks like there are more."

Guilford sighed then looked up. "For some reason Jenkins felt that your grandfather's wand should have gone to him. But warlocks and their wands have to agree to partner. That wand was bequeathed to you and it wouldn't partner with Jenkins, which made him mad. I didn't believe he would try to kill over it, but I guess I was wrong."

From the corner of his eye Jason could see Catie's face, now full of fear and anger. This was not how he wanted to tell her about what happened during his training.

"People were trying to kill you? When were you going to tell us about that?"

"A lot of things happened during training," Jason said, "including that I killed Jenkins and his minions in the end. Something, I was planning to discuss with the family in private."

"This just keeps getting worse," Catie said, her look softening, "but if you killed them, then the wizard they encountered was not part of his scheme?"

"I don't know," he answered.

Guilford turned to Kraskat. "Do you know what the wizard was trying to do?"

"I don't think it was a wizard that did this," Jason interrupted. "The handle on this requires a warlock to use. My guess is that the person was either a failed warlock trainee or someone with just enough talent to qualify for the warlock test but failed."

Guilford nodded. "Jenkins was a seeker for a long time and could have recruited candidates he knew wouldn't make it as a warlock."

He shook his head, this was concerning, and they really needed to return to the Castle and discuss it with the head of the Castle, Mistress Nelson.

"We do not know what he was doing but whatever it was, it was destroying everything around him. He was killing the grass, trees, everything," Kraskat said.

Guilford nodded. "What he was trying to do does worry me. There is a cult, which calls itself the One Realm, which believes that there should only be one realm and over the centuries they have tried to find ways to remove the barriers between all realms. We don't know exactly what will happen if they were ever successful, but we believe it would result in complete destruction of everything. Obviously, we have been tracking these nuts down before they can do any damage. It sounds like they have a new plan."

"Yes, and somehow my grandfather's wand is important to them," Jason added.

"Do you know why?" Guilford asked.

"I don't. I was hoping you did." Jason turned the subject back to his visitors. "So how did you find me?"

"We were really trying to find Master Guilford," Kraskat said.

Jason was surprised at the response. But it made sense since the Ramscians knew Guilford.

"We don't have the magic that a warlock possesses, but we do have some. We are good at tracking and when we picked up Guilford's scent, we followed it here," Kraskat added.

Jason's daughter, Kira spoke up, "Then you must have used magic to conceal yourself from everyone here?"

Kira along with her brother John, had always shared Jason's love of magic. Jason knew that both of his kids hoped that they too were magical. Jason wanted to know why Kira had asked the question but decided to discuss it with her later. Guilford gave Jason a quick look but kept quiet.

The four nodded in agreement. "To the average person we look just like ordinary people. Just a little shorter than most," Bill responded.

Jason was about to ask another question when the mirror in the living room rippled, and Rita stepped through. The mirror was magical, and Jason had used it to travel to the Castle for his training. She walked into the kitchen but stopped when she spied the four Ramscians. She smiled and looked to Jason. "You just have to stir up the pot wherever you go."

Jason shook his head. "I just came home. They found me. Everyone, this is Rita. She is my Warlock Personal Assistant."

Rita had been his valet at the castle and was now assigned to help him establish himself as a warlock on earth. Jason wasn't sure but she looked to be in her late sixties with her hair gray. She had been instrumental in teaching him many advanced spells that saved his life during several firefights. He later found out that Rita had once been a warlock but when she was about to die, became an extension of the Castle. He wasn't completely sure what that meant but she was a trusted friend.

"Why are you here? I thought you were working on getting us office space," Jason asked.

"I am, but my first priority is to get this house secure and setup," Rita said. She noticed Catie eyeing her suspiciously, "Also, since we will have construction crews at our service, if there are any updates to the house you want to make, we can do that. They will do the work for free."

This caught Catie's attention and she started listing off what she wanted done to the house.

Kraskat interrupted. "We very much appreciate your hospitality, but we have been gone a long time and our families will be worried. Can either one of you take us home?" With the mention of going home the other three lowered their heads. They looked homesick and Jason could see that they must have had a rough couple of weeks.

"I should be the one to take you home as Jason probably has not traveled to your realm," Guilford said.

"No, but I would like to go with you," Jason said.

Guilford agreed. "We can travel there together but first we need to alert the Castle, most likely we will have to return there soon."

The four Ramscians gathered near Guilford.

Guilford sent a message via his wand to Mistress Nelson explaining the situation, then opened a portal and the group Stepped through. Jason sensed the magic Guilford performed and felt confident he could repeat the procedure. The Step took longer than most he had taken, and he could feel his wand helping to guide him. Lights and images raced past, and Jason enjoyed the show.

They landed in front of a short, squat house painted bright colors with a flower garden around it planted with flowers of every color. The Ramscians quickly lost their human camouflage. They heard a scream coming from the house then a very short female Ramscian ran out and tackled Kraskat.

"Jason, this is my wife Nashkin," he said as he held his wife for a minute. She looked to Jason, cocked an eyebrow, then waved to him. Nashkin was a good foot shorter than Kraskat and she got up on her toes to give her husband a kiss. Other Ramscians came out, all about the same height as Nashkin. It seemed that for Ramscians, Kraskat and his friends were tall. They spoke in their language and Jason decided that he would like to visit again and would have to learn their language.

They were welcomed into the house, but Guilford declined, stating that with what had happened, they needed to get back. They said their goodbyes then Guilford Stepped, leaving Jason behind.

"Well, I guess I am on my own. It was a pleasure to meet all of you and I hope to visit again soon," he said.

Kraskat stepped forward and offered his hand. "I want to thank you again for your hospitality. You make the best pancakes. Maybe you can come back and show my wife how to make them?"

Jason shook Kraskat's hand, "I would love that." He opened a portal and Stepped back to his house.

Chapter Two

Returning home, he found a smiling Guilford waiting for him. Jason guessed he'd passed an unofficial Guilford test.

"I really think it's time you catch me up on what happened during your training," Guilford said.

Jason wasn't sure his family should hear everything that happened, but Rita encouraged him to tell them everything.

Jason took a deep breath and began. Everyone was quiet as he related what had happened during training, hitting only the highlights. Catie and the kids looked shocked when he told them about having to kill a Castle employee named Tom. Jenkins had sent Tom to kill Jason and retrieve Jason's wand. During a firefight, he had killed Tom but not before Tom had almost killed Rita by blasting through a door.

Guilford interrupted when Jason talked about his encounter with the Lion's Hunter, a large magical creature that looks like a cross between a lion and a rhino. It almost killed him several times before Jason was able to make a temporary truce with it.

"You do have a way of attracting trouble, that's for sure. The good news is that this realm is extremely well guarded, it would take several masters to bring the Lion here," Guilford said.

Jason continued telling them about his time at the Castle but was interrupted by Guilford again when he heard about Jason killing Jenkins. "You killed him by stabbing him?"

"I did stab him but according to Mistress Nelson, he died because my wand defeated his wand."

Guilford nodded, waving for him to continue.

He ended his tales with the part he knew would trouble his family. The announcement that Tess, John and Kira's mother, may still be alive. Jason could see the hurt in John and Kira's eyes. Their mother was alive and had not come back to them.

Kira's eyes were full of tears and she walked to her dad and hugged him. "Why did she leave Dad? Why didn't she say goodbye?" Kira tried her best not to completely break down.

"I don't know, honey. Something must have happened. But I don't know what. We may never know," Jason said as he held his daughter. Tess had disappeared over ten years ago. Initially the police accused him of killing her and hiding her body. Jason spent a month being grilled by the police and his friends abandoning him. Eventually Tess was spotted in Mexico and supposedly died in a fiery car crash. The police cleared him of all charges, but the damage had been done. Just prior to Jason leaving for warlock training, assassins had tried to kill him and his family. He now suspected Tess had sent the assassins.

An awkward silence filled the room. Jason strained to think of something to say. Finally, his son broke the silence. "Do you think whatever was going on with the cult group ended with the death of Master Jenkins and his cohorts?"

Jason looked at Guilford and saw worry in his eyes. "Whoever the Ramscians encountered died a couple of weeks ago and this could be over. But," Jason hated to add this part, although very obvious, "we have to assume that it isn't over, and we will need to investigate."

Guilford excused himself, stating he wanted to go home. He would go to the Castle first and would be in touch. The security detail would remain until Jason could get his house in order. He then disappeared through the mirror.

It was quiet for a moment until Rita spoke up. "Jason, we have a lot of planning to do and we should get started. Part of this will affect your family so they should be present, at least for the first part."

"Well then, let's get started," Jason said and sat down at the kitchen table.

When they were ready, Rita began. "While you are working on establishing your new career, we need to plan for your team also, including me. We will need to find homes for everyone, preferably nearby. I can contact a real estate agent and start looking for homes in the area."

"I know a guy that buys houses in the area and flips them for a profit. He's always remodeling a house or two in the neighborhood. I'll give him a call," Jason said.

"That will help," Rita said. "As for your house, arrangements will be made to provide maid service, lawn service, and maintenance. This will allow us to maintain security personnel at your house without raising any suspicions.

"Would they be warlocks? Or warlock trainees?" Jason asked.

"Some would be, but there are those from other realms who work closely with warlocks and have willingly become magically bound to protect warlocks. These people consider it an honor to help," Rita paused. "Why did you ask about trainees?" As she asked, a look of realization came over her. "You think Jenkins was using failed trainees. That would make sense given the half-wand hybrids we found."

Jason nodded. "I do. But let's move on as I need to discuss this with the masters."

Rita hesitated then continued. "We will have to rework your security procedures for the house, cars, and everything else you own. Also, the charms you put on your family will need to be redone. Each member of your family is a warlock candidate. Just being near you, they will increase in power, making them easier to detect. I suspect within the next few years each of them will have to go to training."

Kira and John smiled. Obviously, they thought being a warlock was a great idea.

"It would have to be after college," he said. Catie quickly agreed.

Jason's feelings were divided. His training had almost killed him, multiple times. He'd also learned how to kill, something he wasn't proud of. On top of that, Jason being a warlock put his family at risk. On the other hand, having his kids trained would allow them to defend themselves if something were to happen. He struggled with the concept of Catie becoming a warlock. He'd already lost one love to magic, he couldn't survive a second. As he was considering this, he received a message on his wand from Guilford.

Meeting tomorrow at eight a.m. in Mistress Nelson's office. You can tell your family but no one else.

Master Guilford

He had expected the request but not the level of secrecy. Obviously, they were worried about spies at the Castle.

"Jason, what is going on?" Catie asked.

"I was hoping to have a few days off before I officially started being a warlock, but I have to go to the Castle tomorrow to discuss what happened today."

Catie frowned ominously but kept her comments to herself. He knew they would continue this conversation later in private.

"That does bring up a few things with the first being we need to setup a few new rooms in your house. I will need a quick tour of the house before I can make my recommendations," Rita said with a look to Catie.

"I can do it and we can go over some of the remodeling I want on the house." Catie got up and took Rita on a tour.

As soon as the two were gone, the kids peppered him with questions about his adventures at the Castle. Having to tell the kids about their not-so-dead mother still weighed on Jason and the grilling about magic and life at the Castle gave him a temporary reprieve.

"Is the Castle magical? Can we visit?" John asked first.

Jason took a breath, "Yes, it is magical, but I am not sure if you can visit. I will see what I can do." He then went into detail about the Castle. When he described Mistress Nelson's office, including the ceiling with a view of space, they were both impressed. They demanded that he do the same in his office.

"Is Rita a warlock? Can she do magic?" Kira asked.

"Rita isn't a warlock, but she can do magic. I really can't tell you anything more about her. You will have to ask her, but I am not sure she will answer all of your questions." It was the best reply he could come up with.

"Rita mentioned adding rooms to the house. Do you know what that means?" John asked.

"At the Castle, I have a special room for training that is enhanced to help me learn spells, especially spells that could go wrong. Also, I am assuming that my equipment will need to be in a secured area."

Both kids had more questions and he answered them as best he could. Eventually they both insisted on him performing magic for them. They looked so eager sitting in their chairs he decided to try something different. Drawing energy, he sent it around their chairs, promptly lifting them into the air. He conjured up a couple of oars so the kids could move themselves around the room.

Catie and Rita returned to find both kids floating in the air. The kids pretending to row their chairs with their oars. Both women tried to keep a straight face but eventually burst into laughter. Rita decided to join the fracas by sitting in a chair, conjuring an oar, and joining them. Even Catie couldn't resist, making a big show of sitting in a chair. Jason then sent energy around her chair, gave her an oar, and sent her on her way.

Everyone roared with laughter as they floated around the room, bumped into each other, or just spun in circles. Jason quickly joined in the merriment, leading them through the house. As the laughter eventually died down, he returned everyone to the ground. Hearing his family laugh and watching them goof off did his heart good. It went a long way toward making him feel better and he wished it could go on forever.

Finally, Rita brought an end to the fun. "Jason, I want to go over the modifications we will need to make for you. Then I need to start looking for homes for your team and office space for your new business, whatever that is going to be. It would be best that we keep your warlock business separate from your home life. You may have a lot of unusual visitors and you don't want that kind of traffic coming to your home."

"As for my new business, I have an idea and will go over it with you when I am ready. Until then, let's start with the modifications for my office," he said, and led Rita to his home office. It needed some cleaning, its typical condition. Cups, papers, and an assortment of books scattered across his desk. Bull, who normally slept under his desk, got up to greet his assistant.

"It is good to see you again, Bull." Rita scratched his ears. In response he jumped up to give her face a lick. She conjured a handkerchief to wipe herself.

"My first recommendation is that we add a hidden office behind that wall where you can store your equipment, your book, and other items. Additionally, your Testing Room can be there also."

Rita pointed to an outer wall with a window. He had an idea of what she was thinking about and nodded in agreement.

With a wave of her hand, the wall magically rotated out of the way, opening up to another room. The room looking similar to his room at the Castle. On one side, stood a wardrobe closet along with several of his uniforms. A doorway off to the right opened to what he assumed was his training room. A fireplace, with a crackling fire, sat on one side of the room, with a large desk and a sofa nearby. His portal mirror now stood in the corner.

Catie walked to the fireplace. "I like it already," she said as she warmed her hands by the fire quickly joined by the rest of his family.

Bull trotted in and laid down in front of the fire.

"I think the room has been officially Bull-approved," Catie said and they all laughed.

Jason looked around. It all looked great, but something was missing. A little redesign seemed in order. He walked to one wall concentrating on what he wanted. Pulling energy, he cast energy out creating a monitoring station on one wall, complete with several displays. The displays came alive with data coming from the warlock data center.

A quick review of the monitors told him the system was working well. The data center looked to be actively watching an event in South America, processing a large amount of data. A team, including several trainees, were investigating. Jason would have liked to join them, but it wasn't his place. He made sure that he would receive updates on the incident.

Jason dedicated a couple of additional displays to the security of the house. Creating a dozen drones, he sent them outside to monitor the house. These were specifically looking for magical entities along with non-magical intruders. During his training he had learned to create magical drones. Later Katan, the head of the warlock data center, and he, created versions of the drones to help monitor the warlock data center. The displays came alive with images from the drones. The images coming from around his house and property. He sent several more to monitor the roads near his home. If anyone or anything magical came his way he would know ahead of time.

Jason liked what he created but had promised himself, and his kids, to create something like what he had seen in Mistress Nelson's office. Not completely sure how she had made hers, he decided to improvise. Opening a small portal, he sent a drone through it. Within a few seconds the ceiling of the room was now a view of earth from space.

"Now that is truly awesome," John said as the group stared at the ceiling.

"I agree," Jason said, putting his arm around his son. "This is what I hoped magic would be like."

He had to admit it was pretty cool-looking. He wasn't sure how long his drone would last in space but for now it worked. When it failed, he would probably just use a feed from NASA. But his drone gave him a much higher resolution image than what NASA could provide. He would have to ask Mistress Nelson how she created the view in her office. Taking a breath, he could feel his magical energy reserves had dropped. With a little time and something to eat, his reserves would refill quickly.

Rita reviewed the changes to the room, nodding in approval. "You have come a long way."

Jason smiled. That was a huge compliment coming from Rita. Before he could say anything, Rita started back to the entrance. "Enough with the frivolities, we need to get back to work."

As he ushered everyone out of his new warlock office, the wall returned to its normal position. He thought he should add a door to enter as opposed to having the wall move and laughed at himself. With moving walls and hidden rooms, the issues he now dealt with were straight out of a mystery novel.

For the next hour Jason and Rita were busy modifying the house. He added a secondary shield over the house to further protect it. His house could be hit by a missile or a swarm of locust and they would be fine.

He worked with Rita to create emergency portals in each of the rooms. This would allow his family to escape to the Castle if the need arose. Anyone in the family could activate a portal by calling for it or pressing on a specific wall.

Jason started reviewing ideas for his new company with Rita when security alarms went off. Checking a readout, his security system notified him that three cars with magical entities were en route.

"Right on time," Rita stated as she headed out the door, motioning for Jason and Catie to follow.

Outside, Jason watched as the cars pulled into his driveway. His drones told him that there were magical entities in the vehicles, but no weapons were found.

The drivers approached and Rita gave the first driver a hug before holding a quick conversation with him. She signed some paperwork, and the first driver handed her three sets of keys and then waited. Rita came back to Jason and Catie and handed each of them a set of keys.

"Jason, the Castle decided that you need new vehicles specifically adapted for your new role. You and Bull get a new truck."

Bull barked enthusiastically then ran around the new truck. He then marked the truck in his own special way. Jason just shook his head then approached the truck himself. Opening the passenger door, Bull immediately jumped in, making himself comfortable. A red 4x4, the truck seemed to have every feature imaginable. It even featured a remote start he could activate via magic. He climbed into the driver's seat and the truck's system came to life without him doing a thing. Bull repositioned himself in front of a vent, enjoying the A/C.

While Jason inspected his new truck, Catie gave the parked SUV a once over.

"Rita, I have to warn you. I like my cars fast and fully loaded," Catie said.

"Then you will love this car. Not only does it have every feature you would want, it has a zero-to-sixty that will leave just about anything else in the dust," Rita said.

Catie smiled. "Including Jason's new truck?"

"You'll have to find that out for yourself," Rita said, smiling.

"I will and will let you know," Catie said with a wink.

Jason overheard her remark and laughed, guessing a trip to the local racetrack was in their future. Sensing both vehicles, he found quite a few magical enhancements. He understood most of the enhancements but a couple he wasn't quite sure what they did.

"So, give us the run down on all of the fun stuff," Jason said.

"The vehicles have been magically enhanced to make them faster and safer. The motors are electric but powered by magic. When you're at home, you will need to plug them in as if you were charging. Both have reinforced bodies, able to withstand colliding with just about anything this planet can offer up. There are various weapons to protect you, along with enhanced communications to the Castle. We also upgraded the sound system." Rita smiled at her last comment.

As if on cue, the stereo in his truck started blasting. Bull sat up and began bouncing his head to some heavy metal music. "Looks like Bull approves," Jason said, and they all laughed.

John and Kira joined them, eyeing the new vehicles with a bit of envy. Rita turned to them, "We have new vehicles for you two pending approval from Jason and Catie. The Castle feels it's imperative that you two have vehicles that can protect you but ultimately it's their decision."

Jason and Catie looked at each other and Jason spoke up. "I agree with the decision to get them vehicles, but we have the final say on what kind of car they get."

Looking to Catie, she thought about it for a moment before finally agreeing.

John and Kira were ecstatic. "We thought as much, and four cars will be delivered later for your review," Rita said.

This left the third vehicle, "The last one is mine," Rita stated. It was a two-door red Porsche, she looked at it greedily. Jason laughed, wondering how she was going to deal with the speeding tickets she was about to get.

Their old vehicles were emptied, and the drivers drove off with them.

"I am off to tour some prospective offices," Rita said as she got into her new car. He could hear her accelerate hard when she hit the main road.

For the first time since he returned, it was just the family and they headed back into the house.

"Are you hungry?" Catie asked.

"One thing you will find is that warlocks are almost always hungry."

"Then I guess your pay raise will come in handy then," she replied.

They all moved to the kitchen with Catie and the kids updating him on everything that had happened while he was gone, which wasn't much. He filled them in on some additional detail from his training. He talked about the friends he made and some of the things he had learned. If the kids were going to attend warlock training, they should have an idea of what they were getting in to.

Finally, the conversation came back to Tess.

"Dad, I have a confession to make," Kira said.

"Yes...?" Jason replied.

"Last year, I thought I saw a woman near school that looked like Mom. I turned away for a second and she was gone. It has happened a couple of times since then. I thought it was just because I missed Mom," Kira said fighting back the tears.

"I saw her too," John said. "I just didn't want to say anything. I thought I was just seeing things."

"You need to tell me right away if you see her again. We don't know what happened to her and magic can change people. Please be careful if you see her again." Tess was watching the kids and Jason was concerned. He would ask the Castle for security teams to shadow the kids in case Tess tried something.

Talking about Tess with his family was ripping him apart and he needed to change the subject before he broke down. "Now, let's move on to a different topic. How are your classes going?" Jason asked.

As Kira and John discussed their classes, Jason scanned his family to see how much power they held. John and Kira were clearly powerful and indeed warlocks. Catie held power but differently and he quickly recognized her power as matching that of a wizard. That could make things difficult. Warlocks hid their existence from just about everyone on earth. Most wizards thought warlocks were just a myth. Only a few in the wizard's administration knew or even communicated with warlocks. This made socializing, let alone marrying, a wizard forbidden. It wasn't going to stop him from marrying Catie, but he would have to hide her powers until he could figure out a solution.

He spent the rest of the day with his family and getting used to life as a warlock. While his lawn didn't really need to be mowed, he got out his riding mower. There was something about the simple act of mowing that eased his mind.

Bull was happy to be back, running around with the other dogs and generally getting in the way. At one point, Jason worried because he couldn't see where his dogs had gone until he found them lying on the back porch, sunning themselves. He grabbed a chair and joined them. Taking out his phone, he decided to call his friend Curt to see if he had any homes available.

"Hey Jason," Curt said as he answered. "What can I do for you?"

"Well, I was wondering if you have any homes in the area for sale. I'm looking for some investment properties."

"I got one, but I don't think I'd feel okay selling it to you. Actually, not sure I can sell it to anyone," Curt said.

"What's wrong with it?" Jason asked, his interest piqued.

"You know I don't believe in that magic and curse stuff?" Curt asked.

"Yeah, go on."

"Well, I might have to change my mind. I am almost to the point where I believe the house is cursed. Every bit of electronics that goes into that house eventually fails. Stuff gets moved and it feels like you are being watched when you are there. I know it sounds silly, but it's the truth."

"I believe you. Where is this house?" Jason asked.

"Well, that's the kicker. It's next to your woods."

Jason bit his lip. He knew the house Curt was talking about well. It used to belong to his grandparents and his parents had sold the house and the lot for a considerable sum. His grandfather's sister and her husband had also lived there before they too passed away. Being next to his woods he suspected that the entities in the forest were probably the cause of Curt's problems.

"Can I go over and take a look?" Jason asked.

"Sure, it's empty. I'm not in town so I can't go with you. But be careful, I'm not sure it's safe there," Curt added. Curt was ex-special forces and still looked like he just stepped out of an action movie. For him to be spooked meant that something was seriously wrong.

"I'll be careful," Jason promised and hung up.

Jason stuck his head in the house, "Catie? I am taking a quick drive over to look at a house. Want to come?" He wasn't sure she should come but it might be a good thing to have someone else there just in case.

"You go ahead. I have some work to catch up on," Catie called back.

"Okay. I'm taking Bull," Jason said.

Bull stood and walked over to Jason. *Where are we going?*

Going to see a haunted house that I want to buy, Jason replied as they walked to his new truck.

I knew life with you would be interesting, Bull said. With a single leap, he jumped into the bed of the truck.

Jason climbed into the driver seat as the truck powered up. Powered by magic, it was quiet but when he pushed the accelerator, he could feel the power. A minute later, he pulled into the driveway of Curt's cursed house.

Getting out of the truck, he used his senses to survey the house. He found a large entity in the house, its energy seemed dark. There were several other entities moving about the house, but they were small, about the size of a large rat.

"Well, this is interesting," Jason said.

I am not sure what that thing is, but I would be willing to bet that is the cause of the problems here, Bull said.

"You think?" Jason said sarcastically. "I guess I need to go inside and ask it to leave."

Somehow, I don't think that is going to work. But bonus points for being polite, Bull quipped.

23

Jason walked to the front door followed by Bull. As soon as he stepped inside, the large entity flew straight at him, slamming into his shield. When it couldn't get through it flew back and assembled into what looked almost like a man. It was semitransparent and completely black with two dim orbs where the eyes should be. What little detail that could be made of the face looked like the thing was scowling.

"Wizard. Leave my house or I will kill you," the entity growled.

"That isn't a very nice way to greet someone. Plus, I'm not a wizard," Jason said.

"Then you're a warlock. Good, so am I," the entity said.

Jason scanned the thing again. Whatever it was, it was not a warlock.

It knows about warlocks and thinks it is one. Any idea of what it is? Jason asked Bull.

No idea. It is unlike anything I have ever encountered, Bull said.

"I don't think you are what you think you are. You may have been a warlock at one time but not anymore. What is your name?" Jason asked. He was trying to buy time to figure out a plan other than killing the thing.

"I am a warlock," the thing yelled. The orbs of the eyes started pulsating. As they did, the rest of the body also pulsed but when the eyes beamed bright, the body went dim. It was as if the creature didn't have enough energy to fully power itself.

"Okay, you are a warlock. Then what is your name?" Jason asked again.

The entity's eyes returned to normal, with it so did the body.

"I, uh...do not remember," the thing said. The scowl left the entity's face. It looked at Jason almost expectantly.

"Look, I know some people that can help you..." Jason started but was cutoff.

"Noooo!" it screamed.

Jason felt something fly by him as one of the orbs from the forest circled him and the other entity.

"Is it you?" the entity yelled, as the orb flew around it.

Jason sensed the entity ramping up power.

Jason, the orb cannot defend itself... Bull warned.

Jason aimed his wand at the entity and tried to put out a shield to protect the orb, but it kept flittering about. Just as Jason sensed the entity would fire, he fired.

Jason's blast hit the thing and sent it to the ground. For a second the entity became blurry and then split into two. The first he recognized as his grandfather's brother-in-law, Josh. Jason still had a picture on his desk of his grandfather with his sister and Josh. The other half was in the shape of a person with no discernable features.

Josh reached out with his hand toward the orb that now hovered in front of him.

"I love you," Josh said to the orb, then disappeared.

The other image reached out to the orb, *I never meant for this to happen,* then disappeared also. In its place a wand now sat.

Jason could feel sadness from the orb as it hovered. It started to fly away but stopped in front of Jason. *Thank you,* Jason felt more than heard from the orb, then it flew away.

"Do you know what just happened?" Jason asked Bull.

No, I do not understand any of this, Bull replied.

Jason scanned the house again finding only traces of magic. Nothing else magical remained in the house.

"Well, it looks like the house is now clear," Jason said to Bull.

I would put up a shield to keep anything new from taking up residence, Bull suggested.

"Good idea," Jason said.

Jason cast a shield over the house then he walked over and picked up the wand on the ground. He felt for its energy but there was none.

The wand is dead. You can return the wand to the Castle and it will be melted down to make a new one, Bull said. *But I would wait until you better understand what is going on in your forest. Returning it now might cause unwanted questions.*

"If you say so," Jason said.

Jason wrapped the dead wand in a towel and placed it under the seat of his truck. He then called his friend Curt, making a more than generous offer for the house and property.

"Jason, I will accept your offer but are you sure? Bad things seem to happen in that house," Curt said.

"We performed a mini-exorcism, and the place is fine now," Jason said. "Let me know if you have any other properties in the area. Especially any near my woods. I would like to reclaim the property my grandparents once owned."

"I don't have any more as of yet," Curt said then added. "But will have another soon. In the meantime, I am pretty sure the Morrisons on the other side of your house are getting ready to sell. Old Mr. Morrison doesn't like me and would burn the house down before selling it to me. You might have better luck."

Jason gave the Morrisons a call and made another generous offer. The Castle had offered to fund any acquisition, so he didn't feel bad about being a little generous to others. They quickly accepted. With these purchases he now owned most of the land his grandparents once had. He vowed to purchase the rest.

He now had houses for Rita and his guides, one task done. He let Rita know of the two acquisitions so she could concentrate on finding office space. The rest of the day he immersed himself in home life. His kids were doing their best to be upbeat and happy about his return, but he could tell the news about their mom was on their mind. That night, Jason climbed into bed and waited. Catie had been quiet about the revelation and he knew it would come out soon.

"Jason," Catie began, then paused. She took his hand and held it for a moment. "With Tess still alive, where does that leave me?" A tear formed in her eye and it almost destroyed him. He had put her through so much and it seemed it would not stop.

"With me," Jason said. "My plan was to come back and propose to you. But with Tess out there, I am afraid that if I do, she will target you."

"Really?" Catie said trying to suppress her tears. "You were going to propose?"

"Yes. Ring and everything," Jason said. "But Tess has already tried to kill us once. If she hears we are engaged, she may try again."

"What if we only tell the kids? We could tell everyone else once Tess is gone," Catie said.

Jason stared at this incredible woman. Her smile alone wiped out all of his doubts. Getting up, he walked to his dresser and pulled out a small case.

He climbed onto the bed trying to get on one knee. He opened the case. "In that case, will you marry me?"

Catie burst into tears. "Yes, Yes, I will!"

Jason placed the engagement ring onto her finger then kissed her. After a few minutes, they woke up the kids and told them the news. John looked excited but Kira seemed torn.

"When will you get married?" John asked.

"Once the issue with your mother is resolved. Until then, no one can know we are engaged. If Tess finds out, she may try to have Catie killed," Jason said.

The smiles on both kids' faces disappeared.

Jason's heart sank. "Look, I don't know what happened to your mom, but she is different now. Something changed her and she is threatening to do a lot of damage. I love Catie and we will marry once things are settled."

Both kids nodded. He hugged them and they went back to bed.

Later, Catie was looking at her ring when a dark look came over her. "What are you going to do about Tess?"

"I have to stop her before she destroys everything. I will try to capture her but if I can't, I will have to kill her," Jason replied.

"Good, because I have a bad feeling it is either her or me," Catie said. She kissed him again.

"Now, let me show you how much I have missed you," Catie said as she removed his night shirt.

"In that case, we should plan on sleeping in, as this is going to be a long night," he said as he pulled her closer.

Chapter Three

The next morning, Jason woke early, showered, and made himself some breakfast. He hummed as the eggs and bacon cooked.

"Hopefully, you made enough for me?" Catie asked as she walked into the kitchen.

"Of course, plenty," Jason replied, then quickly added additional eggs.

"Right," Catie laughed. "I think we are going to need to add another pantry to store enough food to feed you."

"Probably," Jason said as he put the food on two plates. "I have some things I need to check on for the Castle and will be in my warlock room if you need me." He put his arms around her and pulled her close.

"I would think after last night you would be worn out," Catie said giving him a playful kiss.

"Having a boyfriend who's a warlock has its advantages. One being an increased stamina."

"You call that increased stamina?" she teased.

"Ouch."

"Well, I look forward to your 'increased stamina' tonight," Catie kissed him one more time. "But I'm starving and have to start getting ready for this morning."

"If you change your mind, I'll be in my office," he said. He took his plate and went to his new warlock office. He tried to not devour his breakfast, but it was gone by the time he got there. He dressed in a uniform before checking the monitors to see if there was anything going on.

A team had been sent to South America but reported all was quiet. He found one of his teammates, Dod, had been assigned and was tracking something magical. Jason knew she'd be ecstatic being involved in the hunt.

He decided to go through some of the exercises that Master Zhang had taught him. His body went on autopilot while his mind wandered, considering recent events. After thirty minutes, he felt much better and his mind seemed clear.

Entering the kitchen, he found his fiancé making coffee.

"Did they teach you to drink coffee while you were at the Castle?"

"Nope, still a soda guy," he said with a smile. "I'm headed back to the Castle; I have to know if this cult group thing is over or not."

"Is there ever going to be a time where there isn't someone trying to kill you?"

"I hope so, it could be this thing is already over. I just have to make sure." This seemed to satisfy her for the moment, but he knew she wouldn't let it go. He gave her a kiss telling her he would return when he could.

"You know the reverend is not going to be happy, this will be the third Sunday you've missed," Catie said.

"Ooh, yeah. I forgot today was Sunday," Jason shrugged. "Nothing I can do about it. You and the kids going?"

"Yes, we're going to the late service and staying for lunch."

Jason wished he could join them but that wasn't an option. He did have to wonder how being a warlock would affect his view of his faith. While important to him, figuring that out would have to wait. There were too many pressing issues to deal with. He returned to his warlock room, closed the wall, and stepped through the mirror.

As he emerged in Mistress Nelson's office, he was promptly greeted by her guards Dax and Solis, their deadly staffs pointed at him. Both relaxed when they identified him and stepped back. Mistress Nelson, who sat at her desk reviewing documents, didn't even look up. He wasn't sure if this was always going to be his greeting, but he needed to be ready the next time he entered her office.

Guilford was already there along with several other masters including Sophia and Kien. He had met the two during his warlock training. His first experience with Master Kien was during Jason's shield test. Jason was pretty sure that Kien had tried to kill Jason during the test, but they had since become friends. Sophia had tested Jason on other items and had helped him with his magic. The last time he had seen the two was when he helped the two drunken masters back to their rooms after a celebration in Jason's honor.

They greeted him and he asked what had happened since he went home. When he first arrived at the Castle, time had been adjusted and several months at the Castle had only been a few days at home.

They all looked at him and Master Sophia spoke up. "When you left, the Castle readjusted it's time to match your realm. It has only been twenty-four hours since you left but a few things have happened. Once the Wizard's Ambassador arrives, we can update everyone."

Two minutes later, the ambassador arrived and after some quick introductions, Mistress Nelson began the meeting. "This is what we know, there have been multiple reports of attacks on the borders separating the realms. We have been lucky that each time this has happened, it has been thwarted. Twice, the perpetrator was almost apprehended. The Ramscians stopped one attacker and recovered their wand. In another instance, a warlock encountered an attacker and was able to disable him. Before he could bring him in, the attacker killed himself. Several more arrived and retrieved the body but the warlock was able to recover the wand and it was the same as the others." She stopped to give everyone a chance to digest what she said.

The ambassador was first to speak. "Do you have any idea who the attackers are or where these wands are coming from?"

Jason looked toward Guilford and he nodded back. Jason spoke up. "Guilford and I believe the attackers were originally candidates to become warlocks. They probably wouldn't have made it as a warlock, but held just enough power to use a modified wand. It seems the warlock handle is used to manipulate the wizard portion of the wand. Someone with just a little warlock power can now become a wizard, albeit not very powerful."

The head mistress continued. "That aligns with what we have found. While Jenkins was a Seeker, he identified quite a few candidates that were not strong enough to become a warlock. In light of recent events, we decided to reach out to them. Several are dead or missing. Also, it seems that Jenkins had access to the records of the other Seekers and some of their failed candidates are dead or missing. We suspect that anyone not willing to join Jenkins' mission was eliminated."

"That answers the *who* but not *how* they are getting their wands," Jason said.

The ambassador shifted uncomfortably. "You may not know this, but the wizarding world had several conflicts as factions vied for control. We put all of these down, but one faction secretly amassed a store of wands and other weapons. We raided their compound and broke up the group. A search of the compound turned up a lot of conventional weapons, but we found almost no wands. Captured faction members said their wands had been stolen just prior to our attack. Without their wands, they couldn't defend themselves. They didn't have a complete count on their stockpile of wands, but we are guessing between thirty-to-fifty wands."

That explained the wizard portion of these hybrid wands, but Jason still wondered where the warlock portion of the modified wands came from. It was now Master Kien's turn to look uncomfortable.

Their eyes met for a second and Kien relented. "I can explain the warlock portion. The process to make our wands is strictly guarded and only a limited number of warlocks have access to order new wands. Jenkins was one of them. Jenkins assigned a senior to work in the order processing of new wands and placed several orders of ten wands each. The senior picked them up and bypassed some of our protocols, delivering the wands to Jenkins then burying the information about the whereabouts of the new wands. When we tried to arrest the senior, he died suddenly. At first, we thought it was suicide but later we determined that he was killed. A device had been embedded in his chest that was remotely activated. When activated, it blew out his heart."

"Do you know how many wands he received?" Jason asked.

"From what we can tell, he got forty wands. We are not sure how many he kept intact and how many he modified to work with the wizard wands."

Jason thought for a second. "With the wands we have recovered we have to assume that at least thirty are still out there."

Everyone agreed.

"We have a team secretly working on a spell that will disable the combined wands." Master Kien waved his hand, bringing up a video that showed a warlock casting a spell at a combined wand, which caused it to explode.

"Unfortunately, it only works when you are close to the wand. Ambassador, we will share what we learned in hopes that maybe your researchers can come up with your own version."

The Ambassador spoke up. "We will have our best try to duplicate the spell. But tell me, why is your team secretly working on the spell?"

Jason suspected he knew the answer but kept quiet.

Master Kien took a breath. "Since we found out about Master Jenkins, we have been quietly investigating how he was able to bypass our security measures and go unnoticed. We have found one master and several warlocks who had been working with him. We haven't rounded up everyone as we are still investigating. It seems that every time we think we have it wrapped up, we find more people involved."

The Ambassador nodded. This didn't seem to surprise him.

After a moment, Mistress Nelson broke the silence. "So, what we know is that Jenkins was part of a plot to create weapons and recruit a small army. It also looks like whatever plans they have, they have continued. We have to assume that either Jenkins was not the leader or someone else has taken the reins. We need to stop these attacks and capture some of their people to get more information. I am ordering the data center on full alert." She paused. "Also, any warlock assigned to check out suspicious activity needs back up. I don't want any warlock getting ambushed. Anything else?"

Everyone agreed with her comments and no one added anything.

"Meeting dismissed. Senior Jason, please stay so we can discuss your staffing situation." She walked around her desk to shake the Ambassador's hand. Two staff members led him to the mirror Jason had come through. He Stepped through and was gone.

The Mistress sat in one of the high-back chairs and looked at Jason. "Things have changed very quickly, haven't they?"

Jason sat down and leaned back in his chair. "Yes. It seems like just yesterday I found out I was a warlock. Now I have a small team and am hoping not to get killed by a bunch of nuts."

"Aren't we all!" she retorted in a rare show of informality. She laughed for a second and took a breath.

"Back to the business at hand. Normally we would fill your team with guides or other magical beings. Eventually, as a master, you would add trainees, seniors, and even some masters to your team. But you aren't the average senior and things are happening that require a different approach. I was hesitant to make changes, but the Castle was very adamant about its recommendations for you."

Jason took a breath and held it. Mistress Nelson had to know her statement would trigger some questions.

"When you say the Castle, you mean the Castle itself?" He had always known the Castle was a living entity but now it seemed it held direct influence on warlock life. The implications were tremendous. He found himself leaning forward, scooting to the edge of his chair. He caught himself and tried to relax.

She smiled and simply said "Yes." The Cheshire-cat-smile she now held disturbed him more than it should. She was toying with him but that wasn't new. She had always only revealed the bare minimum of information he needed to have.

"To say that the Castle is a magical being or soul isn't quite right." She frowned as she pondered how to explain this to Jason. "No one truly understands the Castle. My feeling is that it is a single consciousness formed from many. Many feel that as warlocks pass on, they may join that collective, augmenting the single consciousness. I have spent hours discussing this with the Castle and I am still no closer to understanding."

"Discussing?" he asked, he sat on the edge of the chair again but didn't care.

As if to answer, a form appeared in the chair next to him. It continuously morphed, sometimes male, and sometimes female. The robe it wore also slowly changed color. The image shook its head and let its hair down. The face of a bearded man came into focus.

For now, Jason guessed he would just call it the Castle.

The Castle spoke. "Yes, Jason, discussing. I know you have a lot of questions and once this situation is resolved, I will answer as best I can. I will warn you now that my responses will not always answer your questions but will tell you what you need to know. For now, we need to get back to the matter at hand. Mistress Nelson?" the Castle nodded to her.

Mistress Nelson nodded, took a deep breath and started, "Jason, we are breaking protocol, and we are assigning some of the more advanced trainees directly to you. Guilford will monitor your performance, but I expect updates from you. You have your choice of trainees, but I believe we already know your choices."

He smiled, at least some things were going his way.

Chapter Four

It had been a week since he met with Mistress Nelson and Jason still pondered his encounter with the Castle. The fact that the Castle was both a place and an entity still confused him. Plans for his new company were making great strides and Rita found office space on the top two floors of a fourteen-story building. The building was part of a large outdoor mall, which excited Rita. One main advantage was the constant foot traffic around the building from morning until late at night. Perfect for what they needed as it would help cover their comings and goings.

"The mall has several popular restaurants, stores, and a movie theater," Rita reported, clearly enjoying herself.

Jason staked out a corner office with a great view of the city. If this was his company, he wanted to enjoy the perks. Tomorrow, he would move in after his office furniture was delivered.

Mistress Nelson and the masters continued their investigation into Jenkin's exploits. Jason wanted to help but Mistress Nelson told him to concentrate on things on earth. Though his trainee selections did not surprise anyone, they still had not arrived. A fact which bothered him. "Be patient. They will be along once they finish some tasks," Mistress told him.

In the meantime, he worked with his guides, Katrina and Le Anna, during the week to prepare them for whatever may come. His guides had been assigned to help him at the beginning of his training. Their role was to make sure he had everything he needed, answer any general questions he may have, and to assist him as needed. They were magical, just not as powerful as a warlock.

Using the Testing room at his house, he ran them, and himself, through multiple tests including firing at moving targets, firing while being fired at, and close-quarter combat. Guilford and the Castle monitored their progress and gave him several exercises to increase their magical strength. They also started a physical exercise routine to keep them as fit as possible.

After running through his exercises, Jason decided to end the session with one last shot, once again using his Testing Room.

"Okay, I am going to use as much of my energy as possible," Jason said out loud to warn the Castle and the others. Putting everything he had into his shot, he fired at a target setup by the Castle. His shot obliterated the target and continued on, hitting the far wall. Jason ramped up his shield as the explosion sent debris and him flying, landing hard on the ground.

"That's going to leave a mark," he said as he stood gingerly and brushed himself off. An image of the Castle appeared, looking very irate.

"Sorry," Jason added, hoping the Castle wasn't too mad.

The Castle gave him another nasty look and then disappeared. It took a full day to rebuild and reinforce his Testing Room for future use.

Work on his house began with a swarm of construction trucks parked in his driveway. Along with the daily parade of construction vehicles came an old sedan with a sign reading 'Maid Services.' Every day, an elderly lady slowly pulled into his driveway and parked wherever she wanted. It didn't matter if she blocked every single truck. Once parked, she would open her trunk, pull out her cleaning materials, and amble into the house. All the construction workers seemed to know her and stayed out of her way.

Even Rita seemed a little leery of her. The first day the maid went straight to the front bathroom and started cleaning. Jason wondered who was faster, a sloth or her but by the time she was done, the bathroom sparkled. He was afraid she would try to clean his office next, but she went to work on the kitchen. By Friday, half the house was surgically clean.

Jason asked Rita about the woman and only received a "You don't want to know." The maid did a great job and he let it go.

On Sunday, the family dressed in their best, and left for church. They were members of a church they used to attend regularly before this whole warlock business started, and Jason wanted to restart their visits. His drop in attendance had earned him a disapproving look from the church deacon when he ran into him at a store.

Catie and Jason had held several conversations about his faith and his new role as a magical being. Despite everything, he decided that being a warlock had no effect on his faith. If anything, discovering there truly was magic in the world made the case for his faith even stronger.

They also decided that once the current crisis was clear, that they would get married in their church.

It was a beautiful morning and Jason enjoyed the trip to church. They could have easily Stepped to the church but that would have caused too many issues. He always loved to drive but now that he knew how to Step he felt that driving took too long. Driving did give him a chance to try some of the enhanced features of his new truck. The one he liked best would adjust stop lights, so he almost always had a green light. This made his trips a little faster and a lot less frustrating.

He parked the truck and they walked toward the church hoping for a good sermon and a chance to visit friends. As they approached the church, he started getting a strong vibe and his magical senses tingled. Hesitant to intermix his personal life with his warlock life, he tried to ignore it.

As they neared the entrance, the church secretary greeted them. "Jason and Catie, so good to see you. Especially you Jason, it has been a while," she said with a disapproving look.

"Yes, it has, but I plan on attending regularly going forward," Jason said.

The secretary's look changed to one of approval. "I have to say you are looking quite well these days. Something must be agreeing with you." She gave Catie an appreciative look.

"Yes. Catie has me on the straight and narrow. Diet, exercise, and some hair dye. It's like I am a new man," Jason said.

"Let us hope it continues." The secretary then turned to walk into the church.

As they followed her, Catie gave him a knowing look. This was going to be a problem he would have to address. As a warlock, his body would continue to reverse age for a short while. According to Master Kien, it wouldn't start aging again until he was at least 150 years old. Even then his aging would be extremely slow.

Entering the church, the strong vibe continued as they walked down the aisle to their regular pew. Jason spotted a man walking toward them and something about him made Jason stop. There were quite a few people in the aisle, and they flowed around him like he was a chair or a column. None looked directly at him, as if they were unaware of his presence. Jason had no doubt this man was causing the vibe he was feeling. He prepared himself for anything but did nothing that was directly aggressive. The last thing he wanted to do was cause a scene in his own church.

The man approached, "Welcome Warlock, what brings you here?" The greeting did not sound friendly and the man did not smile.

Jason looked around, only his family reacted to him being called a warlock in public. Some sort of magic was hiding their conversation.

"Attending church, and you?" Jason asked, desperately trying to keep things civil.

"I am here to ensure the sanctity of this church and the safety of its parishioners. I hope you have no plans to disturb it. Warlocks have a tendency to do that."

"Hmm, they do? And what exactly are you?"

When the man didn't reply, Jason continued, "I have never seen you here before, so I don't believe you are a church member and the fact that you know me as a warlock indicates you are magical." He was starting to not like this man and he decided to poke a little. "Also, as a member of this church and a warlock I would remind you that keeping this church safe is important to me. I hope *you* have no plans to disturb it." Jason stood with folded arms.

"I have been a member of this church for a very long time. Do not mess with me, Warlock. It will not end well for you." The man's voice rose, and Jason could see light in his eyes.

"The last person that threatened me did not enjoy their ending. I suggest you relax and enjoy the sermon. Maybe you will learn something," Jason said, beginning to enjoy this banter as this self-appointed guardian sucked at it.

The unknown man clenched his fists and Jason waited for the inevitable attack. But it didn't come, instead he heard, "Jason, so glad to see you." It was Reverend Jim, one of the church ministers. He walked between the two men saying "excuse me" to the stranger.

The unknown man looked startled at the minister's interruption. Jason sensed something wasn't quite right as everyone else had been ignoring them, but the minister looked directly at the man. The man scowled at Jason and then stormed off.

"Reverend Jim, I'm doing wonderfully and looking forward to your sermon," Jason wasn't sure he would enjoy it as sometimes Reverend

Jim's sermons tended to ramble. But since the minister had just prevented a magical fight, Jason felt it would be ungrateful of him not to.

"You do look good, almost glowing," the reverend said, smiling. "I hope you enjoy my sermon." The reverend then shook Jason's hand and continued on his way.

Once they sat down, Catie leaned over and asked, "Who was that man?"

He hesitated before answering, "Well, he said he kept the church safe, but I have no clue. I'm going to have to research this."

"Everyone around us acted like there was nothing going on. But Reverend Jim seemed to make a beeline straight to you when things got heated." Catie looked around to make sure no one could hear her. "Also, what did the reverend mean by you almost glowing? Does he know you're a warlock?"

Jason didn't respond as he considered Reverend Jim's interruption. Reverend Jim had been with the church for a long time. He no longer took a lead role in church affairs but was very active in the church's outreach program. He was a big proponent of an open church policy and it wasn't unusual to have a few of the local homeless in the pews, thanks to his efforts. Jason looked to see Reverend Jim smiling at him. This unnerved him a bit but then the minister turned to respond to a question from another parishioner.

"I don't know. I really don't know," he said trying to collect himself. He was about to cast a spell to block anyone from overhearing their conversation when the vibe he'd felt returned. It wasn't the exact same but close. He turned around to find the source emanated from a young woman staring at him. She looked away quickly, but he was certain she was the source. She sat several pews back and he guessed she was sent to keep an eye on him.

Well, two can play that game. He pulled energy and created a camouflaged drone the size of a bee and sent it to land on the wall near her. Now he could watch the watcher, but he hadn't shielded it. While no one could see the drone, she could sense it. This seemed to upset the woman as she would look at Jason then the drone. He was probably going to pay for his antics, so he wanted to enjoy it as long as possible. Before she could decide what to do about it, a voice spoke out. "The Lord be with you."

Services started. Jason sensed she didn't want to draw any attention and sat with an irritated expression. Giving Jason the occasional scornful look.

Between the unknown man and the now-irate woman, Jason was sure this was going to be the best sermon ever.

When services ended, the woman got up and disappeared into the exiting crowd. After visiting with friends, they headed home and as he expected, they were followed. His drone continued following the woman from a safe distance and was currently attached to the rear window of her car.

"Looks like we are being followed," Jason stated.

Catie and the kids spun around to look.

"She's driving a yellow hatchback, obviously she's not worried about stealth," Catie said with a short laugh. "So how do we get rid of her? Hopefully, you're not thinking of using some of your truck's weapons. Right?"

"Of course not," he lied. He sorely wanted to try out the truck's defenses. Searching for another idea, he reached out with his senses and found that if the woman did have magic, she was well shielded. His luck changed when he noticed that she hadn't shielded her car. In the distance he spotted two cop cars parked on the side of the road and got a devilish idea. This was going to be fun.

"Watch this," he said. As they got closer to the officers, he reached out with his senses and started flicking the headlights of the woman's car, then honked its horn. Having its intended effect, both cops assumed she was trying to get their attention. They flipped on their lights and pulled around behind her. Jason's last view of her was the glare she gave him as the cops pulled her over. He assumed that she would use some magic to have the cops move on but by then he would be gone.

John laughed. "Okay, Dad, that was impressive."

The next day saw the kids off to school and Catie gone to work. Returning to his warlock office, he found his guides, Katrina and Le Anna, waiting for him.

Jason sighed, when he had first met his two guides, they had worn some very unusual, if not to mention revealing outfits. Neither were from earth, and the two didn't seem to understand that their outfits were not appropriate at the time. What they wore now wasn't much better. "What did I say about your outfits?" Jason asked, crossing his arms.

"What?" Katrina asked. "I watched lots of commercials of women wearing jeans and shirts with holes in them."

"First they were wearing bra's and underwear underneath, and, uh, the holes were not over, uh," Jason could feel his face turning red. "Well, they didn't show everything the woman had." He blurted out.

"And that's a problem on earth?" Katrina asked.

"Yes," Jason replied.

"But my clothes don't have any holes," Le Anna argued.

"That's true, but a see-through tube top is a problem. Not to mention the slit in your skirt is too high," Jason said. "And should be on the side."

"Oh, but this way it is much more convenient for..." Le Anna started but Jason raised his hand.

"That may be true, but I want you two to blend in here. Not attract every horny male in a two-mile radius," Jason said. "Please change into something less revealing."

Both women pulled out their wand and pointed it at their clothes. "Not in front of me," Jason said a little too loud.

"Sorry," the women replied in unison and walked away.

Thirty seconds later they were back, dressed somewhat less revealing. Jason shook his head and decided it wasn't worth another round of arguments. "What's up?" he asked.

"We have an assignment," Le Anna exclaimed. She was too excited but that was just her nature. As for the assignment, he hoped it would be an easy one.

"Okay, what is it?"

"Not sure, Mistress wanted to brief us when we were all here. You're supposed to message her when you are ready."

He notified Mistress Nelson they were ready and waited. A communications line was open via the data center and her image appeared on the main screen.

"Jason, I have an interesting assignment for your team as it comes from the wizards. They detected an unusual magical source from a house in a state called Indiana. Are you familiar with it? I have not been to earth in a long time."

Jason coughed to hide a laugh. Jason had to wonder how long it had been since Mistress Nelson had visited the US. "Haven't been there in a while, but I am familiar with it."

40

"Good," the mistress continued, "The wizards sent a team to investigate and find the cause. The team tried to enter the house, but a magical field blocked them. They were working on entry when they were called off for a bigger emergency. We scanned the area, and the magical source is very unusual. We would like your team to investigate before the wizards return tomorrow. Information and location are being sent. I am also sending the rest of your team to assist and learn."

Jason smiled at the news as he had been looking forward to this. Additional information appeared on his monitors.

"Got it, we will investigate. Our office isn't ready yet, so please have them meet me at my home office. We can travel together to the site," he said.

The Head Mistress nodded and then cut off communications.

Jason read through the information sent, very curious about what they were heading into. The site was a residential home. The family that owned the house had just moved there a couple of months ago. Over the last few weeks, they'd called the police multiple times about intruders but each time none were found. The police noted that during each visit, the family was extremely agitated. During the most recent visit, the father became violent and is currently locked up for a psych evaluation.

During the arrest of the father, both mother and daughter fainted. EMTs were called and they were taken to the hospital with an undetermined diagnosis. The doctors were doing their best, but both were rapidly declining, and their prognosis was poor.

His security system notified him that Gail, Dod, and Weston were requesting permission to enter. He quickly granted access.

One of the issues he'd encountered, was that the Castle and all warlock sites were wide open. Once he gained access to one spot, he could go anywhere within the Castle network. The Castle had always been relied on to identify intruders and stop them. But after an assassin had bypassed security and attempted to kill Jason, the Castle's security team knew they needed additional security.

Part of the new security was that everyone needed to be identified prior to entering the Castle or another warlock's home. This caused some slowing of Castle employees entering for work but had already nabbed a couple of people attempting to sneak into the Castle. Most of these were people just trying to escape some situation or hoping to find work somewhere else.

Dod, Gail, and Weston emerged from the mirror. Jason was happy to see them and gave each a hug.

Jason dove into their current situation. "As you know, we are now a team. As assignments come in, I will assign some or all of you. Also, we have started a training program to improve our magical and physical strength. You will be expected to participate. One thing I want to point out, while I do lead this team, I do want your input. This is a team, our team. Any questions?"

When there were no questions, "Well, tell me what's been going on?" He was eager to hear what they were up to and see if he could learn any additional information.

Dod went first. "Well, we cleaned up the cat mess that you left. Damn that stunk. Since then, I've been on several missions with masters but haven't really seen any action. I did some tracking work for one, but we lost the trail. I'm hoping that partnering up with you we'll see some action."

"What were you tracking?" Jason was intrigued why a trainee, even one as talented as Dod, would be used to track something magical.

"They were looking for some Kimian escapees from another realm. The escapees tried coming to earth but since their planet's average temperature is 120 degrees, our planet was too cold, and they promptly left. I found their tracks and if they would have called me earlier, we would have caught them before they left our realm."

Gail continued the update. "By the way, thanks for leaving the cat-mess."

Jason had to chuckle. He had been sent to investigate a magical being that was killing the locals and had killed some wizards. When he killed one of them, the body of the huge cat-like creature had fallen on him. After almost being smothered to death by the big cat, he was glad to have gotten away from it.

"Anyhow, Weston and I were teamed with some masters investigating those hybrid wands. We've learned a lot. Our team was the one that discovered the spell to disable those wands," Gail said proudly.

Weston couldn't contain himself. "The magic used to merge the two wands is impressive but the magic we created to de-couple them is quite a feat." Weston was in his zone and becoming very animated.

Dod cut him off. "I haven't heard about these wands, are they the reason we're here?"

"We need to hold off on that conversation for now. Dod, I'll fill you in later. Weston and Gail, I want you two to lead the training to teach the team the spell to disable those wands. Can you do that?"

Both nodded.

"But first, where are your guides?" he asked.

"My remaining guide will be here soon, the other disappeared when they started investigating all of Jenkins' links. As it was, my remaining guide has gone through a lot of interrogation," Dod said.

Weston nodded. "I lost one of my guides also, he is currently in lock up. He tried to escape and when cornered, he fired on Master Kien. That was a very bad idea and he barely survived. The other finished her security review and will be here soon."

This troubled Jason. It looked like the One Realm cult had infiltrated the Castle staff much more than expected. He asked Gail about hers.

"Mine will be along after they pass their security reviews. One should be here any minute, the other I am not sure about when he will be here," she replied.

"When they show up, we can bring them up to speed. In the meantime, I need to inform you of your assignments." Jason reviewed what they knew so far and started going over his plans.

"Weston and Gail, I want you to go to the hospital and figure out what is wrong with the mother and child. After that, find out what is going on with the father. Le Anna, I want you to accompany them."

Turning to Dod, "Dod, you will come with Katrina, Bull, and me to investigate the house. I need everyone to please keep a low profile and keep in touch. If something starts to go wrong, call for backup. I will do the same. I suspect we are all in for some fun."

Gail and Weston's guides arrived shortly and looked like they had been through hell. Jason wasn't sure how much help they were going to be if things went south. He would have liked to have given them a day to rest and recover but he wasn't sure if the mother and daughter would survive until then. It was noon and he decided to give everyone a bit of a break by taking them out to lunch.

Since it involved food, there was an intense debate on where to go and Jason declared that as their leader, he was selecting a local Mexican restaurant.

Over dessert, he looked over his team. They had gone through a lot; each had physically changed since training started but none more than

Gail. The first time he saw her, she was round, her gray hair almost white. Over the course of training, she lost her excess weight and was now in incredible shape. She still had some gray hair, but it was disappearing. Her face, once wrinkled by age, was looking younger all the time.

Weston had also changed; no longer the scrawny, awkward guy Jason first met. He had put on quite a bit of muscle and his movements were much more graceful. Compared to Dod, he was still clumsy but overall, he had changed a lot.

Dod had changed also as well, but not so much physically. She was in better shape than when they started but her growth was more mental. She was now comfortable being part of a team, asking for help, and relying on others. While she still had a bit of a chip on her shoulder, she was much more relaxed.

As for himself, he liked who he had become. When he first found out about warlocks, he hadn't been keen on the idea of becoming one. Now, he was at peace with that decision and looked forward to the long life that he hoped to have. He just needed to figure out how to make sure his kids and fiancé became warlocks. Outliving his loved ones was not something he wanted to experience.

"Okay, time to get back to work," he said to a general consensus of groans and complaints.

"We don't have time for a second dessert?" Dod asked.

"Don't you mean third dessert?" Jason asked.

"I might have lost count," Dod said playfully.

"We have people waiting on us. We can run by Geos once we are done with this assignment," Jason said. Geos was a bakery that had gelato and lots of other decadent treats. The group happily agreed.

After they returned to his house, and concerned about the family's condition, Jason sent Le Anna and her group off.

Le Anna, Weston, Gail, and their guides Stepped to the hospital. Jason's team Stepped to a spot near the reported house where they would not be seen. Arriving near a river that provided some cover. They walked to the house to scope it out.

The house was a two-story home with a well-manicured lawn and two SUVs in the driveway. As they approached it, they could sense some sort of shield around it.

I think I recognize this type of shield. I hope I am wrong as it would be a bad sign, Bull said.

"How bad?"

Bad enough. When we know more, we will need to discuss. For now, we need to get into the house.

They scanned the house but kept walking trying not to raise any suspicions of the neighbors. As it was, no one was around, and an eerie silence blanketed the neighborhood.

"This neighborhood is creepy," Katrina said, casting her eyes about. She had her hand on her wand, seemingly ready for anything.

Agreed, Bull responded.

Jason looked at each house for signs of life and saw none. All curtains were drawn, and no one was outside.

They walked past the house and around the corner, now out of view of any prying eyes. They Stepped to the backyard of the house. Jason spent a minute sensing the shield, figuring out how to get past it and finding no solution. He decided the only way was to use his energy to cut a hole in the shield. He thought it would be quick and easy. As he started to cut, he quickly found it took more energy than he thought it should.

"Bull, stay here and keep an eye out for anyone approaching. If anything goes wrong inside you will be our back up."

Easy enough. Be careful, you may encounter some powerful opponents if I am right. The dog partially morphed into his wolf form. The hole Jason cut was not large enough if Bull took his full form, but somehow Jason didn't think that was going to be a problem for Bull.

Jason didn't want whatever was in the house to get out, so he raised his own shield around the house, locking in whatever was in the house.

"Katrina, Dod, let's get to work." He was excited to start another adventure and hoped this would be easy.

He checked his shield and walked through the hole. He found the house's back door unlocked. They entered the kitchen and immediately sensed the presence of multiple magical beings throughout the house. What they were, he did not know. Initially, they kept their distance. He signaled Dod to check the rest of the kitchen and garage. He sent Katrina to check the bedrooms.

He entered the living room and stopped in front of a rather ugly mirror. There were multiple beings trying to hide in the room. He stood and waited, interested in what they would do. Eventually one approached him, stopping a few feet behind him. He could feel its presence almost as if it wanted him to. He closed his eyes and waited. When the entity did not move, he opened his eyes. In the mirror's reflection, he now saw a ghost like image of a woman with half of her face rotten off. It would have been impressive if Jason hadn't seen the exact image in a popular horror movie. He guessed that the entity was trying to scare him away.

Oh, this was going to be fun, he thought. Jason slowly closed his eyes then powered himself up, feeling the blue aura surround him. He could instantly tell where each being was and how powerful it was. Using some energy, he reached out to the nearby stereo, cranking up the volume and letting loose with a song from one of his favorite rock groups. Just as the stereo started to blast, he opened his eyes with them lit to full brightness. He had to admit that his glowing blue eyes looked cool in the mirror.

Between the sudden blast of music and his glowing eyes, the thing behind him realized it was in trouble. It tried to fire something at Jason which bounced off his shield. Jason returned fire, killing it. Suddenly, there were blasts coming from every direction. From the other parts of the house, he could hear both Dod and Katrina firing. Dod let out some sort of battle cry sending a chill through his bones. Every being in the room paused for a moment, then resumed firing on Jason. His shield took several blasts, but the shots were not very powerful.

Just in case, he dove off to the side, landing behind a sofa. He returned fire on the beings while the sofa took a severe beating. Luckily for Jason, it was a thick sofa with a solid wooden frame. He made a mental note to get one for his house.

One of the beings tried to flank him and he fired, hitting it square on. The thing was knocked back against a wall, but surprised Jason when it headed straight back at him. A second shot killed it. He eliminated two more before the rest gave up and tried to leave.

The entities were now trying to escape but his shield blocked them. He killed the last of the entities when he heard Dod yell, "Jason, garage!"

Jason headed to the garage and met Katrina along the way. Katrina was bleeding from a cut on her face, but she had the biggest smile he had ever seen. There was no time to discuss as they ran to the garage.

Entering, they almost ran over Dod who pointed her wand toward the center of the garage.

A ring of seven stones sat in the center, each emitting a bright, white light. In the middle of the ring, stood a partially melted human giant about ten feet tall. As it took huge breaths, its body expanding and collapsing, with an awful sound. The giant turned toward them and roared. It then spun around, grabbed a shovel, and threw it at Jason. The shovel bounced off Jason's shield and clattered to the ground. To be honest, Jason felt it was probably one of the ugliest things he had ever seen, and it deserved to be angry.

"You should not have killed my spawn," it screamed, spewing some rotten-smelling liquid everywhere. "You will pay for this and then I will make your people pay for their heresy."

Jason guessed it smiled, but the mouth was so misshapen he wasn't sure. He ramped up his power and was about to fire when Bull, in full wolf shape, crashed through the side of the garage. The dog pounced on the giant, knocking it to the ground. Instantly, he was on top of it and had the thing's head in his mouth. With a quick pull, Bull ripped its head off. To everyone's disgust, he settled in for a snack, starting with the head.

Bull paused. *I claim the kill, but will share if you like.* Looking at each of them. *You should try it, it's quite delicious.* Bull then ripped off one of the giant's arms and tossed it to Jason.

"Thanks, but no thanks." Jason fought to keep his lunch down. In retrospect, his selection of Mexican food for lunch may not have been the best. "What can you tell me about those stones?" he asked, trying not to watch the carnage Bull was creating.

I can but first you need to destroy them, now. Without hesitating, Jason started firing on the stones. They took quite a bit of magical energy to destroy. Dod and Katrina joined in, each working to destroy one. When they combined their efforts, they destroyed the stones faster, but it still took a while. Jason used a considerable amount of his energy on each one. He worried that it was taking too long when the last of the stones disappeared. A circle burned into the ground now sat where the stones had been.

"Damn! Bull do you know where the last one went to?" Dod asked.

Between bites, Bull replied. *I believe it returned to its owner, where exactly that is, I could not tell you. I can tell you that it is very difficult to create those stones and they are hard to destroy. You did well to destroy six.*

Jason noted a small chunk of one of the stones by his feet. He casually picked it up and put it in his pocket. He would give it to Weston later to review. Bull saw him pick it up but said nothing.

From behind, someone shouted, "What have you idiots done?" It was the young woman from church. She stomped around the room, looking for something. "The portal stones, where are they? Tell me you didn't do something as stupid as let them go."

Jason had not detected her arrival and wondered how she got through his shield. It had been meant to keep things in, but still should have kept her out or at least let him know she'd arrived. If he had drones recording the event, he would have been alerted but he had failed to do that. Another mistake to correct for his next mission. He created several drones to start scanning and recording the results.

Bull stopped chewing and looked at the new intruder, *Calm down, they did well. If it will help you feel better, I will share my kill*. The woman looked at the carcass with disgust and was about to say something nasty when Bull cut her off.

Careful. I know your maker and he will not be happy to hear how rude you have been. Lysion and I have been friends for longer than you have existed. Also, I rescind my offer to share my kill with you. You will have to find your own. Bull returned to his meal.

The newcomer looked startled and took a breath. "I apologize for my rudeness." It was clear she was saying this only to Bull. "My name is Gatron and I have been hunting the creator of those stones. I was very close to finding them." She looked around. "Please tell me you have the stones."

Katrina spoke up, "You have been searching for whoever created those stones?"

Gatron nodded.

"And this is the closest you've gotten?"

Gatron nodded again but a look on her face told Jason that she had started to figure out where this was going.

"Yet, on our first trip we killed that thing, and destroyed six of the seven stones. You're welcome." Katrina said triumphantly.

Gatron's anger started to reappear as she turned red in the face. Jason cut her off before she did something stupid. "I recognize the burn pattern on the floor from my studies. That thing used a God's portal to come here. Those portals are very hard and expensive to make. Why did it want to come here so badly?" He wanted to keep her talking and get as much information as possible.

Gatron spun to look at him then paused before she started. "It belonged to a people called the Meathonians. Our people and theirs consider earth a holy place. We believe that humans are part of this holy place. They do not. They feel that humans must be eliminated before they destroy the planet." She looked a bit worried when stating this. "Do you have any of the stones?" Gatron asked, continuing her search.

As Katrina said, six were destroyed and one has returned to its owner. Bull responded.

Gatron stomped around the room. "I would have had them if it were not for you four."

This was enough. Jason was tired of her rants and needed to end them. He ramped up what was left of his energy and stepped in front of her.

"If it wasn't for us, that thing was about to go on a fun trip through this neighborhood. If we had waited for you, it would be gone and so would the stones. You showed up too late and we did the best we could." Jason walked away with Dod and Katrina following. Bull picked up his meal and disappeared.

"We're out of here," Jason said a little too loudly as he tried to reestablish his authority.

Just as they were about to Step back to his house, Gatron yelled, "Where are you going? Who's going to clean up this mess?"

Jason replied, "It's time for you to make yourself useful."

They Stepped back to his office to find Bull absent. Katrina and Dod were laughing about how upset Gatron looked when they left but Jason couldn't join in the laughter. Gatron was a hot head who seemed to have a lot of power, never a good combination. He decided there was nothing to be done about that now and reached out to Bull. Bull responded by asking Jason to join him alone, sending him a mental note on where he could be found.

"Bull wants to talk to me about something. Find out how the other teams are doing and wait for me to return. If there is an emergency let me know right away," he told Katrina and Dod then Stepped to where Bull was.

He landed in a clearing surrounded by a row of trees, a type of which he had never seen before. The ground was an interesting shade of blue and resembled a form of clay. He could feel that he was in a different realm. The area looked like nothing he had ever seen. Bull stood in the middle of the clearing with the remainder of his kill. Quite a few creatures were on the edges of the clearing; several were licking their lips waiting for their chance at the carcass.

You do not need to worry about the others. This is part of nature's cycle. After I am done, the larger creatures will clean what they can from the carcass then leave so the smaller creatures can eat.

Jason wasn't too worried about the creatures around him with Bull around. He was more concerned about why his companion had called him here.

"If you wanted us to have lunch together, I would have brought along something to eat."

You need to expand your palate. Many consider this a delicacy. Bull said, licking his lips.

"I will take that under advisement. Did you want to discuss something in particular?" Jason wanted to get to what was bothering Bull.

You have involved yourself in something that is much bigger than you or even the warlocks. Bull stared directly at Jason and he could tell the Laciter was worried.

"Is Gatron an angel?"

An angel as in your Bible? No, at least I do not believe so, but it is complicated. Her people are deeply religious and are zealots. They are called the Zycros and are ancient beings. This thing we killed belongs to the Meathonians as Gatron mentioned. It is one of their pets we killed, very strong, thick skinned, and has some magic. They are very devoted to the Meathonians and will fight to the end to protect them. The Zycros and the Meathonians have opposing views on just about everything and each is an extremely powerful race. This makes both very dangerous to themselves and everyone else. They will not hesitate to wipe out anything or anyone in their way if they feel it benefits them or hurts the other.

"You said you knew her creator, how do your people come into the picture?" Jason was hoping to learn more about Bull and his people.

My people once tried to mediate peace between the two nations. It worked for a while, but we found that they were not really interested in peace and used the treaty to regroup and prepare for war. When my people decided to leave, the two groups openly declared war on each other again. My people put up as many barriers as possible to shield others from their war. Still, many innocent lives were lost. Both sides are weak at the moment and with the warlocks putting up additional barriers, the two sides have been separated for the past thirty years.

"Why did your people leave and where did they go?" Jason didn't expect an answer but had to try.

Bull looked at him for a moment. *There were many reasons for them to leave and where they went, I cannot tell you. Even if I knew, I cannot risk that information getting to the wrong people. When I am ready to join them, I will know where to go.*

"Then why are you still here?"

There are some of us who have things we still need to accomplish. I am one of them. Though my people have left, we have not shrugged our responsibilities.

Jason thought for a moment then spoke. "I would have thought that Gatron would have been relieved that we destroyed six of the stones, but she seemed upset about not getting her hands on one of the stones. What am I missing?"

The power required to create a single stone is immense. As you saw, it took seven stones to power a god's portal. It also takes a considerable amount of energy to maintain even one stone. While the Meathonians are powerful, they do have limits. To have created seven stones and to use them means either that the Meathonians have found another power source or someone is helping them. Gatron hopes that by examining the stones she can determine the power source and find where they are being created. If they can create more stones, then war between the two is inevitable and everyone on earth will be in danger.

"Two very powerful opponents fighting each other on earth would be a catastrophe," Jason agreed. He considered the problem for a moment when another thought came to mind. "Those other things we fought in the house, what were they?"

I do not know, Bull said.

"This all has to tie back to Tess somehow," Jason mused. He didn't have any evidence, but his gut told him he was right.

Bull took another bite of his meal and then walked away. *I am full. Since you don't want any, I suggest we leave to allow the others to eat. As for the connection to Tess. I agree, she is involved but I don't know how. I am certain it will be revealed to us soon.* Then Bull disappeared.

Jason remained, pondering Bull's comment but when some of the larger creatures crept out of the shadows, he decided it was time to leave and Stepped back to his office.

He found his entire team waiting for him. Katrina and Dod looked happy but Gail, Le Anna, and Weston looked tired.

"So, what happened? Were you successful?"

Gail and Weston looked at each other and Gail began. "The overall results are that the mother and child are getting better and will survive. The father is better but may never be one hundred percent again. The Castle is sending a specialist to see if they can help."

"Good news. Now tell me the details," he said.

This time Weston continued the report. "Per your orders, we went to see the mother and child first. What we found was that each had something inside them trying to take control of their body. The things weren't successful, and their bodies were waging an all-out battle, trying to expel the things. I have read about things like that and we came up with a spell to extract the things and eliminate them."

"Once the things were gone, the mother and child immediately started to improve. I helped as I could, and they should recover completely. Gail and I may need to visit them again," Le Anna added.

"Do you know what the entities were?"

"I don't but Mistress Nelson seemed to know. She wanted to discuss this with you," Weston said and shifted to a more comfortable position in his chair.

"As for the father, getting into the hospital and getting to him was difficult. It took a lot of work to get in and we had to get our data center involved to help bypass some of their security protocols. Once in, we found the father's situation to be completely different. With the mother and daughter, the thing inside them tried to take over their entire body. With the father, the thing only attacked his mind. His mind was fighting back but losing. Extracting it was difficult, but we did it. Unfortunately, his mind still has all of the memories of the attack and he is having a challenging time coping."

"We talked with a specialist from the Castle who will try to wipe his memories. He thinks he can help but some of these memories are very traumatic and he may not be able to completely fix the father. Hopefully, you were more successful?" Gail said.

"Yes, we rid the house of the things that were attacking them and stopped a threat temporarily," Jason then related everything that had happened but did not include his entire conversation with Bull.

Gail shook her head. "Leave it to Jason to have the exciting assignment."

"Yeah, I don't think I was destined for a quiet warlock life. Changing subjects, its late and you are all welcome to spend the night if you don't mind the couch," Jason said.

"We can't, we still have to get back to the Castle and do our reports. Also, I would like to sleep in my own bed," Gail said. Gail and Dod hugged him and left with their guides.

Weston was about to leave but Jason stopped him. "Weston, can you stay for a couple of minutes? I have something I want to talk to you about."

Katrina and Le Anna left while Bull returned to his bed in Jason's home office.

Weston waited as Jason pulled out the piece of stone he picked up, "I need you to quietly research this stone. I need to know everything about it," Jason said, handing the stone to Weston.

Weston slowly turned the piece of rock over and over in his hand. "I have never seen anything like this." His eyes widened in surprise.

Jason noted a blue tint in his eyes. "Is it magical?"

"Not sure. It's almost the opposite of magical," Westin said in awe. "Everything has some magic in it, from the bug on the floor to the tallest tree. This thing not only has no magic in it, it's impervious to magic. I have read as many books as I can from the Castle's library but have never read about anything like this. I need to get it back to the lab and let the other masters help me."

"You can't tell anyone about this for now, but I will let Mistress Nelson know," Jason cautioned.

Weston left with the stone and Jason enjoyed the quiet for a moment. Deciding he needed more information; he sent a request to Mistress Nelson for a conference. He wasn't surprised when she immediately appeared on his central monitor.

"I have been following your exploits and look forward to your update."

"I'm not really sure you will be after I add to your list of things to worry about," Jason said grimly.

"I'm assuming you are discussing Gatron and Bull?"

Jason should have known she would already know about what was going on.

"Yes, it seems like this realm is becoming a battle point for two powerful entities. It also looks like I have put us directly between these two forces. I think Gatron's side may be a little friendlier but not by much.

Pretty much we are stuck between a rock and a hard place." He sat back and yawned. It had been an eventful day and he just wanted to sleep.

"We were already in that position prior to your efforts but if there was any doubt, you removed it. However, you had no choice and did what any team would have done." The Mistress smiled and reclined back.

"Do you think this is related to the wands and the missing trainees?" Jason hoped it wasn't as it would make things much more difficult.

"I am not sure. Normally both the Meathonians and the Zycros are too egotistical to team up with warlocks or wizards. But if either side were offered something enticing, they may consider an exchange." She held a troubled look which bothered Jason.

"You mean like a power source to create those stones?"

Mistress Nelson sighed. "Exactly, I don't believe it is a coincidence that the Meathonians suddenly found a new power source at the same time Tess and her group came out into the open."

"We might have caught a break. I found a small piece of one of the stones used in the God's portal. Weston is going to research it, but I told him to keep it quiet for now," he said, hoping she would agree.

The Mistress nodded. "The Castle detected it when Weston returned. We are monitoring it closely and will take action if we think it is a danger."

Jason would have to alert Weston that the Castle knew about the stone.

"Back to our predicament. One thing to keep in mind, both of those groups are powerful. In a fight, you could stand toe to toe with most of them, same for Dod. Weston and Gail would be at a slight disadvantage. Your guides would stand little chance, even with the added strength training. Keep training hard, including challenging your minds and you will improve your chances," she said and leaned forward to end the link.

Jason raised his hand. "Wait."

Mistress Nelson paused.

"Weston said you might know what those things were that attacked the family," Jason said.

"Not exactly. About a century ago, the wizards reported something similar but couldn't find who was causing it. The wizard ambassador at the time asked us to investigate. We determined it was a Meathonian researching ways to use humans for battle. The humans experimented on were put through living hell, both physically and mentally. We tracked down the Meathonian only to find that he and his staff had been eliminated by the Meathonian government. What he was doing was considered heresy and his death was a gruesome one. We thought that the research had ended with him but evidently not."

"Looks like someone resurrected the research and we need to end that research now," Jason said.

"Agreed," Mistress Nelson said and hit a button. The communication ended.

Chapter Five

Jason sat in his new corporate office reviewing sites for possible acquisition. It had been a couple of months since they moved into their new space and things were still getting setup. He'd left most of the prep work to Rita and his team. He needed to get his business going and start acquiring companies and properties to make sure his company did not draw any undue attention. A company that did nothing but employ a lot of workers would eventually attract someone's interest. Relying on magic to keep unwanted attention away seemed careless to Jason.

He now had two main roles. One was to hunt down Tess and deal with any event related to her. The other was to develop his business and make it profitable if possible. Actually, the goal was to make a little profit but not enough to attract attention.

To track Tess, he set up bots to watch all incoming data at the data center along with news stations, police, military, and fire communications. If something came up, he would know quickly. For the last two months, all had been quiet.

As for his business, he wanted it to address one major issue that had been bothering him. With the number of security cameras setup by banks, businesses, the government, and even private citizens, it was hard to Step somewhere without being detected. The problem was worse in large cities as it seemed that every corner had at least one camera.

The solution he came up with was to buy companies with sites all over the country but were mostly ignored by local residents and businesses.

Through his company, they began purchasing several chains of self-storage facilities throughout the country. Self-storage facilities were common enough that no one paid attention to them and building one in a sparse area wouldn't raise any undue attention.

For each facility, he set aside several storage units dedicated to allowing warlocks to travel and leave relatively undetected. Each facility was monitored by Castle security and would only require hiring locals to run the front desk during the day.

As it turned out, it was a lucrative business, and the Castle was very happy to make this happen. It would also give him an excuse to start traveling across the country to investigate new sites.

He was planning a trip to scout out a new location when he received an alert about some unusual activity in a very remote area of Iowa. He opened a portal and sent a drone to do some forward reconnaissance. His monitors lit up with a video feed of a wizard performing magic. The wizard was firing a spell into the air at an invisible wall and causing shockwaves across the area.

Jason zoomed in and found he was using was one of the hybrid wands. He alerted the Castle. "We have an attack," Jason shouted, but then realized most of his team was out of the office.

Katrina followed by Le Anna ran down the hall. "What's going on?" Katrina asked.

"We have a wizard attacking a realm wall. I alerted the others, but we will be first on the scene. Ready?"

Both his guides nodded, and they Stepped to a spot near the wizard. Jason was about to fire on the wizard when he felt a power surge. "Duck!" They jumped out of the way just as blasts came from two hidden wizards. Jason rolled and returned fire to scatter the attackers. He then amped up and fired on the wizard that was still firing at the wall. It hit him directly and sent the wizard tumbling to the ground. An explosion came from somewhere near where the wizard went down. This gave Jason some cover and he released Eagle wanting to get a better aerial picture. Eagle was a magical being in the shape of a bald eagle. Jason had created him when he was being hunted by the Lion's Hunter. He had been Jason's eye-in-the-sky to alert him if the Lion was nearby. Dod still ribbed him about Eagle's name but Jason thought it was perfect.

Katrina and Le Anna Stepped behind the two wizards who had ambushed them and hit each with a blast, dropping both to the ground in a heap. The guides dragged them to their feet, magically bound the wizards, and recovered their wands.

Jason jogged to where the wizard that was firing at the realm wall had gone down. "Damn," was all he could say. The wizard had taken the full impact of the blast, with his body parts spread over the area. Jason walked back to where his guides were. "Not much left of the other wizard. I wouldn't go over there unless you have a strong stomach," Jason said, shaking his head.

"Well, at least we caught two of them," Le Anna said. "Do you want to talk to them?"

"Sure..." Jason's words were cut off by two small explosions and the two wizards dropped to the ground. "Or maybe not," he said, as he approached the now dead wizards. The two remaining attackers now had large holes in their chest.

"Suicide packs I'm guessing," he said. Jason wasn't completely sure suicide pack was the correct name as a fourth person had probably activated them. The wizards may not have even known they had them.

On a hunch, he sent his senses out and found a trace of a fourth person, most likely a warlock. Not strong, but definitely a warlock, either a failed trainee or a trainee candidate. He sent Eagle, who had been circling the area, to investigate but whoever had been there was gone.

"Son of a..." Jason caught himself after a look from Katrina. "We walked into that one. I can't believe I was so stupid," he yelled to no one in particular. In his hurry to get to the action, he'd led them into an ambush. He should have also been prepared for the suicide packs.

He notified the Castle asking for a team to take the bodies and help with the investigation. Guilford appeared first and after getting Jason's report, spent the next several minutes telling Jason how stupid he had been. His lecture was cut short when Ambassador Silvers arrived.

Silvers was the wizard's ambassador to the warlocks and Jason had met him during his training. Things had worked out well and Jason considered Silvers on his side. They walked over to greet the ambassador and the two men with him. One of them was a man named Oliver who Jason met during a mission to kill two Bachrachts which were large cat like creatures. Oliver's memory of the incident had been wiped and he would not recognize Jason. The other man Jason didn't recognize.

"Jason, Guilford, let me introduce Oliver and Wren," said Ambassador Silvers. They shook hands. "Both are part of our Special Services group. They know about the existence of warlocks and the wizarding connection to them. They will keep your secret. Mistress Nelson is aware."

Jason nodded but made a mental note to discuss it with Mistress Nelson.

"Can you give us an update?" Silvers asked.

Jason started. "We detected some unusual magic, and I sent a drone. I saw someone firing into the sky at a border wall. We alerted the Castle and came here directly. When I fired on him, it caused some sort of explosion that killed him. We encountered two additional attackers and disarmed them. We were in the process of securing them, when a spell was sent that caused some sort of explosive device in their chests to explode."

"Any idea on who the fourth person was?" Oliver asked.

"From my senses I gathered it was a very weak warlock," Jason responded. The group walked over to view the bodies.

"Do you recognize any of them?" Guilford asked.

The ambassador looked at them closely along with Oliver and Wren. "I don't recognize them, but I will have my staff do some research." Wren took out his phone and took pictures of the dead men.

"I don't recognize any of them," Jason said. Using his wand, he sent pictures of each one back to the data center for identification. "If your team can't identify them, maybe ours can."

The ambassador said quick goodbyes and disappeared with his team.

"Okay, get your team back home and write this up. I want to know what you will do differently next time," Guilford said sternly.

"Yes, sir," Jason said. He turned to leave but Guilford put his hand on Jason's shoulder.

"Jason, as a leader you have to be ready for any situation. The mistake you made has been made countless times by new warlocks. The problem is you don't have the time to make the common mistakes. There is too much at stake now." Guilford patted Jason's back.

Jason nodded and Stepped back to his house. He should have returned to his office but felt the need for some quiet time to think. He would return to his office later and make the drive home to keep up appearances.

As he was leaving his home office, his security system notified him that a delivery truck had pulled up and was dropping off packages. He had been waiting for these. Each of his sisters had a box of his grandfather's belongings and he'd asked if he could borrow them. He put the two new boxes next to the box he already had and started investigating.

Before he'd left the Castle, he'd learned his wand had belonged to his grandfather and the One Realm group wanted it. Mistress Nelson ordered him to learn as much as possible about his grandfather and his wand. If the One Realm group wanted Jason's wand, they needed to know why.

Opening each of the boxes, he found old pictures, a baseball mitt that had belonged to his grandfather, several of his favorite books, and other items. On a hunch, he used his magical senses to scan the boxes. He found that each box contained a magical item. Pulling each from their box, he found three pieces of a doll. He assembled them together, but nothing happened.

Reaching out with his magic, he touched the doll and infused energy into it. The doll started to shake then displayed a 3D image of a person, too blurry to make out initially. Once the image cleared, he recognized the image as that of his grandfather.

"Grandson, it is so good to see you again," he said, walking over and hugging him. He was not completely solid which made the hug awkward.

"Grandpa Wes! Is it really you?"

His grandfather had always been special to Jason and he had deeply missed the man when he passed away.

"Yes, Jason it is me, but not all of me. I have longed for the day when we could talk again."

Jason felt happiness coming from his wand and it left its case on his hip.

"Old friend, it is good to see you too," his grandfather said to his wand, gently holding it. He released it and it returned to Jason.

"What do you mean by 'not all of me'?" Jason asked.

"Jason, sit down so I can explain. You may need to give the doll a little more energy to keep this image going," he said, and Jason complied.

"Thank you," he said when Jason was done adding energy. "Let me explain. As you probably know by now, your grandmother and I were both warlocks and we lived a very long life. Your grandmother was a very talented warlock and discovered many new spells. I, on the other hand, was much more talented using my wand to protect this realm. Long before she died, your grandmother had discovered how the Castle kept warlocks alive after they die."

"My valet, Rita, is one," Jason said.

"Rita? I knew her before she died. Very talented. It's horrible about her family. I guess it doesn't surprise me she was assigned to you." His grandfather said. "But back to the subject. Your grandmother Sue figured out how we could continue on to help you without being reliant on the Castle. Also, without the side effects that usually occur."

"Side effects?" Jason asked.

"Yes, the research available from the Castle showed that insanity was an inevitable outcome for anyone that continued on after death." His grandfather went on. "Your grandmother kept researching and found a way for us to continue to help you that wouldn't end with us going insane."

"And she is sure it will work?"

"Yes, she is sure. She said the fix was not that hard. In fact, she suspected that the Castle researchers knew the fix but purposefully hid it to discourage warlocks from using it."

"Does this make you immortal?" Jason asked.

"No, the spell will allow us to continue on, in a limited state, but will eventually give out. Once the spell fails, we are gone."

"I'm glad you are here, but you mentioned you did it to help me, why? And why were you worried about being reliant on the Castle?"

"The group that you call the One Realm was forming and I knew they would try to destroy all realms in their quest. The only wand that knows how the realm borders work, is yours. We learned that knowledge repairing the damage to a realm border. Knowledge that I knew you would need. That meant we needed to live longer to help you, but our bodies were failing, and I knew I was not up to taking them on by myself. So, your grandmother cast the spell on herself first and she became part of the forest behind the house. I followed shortly."

"When I was in the forest, I sensed several entities, not just two. Who are the others?" Jason asked.

"That I can't tell you. I created the entity talking to you just prior to my death. I only put enough information in it to help you connect with us in the forest. When you talk to the real me, I will explain. But my time is running short as this entity will not last much longer. Take the doll to the forest and it will help you connect to your grandmother and me."

"You didn't answer the question on why you were worried about being reliant on the Castle."

"It was because your grandmother and I had our suspicions that the Castle had been infiltrated and that some of the masters may have been working for the One Realm group," his grandfather replied.

"And how can I trust that this is actually you? This could be a trap." Jason didn't believe it was a trap but needed to be sure.

The imaged laughed. "Good point. I was left with two pieces of information. First, do you remember the magazine you found in the back of my closet? I never moved it after you found it the first time."

Jason blushed; he had found a mild porn magazine in his grandfather's closet when he was a kid. Fairly benign porn, considering the stuff on the internet now, but it was the first time for him to see a naked woman.

"The second?" he asked, trying to change the subject.

"You once told me that magic is what you were born to do," he said.

Jason had to turn away as a tear came to his eye. Only his grandfather would know that.

"Your response was 'then fulfill your destiny'," Jason responded.

"Good, we have that clear. Now, take the doll to the forest. There are magical items in it that your grandmother needs to finish her spell. I had just collected the last item but was pretty sure I was being followed. I hid them in the doll just in case and I created this entity in case something went wrong. I guess something did go wrong and I died before taking it to her. You must get this to us in the forest, without it we won't be able to help you. Good luck, grandson. Know that your grandmother and I love you." And then he disappeared.

Jason tried putting more energy into the doll, but the image would not return. He could feel sorrow flowing from his wand. "Yes, I miss him too, but we will figure out how to connect with them," he said.

The sense of sorrow from his wand turned to happiness, *Thank you!*

He wanted to go to the forest, but Guilford was waiting for his report and he needed to do some research. He Stepped back to his office at work and found an urgent email from the Data Center.

Opening the email, multiple 3D holographic images of the three dead from the attack. From what he read, each had been possible warlock candidates, not wizards as he first thought, and all disappeared in the last year. Concerning him the most was one of the attackers was also in the picture with the woman that his hacker group identified as Tess. His supposedly dead wife.

Replying back, he asked the Data Center to send the list of all warlock candidates that had been evaluated over the last two years. He wanted to go after Tess, but he didn't want to tip his hand yet.

He decided he needed to reach out to Katon to warn him. Using his wand, he called Katon.

"Jason! So glad to hear from you. How are things going?" Katon asked.

"Not good, almost got ambushed today and things seem to be escalating," he replied.

"Yeah, but I heard you guys recovered well."

"Thanks," Jason responded.

"I am assuming this isn't a social call, what's up?" Katon asked.

"Yeah, not a social call but first, we need to use a secure connection," he said. Jason and Katon had borrowed some encryption techniques from the IT world and came up with a way to encrypt their wand communications.

"All set. Now what is so important that we have to talk on a secured line?"

"I have sent in a request to the Data Center to provide a list of all warlock candidates over the last two years," Jason started.

"Yes, I'm aware." Katon replied.

"I want to add that I need to know how many of them ended up working for the Castle in any way. This request may actually help us find the ringleader of the One Realm. The ringleader was working with Jenkins and possibly others in the Castle. And I am worried that..."

Katon finished his sentence, "And you are worried that some of the others may be working in the Data Center."

"Unfortunately, yes."

"And you want me to keep an eye out to try and capture this person or persons."

"More than that, you need to be careful of these people. If they find out you suspect them, they will not hesitate to kill you," Jason said as bluntly as possible.

Katon hesitated for a moment. "Ah, I see your point. I think I need to increase security in the operations room."

"That would be a good start. Trust no one. Also, if a curvy brunet shows up in your research, do not investigate her. Send the information to me and say nothing to anyone."

"Wow, true cloak and dagger stuff, would be fun except it could lead to my death. I thought IT was a safe career choice," Katon mused, trying to lighten the conversation. It didn't work.

Jason hung up and started on his report for Guilford. Two hours later he was done and drove home.

Back home he immediately headed to his home office as he needed to warn his hacker group. If they continued searching for Tess, she would track them down and kill them.

The hacker group had always been paranoid about the government coming after them. They had given him a web address to go to if Jason suspected that they were after them. Using an old laptop, he opened up a browser and went to the site they gave him. He had a prearranged message that he was to enter in a single text box. He added "If in peril, call me" then hit Submit. He hoped they would understand his addition to the message. If his ex-wife or her group went after them, their only chance was for him to rescue them. Afterwards, he destroyed the laptop knowing all too well that it was probably infected.

Two hours later the website that contained all of the information on the grail search for his wife was gone. The Round Table hacker group had received the message and had gone underground.

After dinner with the family, he took his grandfathers' doll out to the forest. As he entered the forest, the orbs approached. They swirled around him and he could feel only joy. His wand left its holster and joined the orbs spiraling around. He held up the doll and it too was lifted into the air.

"Will you be able to use that to communicate with me?"

Yes, was their reply.

"How long?"

Not sure. Days, weeks, they replied.

"Hmm, I was hoping for a little sooner than that, but I will wait." His wand returned to his holster.

"Grandma and Grandpa, I hope you are there. I need to know everything I can about realm borders and how to prevent their destruction," he said.

The orbs swirled around him for a second, then left with the doll.

For the next several weeks, things were quiet. None of the missing warlock candidates had shown up and no more attacks occurred.

Weston continued his research on the stone Jason had recovered. He had learned a lot about it and even theorized how to recreate the storage device.

Jason and his team continued their training under Guilford and Rita. Jason pushed them to learn as much as possible and to become as strong as they could. Dueling was a daily affair, and his team was getting better. Jason continued to be the strongest, but the others were learning how to balance the scale.

While Guilford concentrated on combat training, Rita concentrated on technical items. She taught them how to erase someone's short term memory of an event. It was fairly limited but useful. Traumatic events were hard to remove and anything that occurred more than thirty minutes prior was difficult to erase. There were techniques for those types of memories, but they required in-depth studies they did not have time for.

"The next thing I am going to teach you is how to temporarily slow time," Rita said.

"That sounds like fun, will it take long?" Jason joked. A general groan from the group let him know they did not appreciate his dad humor.

"Actually, Jason, you have already done it. Unintentionally, of course," Rita quipped.

"Uh, I have?" Jason asked. Thinking about it, he realized she was talking about when he tested for his attack spell. During the test, he was required to pull together Fire and Ice energies. When he did, it caused an explosion and time had slowed.

"My attack test," he said, and she nodded. "But I didn't do it on purpose, and I am not sure how I did it."

"Doesn't matter, once you have done it, it is easy to recreate. Everyone bring up your senses and be ready. Jason, I will join our energies and show you," Rita said. Guilford turned away, looking uncomfortable but said nothing.

Rita noted Guilford's actions but ignored it. She reached over and touched Jason. He could feel her energy mingle with his.

Ready? He heard in his head.

Yes.

Concentrate on someone and put energy into your senses, he heard.

He looked at each of his team and selected Dod. Concentrating, he poured energy into his senses. He could feel Rita shaping the energy and understood what she was doing and joined in. Everyone around them, except Guilford, slowed to a crawl. A leaf that had been floating down from a tree, hung in mid-air. He reached up and plucked it.

As Jason walked behind Dod, Guilford followed his movements with his eyes. When Jason waved to Guilford, he waved back.

Jason was using a lot of energy to maintain the spell and released it before he ran out of energy.

"Where did he go?" Dod asked and spun around. Spotting Jason, "That was cool!"

"Yeah, it was," Jason said, turning to Guilford. "But how were you able to track me?"

"The magic to slow time is well known by warlocks, even the more powerful wizards can do it. It can be felt once you know what to look for. Once you know, it is easy to match."

Rita interrupted them. "I think I need to return to the Castle." She looked pale and almost transparent.

"I will take you," Guilford said opening a portal and pulling Rita through it. They both disappeared.

"What just happened?" Gail asked.

"Rita is an extension of the Castle and can only last so long away from the Castle. My guess is that she used too much energy helping me slow time," Jason said. He worried even though past experience told him she would be fine.

He was about to end the training session and go check on her when a message popped up on his wand

A border wall attack is starting, sending location, it was a message from the Data Center. Since the last attack, a team had been working on a better way to detect when a border attack began.

"Alright. We have another situation, and I am assuming they have laid a trap for us. Time to put our plan into action," he said. Bull appeared next to him.

He conjured up Eagle, opened a portal, and sent him through. Along with the satellites the Data Center had tapped into, he would provide reconnaissance information.

The team at the Castle is ready and waiting on your command, Bull said.

"Shields up. On my mark. 1, 2, 3, Step!" he yelled.

They Stepped and he immediately ducked for cover as a barrage of fire came at Jason. He was the only one near the enemy as planned. Jason quickly detected five magical beings, most likely failed trainees, behind a nearby tree stand. Another group hid behind two large boulders.

"Where are the rest of them?" a woman's voice came from behind the boulders. Before any of her companions could answer, Jason's team appeared behind them and laid down a crosspatch of fire that downed several of the attackers before they knew what was going on.

Jason Stepped to a position behind the boulders, stood, and opened up a series of rapid-fire sequences clearing out more of the attackers. Another group of attackers appeared only to be slammed into by Bull. Weston mopped up the few that still stood. Jason was assessing the situation when he felt Eagle being attacked.

He looked up to see a huge vulture attacking Eagle. Jason fed Eagle energy allowing him to grow and match the size of the Vulture.

Thank you, I will handle this thing, Eagle said.

Jason jumped in surprise. When did Eagle start talking?

"Jason, we need help!" Dod yelled.

"Bull!" he yelled and Stepped to where Dod and Katrina were. Katrina was on the ground and not moving. Two warlocks were also down, blood everywhere. Dod was firing at someone behind a large rock. Jason's anger raged as he ramped up his power and waited. To his surprise, Tess stepped out from behind the rock and fired at him. He hesitated but managed to use his energy to divert the shot away from him. Raising his wand, he returned fire, hitting her, and Tess went down.

He was surprised when she stood back up and returned fire. This time he couldn't divert the entire shot and his shield saved him, but he still went flying, landing hard on the ground. He rolled and fired with a heavy dose of energy, more than he should have but he needed to end this. Tess diverted the energy, but she diverted it into a nearby boulder, which blew up and knocked her down.

Jason prepared to fire again when she disappeared. He started shouting commands that they'd practiced and prepared for.

"Shield the area," he yelled to two masters who came running up.

Opening a line to the Castle, "Castle, we have multiple wounded coming in. Tell Gail and Weston, I need them here now," he yelled.

Between battling Tess and seeing Katrina hurt, Jason's emotions were trying to take over and he fought to remain calm. His team needed his full attention to get this situation under control. He could break down later.

Gail appeared first and went straight to Katrina, pulled her wand, and started assessing her injuries. She then looked at the other two downed warlocks. "Dod, can you help me get them to the Castle?" she asked.

When Dod nodded, the two levitated the wounded and Stepped them back to the Castle.

Mistress Nelson and Master Kien arrived. Guilford was hog-tying the remaining captives and Jason jogged over to meet them.

"Jason, what in the beast's hell happened here. This should have been a dunk slammed," Mistress Nelson said, almost yelling at him.

"It would have been a slam dunk," he yelled correcting her. "if it hadn't been for Tess showing up!"

His energy started to surge, and he slammed his fist into a nearby boulder. His guide was severely injured, two other warlocks were hurt, and Tess turned out to be much stronger than he expected. This situation was his fault. He stared down at the rock, now with a crack down the middle. His hand hurt but the pain felt good. He could feel his body healing his hand and almost stopped the process. Luckily, the logical part of his brain won out and his hand finished healing.

"Dragon's ass," Master Kien sputtered, stomping around like an enraged bear. "Did we capture any of her people?"

"Yes, we captured four, twelve died in the battle. We were about to take them back to the Castle," Guilford said.

"Good, we can interrogate them and find out what the heck is going on," Mistress Nelson said angrily.

"Wait, I don't think it's a good idea to take them straight back to the Castle," Jason said. This was too easy. Tess would plan in multiple steps. She had known they were coming so why didn't she kill her fighters when she had a chance.

"I think that is what Tess wants us to do. Is there someplace else we can take them until we can be sure she didn't set another trap?" Jason said.

Mistress Nelson was about to answer when a huge, dead, vulture slammed into the ground near them. Eagle landed next to it with a crash. Blood dripped from several open wounds, but he looked very satisfied at his work.

Does anyone want to share in the feast with me? Eagle asked.

Almost everyone declined except for Bull.

I would be honored. It is a good kill you have there, Bull replied. Eagle's back straightened as the big bird stood taller. Through Jason's connection with Eagle, he could sense its pride.

"I will leave the feast to you two, but it is a good kill," Jason said. Eagle nodded back, the sense of pride coming from the bird almost overwhelmed Jason. The two started in on the kill and everyone returned to the prisoners to avoid watching the carnage.

Approaching the four prisoners he found three women and one man. Jason noted with pleasure they were watching Bull and Eagle rip apart the dead vulture. They held a nervous look and Jason decided to play off this.

"Once they are finished with it, they are going to use you four as dessert." He sent a mental message to the two animals who responded by howling and screeching. The four prisoners went pale.

"Please keep your shields at max," he told the two warlocks guarding the prisoners. He turned his attention back to the prisoners. "My guide is injured and so are two others. To make it worse, my ex just tried to kill me. To say that I would be just as happy to let those two eat you is an understatement."

He was about to further threaten them when he felt a power surge. One prisoner, a woman, began screaming, "get it out, get it out." Jason opened a portal and sent the four through it with their dead companions to a spot several hundred yards away. Just as he closed the portal, the prisoners exploded, wiping out a football-sized area. Even though they were quite a distance away, everyone still felt the shock wave.

"We need to clean up quickly and get out of here, someone is going to detect that explosion and send a team to check it out," Guilford said.

"Everyone needs to leave now; I have a team that will repair the area before the local authorities arrive. They will find a natural gas leak that exploded but we all need to return to the Castle now," Mistress Nelson commanded.

They all Stepped, and Jason landed in his room back at the Castle. He looked around his room for a minute, hoping to clear his mind. Nothing had changed since he had left. He looked out his magical window that displayed scenes from places all over this realm and others. He could see a beautiful sunset from a place he did not recognize and tried to enjoy the beauty of it.

He quickly realized he was avoiding the task in front of him and decided he needed to get moving.

"Castle, where are Mistress Nelson and the others?"

You are to meet them in her office, the Castle responded.

"Castle, please scan any person or item returning for any type of explosive, listening, or tracking devices," he asked.

That was already done prior to your arrival. Multiple devices were found and removed. We continue to do new scans to find anything we may have missed, the Castle responded.

Jason decided for now, they should be safe. While Tess did plan ahead, it was usually only two-to-three steps. She felt any farther out was too unpredictable.

"Do you know the status of Katrina?" he asked.

She is in critical condition but is expected to recover. One of the two warlocks brought in is also in critical condition. The other is currently being treated and prognosis is unknown.

"Damn," was all he could say.

Mistress Nelson wants you to meet her in her office now. Dod and Weston will be there. She has instructed you can visit your injured guide after you meet with her.

Anything Jason had to say at that point would probably not go over well with the Castle. He bit his lip instead. He took one last look around and longed to take a nap in his bed or even soak in the tub. He shook his head, neither would help Katrina so he headed to Mistress Nelsons office as fast as he could.

Arriving, he found a contingent of masters all talking rapidly. Mistress Nelson was conversing with Guilford and Kien. They looked up when he approached.

"Bull and Eagle?" Kien asked.

"After the vulture was cleared of explosives, they took it to finish off their meal. Bull is helping Eagle heal and will join us shortly," Jason stated.

Dod came into the room and went straight to him. She enveloped him in a hug, and he held on to her as she started to cry. The room went silent as she sobbed.

"I'm sorry, I tried. Katrina had her shield up on max but took a full blast. If it wasn't for your damn insistence to strengthen our shields, we would both be dead," she said. She pulled herself away from Jason.

"Yeah, I can be a task master when I want to be but right now, I need the full story, what happened?" he asked.

"Mistress Nelson, can you help me show them what happened like you did with Jason?" Dod asked.

"Yes, but are you sure you are up to this?"

"Oh, hell yes," Dod stated, her moment of tears replaced with the anger Jason knew she held.

Mistress Nelson walked over and put her hand on Dod. Dod closed her eyes and a look of intense concentration came over her. After a minute, an image was projected in the middle of the room.

When they spotted Tess, Dod and Katrina came in from one direction and several other warlocks came in from two other directions. This left Tess in a three-way crossfire. But from the look on her face, she wasn't worried.

One of the warlocks ordered Tess to drop her wand but instead she rapid-fired on both warlocks. Several more of Tess's army appeared and also fired on the warlocks. For thirty seconds, it was a firefight as the warlocks took hits and two went down, but the rest managed to kill Tess's followers while she hung back, coordinating her forces. With Tess's followers gone, Katrina pointed her wand at Tess and open fired, hitting her, and knocking her back. Jason immediately saw Katrina's mistake as she used too much energy and her shield was weak. Dod tried to extend her shield to Katrina when Tess fired. Dod's shield was probably the only reason Katrina still lived. When Katrina went down, Dod's eyes flashed in anger and she fired on Tess, hitting her. He could tell that Dod had hurt Tess and she returned fire. Dod both dodged the shot and used her energy to guide it away from her.

Dod grabbed Katrina and pulled her behind a rock and called for help. Three seconds later, Jason appeared, and the image stopped.

Jason projected his own memory. It began as Tess reached down and touched something on her belt. The way she stood taller made him think she somehow had just reenergized herself.

"Weston, I need you to look at that thing on Tess's belt. Something isn't right," and Weston nodded and approached the image. Weston examined the image but looked puzzled.

Jason continued replaying his memory, stopping after Tess got up from the first time he fired on her. Examining her closely, he could see she was hurt by the way she held her arm and the blood coming from a cut on her shoulder.

He continued the image to the point where Tess deflected his second shot into the boulder and it exploded, sending her flying.

"I need to go back there right now," Weston yelled and before anyone could say anything, he disappeared.

"Dammit Weston," Jason yelled and was about to Step to the scene when he received a message from Weston that he was now back at the scene and he would return in a moment.

Jason continued replaying the memory. He could see Tess land hard but then he saw something he did not expect. Another person appeared, grabbed Tess, and disappeared. Another warlock had Stepped into the battle and saved Tess.

He backed up the image trying to see the unknown warlock's face but whoever it was, kept his back to Jason.

"Any idea who that is?" Jason asked the group, pointing to the back of the man picking up Tess.

"There is something familiar about this person, but I just don't know what," Kien said.

Jason continued his replay to the part where Tess's followers had blown up.

"Pretty cold hearted to blow up your followers. But didn't we have a shield to prevent that from happening?" Master Sophia asked.

"We did, but she didn't set them off remotely. I think they were on a timer. Those people were going to die either way. The question is, were they meant to kill us or was it part of the process to break down the realm border?" Jason pondered.

"What do you mean Jason?" Mistress Nelson asked.

"For the last attack it took us nearly fifteen minutes to detect the event and then another five minutes to mount an attack. This time we detected the event as soon as it started. Instead of being there in twenty minutes, we were there in two," Jason said slowly, trying to work out the pieces of the puzzle in his mind.

"I'm guessing Tess believes that to bring down the border between the realms she needs to expose the border, weaken it with a spell, and then use a blast to finish it off. But we cut off the spell early so the border was hidden and protected when her followers exploded," Jason continued.

"We need to be careful. Next time Tess may try to use our own firepower to destroy the realm border," Jason said finally understanding where Tess was going with this.

"I think I might be able to help," Weston said walking into the office. "I saw the spell the wizard was using to weaken the realm wall and I think I know how to stop it."

"Your ability to see magic is coming in handy," Jason said.

"Yeah, it sure has. When I first met you, I thought everyone could see spells. But I was wrong, I can see them, Gail can see a little. But so far, we are the only ones I know about," Weston said.

Jason detected a bit of pride in his voice. Being able to see a spell would go a long way toward understanding a spell and recreating it. Jason had learned several spells with Rita's help. Since she was no longer human and now a magical being, she could show Jason the inner workings of a spell which allowed him to master them faster. Being able to see magic and how it works would be a much faster way to learn.

"And you think you can come up with a way to block the spell?" Mistress Nelson asked.

Weston scratched his head. "Yes, but it will take me some time. If Gail and a few of the warlocks I worked with before could help, it would speed the process."

"Where is Gail?" Jason asked.

"She is assisting our medical staff with the wounded," Master Sophia responded.

This didn't surprise him; Gail had a gift for healing. He secretly hoped she was working on Katrina.

"When she is done aiding the wounded, she can join you. Whoever you need to figure this out, just let me know. Please get started now," Mistress Nelson said.

Weston nodded. "I have one other item that may help," he said and handed Jason a small pack.

He instantly recognized it as the pack that Tess had touched and seemingly reenergized herself. He could feel remnants of magic in it, but it felt different. He knew this magic but couldn't remember where from. He handed the pack back to Weston.

"Something about the magic in it feels familiar. I am guessing that is how Tess refreshed her power," Jason said.

"It should feel familiar," Weston said, "it's made from the same basic material that is in the portal stone you found."

Of course. The remnants of magic in it were the same but the material felt a little different.

"Could we use that pack?" Jason asked.

"We could, but we have two problems. First, it does not store typical warlock energy. If it did, it would hold only a small amount. Not enough to do much good. It takes two different power types, and the material helps fuel whatever fuses the two to create warlock energy. This fusion creates a considerable amount of energy, I'm guessing. The problem is I don't know what energies are used to fuel the device," Weston said.

"The second problem?" Jason asked.

"The device that mixes the two energies and delivers it to the user is missing," Weston said.

"For the energy issue, I might have an idea on who to ask," Jason said mulling over his idea.

"I will work on the second problem," Weston said.

"Her ability to replenish her energy is a concern, especially if her followers were able to also. If we end up in a war with Tess and her followers," Mistress Nelson said, "it would be a significant advantage in battle. Weston, please take it back to your lab and continue your work with the other masters."

"Jason, any luck on learning more about your grandfather's wand?" Mistress Nelson asked.

"He left some magical clues for me to solve and I'm working on them. Hopefully, I will have some answers soon," he replied.

Jason kept the fact that his grandparents were not dead a secret. He wasn't sure how the warlock world would take to finding that his grandparents still existed. Plus, he didn't want Tess or anyone from her group to know. If they found out, they would be at his house in no time.

"Jason, they know about your wand. I wouldn't be surprised if they set a trap, targeting you, during the next attack," Kien said pulling Jason from his thoughts.

"Yeah, I thought of that. My guess is that Tess was setting up a trap for me, but I arrived too soon. She also might have expected me to go after her first. I will be ready next time. I suspect we have some time before the next attack. She has to recover, go over every detail from the attack, then plan out every detail for the next one," he said.

Tess was good at planning for every possible contingency. But it also meant that if he came up with an unusual angle, it typically blew up her plans. They used to play board games and she won a lot. But he won his fair share by being unpredictable.

"I know we have to plan for the next attack, but it can wait. I need to see my injured guide," he said with a look that made it clear he was not going to be denied. When no one challenged him, he left.

Arriving at the infirmary, he found Le Anna sitting next to Katrina. Katrina was lying in bed with bandages that covered her from her knees all the way above her chest. She looked tired and grimaced in pain. Gail was examining her with her senses, and he could detect she was trying to heal her. He waited until she stopped then headed over. As he approached Katrina pulled her blanket over the bandages. Jason sensed some embarrassment from Katrina and approached slowly.

"Katrina, how are you? I have been worried sick about you," he said taking her hand.

"The medical staff say I will be okay," Katrina said groggily. "Just some scarring and other things I will have to deal with." Tears ran down her face and she wiped them away. She looked at Jason but quickly turned away and sobbed. "I'm sorry, I'm just really tired."

Le Anna gently held her hand.

He was about to ask what the issue was, but Gail shook her head then nodded toward a person standing nearby. Dressed in a lab coat and carrying a clipboard, Jason assumed he was a doctor. Jason went straight to him.

"Excuse me, are you treating Katrina?" he asked. He needed to know why they weren't healing Katrina. He was mad at the doctors but letting his anger loose would help nothing and he did his best to suppress it.

"Yes, I am Master Ryhsan and I am the head healer here. What can I do for you?" he said.

"Katrina seems very upset. She mentioned scarring and other issues, why aren't you healing her?" he asked.

"It's because she is not a warlock," he said, Jason geared himself up for a full-on explosion when Gail spoke up.

"Jason, it's not what you think. Let him explain," she said.

Jason drew a deep breath to steady himself. "Please continue."

"Typically, when a warlock comes in injured, we just add to their energy so they can heal themselves. Some injuries warlocks cannot heal by themselves and we actively heal their wounds for them. She is not a warlock and while we can heal her wounds, and even keep the scarring to a minimum, returning her body to her original state is not something we can do. We can get close, but I'm sure it won't be enough. She was badly burned and the type of reconstructive healing she needs is beyond what we can provide here. There are some retired warlocks that may be able to do it, but they often want a lot for their services. Usually in the form of warlock currency. Even on a Senior's salary, I am not sure you could afford their services." Ryhsan looked down. "I am very sorry."

"Jason, I will research this and figure out a way, but it will take me a while," Gail said. Her eyes were bloodshot, and tears ran down her face.

It took Jason only a moment to realize that with the bandage across her body, it could only mean one thing.

I know your upset, but do you mind not squeezing so hard? His wand said. He had unconsciously been gripping his wand, evidently too hard.

Sorry, he said relaxing his grip, *I need a way to help Katrina, but I don't know how.*

I heard what the healer said, and I know a way for you to help, his wand said.

How? Jason asked.

Do you remember the wands you sold to the ambassador? His wand asked.

Damn, of course. Thank you, Jason said.

"Castle. Please show the healer how much credit I have from the wands I returned to the wizard's ambassador," he asked. During a battle he won, he received ownership of several wizard's wands. The wizard's ambassador had offered to pay handsomely for them. It was only recently he had found out how much.

The Castle displayed the amount, and the healer took a step back. "It will take about half of what you have." He paused for a moment. "Are you sure?"

"I would gladly give it all up for any member of my team," he said a little too loud. He was fighting back his emotions and on the verge of breaking down. He couldn't even imagine the pain and anguish Katrina must be going through. The very thought was destroying him.

"Then we will make it happen. Thank you, the staff has been distraught that we couldn't do more for her. This type of healing is something we are trying to learn and hopefully we can learn to help others," he said. "I must warn you that she may not be completely healed. This is experimental magic at best."

He started to walk away but stopped and turned, "I hope someday I have a friend like you in my life."

"Thank you. I do want to make sure Gail is part of the process to heal Katrina. We need someone on my team that knows how to do this." Was all he could say.

He left the healer and returned to Katrina.

"I'm so sorry Jason, I didn't mean to cry, it's just..." and Katrina stopped.

"No need to apologize. I just spoke with the healer; they are bringing in a specialist who will do their best to restore you to good as new," he said.

She looked up hopefully. "Jason, they told me it was a lot of money. I can't afford that," she said breaking into tears again.

"I can't afford to not have one of my guides and I am paying for it. No arguments or I will have to write you up," he said trying to add some levity.

All it managed to do was make Katrina cry more. "Thank you!"

Le Anna came around the bed and hugged him.

"If you two make me cry, I will write you both up," he said fighting back the tears. Both women laughed and it gave him a moment to regain his composure. He held their hands for a minute, treasuring his friends. He had almost lost one of them and he swore he would do better.

"I have to get back and figure out our next steps," he said and kissed them each goodbye.

Gail walked him out to the hallway.

"Jason, there is something you need to know." From the look on her face, he knew he wasn't going to like what he was about to hear.

"I believe that what Tess did to Katrina was intentional. The shot she fired was meant to burn her alive. Dod's shield took a huge hit. Tess didn't just want to kill Katrina, she wanted to mutilate her terribly," Gail said.

"How do you know this?" Jason asked.

"A full shot would have contained both fire and ice, but her shot had no ice component. She wanted Katrina to burn," Gail said shakily.

Jason pondered the situation for a second. "I see your point," he took a breath trying to fathom how anyone could be that evil. Never in a million years would he had expected Tess to do something like this. Something changed her and he wanted to know what.

He shook his head to pull himself together. "Either she is trying to get back at me or she is trying to provoke me. Once she hears that Katrina can be fully healed, Tess will try again. Instruct the healer to tell no one about the reconstructive surgery. To everyone outside of this room, Katrina is horribly disfigured and there is no hope."

"I will make sure that the medical staff knows that breaking our secret will be very painful," she said with a determined look on her face. "One last question," she paused then looked him directly in the eyes, "what you said about giving it all up for any member of your team. Is that really true?" Gail asked.

For probably the first time since he met her, Gail did not have her usual self-confident look. The tears in her eyes and look of sorrow completely disarmed him. Gail always carried herself like she knew who she was, where she was going, and what she needed to do. This was not that woman standing in front of him. The attack on Katrina had shaken Gail to her core.

"To save Katrina, Le Anna, Weston, Dod, or you, I would gladly give up everything. This I promise," he said.

"Thank you," she whispered and hugged him, holding him tightly. When she released him, she wiped the tears from her eyes and straightened her shoulders. "I knew you were a leader I could put my faith in. Just know, I will always be there for you too." She turned to check on Katrina.

Jason leaned against the hallway wall for a minute, trying to keep his emotions in check. He had a team that believed in him and a woman he once loved who now wanted to kill all of them. Could his life get any crazier? Better question, was he really the person they should be following? So far, the only answer he could come up with was no and this had to change.

He shook his head to clear it. He needed a plan to save them and one was forming. His first step was to be return to Mistress Nelson's office to set things in motion. He made a beeline back to her office, ignoring all that he encountered. Walking in, he marched to her desk. "I'm forming a plan to take out Tess and her group, and will need resources," he said. He wasn't sure how Mistress Nelson would react to his taking control.

Mistress Nelson paused. "You think you can stop Tess? Maybe even kill her if necessary?"

Her questions didn't surprise him, but it still shook him. He took a deep breath. "Yes, I believe I can stop Tess and end this madness. If I have to kill her, so be it. I will capture her alive if I can, but right now my priority is saving the realm," he said as confidently as he could.

Mistress Nelson stared at him for a minute. "All right. As of this moment you have access to any resource you need. Know this, if I see any weakness in your ability to stop Tess, I will take over," she said, holding eye contact with him.

"Fair enough." He had expected as much. "Right now, I need four of your best warlocks to guard Katrina. Tess will come after her if she finds out Katrina survived. Also, I need to redirect the full processing power of the data center."

"Done, I know the ideal warlocks that will fit the bill for guarding Katrina. I will also let Katon know you will be needing the services of the data center."

Twenty minutes later he was standing in the middle of the data center operations area. Every eye was on him as all work had halted. More than a few staff were upset they had been assigned to work for him. Katon stood uneasy next to him, having his staff idled was not sitting well with him. Jason had met Katon during Jason's training. Katon was also a Senior and currently led the Data Center. The young man held a vast knowledge about technology and Jason, having spent most of his life in IT, took instant liking to him.

"Today, for the second time, my not-so-dead-wife Tess and the group called 'The One Realm' has tried to bring down the barriers between realms. We stopped them again but at the cost of three people in the infirmary. One person, one of my guides, is badly burned and scarred for life," he paused to let that sink in. Many of the hard stares he received softened when he flashed pictures of those injured on the central display for everyone to see.

"Today we are going to use the talents of this group to save the realm and destroy this rogue group." Many in the group sat up straight, eager to hear more.

"You have the technology, knowledge, and skill to give us the information we need to nail this group. I believe in you. Do you believe?" he asked.

There was a general murmur as everyone started talking. Finally, Katon stepped up. "Are we going to nail this bitch and her army before they kill everyone we love?" he yelled.

The entire room erupted in a resounding, "Hell yeah!"

Jason eyed Katon for a moment. Realizing what he just said about Jason's ex-wife, Katon turned red.

"Sorry, no disrespect intended," Katon said staring at the ground.

Jason waited a moment and continued. "Thank you for your support. Here is what we are going to do. You will form into three teams. The first team will review the first attack and determine why they selected that particular location. Starting three days before till three-days afterwards you will review every bit of data. If there were a higher-than-average number of toilet flushes in the area, we need to know about it. The second team will do the same for the second attack and the two teams will share data. The third team is going to use every bit of technology in this world to track Tess and her followers. A hacker group called The Round Table did it and so can you. Any questions?"

When there were no questions, he continued, "Katon will identify the teams and you will start now. This will be a round-the-clock-operation. All leaves canceled and as much coffee and pizza as you can eat. Now let's get going!"

Jason knew he would be in the way and left as soon as he could.

Chapter Six

The data center staff were working hard on their research and Katon promised results soon. A retired warlock had been selected by Master Ryhsan that he felt could heal Katrina completely. As expected, his price was high, but Jason didn't care. Between his warlock salary and the income from the business, he had no money issues. Katrina's treatments began immediately, and she responded well. The healer didn't know when she would finish her treatments. This was experimental magic, and he wasn't sure when, or if, she would be healed.

Jason had established a monthly team lunch allowing each person to select a restaurant. With the group consisting of his team, their guides, his guides, and Rita's aides, it became more of a social event than just lunch. Most of the ladies and some of the men would spend days figuring out what they would wear. Even Gail, got in on the action as she reviewed her possible choices with Weston, which usually went along the lines of him liking every outfit. Eventually, Gail would give up and ask someone else. Weston had a complete blind spot to both fashion and Gail. She could wear a paper bag and Weston would say she looked beautiful.

Rita coordinated the outing, with each team member getting to pick a lunch spot. This month was Katrina's turn, and she picked a buffet restaurant called the "Southern Imperial Buffet" which combined traditional southern food with specialties from across Asia. Most of the group moaned at the selection. Previous locations had been expensive, upscale restaurants and a buffet wasn't quite in line with the rest of the team's expectations. But with Katrina in a wheelchair and still recovering from her injuries, no one argued. All were just happy to have her with them.

Using magic burned a lot of calories and the group had been training hard. Jason was a little worried as his team looked a little thin and he had been having food brought in to help stop the weight loss. The typical warlock could out-eat the average person. An all-you-could eat buffet was perfect as the group could eat as much as they wanted, and the bill would be reasonable. With the company doing well, he didn't mind the cost, but it wouldn't be a bad thing to spend a little less on lunch every once in a while. Okay, he was a bit tight with money.

Rita had negotiated reservations and when the group arrived, they found their seats waiting. Wasting no time, they swarmed the buffet. It was like a plague of locust descending on the food and by the time they sat down, the serving tables were almost empty. The owner of the restaurant, a short, heavy-set woman with a tan complexion, gave the group a nasty look until she saw that everyone cleared their plates. Many commenting on how great the food was. This put a smile on the owner's face, and she ordered her staff to keep loading the buffet.

The group again, descended on the replenished buffet and started filling their plates. "Dod, you have to try the green beans," Gail remarked.

"Try the beef tips, they are wonderful," someone added.

Le Anna walked over to the owner and gave her a hug. "Thanks for making this lunch spectacular for my friend." She pointed to Katrina. She then walked off, leaving the owner in tears. The owner started yelling at her staff to get more food out. The head chef came out and watched with wide eyes at the horde decimating his buffet. The owner said something to the chef and nodded toward Katrina. With a determined look, the chef returned to his kitchen. War had been declared and the look on his face told that he would not lose.

Immediately, the sounds from the kitchen doubled with pots and pans clattering, cooks yelling at each other, and orders shouted to move faster. The kitchen staff now knew the challenge and they didn't plan to lose. A steady stream of food began flowing from the kitchen. So much so that every employee was enlisted to get the food to the buffet. Bus boys, waiters, even the hostess were carrying pots of various dishes to the buffet. But as fast as the food came in, his team was all over it, only slightly slowing to allow other patrons to get some food. It was a pitched battle as his team had also picked up on the challenge and took advantage of every bit of food they could put on a plate.

Eventually, the pace of his team refilling their plates slowed and the sounds from the kitchen diminished. The chef came out to review the situation. He was sweating heavily and looked slightly out of breath. As he surveyed the buffet and the table of very full customers, he smiled. He'd won his war.

Jason had been waiting for his staff to get their final fill before getting more food. With everyone seated and eating, now was a good time and he made his way through the tables to the buffet. As he approached the bar, he noticed a young man filling his plate. The man stood a little over five feet with dark brown hair and fair complexion. Something about him, caught Jason's attention and Jason used his senses to scan him. Surprisingly, the man held some power. Weak compared to anyone on his team, but Jason had to wonder how he would have looked prior to going to the Castle.

The young man looked up as Jason approached and Jason could feel him scanning Jason. It was very different from anything he'd felt before. The man put on the biggest smile, "Hello! You are special like me."

Jason smiled back. "Hello. Yes, I am," he replied. He recognized that he had Down syndrome, which set off an alarm for him. He remembered Mistress Nelson's early comment about eliminating those with limited power since they could be dangerous. How would she view this person? For now, he decided to keep his discovery a secret.

"My name is Jason, what is yours?"

"My name is Steven, very nice to meet you." He put down his plate and shook Jason's hand vigorously. When Jason first met Weston, Weston had almost hit him in the face trying to shake his hand. Weston meeting Steven could be an interesting, if not painful, event.

"What's your favorite food here?" Jason asked.

"I like making tacos. Tacos are my favorite," Steven replied.

Jason wasn't a hundred percent positive that Steven knew he was magical and decided to give Steven a test. "Can you tell me if any of my friends are special like us?"

Steven looked over his friends, "They all are. I have never seen so many special people in one place," he paused, "And I have never seen anyone glow like the lady in red."

Rita was the only woman wearing red and it confirmed that Steven could see magic. What made it unusual was that every one of them had camouflaged their magic. Steven should not be able to see their magic, yet he could. This was unusual and could have its advantages.

Several at his table were watching and some even scanned Steven. Steven didn't seem to mind, even looking at each person scanning him. Dod stood and walked over.

"Jason, looks like you made a new friend." She offered her hand to Steven. "My name is Dod."

"My name is Steven. You are very pretty," he said excitedly. Steven very much liked Dod, that was clear.

"There are so many special people here. Is that man over there your friend also?" Steven asked, pointing to a man sitting alone at a nearby table.

Jason scanned the man; he did have magic that was well hidden. Jason watched as the man pulled out his wallet, dropped some money on the table, and stood to leave.

"Excuse me sir," Dod called out. The man took a quick look at her and ran into the nearby restroom door.

Dod walked quickly after the man. Jason followed, trying not to run. He managed to stop Dod before she entered the men's room.

"What?" she asked.

"Are you really going to go into the men's room with everyone watching?"

With the stranger running into the restroom, then Dod and Jason following, every eye in the restaurant was on them. She turned and entered the women's room. Jason put his hand on his wand, ramped up his shield, and entered the men's room to find it empty.

A quick scan found residual energy that indicated it was a wizard they had encountered. He left the restroom and headed back to the buffet where Steven and a woman in her mid-thirties stood watching him. Dod joined him as he approached Steven.

"How is your friend? You look worried about him," Steven asked.

"Uh, he isn't feeling well and went home. Who is this?" Jason asked, trying to change the conversation.

"I'm Carol, Steven's mother. Nice to meet you." She seemed a little wary of Jason as she put her hand out to shake. She stood about five-foot-six with brunette hair. She wore scrubs and he guessed that she worked in the nearby hospital.

"My name is Jason Canin, and this is my friend and coworker, Dod," he said, introducing her. Steven's mom relaxed a little upon meeting Dod.

"Nice to meet you," Carol replied.

Jason waved his arm toward his team. "We're here for a team lunch. We've had a good month and are celebrating."

"Oh, where do you work?" Carol asked.

"Castle Investments," Jason replied. He thought the name was quite clever though no one on his team agreed. "I am the CEO and Dod is one of our vice presidents. We own quite a few investment properties including self-storage facilities across the nation, along with several other companies."

"Are you hiring? I need a job," Steven interjected.

"Sorry about that," Carol said. "Steven really likes to work but lost his job when a new manager came in."

Steven frowned. "She didn't like people like me." For the first time since meeting him, Steven was not smiling.

"Actually, we are," Dod piped up. "A couple of our clerks left for college and we are very short handed. We pay well but expect everyone to work hard. Are you interested, Steven?"

Jason wasn't sure about Dod's idea. But having Steven close by made it easier to watch him until they could figure out how to keep Mistress Nelson from eliminating a potential threat.

"That's a great idea. Steven, you would be helping us tremendously. Plus, we special people like to stick together," he added. If Jason could harness the power of a smile, he would have hit the jackpot with Steven. His smile seemed to radiate throughout the restaurant.

"Yes, I would like that," Steven almost shouted.

Jason reached into his wallet and pulled out a business card. "Okay, here is my card. Be at that address at nine a.m. on Monday. Work hours are eight to five, Monday through Friday.

Dod jerked a thumb in Jason's direction. "He pays well, and you will get full benefits."

"Thank you so much," Carol said, shaking Dod and Jason's hand.

Dod and Jason returned to their table. "Now I just need to figure out how to keep Mistress Nelson away from him," he said, sitting down.

"We'll figure it out," Dod replied.

"Did anyone get a good look at the mystery wizard following us?" Jason asked.

"I did and should be able to recreate an image of him," Weston said.

"No need," Gail stated. "I took his picture with my phone and sent it to the Castle data center to track him down."

Weston smiled at Gail. After a few seconds, it started to become awkward and Rita nudged him. "Sorry," Weston cleared his throat. "I got a good look at the magic he used to hide himself. It's very impressive magic and I think I can use it to improve our camouflage."

"We should get going, I want to know more about this man and why he was following us," Jason said.

The sorrowful look on Katrina and Le Anna's face made him stop. The owner of the restaurant was approaching with dessert and the ladies felt no meal was complete without dessert. It was a cookies and cream bread pudding and looked wonderful. "Okay, after dessert," he said. Katrina rolled her wheelchair over and gently hugged him. "You are the best boss in all the realms."

"Yeah, I know," Jason said jokingly, trying to keep his emotions in place.

As the group raved of over the food, the owner became elated.

"Best dessert ever," Le Anna kept saying.

The owner kept fussing over Jason's guides. "Look how much they ate. You need to pay them better."

"Jason is a great boss, and he pays us well. We just got off a diet and we were very hungry. Not to mention that the food was delicious," Le Anna said.

Reality was they used their magic a lot which resulted in a metabolism of a hummingbird. Everyone at the table could eat a seven-course meal twice a day and never gain an ounce.

The owner promptly gave the two guides several plates of food to take back. Jason was offered nothing. But when the owner saw the tip, he got his own plate. As he was saying goodbye he whispered, "Those two are like my daughters and mean the world to me. Believe me when I say I take good care of them. Everyone at this table is family to me."

The owner smiled. "You are a good man, please come back soon."

Arriving back at their office, he was handed a folder as he walked in the door. It contained information about the mystery man they encountered at the restaurant. He was a wizard who disappeared six months ago. The wizarding government had been searching for him and was very interested in Jason's encounter with him.

The strange thing was that where wasn't anything unusual about the man. He seemed to be an average wizard working at an accounting firm and one day disappeared. His family and friends had no idea why he disappeared and hadn't heard from him. So far, the Castle's data center's initial efforts to track him down had turned up no new leads. Jason ordered any information they discovered be sent to the wizards. Hopefully, they could turn up something. Jason handed the folder to Weston, who quickly scanned it and gave it to Gail.

"What about that hacker group that sent you that information? Can they help?" Weston asked.

"Not sure but maybe." The more Jason thought about it, the more he was sure they could help.

"You never told us how you got involved with them," Gail said, "time to fess up." She took a seat and made herself comfortable. Jason wasn't thrilled about talking about it, but Gail had made up her mind and nothing was going to happen until she heard the story.

Jason grabbed a chair and sat down. "When Tess went missing, I became desperate and tried just about every avenue to find her. I heard about some hackers that could scan a picture of someone then use all sorts of video streams from airports, ATMs, anything they could hack and run facial recognition software against the picture. I paid them a bunch of money to find Tess. They never found her and to this day are still searching. They took the money I gave them and used it to start hacking full time. They call themselves 'The Round Table' or TRT for short, as they have a fascination for King Arthur."

He took a deep breath. "They were the ones that sent that picture you saw in Mistress Nelson's office. When I first saw it, I didn't think it was Tess. Now that I know about magical disguises, I'm certain it was her."

"So, what's our next step?" Weston asked.

"I need to know more about who this wizard is and why he was following us," he replied. "And I am going to need some help. But first, I need a laptop that I can get rid of."

"We have several we were about to pull the hard drives on and recycle," Dod said. She walked over to a stack of laptops, grabbed the top one, then handed it to him.

"Thanks." Jason tucked the laptop under his arm and headed out to a nearby internet café. Jason knew that any machine or network he used would be compromised quickly once he started. He didn't want to risk doing this on the company network. The local internet café's network was so infested with malware there wasn't much the hacker group could do to it. He would have to destroy the laptop afterwards.

He was going to take a chance and contact someone from the hacker group. The TRT had gone underground with Jason's warning but he had ways to reach them.

If anyone could track down the wizard that had been trailing them, it would be the TRT.

He found a spot in a corner of the café, which would give him a little privacy. The website he needed to go to was home of some of the most far-fetched conspiracy theories on the web. It surprisingly did a brisk business. It seemed that these days the stranger the allegation, the more likely someone would believe it. Navigating to the site the headline read 'Is Elvis the Pope?'

He paid for an ad titled 'Looking for a King for a New Country' with a credit card with a one-hundred-dollar limit. No doubt the card's information would be stolen and used in short order. After placing the ad, he called the credit card company and put a hold on it. He also removed the battery from the laptop. By now it was sure to have all sorts of interesting software installed on it. He headed back to his office as he knew it might take a couple of days for the TRT to respond. Getting off the elevator, he went straight to the area set aside for the team to duel. Using his wand, it only took one quick shot to destroy the laptop.

Monday morning, Steven arrived at eight-thirty, concerned he would be late for his appointment. Jason was intrigued with Steven and what he might be able to do. He had setup some tests that he hoped would tell him what he needed to know. As part of the first test, he sent Le Anna, Dod, and Weston into the Testing Room and told them to camouflage themselves.

"Hey Steven, ready to work?"

"Yes." Steven's smile lit up the room.

"Okay, I'll take you to where you will be working, but I need to make a quick stop. Follow me," Jason said, then started off.

Jason led Steven to the Testing Room. Opening the door, he motioned for him to go inside. He followed and closed the door.

"Hmm," Jason said. "I thought this room was empty, but I think there is someone here. Can you tell me if you can detect anyone?"

Jason didn't want to actively scan to see where everyone was hidden but he could feel Le Anna standing nearby. He was pretty sure where Weston was, but had no clue where Dod hid. Dod made it a goal to be the best at tracking and evasion. Eventually getting to the point that even when Jason used all of his magic to find her, it was still difficult.

"Yes. There is someone standing over there," Steven said, pointing to where Jason thought Le Anna was.

Le Anna dropped her camouflage shield. "Hi Steven, my name is Le Anna."

"Nice to meet you," he responded.

"Very good. Anyone else you can see?" Jason asked, hoping he did, in fact, see the other two.

"I see a man standing over there. His cloak is really good," Steven said.

Weston dropped his shield. "Dang, I thought I had it mastered. Nice to meet you."

Jason could feel Steven actively scanning the room again, he seemed to be concentrating on one corner of the room.

"I think I see Dod. She hides well," Steven said, pointing to a corner.

Dod stepped out of the shadows. "That was really good. How did you find me? I thought my shield would hide me."

"Your shield shakes a little and it turns different colors, but just a little," Steven replied.

"He's right. While we were waiting for Steven to come in, I was watching your shield. It slowly changes shades of colors. When it does, it vibrates," Weston said.

"I can help you fix it, if you want?" Steven said.

Dod hesitated for a moment. "How would you fix it?"

"I don't know. I just know that I can touch it and fix it," Steven said.

"Are you sure? That would be impressive, but I have never heard of anyone that can do that," Jason said, not sure he liked where this was going.

Weston stared intently at Steven. The man smiled back.

"Actually, I have," Weston said, still giving the newcomer a once over. "I've read of those who can actually touch magic and morph it as they want. As far as I know, there have only been three documented cases of this."

"Okay Steven, I will let you do this but please be careful," Dod said.

"Are you sure?" Jason asked.

"Yes, I'm pretty sure." Dod gave Jason a nervous look. "Will you fix my shield, Steven?"

"Yes," Steven said. "You need to bring it up for me to fix it."

Dod took a deep breath, looked at Jason. "Here goes nothing," Dod said, then disappeared.

Steven stared at where she had been standing and bit his lip. He seemed to be concentrating hard on something and even tilted his head a couple of times. Jason scanned for Dod and found her. Watching closely, he could barely see the color changes Steven and Weston talked about.

"Okay, got it," Steven said. He walked to where Dod was shielded and put up his hand.

Jason used his magic to observe as Steven's magic connected with Dod's shield. At first, nothing happened, then there was a quick flash.

"Whoa!" Dod squealed, and reappeared. She jumped around and shook her hands.

Jason rushed over. "Are you okay?"

"Yeah. That was. Wow. Not sure how to explain it. Just intense."

A frown formed on Steven's face. "Did I hurt you?"

"No, you just surprised me," Dod said, patting his shoulder.

"Your shield should be fixed. Try it," Steven said with a smile returning to his face.

"Okay. Hope this works." Dod disappeared again.

Jason used his magic and could not find his teammate. He pulled as much energy as he could and scanned again. This time he could only find a faint outline of her.

"That is amazing, you are truly hidden," Jason stated. "Weston?"

Weston stared intently at where she had been standing. "Wow, I see what you did. That is amazing. I hadn't thought of doing a shield that way."

Weston looked to Jason. "I can recreate what Steven did and teach everyone else how to do the same."

Dod reappeared. "Thanks, Steven, for fixing my shield."

"You're welcome."

Jason had one more test but wasn't sure it was a good idea. He decided to ask his wand for advice. *I would like to see if he can use a wand, but not sure that is a good idea.*

It is a good idea; it is a standard test for those candidates we are not sure about. But in his case, I would not test him with a warlock's wand. I doubt it would work and may cause issues. I suggest using Le Anna's wand for testing. If she will allow it, his wand said.

Good idea. Let me ask her.

"Steven. Can you stay here for a minute while I talk with Le Anna?" Jason asked. Steven nodded and Jason motioned for his guide to follow him out the room.

After closing the door, "We need to test him to see if he can use a wand. My wand doubts he can use a warlock's wand. He might be able to use yours, but only if you are okay with it."

Le Anna thought for a second. "He can try with mine but only for one test." Le Anna looked uneasy about her decision.

"Are you sure? It's perfectly okay to say no. I will completely understand if you don't want him to use it."

Le Anna took a deep breath and nodded her head. "I'm sure. I don't know how I know, but I do know this is important."

"I appreciate it, this means a lot," Jason said. He walked over to a desk and grabbed a book off of it. "Let's go see what he can do."

He opened the Testing room door and followed Le Anna in.

"Steven, I have one more test for you. Le Anna is going to let you use her wand for just a moment. You must promise me that you will be extremely careful with it. Do you promise?"

He nodded. "I promise. Thank you, Le Anna."

Le Anna pulled her wand and gently handed it to Steven. "Please be careful."

Steven raised the wand up to his face and studied it closely. "It is a very pretty wand. You are very lucky," he said, causing Le Anna to smile.

"Do you think you can use the wand to levitate this book?" Jason placed the book at his feet.

Steven looked at the book and then back to the wand. Jason could feel him talking to the wand but didn't want to eavesdrop on their conversation. After a minute he looked back to Jason.

"I think so, Le Anna's wand and I have worked out how to do it." Steven lowered the wand, pointing it at the book. He held his breath and his brow furled as he concentrated. Jason could sense his magic flowing from him, through Le Anna's wand, and toward the book. The book began to shudder and rise into the air, almost an inch off the ground. Jason kept trying to will the book higher. Steven began to sweat as the book continued to slowly rise. It made it almost a foot off the ground when he let out his breath and the book dropped to the ground.

Everyone applauded and Jason added a "good job" as he gently slapped his back.

"The book didn't move very far," Steven whispered, handing the wand back to Le Anna.

"Don't worry about it. It was your first try. With practice you will get better," Weston chipped in.

"I think that was a success and probably enough for today," Jason began. "Dod, why don't you show our newest employee where he will be working. I'll catch up with you later."

"Steven, this way," Dod said, leading him out of the room.

"I need to get back to work, we have a new location opening soon," Le Anna then left the room. Only Weston and Jason remained.

"Okay, can you tell me what just happened? Steven fixed Dod's shield but could barely lift a book, what gives?" Jason asked.

Weston took a breath. "Steven is definitely a warlock but a special kind of warlock."

"What do you mean by 'special'?"

"As I mentioned, there have been only three others in all of warlock recorded history that were like him. There is no official term other than some use the word 'empath' to describe warlocks like him."

"Go on," Jason urged, intrigued.

"Okay, so you know I can see magic. It helps me recreate spells or create counter-spells when you can actually see what the magic is doing," Weston said.

"I think I understand the basics."

"Steven is on a whole different level. Not only can he see magic, but he inherently understands it. This allows him to do things like change Dod's shield. What he can teach us will fundamentally change our approach to magic." Weston began pacing back and forth. "Instead of trial and error, we could understand what magic is doing and change it as we needed. This is an amazing find," Weston declared, almost hugging Jason.

"Doesn't that also make him very dangerous?" Jason asked, his nagging feeling was getting worse.

"Yes, but he does have his limits. You see, I have found that magic has a balance." Weston stopped pacing and looked to Jason. "I can see magic but magic balances that with me struggling with certain spells and I will never be as powerful as you or Dod. Dod is great at hiding and tracking but will never be as powerful as you and has other limits. You are a great leader, and also very powerful but subtle skills will never be your strength."

Jason nodded. He prided himself on knowing his limits and relying on his team. "So, what is Steven's weakness?"

"He has almost no power. As your wand pointed out, he can't use a regular warlock wand. He even struggled using Le Anna's. A special wand could probably be created for him, but he will never be able to use magic like we can. In a fight, if he couldn't disable or divert his opponents magic, Steven wouldn't stand a chance. Even against Le Anna or Katrina."

"So, we need to protect him so he can help us better understand magic?"

"Exactly. There is one other issue that is probably worse." Weston looked down at his feet and paused.

"Yes?" Jason asked slowly.

"According to the history books, the last three empaths' went crazy when they got older. Usually in their fifties," Weston said. "Each were eliminated when they started attacking others. Needless to say, being able to modify another's magic makes it easy to kill them. But only if the Empath can touch them directly. Also, I don't know if his Down Syndrome helps or hurts him."

Jason sighed; would anything ever be easy?

"Well, Steven is young so we have some time, but we will have to watch him," Jason said, pondering the issue. "Okay, one more question. When Steven touched Dod's shield, she jumped and dropped her shield. Do you know what happened?"

"Basically. He touched her core magic and shifted it. That must have been a shock. Remember when you linked to Dod and mine's magic to help us with our shields?" Weston asked.

"Yes," Jason said, just a little uncomfortable. It was a rather personal experience. Helping Dod, it was the first time he had done it and it was an unnerving event. When he helped Weston next, he learned to keep himself separate from Weston's magic.

"It's like that but not quite so personal. Even still, this was probably the first time she had experience anyone touching and changing her magic. Probably scared her. For now, I am going to hold off on him touching my magic until I'm ready."

"Okay, let's keep an eye on him. Work with him as much as you can but no one other than those that were in this room can know about his abilities," Jason warned.

"Even Mistress Nelson?"

"Especially her. I don't want to risk her eliminating Steven for being different." How long could he keep Steven hidden?

"Do you really think she would do that?"

"My gut tells me no but some of her earlier comments worry me," Jason said. "I better get going and see how he is doing. Please keep digging and find everything you can on previous empaths."

Weston nodded and headed out the door. Jason took a breath and followed.

Dod had given Steven the job of organizing all the materials being shipped to each site. She'd assumed it would take all day, but he finished by lunch. Dod gave Steven more work, elated that he could pick it up so quickly. The Empath apparently liked to work and dove into it.

At lunch, Dod and Jason took their new co-worker to a nearby restaurant.

"Steven, remember the man in the restaurant where we met you?" Jason asked.

"Yes. He was trying to hide himself like you were."

"If you ever see something like that again, please let me know," Jason said.

"You mean like that shop?" Steven pointed to a boutique. It sat across from the entrance to the building where their offices were located.

"People there are hidden?" Dod asked.

"No, the shop is hidden. They don't want anyone to see inside but I can," Steven said excitedly then frowned. "I'm not supposed to, Mom says it isn't polite to be nosy."

"I agree with your mother but in this case, I think it's okay. Can you tell me about that place?" Jason asked.

Steven hesitated, obviously not comfortable with the request. Dod jumped in to help.

"It's okay to say no. But we are worried about people watching us and trying to hurt our business," she said softly.

Steven nodded and studied the boutique. "There are three special people in there. They keep trying to see into our building, but they can't. Your shield is blocking them. They keep trying new things."

"Thanks, that helps. Dod why don't you two order some lunch. I have to make a quick phone call and will join you," he said.

Dod nodded, taking Steven into the restaurant. Jason then dialed a number that connected him to Master Kien.

"Jason? Hello. Are you there? Speak!" Kien said, answering the phone. Master Kien wasn't quite up on phone etiquette, but Jason ignored it.

"Kien, yes it's Jason," he said.

"Okay, I don't trust these cell call-things. Can't you just use your wand?" he said, irritably.

"I'm not sure that talking on my wand in public would be a good thing."

"If you say so," Kien replied.

"When was the last time you spent any time on earth?"

"Hmm, I think William McKinley was president. Very nice guy by the way," Kien replied.

"You do realize that was over a hundred years ago?"

"Have things changed that much?" Kien asked. He sounded genuinely interested.

"Ah, yes, things have. I think you need to spend a little more time here. But that isn't what I called about. We have discovered a small shop across the way that may be watching us. Multiple magical entities inside," he said sending the coordinates and pictures of the shop.

"Hmm, we will be there in an hour," he said, hanging up. Jason needed to teach Kien how to properly end a call.

They finished their lunch and arrived back at work to find an upset Kien pacing the hall in front of Jason's office. When Kien saw them approach, he stomped over. "Where have you been? I have been waiting."

"You said you would be here in an hour. It's only been forty-five minutes. Why didn't you call me when you got here?" Jason replied.

"I thought it had been an hour. I guess I misjudged the time," Kien said avoiding eye contact.

"We need to get you a watch," Jason replied, then led him into his office. "There, that boutique down there." He pointed out his office window.

"It looks like any other shop," Kien said. "What makes it a boutique?"

Le Anna walked in and set a stack of files on Jason's desk. "A boutique is a small retail store that focuses on selling unique items."

"For the love of dragons! Really? Can we just concentrate on the task at hand?" Jason said, giving Le Anna a pointed look.

"I just wanted to know the difference. Thanks, Le Anna," Kien said. Le Anna looked about to add something else, but Jason frowned at her. She remained quiet.

"Do you have a plan to address the possible spies across the street or are we going to go shopping for bath salts next?" Jason asked, trying to get back to the task at hand.

"I know a perfect..." Le Anna began but stopped when Jason rounded on her.

"Why don't you check on the monthly report of prospective sites. I need that now," he said, glaring at her.

"Okay," she squeaked and ran off.

"You have something against bath salts? They can be quite soothing," Kien said.

"Who are you and what have you done with Kien?" Jason asked. He shook his head and leaned against the wall. Things were so far off the rails the only thing he could do was wait it out.

"Just because I like bath salts doesn't mean anything," Kien stated, suddenly finding his shoes interesting.

"The first day I met you, you tried to kill me and now you are asking me about bath salts. You don't see anything wrong with this?" Jason asked, amused. Kien stood well over six feet, all muscle, and could probably wrestle a bear and win. To have him talk about bath salts was completely out of character.

"In my defense, I haven't spent much time on earth in the last one hundred years. As for trying to kill you, I knew the Castle would protect you and you were never in any real danger. We needed to speed up your bonding with your wand and I took a calculated risk. You lived."

"Well, good to know that you weren't really trying to kill me. But can we get back to the boutique across the street?" Jason asked.

"We have scanned it as much as we can without tipping off the occupants. Our security camera's show they come in around seven a.m. and leave at eight in the evening. Foot traffic is very light at seven a.m. and we will raid them tomorrow morning," Kien said. "How did you pick up on it? If we hadn't done an intense scan, we would have never seen it."

"A combination of a bit of luck and some effort by Dod," Jason said quickly, not wanting to discuss Steven quite yet. "Will you need anyone from my team in the raid tomorrow?"

"We can use your team as a ruse and as back up. In the meantime, I am going to catch up and see what this modern earth has to offer," Kien said.

"Perfect, Catie would love some bath salts."

"Great! I will pick up some...," Kien said but stopped when Jason started laughing, "oh, very funny."

"Actually, she would like it and she can probably give you some insights into the best ones." Jason sat down at his desk feeling satisfied. It wasn't often he got the best of Kien.

An hour later he received a call from Catie.

"Jason why is a bear of a warlock named Kien here asking me about bath salts?" she asked with a bit of amusement in her voice.

"Despite his weirdness he's a good guy. He just hasn't spent much time on earth lately," he said between bouts of laughter.

"Okay, just checking. Love you." Catie hung up.

The next morning the teams were in place. Several members of his team sat outside a coffee shop to the far right of the boutique. The assumption was that the spies would be so intent on listening in on his team's conversation that they would be distracted enough to allow the other teams to approach.

Jason sent Steven with Rita to purchase supplies to keep him as far away from Kien and the others as possible.

Two men and a woman entered the boutique earlier, but the store hadn't opened yet. Jason's team planned to sit in an open spot to discuss inane items that employees would normally chat about. Weston was to watch for signs that they were being monitored and given a code phrase to use when he detected something. He carried a wireless transmitter so Jason and Kien's team could wait for his signal. They didn't want to use anything magical to tip off the unknown spies.

After a half hour of mundane chatter, Weston broke in with, "Hey guys, I forgot to tell you. I think I found my new car."

Kien yelled to his team, "That's the signal, go!"

Down the street a warlock waited in a car. With the signal, the driver caused the car to backfire loudly. While the few people on the street turned to look at the car, Kien's team entered from the front and the rear of the boutique. Jason immediately detected wand fire. It seemed to be a mixture of wizards and warlocks. Jason ran out of his office and hit the elevator button then decided the stairs were faster. He bolted down the stairs as fast as he could, he wanted to Step but there were enough cameras in the building that one of them might pick it up.

He ran across the street just in time to meet Kien's team running out. A loud thump reverberated inside, and they slowly reentered. Inside, the place was a mess with broken figurines everywhere. Smoke filled the room and one of the masters was using his wand to put out a small fire.

The center of the room looked to be the epicenter of the explosion. Blood and body parts were splattered everywhere. The remnants of a warlock shield hovered in place in the center of the room.

"We entered and the three immediately started firing on us," Kien began. "They had a pretty strong shield, but their wands were not that strong. For wizards, they were pretty weak. After a couple of blasts from us, their shield fell apart. One put up his hands but the other two kept fighting and went down quickly. Before we could get to the third, he started screaming and we detected a power surge. I put up a shield around the room and we ran for it. Good thing too."

Weston entered and began searching through the shelves. "Ah hah," he said, and pulled a small pack from a shelf. Carefully, he removed the wrapping, "This must have been powering their camouflage shield, the residual energy in it is amazing."

Jason picked up the pack and inspected it. As he suspected, it was made of similar material as the rocks the Meathonians used.

"This definitely means they were working for Tess and she has acquired more material," Jason said.

"I believe the unit was created with help from a spell," Weston said. "Maybe Steven could look at this. We may be able to recreate that spell with his help. His ability to see magic amazes me."

Jason had been trying to shut Weston up, but it was too late.

"Jason, who is Steven?" Kien asked with a frown.

Weston, realizing he just let the secret out, stuttered, "I need to get back to the office." He attempted to walk around Kien, but the master stepped in front of him.

"We need to discuss Steven, but not here and we need Mistress Nelson," Jason said. "Until we discuss with her, no one goes near or touches him."

Kien glared at Jason, his bushy eyebrows furrowed.

"So, did you find any good bath salts?" Jason asked with a smile. Hoping to change the subject.

"Your ability to cause trouble wherever you go knows no bounds, does it?" Kien asked.

"Like I keep saying, it is one of my unique warlock abilities," Jason mused.

Back in the office, Kien and Jason waited for Mistress Nelson's arrival. They had said nothing to each other since leaving the boutique. Kien held an animated conversation with Mistress Nelson via his wand and she was not happy with Jason keeping secrets until she arrived.

She Stepped to a designated spot and headed straight to his office. Dax and Solis accompanied her and immediately set up guard outside his office.

"Did you have to bring those two?" Jason asked, pointing to the two giant bodyguards.

"Yes, for all I knew, you were going to introduce me to another Lion's Hunter," she said in a huff. "So, let's get to it. Who is Steven?"

Jason related the story from his encounter of meeting the Empath. He left out his Down syndrome.

"This is great news, Jason. He sounds like he would be a great warlock candidate. So why all the secrecy?" she asked.

"Can you ask Dax and Solis to stay away from him? I don't want them scaring Steven," Jason asked.

"Dax. Solis. Back away from the door. Someone is coming through who is a friend," Mistress Nelson commanded, and both stepped back.

Jason signaled Rita to return to the office, shortly returning with Steven. As he approached, Steven eyed Dax and Solis closely.

"You guys are big," he said with a shy smile. "But I like your off buttons."

The two guards looked at each other bewildered, letting him pass. Meanwhile, Mistress Nelson looked shocked at the statement.

He approached Kien and Mistress Nelson. "Hello, my name is Steven. You are special like me."

"Steven, it is nice to meet you. Can you tell me how you see their 'off' buttons?" Mistress Nelson asked.

"I don't know, I just do. It's obvious," Steven said.

"Is there anything else you see right now?" Kien asked.

"Besides you being special?" he asked and Kien nodded. "She has two wands. One is weak and looks very unhappy."

Kien frowned but Mistress Nelson just about fell out of her chair. Her face flushed red, she tried to speak, but just stammered.

Jason was concerned that she may be having a heart attack. "Are you okay?" he asked, rushing over to her.

She nodded but said nothing. After a moment, she reached behind her back and pulled out a hidden wand. While it looked similar to his, it was much more decorated with designs etched on the handle and blade.

"What else can you tell me about this wand?" she asked, her voice barely above a whisper. She tried to hand Steven the wand, but her hands shook badly.

Jason took it and handed it to him.

He seemed spooked and reluctantly took the wand. Turning it over and over in his hand, his smile disappeared. He looked sad then quickly handed the wand back. "I don't like to touch stuff like that, makes me feel weird," he said, running his hands up and down his body.

"Steven, did you learn anything about the wand?" Jason asked. "I think it would help Mistress Nelson."

Steven stood quietly for a second. "Yes, it belongs to someone else. Someone who is lost, and it wants to go looking for him."

Mistress Nelson began crying, which upset Steve even more.

"See. That's why I don't touch stuff like that. It's bad!" He started pacing and wringing his hands.

Mistress Nelson immediately stood and walked over to him. "Steven, no, you did a good thing. These are tears of joy," she said, hugging him.

Steven relaxed into the hug. "So, I did good?" he asked, still holding the Mistress.

"Yes, very good," she responded.

Jason gave them a minute. They needed to finish their conversation about Steven's fate, but he didn't want him anywhere nearby. "Steven, I need to talk with Mistress Nelson and Master Kien. You can go back to work."

On his way out, Steven waved to Dax and Solis. Jason could tell he was sensing them. He smiled and said, "Goodbye."

To Jason's surprise, the two guards smiled and waved back.

It was a minute before Mistress Nelson could compose herself.

"Jason, why have you been hiding such a valuable person such as Steven?" The Mistress asked.

"Because of you," he said, sitting down.

"Me, why?" she asked.

"The first day we met, you told me how those discovered with some magic but not strong enough to become warlocks were eliminated," he paused, "I will not let it happen to Steven." This was it, he thought. If she was going to kill Steven, he would have to protect him. He doubted he would be able to defeat Mistress Nelson, but he couldn't let him die simply because he was different.

"Jason, I am sorry you thought we might harm him. It's my fault, I should have given you more information. We only eliminated those who were already on a path to use their power for evil. We would never hurt someone like Steven."

It was Jason's turn to almost fall out of his chair.

"I have heard of others with similar skills. They can see and communicate with magic like no others. They usually have little ability to actually use magic, but their abilities have allowed us to learn about magic in ways we never thought possible. I never thought I would get to meet one," she said, putting a hand on Jason to reassure him.

"Well, good," he said a little louder than he meant to. He took a breath to gather his thoughts. Knowing that Steven was not in danger took a huge weight off. "So, tell me about this wand of yours?"

"I'm interested as well," Kien added.

"Well, I guess you deserve the truth. About a hundred and fifty years ago I met someone who I thought was a Keorian named Nemal," she started. Jason had met a Keorian in the Castle staff cafeteria. They looked fairly human but had pink eyes and razor-sharp teeth.

"Except Nemal wasn't a Keorian, she was actually a Welsex," she looked at Kien and Jason to see if they recognized the name.

Jason shook his head. "Never heard of them."

"I know they inhabit a very large and powerful realm, but have never met one to my knowledge," Kien said.

"Welsex's are a shape-shifting race, they can become whatever species or sex they need to blend in with their surroundings. The transformation takes months, but they truly become whatever species they need to be," she said.

"Nemal and I fought many battles together, along with your grandfather, Jason. We spent a lot of time planning raids, fighting together, and drinking to forget. Over the months, Nemal became human and a male. She hid her transformation to become a male until it was complete."

Mistress Nelson shifted in her seat. This was personal, and she wasn't comfortable sharing.

"And you fell in love?" Jason asked to help her along.

"Yes," she blushed. "When he announced that he was now a human male and in love with me, I didn't know what to say and he kissed me."

There was obviously more to it than a kiss, but Jason didn't push.

"For a while I struggled with the fact that Nemal had been my best female friend and now Nemal was my lover," she turned even redder when she let that slip. "Nemal helped me get over my insecurities and see that love is love and it didn't matter what he had been before."

She had tears in her eyes and was barely holding on. "Our final battle together was on another realm. We were winning and just about convinced our enemies to surrender, when one decided to kill himself, and everyone around him. He armed a very destructive explosive with a timer, and we couldn't disarm it. I put a spell on the device to slow it down. Nemal grabbed it and tried to Step away. Something about Nemal's Step reactivated the timer. He tossed it and tried to Step away, but the blast wiped out everyone in the area. I barely survived."

She stopped and sobbed for a moment. Kien put his arm around her and held her. Eventually she regained her composure.

"We searched and searched in hopes of finding Nemal. We hoped he'd Stepped successfully but we found only his wand. After fifty years of searching, we finally gave him up for dead."

"Why after fifty years?" Jason asked.

"It's part of the secrets of our wands and I can't tell you," she replied.

Jason's frustration with the warlock secrecy boiled over. "We have a very powerful warlock who is close to being able to bring down the realm borders, and you are doing the cloak-and-dagger secrets about wands? There may be information you have that might help." Jason tried to calm himself. It seemed that even basic knowledge, that all warlocks should know, was closely guarded.

"I have neither a cloak nor a dagger. I guess my wand is somewhat like a dagger. Kien?" she asked looking to Kien.

"No, I have neither," he responded.

"Dear lord. You two need to spend more time on earth," Jason shook his head. How could someone as powerful and knowledgeable as Mistress Nelson be this clueless?

"You are right, we do need to. Catie and I found the most amazing shop down the way with the most fantastic bath salts," Kien said. "The Himalayan bath salts smelled wonderful."

"Oh, I do love them. It has been ages since I had some," the Mistress said.

Before he could interrupt, Kien and Nelson were in full swing talking about bath salts. Jason dropped into a chair, closed his eyes, and rubbed his temples. What did he do to deserve this? "Can we please get back to business?" he finally interrupted the two. "Wait, you went shopping with Catie? My Catie?"

"Yes, you are very lucky. She really knows her bath salts," Kien said.

"Just shoot me now," he said, burying his head in his hands.

"Jason, you really should explore the world of bath salts," the Mistress said. Jason was about to blow a gasket when she continued, "You're so impatient, some bath salts would really help you."

He just glared at her until she continued.

"Oh, all right. As you know, wands are magical entities and become their own beings eventually. Wands get their powers as a result of pairing with a warlock. It is complicated, but wands do not get their power directly from warlocks, but they need to pair with a warlock to access magic. When a warlock dies, often the wand dies shortly afterwards."

"But then why did my wand not die when my grandfather passed away?" Jason asked. His attention fully on Mistress Nelson.

"Most wands die because they are solely bonded to one person. With that person gone, they can no longer access magic. Your grandfather imparted his wish for his wand to try to bond with you. It was a long shot as it rarely happens, but in your case it did. To survive, his wand took on as much power as it could before he died. As it was, it only had enough power for another five to ten years when it bonded with you. Even at full reserve, wands can only last up to fifty years after their warlock dies," she stopped and took a breath.

"Nemal's wand stopped communicating after about fifty years. I assumed it meant that Nemal was gone. I guess I was wrong. I couldn't bring myself to destroy the wand and have been carrying it ever since."

"And for Nemal's wand to be alive after over a hundred years means...," Jason trailed off, fascinated by the implications.

"That Nemal is still alive. Which is great news. But I'm no closer to finding him than I was before," Mistress Nelson said lowering her head.

"Actually, you're wrong there," Jason said. She looked up with hope.

"Steven may be able to communicate with your wand. If anyone could find Nemal, it would be his wand. I can call him back right now."

Mistress Nelson sat for a second. "I am sure you are right about his ability to talk to the wand, but we need to have a discussion about Steven first."

"I thought we agreed he wasn't a problem," Jason said, becoming a little worried.

"We did, but have you discussed the ramifications of becoming a warlock with him? Or his parents?" Mistress Nelson asked.

"Um, no," Jason replied, realizing that in his quest to protect the empath from Mistress Nelson, he potentially put Steven and his family at risk from others.

"Have you shielded him or taught him to shield himself?" she asked.

Jason hung his head. "No."

"Well, we have to do this proper, for Steven's safety as well as ours," Mistress Nelson said. "Before we do anything, we need to speak with him and his parents about the risks."

"That will require us revealing that magic exists to his mother," Jason said.

"It can't be avoided. Eventually he will start talking about it and may even try to show her," Mistress Nelson said, standing. "Better to tell her under controlled circumstances."

"Let me see if I can get his mother to come down and meet with us. According to Dod, his dad left, and Steven hasn't seen him in years."

Mistress Nelson stood. "Please make it quick before something goes wrong." She then walked out of the office with her guards and Stepped back to the Castle.

Chapter Seven

J ason asked Dod to setup the meeting. She reached out to Steven's mother, Carol, and asked her to come in for a recognition ceremony the next day. Steven was going to be recognized as a new employee and they wanted her there. At least, that was the premise. At the appointed time the next day, she arrived and Dod ushered her to Jason's office.

"Thank you very much for coming. Steven will be here in a second as I just have a few things to go over before the ceremony," Jason said. He didn't like lying to her but telling her that her son was magical over the phone didn't have much of a chance of success. There was a ceremony planned afterwards, at least that much was true.

"This is great of you folks to do this for Steven. I am very excited," Carol said.

"Ah, here he is," Jason said as Steven walked in with Mistress Nelson and Dod. "Carol, let me introduce Mistress, sorry Miss Nelson. She will be performing the ceremony."

"Nice to meet you Carol. I am so glad you could make it," Mistress Nelson said, shaking her hand.

"Now let me discuss something that is going to be difficult for you to understand," Jason said.

Carol's smile changed to a look of confusion.

Jason decided to be blunt. He had worked all night trying to come up with a better way of stating it but came up with nothing better. "Well. To be honest your son is magical."

"Oh yes, I quite agree," Carol said, smiling.

"No, I literally mean he is magical. He can do magic and is a candidate to be a warlock."

Carol looked to her son and then back to Jason. "Is this some sort of cruel joke? Because if it..." Carol began but stopped when Jason conjured Eagle.

Carol's eyes went wide as Eagle appeared and spread his wings.

"Eagle, this is Steven, the one I told you about," Jason said.

It is very nice to meet you Steven, Eagle said.

Steven waved to the bird. "It's nice to meet you too."

Jason had worried about Steven's reaction, but he took it in stride. His mother, on the other hand, did not. She kept looking from Eagle to Steven. With the death grip she had on her chair, Jason was surprised the arms of the chair didn't break off.

"Did the bird just talk?" Carol asked.

"Yes, Mom, he did," Steven replied. "Mom, it's true. I have magic. Not like everyone here, but I do have some."

"Thank you, Eagle," Jason said.

It was nice meeting both of you. Eagle nodded and disappeared.

Carol looked around trying to see where Eagle had gone. "That's an impressive trick," she said and nervously laughed. Her eyes darted around the room trying to discover how Jason performed his trick. When no one else joined in her laughter, she went quiet.

Mistress Nelson sat down next to Carol. "I know this is a lot. I've had this conversation with many families over the centuries. We don't always know why some people are magical and some aren't. It just happens. The important thing is that you know and understand because you two have an important decision to make."

"And that is?" Carol asked. She sat up straight in her chair and her tone was business like.

"Being magical attracts attention. Like any other group, we have good people and not so good people. Without the proper training, Steven could attract the wrong type of people who would want to use him. We can train him to protect and hide himself, and you. He could also help us as we defend this planet from those that would destroy it," Mistress Nelson said.

"And what if I don't want him to become a warlock?" Carol asked.

"We can try to remove his powers but that can be dangerous. Especially with Steven, his type of magic is not well known by us. The other option is to cast a spell around him to keep him hidden. It is not foolproof, and he may well be discovered in the future. What some evil person may do to him or to you, I don't want to think about," Mistress Nelson said.

"Mom. I want to be a warlock. Weston says I could be a very important person that can helps others," Steven implored.

"What did you mean by 'his type of magic'?" Carol asked.

"When you saw Eagle conjured, you did not see the magic that did it. You just saw the result. I can see his magic but all I see is energy flowing. I don't understand it. Steven has the unique ability to not only see magic but can understand what it is doing. Over the centuries only a few people have had that ability. We call them Empaths." Mistress Nelson paused. "The downside is that he can't use magic as well as most warlocks."

Carol frowned. "I don't understand."

"An analogy would be that most people know how to drive a car but if you asked them how it worked, how the engine ran, the transmission shifted, etc. they could only give a very rudimentary explanation. But someone like your son could take one look at any car and explain how it worked down to the last detail," Jason added. "The downside for him is that he could barely drive the car."

"And what would be his role?" Carol asked.

"He would be a very important part of my team. He will help us understand magic in a way that few have ever been able to do," Jason said. "We could protect him, and he can help us."

"So, either he becomes a warlock, or we try to hide from the bad guys. That is, assuming you aren't the bad guys," Carol stated.

Jason had to admit she had a point. "That's pretty much it. If it helps, I just recently became a warlock and I had the same decision to make with my family."

"I'm sorry. I am trying to understand but I don't. The trick with the bird was impressive but I just am not buying it," Carol said, crossing her arms. A determined look came over her face. "Also, I think it's cruel that you are playing this trick on my son."

"Well, if Eagle didn't convince you then may be Silver can?" Jason nodded to Dod. After Jason had created Eagle to help him watch for the Lion's Hunter, others had created their own magical pets. Dod had created Silver, a fox with a silver tipped tail.

"Sure," Dod replied. Within seconds, Dod's Silver appeared on the desk. The fox looked around then jumped down and put his legs on Carol's.

"Silver, this is Steven and his mother Carol." Silver made a slight, bark-like noise then jumped into her lap. He immediately curled up and started thumping his tail on her leg. Carol laughed and began stroking the fox. Steven reached over to pet Silver.

"Looks like Silver likes you," Dod said. There was nothing but smiles in the room.

Jason nodded to Dod and with a flick of her wrist, Silver disappeared. This left Carol stroking thin air. The startled look on her face told Jason he had scored a point.

"I have to say that was another impressive trick," Carol stated, but her confidence was gone.

"Then here's a better one." Jason reached out with his hand. "Please take my hand."

Carol stood up and hesitantly put out her hand for Jason. Jason took it in his, opened a portal, and Stepped them to a nearby bayou. Keeping a tight grip on Jason's hand, she stood frozen then slowly reached down and touched the ground. "I guess I believe you now," Carol said, looking around. "But can we go back?"

"Sure," Jason replied. He opened a portal and returned them to the office.

"Mom, did you like the trip?" Steven asked, excitedly.

"Yes, I did, Steven," Carol sat down a little unsteady. She took a deep breath and let it out slowly. "Okay. If Steven wants to be a warlock then that's his decision, and I will accept it."

"Thanks, Mom," Steven bent down and hugged his mother.

"But I want your word that you will do everything you can to protect him and me," Carol said to Jason.

"Being a warlock does include danger, but I and my team will do everything we can to protect him," Jason said. "I will add that I believe that he will help a lot of people."

"So, what happens next?" Carol asked.

"Jason and his team will work with Steven to protect himself and hide his magic from others," Mistress Nelson began. "I will personally come by your home to shield you and the house. Magic leaves a trace, and we need to make sure your house isn't discovered."

"We can work out the details later but right now we have a ceremony to attend," Jason said.

"You are most certainly correct. We must get moving," Mistress Nelson agreed.

"Carol, if you will follow me, I can take you to where the ceremony will be performed. Steven will go with Jason and get ready," Dod said.

Carol stood, hugged Steven, and left with Dod and Mistress Nelson.

"Follow me. We need to get you properly dressed," Jason said.

"But I am dressed," Steven said.

"I know but we have a special warlock uniform for you to wear."

"Really?" Steven asked.

"Yes, now follow me."

Jason turned and walked out with Steven in tow. They entered the locker room and found Steven's warlock uniform, in clear plastic, hanging on a hook.

"You have to use magic to put this on. This time I will do it for you. I want you to watch and maybe next time you can do it?"

"Okay," Steven replied.

"Put your arms out to your side. I will cast a spell to remove your outer clothes and another to put your warlock uniform on. Make sure to watch closely so you can do it later."

Jason had only used the spell to remove his own clothes. Well, Catie's also, but had never used it to put a uniform on someone else and decided to use his wand to help.

Pointing his wand at Steven, "Undress." His clothes separated at the seams, left him, and reassembled, folded on a chair.

"Cool spell. I can do that," Steven said.

"That's good, Steven," Jason pointed at the uniform. "Dress."

The uniform came apart and reassembled onto Steven. It was the trainee gray but had none of the emblems that normally were on the uniform. He decided to ask Mistress Nelson about it later.

"I liked that spell also. I'm not sure I can do that one. This uniform is great. I like the magic in it," Steven said.

"We can help you with your spell casting, but we need to get to the ceremony," Jason said. "Follow me."

Steven followed Jason slowly as he kept admiring his uniform.

"You can check yourself out later. Do you want to miss your ceremony?"

Steven looked worried. "No." He then sped up.

Jason led him to the breakroom. Approaching, it was obvious someone had made some magical modifications. Where normally there was a single door, now two huge doors stood that looked more at home in a castle than a modern workplace. Mistress Nelson's two guards stood on either side.

Jason slowed his step and urged Steven to lead. As Steven got closer, both guards saluted with their weapons then each grabbed a rung and hauled the doors open.

Jason entered after Steven to find the breakroom transformed into a large room that looked strangely like one in the Castle. He felt no spell that would have transported them back to the Castle. Mistress Nelson must have created a copy, he surmised.

Royal banners with the warlock emblems hung on the walls. One large banner floated in the air at the far end. Three crystal chandlers with candles hung from the ceiling. Flower arrangements at the end of the hall stood near where Mistress Nelson and the others waited. A golden rug ran from the door to where they stood. On both sides of the rug, were rows of chairs filled with many from the Castle.

Everyone stood as they entered, and Steven hesitated. Jason whispered into his ear, "Go ahead and lead us to where your mom is."

Steven started walking and when Carol smiled and waved him on, he picked up speed. Halting once he got to his mom.

Mistress Nelson motioned to Jason to stand next to Steven, opposite his mother. She motioned for everyone to sit.

When all was quiet, Mistress Nelson spoke. "This brief, but very important ceremony is to welcome Steven Lopes as a trainee candidate. Steven is an Empath, and his training will be different from most. Please welcome Steven into our warlock family."

Jason began clapping and everyone in the audience stood and followed his lead. Steven smiled at the crowd and waved. Mistress Nelson gave Steven a moment to enjoy the applause, then raised her hand and all went quiet. "I would like all to join us for some food and refreshment."

Jason shook Steven's hand then joined the line to get some food. Carol stayed for a while and then excused herself saying she had to get back to work.

"She works too much," Steven said watching his mother leave.

"Now that your part of the warlock family your salary should be enough to help her," Jason said.

Mistress Nelson interrupted their conversation. "Jason, I think we can have that conversation with Steven as soon as this is finished."

"Agreed. Steven, when everyone is done, we need to meet in my office. We have your first task as a warlock trainee."

"Okay, but when do I get my wand?" Steven asked.

"It might be a little while, Steven. We need to build your strength and we have to create a special wand made for you. I have to get permission before we can start making it. I will meet you two in Jason's office," Mistress Nelson said, then walked off.

Chapter Eight

After the party broke up, Jason and Steven headed back to Jason's office to find Mistress Nelson waiting for them.

"Well, let's get this started. Can I have the wand?" Jason asked Mistress Nelson. She reached behind her back and pulled it out. She looked at it for a second and then handed the wand to Jason.

"Steven, we need you to talk to this wand and tell us where to find its owner whose name is Nemal," Jason said, then offered it to him.

"I don't know if I can. It doesn't want to talk," Steven said, looking at the wand in Jason's hand as if it would bite.

"Tell it that we want to go looking for Nemal and we need its help."

The Empath looked doubtful but took the wand.

Steven held the wand delicately, almost as if he thought he would break it by simply holding it. He stared at the wand and his lips moved as if he were talking to someone.

Jason tried to read Steven's lips. Eventually he made out, "Please talk to me."

Steven jerked, almost dropping the wand. His lips stopped moving but then he nodded before handing the wand back to Mistress Nelson.

"Steven, did you talk to the it? Did it say anything?" Mistress Nelson asked. She sat on the edge of her chair and leaned toward him, the wand clutched to her chest.

"I talked to it. It said only one thing."

"What was that?" Mistress Nelson slowly rose to stand.

"It said, 'Take me to Glassony' I think. It whispered. It's very weak," Steven said. "Does that help?"

Mistress Nelson stared off into space for a moment. "Yes, it does."

Jason walked over and put his hand on her shoulder. "Do you know where this place is?"

Mistress Nelson nodded then turned to Jason as if she was coming out of a trance. "Yes, yes, I do."

"We should leave in the morning as we will need time to prepare," Mistress Nelson said, still staring at nothing.

"We?" Jason asked.

"Yes. Just you and me. Steven is not ready to make that trip. Master Kien is a great master but needs to learn the art of diplomacy. As a Senior, the Glassoners will regard you with respect but will not expect much out of you. With the amount of power you possess, they will not bother with you."

"I guess I need to spend some time tonight learning about them," Jason said, thinking about everything he needed to do before the morning.

"Yes, make sure to talk to your wand as your grandfather spent a couple of months there. Also, start ramping up your reserves. You will need a considerable amount of energy to get there and you will need some after you arrive in case something comes up," Mistress Nelson said.

She walked toward where her guards stood but stopped short and turned. "Steven, thank you. I am not sure how I will ever be able to repay you for this."

"If you could get me a wand, I would like that," Steven replied.

"I will work on that," she said. She walked on and her two guards quickly followed. She waved her hand and the three Stepped away.

"Do you think she can get me a wand?" Steven asked.

"If anyone can, it's her," Jason replied. "Why don't you check to see what Dod needs you to do."

Steven walked away leaving Jason to figure out his next step.

I can help you. You are going to need all the help you can get for this trip, His wand said, interrupting Jason's thoughts.

What do you mean?

The Glassoners are a great ally of the warlocks but they are a complex people. They can easily be offended. Their rules are fairly simple but extensive. I will list the most important ones for you, and you will need to memorize them. During any interaction with them, I can nudge you in the right direction.

His wand gave him a long list which he wrote down and they spent several hours going through various situations and how he should handle them.

I got the list and what to do. What I am not confident in is when to use which rule. There are way too many variables, Jason said, concerned. It appeared even simple things could cause problems. Initiating a handshake to a person who is considered senior to you could cause an insult. The problem was trying to determine if who you were addressing was senior to you. Someone could be older with an official title. But if they worked a person that was lower in the pecking order than who you reported to, you were expected to offer the handshake.

Well, I'm just going to have to wing it and rely on you to keep me out of trouble, Jason said.

You really want to put that much pressure on me? Thanks a lot, his wand replied, and Jason chuckled.

So, tell me about the Glassoners. What should I expect from them, their culture, their country? Heck, I don't even know what they look like, Jason said.

First, while we call them Glassoners, it is not what they call themselves. Most can't pronounce their name in their native language, so they allow the use of the term 'Glassoner'. It comes from their extensive use of material that looks similar to glass. Wherever cement would be used on earth, they use a glass-like material. It is both strong and resilient. As for what they look like, they are human-like, but their features are sharper, almost hawk-like. They also tend to be thin. Many think they are very uptight but in reality, they have a great sense of humor. But their humor is very dry.

I guess that helps, Jason said.

You need to start ramping up your power. Do it now and keep yourself full all day. It will get easier.

Already have, Jason said. He had opened some of his internal gates to fill his energy store. Within an hour, he was full. The sensation unsettled him as he had never held that much power before. He tried firing his wand at a target in his Testing room. The amount of energy available to him was amazing and somewhat frightening, and he struggled to contain it when he fired.

After a few hours, the sensation went away as he became comfortable with holding that much energy. He tried firing a few more test shots and barely struggled with the energy.

The next morning, he stood in Mistress Nelson's office ready to go. Mistress Nelson wore a master's uniform that looked different from what he had seen on her before. Rita stood next to her with another uniform in clear plastic.

"These are our dress uniforms. Rita has yours but please put it on in that room. She says you have a habit of flashing people," Mistress Nelson said, with a hint of a smile.

Rita winked at him as she walked over and handed it to him.

He walked toward the room to change and just before he entered, he turned. "But she said she wanted more excitement in her life." As he quickly closed the door, he heard an "Oh, you…." He laughed and quickly changed.

The dress uniform fit and looked similar to his regular one. Down the outside of the pant legs ran the four warlock symbols in between two red lines. On his chest were small icons that he assumed were awards he had received. He would have to ask Mistress Nelson about them later. On the shoulders, hung braided loops with the four warlock symbols. There was no hood. Instead, the shirt had an overly starched red collar and a knee length cape that was gray with red edging. Overall, he thought he looked quite good in his new formal uniform and tried a couple of different poses in the mirror.

Yes, Mr. Fashion model, you do look good in it. Now just don't say anything to offend the Glassoners and this trip will be a success, his wand quipped.

Jason laughed as he tried another pose. *Easy for you to say. I have a well-earned reputation for finding trouble.*

That you do, my friend. That you do.

Jason took one last look at himself and returned to where the two women waited.

"So, how do I look?" Jason said, putting his hands out to show his uniform. "I think I clean up pretty well."

When Mistress Nelson peered around him, looking in the room he just left. "I mean, I think the uniform looks good on me," Jason said.

"Well, why didn't you just say so?" Mistress Nelson asked.

Rita chuckled and walked over to him. If he didn't know better, he would say she was beaming with pride. She had the widest smile he had ever seen and a tear in her eye. She brushed some non-existent dust off his uniform.

"You look very handsome and I am very proud of you," Rita said.

Without even thinking, he hugged her. She held tight for a few seconds then released him. "Oh, I'm going to mess up your uniform," she fussed, as she dabbed the tears from her eyes.

"It's fine, and thank you for all you have done," Jason said.

"I must be going," Rita said, brushing his uniform one more time. "Make sure he comes back in one piece," Rita said to Mistress Nelson.

Mistress Nelson nodded as Rita left. "I do believe she just threatened me. I must say, I'm quite impressed."

"Rita is not one to messed with," Jason said. Rita and Tess would have got along well, Jason thought. At least the Tess he remembered. Both were passionate, intelligent, and fierce about those close to them.

"We need to get moving. I do not want to be late for our appointment with Eminent Caylon. He does not believe in 'fashionably late' or any other type of late," Mistress Nelson stated. "Are you ready?"

Jason nodded. "My wand spent most of last night trying to teach me about Glassoners and all the ways they can be insulted. My plan? Keep my mouth shut and my answers brief."

Mistress Nelson nodded in agreement. "Good idea," she said as she scanned him. "I see you are ready to travel. You should have plenty of energy to get there and be ready for whatever may come, when we arrive."

Jason just nodded. His nerves were getting to him and he wished they could leave.

"We will Step separately as I want you to experience this on your own. It takes a fair amount of your energy to get there and this way we can share the load. I will show you where we are going but I want you to follow me closely as we Step. Even entering that realm is highly regulated. We need to arrive together," she said, as she opened a portal.

Once he saw where they were going and he opened a similar portal. She linked their portals with a touch and walked into hers.

When he did the same, his portal took off like a rocket. He could feel her pulling away and put more energy into his portal to catch up. As they traveled, he could see their destination, but it never seemed to get closer. He saw flashes of light and could almost make out images of other worlds, but they sped by too quickly.

There was no way to track time but after what he thought was an hour, their destination seemed only marginally closer. He had used a good amount of his energy and fatigue was setting in. If they didn't arrive soon, he would have to stop and rest.

Finally, after what he thought was another hour, Mistress Nelson broke the silence. "We are about to arrive. Prepare yourself and try to land gracefully."

"Thank goodness. Not sure how much longer I could last," Jason said.

He could feel them approach their landing spot and almost stepped out of the portal. Realizing that arriving at the same time as his superior would be seen as a misstep by the Glassoners, he paused. Then easily landed a half-second after Mistress Nelson.

He found himself in a large office near a massive desk with what looked like a royal emblem on the front. Behind it hung a large painting of a man and woman in royal dress. Jason assumed it was a painting of the Excellencies, effectively the King and Queen of the Glassoners. With the décor of a large desk, bookshelves, and chairs, Jason assumed this was a politician's office. The floors looked like blue marble with the walls a milky white. Looking around, he found almost everything except the furniture was made of the same sort of glassy material.

Standing near them was a tall, thin, hawk-nosed man. He stood in front of three men and wore a black suit with a jacket that flowed to the ground. Two of the other men wore similar suits that were a darker gray. By his uniform, the third man was obviously military and an officer of some sort.

Jason became alarmed as the officer kept scanning the room with his eyes. The man appeared concerned about something. Behind the man were two guards and Jason could sense two more guards behind Jason, standing in the corners.

The guards carried weapons that looked similar to a machine gun. From what Jason learned, this was standard Glassoner issue. The weapons were dangerous, especially to weak shields. Each also carried a box that when activated, would generate a modest shield. Nothing most warlocks or wizards couldn't cut through, but it did provide protection from small weapon's fire and some magic. The two guards behind the officer kept scanning the room with their eyes, each keeping one hand on their weapon and the other on the box on their belt.

Jason scanned the room again with his magic but found nothing. Even still, he kept himself ready for anything.

The tall man smiled. "Mistress Nelson, it is very good to see you again." He took a step forward and extended his hand. From Jason's limited training, this meant he saw her as an equal.

Mistress Nelson took his hand and gave it a squeeze, a Glassoner sign of respect, Jason remembered. "It is good to see you too, Eminent Caylon. It has been much too long." She motioned to Jason. "Let me introduce Senior Jason Canin."

The Eminent smiled and nodded to him. Jason took a step forward, nodded, then stepped back. Mistress Nelson's slight smile meant, so far, Jason was doing well. Maybe he wouldn't cause a scene for once.

Caylon introduced the other two men as his aides. He mentioned their names but didn't stop to allow for a handshake or even an acknowledgement. Neither man reacted, acting as if this was to be expected. He turned to the man in the military uniform. "And this is Captain Welxs of his Excellency's service. He has the unenviable task of keeping me safe. He would probably have the most boring job if it weren't for his paranoia," the Eminent said.

A brief look of irritation flashed on the Captain's face but was quickly replaced with a smile. "It is an honor to meet you, Mistress Nelson," the Captain said with a bow.

"The honor is mine, Captain," Mistress Nelson replied.

The Captain turned to Jason, gave a slight bow, then extended his hand. Jason wasn't quite sure this was the correct etiquette but said nothing. The way the man moved, smoothly and with confidence; Jason was sure the man had seen plenty of action. This was a man to be reckoned with.

"With all due respect, Eminent. I believe it is probably his paranoia that makes his job so boring," Jason said, getting a quick smile from the Captain before his worried look returned.

Gripping the captain's hand, Jason leaned in and whispered, "What's wrong?"

The Captain gave him a hard look as if to size him up. "Not sure but there is something wrong. I feel it in my bones," the Captain whispered back. Both men stepped back and resumed their official positions.

The Eminent glared at his Captain for a moment then turned his attention back to Mistress Nelson. "Shall we go to my study. I have taken the liberty of having your favorite coffee brewed fresh."

"That is most kind, Eminent. I look forward to catching up with you," Mistress Nelson said.

The Eminent offered his arm to Mistress Nelson who promptly took it. The guards opened the door and the couple stepped through the doorway, then paused. The two guards stepped around the couple and took point. At a signal from the Eminent, the guards marched forward with Mistress Nelson and the Eminent following.

Jason and the Captain were next side-by-side. As they entered the hallway, he did a quick scan. He found nothing yet intuition told him the Captain was right, something was wrong. He couldn't put his finger on what it was.

Trying to think of what he should do, he remembered something Dod told him. "Always listen. Sounds change when someone is camouflaged nearby. By listening, you can tell if someone is there and where they are."

He listened, augmenting his listening with magic. The answer came to him quickly. Using a low voice, he asked, "Captain, do you have any men camouflaged nearby?"

"No," the Captain replied under his breath.

"One ahead, in the left corner. One in each corner behind us," Jason whispered.

"Protect the Eminent. I think the Mistress can hold her own," the Captain said. Before Jason could respond, Welxs picked up his pace.

"Eminent! May I have a word?" Welxs called.

The Eminent turned with a scowl. The Captain's social faux paus clearly embarrassed him. But Mistress Nelson put a hand on the Eminent's arm, causing a look of confusion on his face.

She had seen Jason grasp his wand and Welxs rest his hand on his weapon. Two of the guards noticed their Captain's agitation and turned away from the officials, weapons drawn, and boxes activated.

Jason had just a second to sense someone powering up, when one of the intruders behind them revealed himself and fired. The guard, with no time to put up a shield, took the brunt of the shot. The second guard opened fire on the intruder, cutting through the attacker's shield and killing him.

Jason realized this was a ruse and started moving, trying to put himself between where he thought the second attacker was and the Eminent. He pulled his wand and jumped, hoping he would be in time to protect the Eminent. As he jumped, he ramped up his shield then fired with everything he had. Time slowed as he flew through the air. As Jason fired, the second attacker dropped his camouflage and returned fire. He watched as the two shots narrowly missed each other.

Time resumed when the attacker's shot slammed into him, destroying his shield, and hitting him in the chest. Jason barely saw the attacker slam into the wall from his own shot, when Jason was launched backwards. He collided with the Eminent, knocking him down, and Jason rolled on the floor. Shots rang out as a battle raged around him.

Jason fought to catch his breath and felt pain intensify in his chest. Jason could see the Eminent trying to get up then felt a huge power surge. His eyes turned to Mistress Nelson who now radiated extreme energy.

"Enough!" She yelled, and a force rammed through the room. The only standing attacker slammed to the wall and fell.

Jason tried to stand and raise his wand, but the pain was immense, and he could barely get on his knees.

"Jason. Stay down. I have this now," Mistress Nelson commanded.

Jason immediately dropped back to the cool floor and poured what energy he had left into healing himself.

Let me help, his wand said.

The wand sent energy into his uniform and it started repairing itself. Jason hadn't realized that some of his uniform had been burned into his skin. When the uniform separated itself from him, it sent a shockwave through him and he uttered a few curse words that he hoped no one would hear.

I know it hurts but you need your uniform mended in case there are other attackers, his wand said.

After a moment, Jason felt a little better. His chest still felt like it was on fire, but he knew he would live.

Jason, the guard. He doesn't have much time before he dies, his wand urged.

Jason looked over to the downed man. He lay on his back gasping desperately for air and bled profusely from his neck. His partner was trying to help but there was little he could do. Jason crawled to the injured guard. Putting his hand on the guard's neck and he was about to start healing him when the other guard pushed him back.

"Leave him be!" the guard yelled.

With the man's life hanging in the balance, Jason didn't have time for this and sent a blast at the guard. The man stumbled backwards several yards.

"I am trying to save him, you idiot," Jason said, putting his hands back on the dying guard. Pushing out his senses, he could feel the severed artery. He put as much energy as he could into repairing it. This was a much more complex repair then he had done before, but the man would die if he didn't try. He could sense the artery begin to pull together and he breathed a sigh of relief when it finally healed.

Next, he started repairing the damage to the man's throat. It took a minute, but at last the guard started to breathe normally. Jason could sense the man still had broken ribs and several cuts, but Jason was starting to feel woozy. Having used most of his energy on the attack and the repair to the guard's neck, he had very little energy left. Healing the rest of the guard's injuries would have to wait. Releasing his connection to the injured man, he slumped back.

The guard's partner approached, slowly rubbing his head. "By their Excellencies! I'm sorry, he's my best friend and I panicked."

"Understood," was all that Jason could get out, just glad that the guard would live.

Mistress Nelson came to him and put her hand on his back. Power flowed in and he felt well enough to stand.

"I need to get back to helping the Captain," Mistress Nelson said, leaving him and rushing back to the Captain who lay in his own blood.

Guards rushed in from all sides, looking for any remaining attackers. The scene became chaotic as orders were shouted then countermanded when someone else arrived. Something had to be done. Jason wobbled a bit but decided to take command of the situation.

"I want this entire facility searched. Every room, every space. Minimum two person teams. Find anything suspicious, lock off the room and call for help," he ordered.

An older man in uniform looked to Jason. "Sir, we don't work for you and it is best you keep quiet," the man said.

The guard jumped when a booming male voice from across the room yelled, "By Kings and Gods, you work for me and you will follow every order he gives. Is that clear?"

The Eminent stepped to the center of the room. With his face a deep red and his furled brow, he looked menacing. The man he yelled at almost fell over backwards while calling out, "Yes, Eminent." He turned to his troops and began relaying Jason's orders. Afterwards, he turned his attention back to Jason. "Arm's Guard Nexon, at your service. Anything else, sir?" Nexon said with a salute.

"Yes, I need this room cleared of everyone except the officials and those needing medical attention. The soldiers are stomping on possible evidence. I want all search teams reporting in every two minutes. Anyone doesn't report in, I need to know. Use your judgement, if something feels wrong, do what you think necessary until I can get involved. I will back you," Jason ordered, starting to feel better.

"Sir. Thank you, sir." Nexon saluted, then returned to his guards, yelling orders.

Jason hobbled over to Mistress Nelson who was healing Captain Welxs. Welxs had taken a shot to the abdomen and Mistress Nelson used an amazing amount of energy to pull his intestines back into the cavity and fixing what she could. The Captain didn't look good with burns over several parts of his body, including his face.

The Eminent watched as Welxs body healed, "Kings and Gods," was all he could say looking at his Captain. His face had gone from a deep red from yelling at Nexon to a slight tinge of green.

Finally, Mistress Nelson released her connection and then stood. "That's all I can do for him now. He will live but will need more care. I'm sure your medical team will be able to heal him completely," Mistress Nelson said.

"Kings and Gods," the Eminent repeated. He looked to be in a trance staring at his Captain. "I thought he was being paranoid."

"Eminent, your medical team needs permission to take him back to their facility," Mistress Nelson said calmly, taking his hand.

The Eminent shook his head. "Of course. Please do what is needed." He took a deep breath. "I am so sorry this happened. I am burned to my core."

"Eminent," Jason said, trying to get the man's full attention. "I need to bring in a couple members of my team to help with the investigation and your protection. They can work in coordination with your staff, but I need to let them know now."

"Considering that you just saved my life, of course. Do as you see fit." The Eminent replied, then looked hopeful to Jason. "Would it be okay if we continue our trip to my study. I could use a tea, or something much stronger."

"Of course. Give me a minute to summon my team. Then I'll escort you."

Using his wand, he sent a message to Dod and Bull, telling them he needed them as soon as possible. He did add that Dod needed to see Rita about a dress uniform. He knew that wouldn't go over well with his favorite tracker and he put it as an order.

"Arm's Guard," he called and Nexon marched over.

"Sir. All teams are reporting in as requested. So far all is clear, but one team just reported something unusual in a linen room," Nexon said with a salute.

"Tell them to seal off the area. I want ten of your best soldiers there now and tell them to be ready for the fight of their lives. Anything tries to get out, have them open fire. You can take me there after we get the Eminent settled," Jason started. "Also, I want everyone out of this hallway and the doors locked. I will seal the room after everyone is out and I want four guards at every entrance. Anything tries to leave have your guards stop it with any means necessary. No one comes in here without my permission. Understood?"

"Very good, Sir," Nexon said. "Sir, do you expect another attack?"

"No, but if they do, I want to make sure they pay for what they've done."

"Believe me sir, my guards would like nothing better," Nexon growled. Turning, he began ordering the rest of the guards out.

Mistress Nelson took the Eminent's arm and escorted him out of the hallway. When Jason got to the end, he cast a spell putting up a barrier. No one could get in or out of the hallway without him knowing it.

The Eminent regained his composure as they walked and started to prattle on about the various artwork and architecture. Jason knew this was his way of pulling himself together. But, he had to admit, it was interesting stuff. At least what he could hear. His senses were on full alert and he tried to listen for every noise. Considering there were at least a dozen soldiers surrounding them, it was hard to hear anything.

The group approached a large set of double doors. Each heavily adorned with intricate patterns. The Eminent slowed and approached the doors as if they were snakes ready to strike. He turned to Jason.

"I assume you want to check the room before we enter?" the Eminent asked, casting a nervous glance at the doors.

"Yes. Please stay here. You five," Jason pointed to the five guards nearest him. "Come with me. The rest protect the Eminent. If there's trouble, take my advice." Every ear turned to him. "Stay out of Mistress Nelson's way."

The guards chuckled then saluted.

Mistress Nelson gave him a smile as he walked to the doors. "Please be careful."

"So now you're worried about me?" Jason asked, feeling his tension drop at least for a moment.

"You? No. Those dress uniforms are hard to create and that one has already taken enough of a beating for one day," Mistress Nelson quipped, flashing a smile and then turning her attention to the Eminent.

"These things are tough," Jason said, thumping his chest. That turned out to be a bad idea as his wounds were not completely healed. Pain soared through him for a moment and he paused to let it die down. He reminded himself he was wounded and could possibly be walking into another firefight. Not being one hundred percent was a concern but there was nothing he could do about it.

He looked around to find his backup, three men and two women, watching him. He took a deep breath, pulled his shoulders back, and decided it was time.

"Let's go see if someone has planned a surprise party for us," Jason said. "On my count open the door. I will go in first. If there are any fireworks, feel free to join in."

The guards responded with "Sir. Yes, Sir!"

"One, two, three. Now," Jason said, and two guards opened the doors.

He walked inside with his shields at max and his wand ready. He could feel his wand anticipating battle, almost wanting it.

Calm down. I would prefer a few minutes of peace, Jason said to his wand.

I'm sorry. That last battle reminded me of the old days with your grandfather. They were good times, his wand said.

Only because you two survived.

Good point, his wand replied.

Jason sent out a magical ping, something that Dod had taught him to find those who hidden nearby. He didn't care if any intruder knew he was searching for them. When he found nothing, he tried listening.

His backup filed in slowly. "Please be quiet for a moment," Jason ordered, putting up his hand. After a minute, he found nothing. His instincts told him there was no one there.

"Please let the Eminent and Mistress Nelson know that all is clear, and they may enter." Jason took a deep breath and slowly let it out. He needed to pace himself and let his energy store refill and his body to heal. If he didn't, he may not survive the next attack.

The two entered and the Eminent went straight for a small bar and started pouring drinks. His hands shook and Jason walked over to help him. Taking the bottle from the politician's hand, he poured a drink and held it up.

The shaken man looked at it. "I think the occasion calls for a double."

Jason obliged and filled his glass along with two more. He handed one to Eminent Clayton and one to Mistress Nelson.

The Eminent held up his glass. "To, uh," his face went blank as he tried to come up with something.

"The Captain," Jason added, trying to help the shaken man.

"Yes, good, the Captain." The Eminent then emptied his glass.

Jason gave Mistress Nelson a look and followed suit, with Mistress Nelson doing the same. Whatever it was, it was smooth. Similar to bourbon and he enjoyed the burn as it went down.

"Another?" the Eminent asked.

"I'm afraid I will have to decline. I still have work to do," Jason said enviously. Whatever they were drinking was delicious and he would prefer a little more time to savor it. "Please excuse me, but I would like to take up your offer at a later time."

"Of course," Eminent Clayton said.

As he walked away, he heard Mistress Nelson say, "I will join you for another, but we should let the first settle a bit, don't you think?"

"Arm's Guard," Jason called.

"Sir?" Nexon answered as he entered the room.

"Two items. I have two members of my team coming and they will arrive in the same place Mistress Nelson and I did. Please have someone there to greet them and escort them to me. Warn your guards that one is not humanoid. Also, let them go wherever they want. They are both excellent trackers and may find clues on the way."

"Yes, Sir. And the second item?"

"Take me to where your guards found something unusual."

"Very good, Sir. This way," Nexon said.

As they walked away, the study doors closed, and Jason felt Mistress Nelson put up a shield. He stopped and turned to admire it. No one was getting through her shield anytime soon.

He turned back and motioned to Nexon to continue on. As he walked, he kept scanning the area but found nothing. Taking a lesson from Dod, he scanned the ceiling, detecting a trail of magic. As they approached a group of soldiers, the trail led straight past them to a door on the other side of the group.

The group parted as the Arm's Guard approached. All except for three individuals who clearly were not soldiers. Each wore an outfit resembling what a scientist on earth would wear.

Without even introducing himself, one said, "These guards will not unlock these doors for us and said they have orders to not allow anyone in. Who gave you that authority?"

The Arm's Guard paused for a moment and then looked to Jason. "Senior Canin of the warlocks gave the order."

The man turned on Jason. "And who gave you that authority, Mr. Canin?"

While Jason didn't know all Glassoner rules of etiquette, he could tell an insult when he heard one. "First, it is Senior Canin to you. Second, before I answer any questions from you, I need to know who you are and why you are wasting my time."

The unknown man huffed as if Jason had just slapped him and looked at his two comrades.

"I," the man emphasized, "am Scientist Wilmon, Scientist Prime of his Excellency's Royal Science Academy. I report to Prefect Barrs, who reports to the Eminent."

The man looked to his two colleagues who nodded their approval. He then turned to Jason with a look that he expected an apology and probably some groveling.

Jason smiled. "My authority comes directly from the Eminent and I am in charge of securing this facility and determining if there is a continuing threat. As such, I expect all of you to follow my orders or I will have the guards escort you back to where you came. Is that clear?"

Jason paused and watched a range of emotions play over the faces of the three. Finally, the Wilmon recovered. "Of course, I was not made aware of the current situation." He scowled at the other two. "Our job is to support your goal as much as you will let us."

Jason would have loved to torture these three as it was clear they felt themselves very important and probably flaunted it to anyone they felt inferior. But with the current situation he needed as much help as he could get.

"Arm's Guard, I want to talk to the guards about what they found," Jason said.

Nexon snapped his fingers at two guards standing off to the side. Both approached and saluted. The two were young and looked nervous. They tried to keep their eyes looking forward, but their eyes kept darting at Jason and away.

"At ease both of you. I'm just going to ask you questions, not remove any vital organs," he said, hoping to get a laugh.

The first guard looked at him. "Do you do that?"

Jason mentally kicked himself, he needed to watch what he said, "No. I don't. Let's not get off topic. First, what is your first name?"

"Jilx, sir," he replied.

"Jilx, tell me what you saw when you went in that room."

"Wilzer and I entered and there were these rocks in a circle. Bright light coming from them, almost blinding. Then I thought I saw something appear out of nowhere and enter the circle. As fast as it appeared, it disappeared. We followed your orders, sealed the room, and called it in."

"Wilzer, anything to add?" Jason asked.

"No sir."

"Thank you. Dismissed," Jason said.

"Arm's Guard, do you have a map of this facility? Specifically, where the attack occurred in relation to this room?"

"Yes sir, I do." Nexon took out a small device and it displayed a 3D map. He found the room was two floors down from where the attack occurred.

"Interesting," Jason commented.

Returning to the three scientists, "I have my own experts coming in," he paused to let that sink in, "but I can use all the help I can get. I will open the door and do a scan. You may do the same, but no one goes in and nothing gets put in that room. Once my experts arrive, you can coordinate with them. Is that agreeable?"

Wilmon looked to the other two and took a deep breath. "Yes, that is agreeable, and I appreciate you working with us."

The disdain on his face and his clenched fist made it clear the man was not happy with the arrangement, but he had no choice. One of the scientists held something in her hand and promptly put it behind her back.

"Good. But let me warn you. If you try to sneak something into that room, I will have these guards insert that item somewhere into your body at their discretion. That would probably be quite painful not to mention embarrassing, so I suggest you heed my warning."

The third person of the group covertly returned what she held in her hand to her pocket and Jason assumed the matter was settled. He would watch closely but he felt his message had been received.

"Arm's Guard. I want you to unlock the door and when I am ready, I will open it. If there is someone in there and we get into a firefight, I want four of your guards to get these three to safety. The rest better back me up. Oh, and make sure none of them shoot me," Jason said.

Nexon chuckled. "Of course, sir. When you are ready."

Jason nodded to the Arm's Guard. He took out a small item and placed it on the door near the handles. He could hear the door unlock. Nexon stepped back and motioned to Jason.

Jason stepped forward and used magic to pull the door open. Leading with his wand, he stepped forward just enough to look inside, finding a small room filled with racks of linen. On the floor, in the center of the room, was a large circular area that looked like it had been burned. The glass-like floor had been melted. Jason's heart skipped a beat. The burn looked exactly as he had seen during the Meathonian attack.

He scanned the area for over ten minutes and found only lingering magic from what he guessed was three-to-four magical entities. He spent another ten minutes listening for anything. He couldn't detect any movement and whomever had been there was now gone.

He stepped back and gestured to the three scientists. Each peeked inside then turned their attention to their hand-held devices. An hour later, they completed their work and Jason ordered the door closed and locked.

The three scientists started conferring with each other, ignoring Jason. After about ten minutes, he felt he'd been ignored long enough. Jason interrupted their conversation. "Please tell me what you found."

A brief flash of annoyance on Wilmon's face was quickly replaced with a look of boredom. "We have found traces of magic from multiple individuals. Once we get back to the lab, we can determine how many individuals. With your permission, we need to take some samples from the room to analyze," the only woman of the group said.

"Thank you for the information. Once my experts get here and have done their initial scans you may. Can you tell me your name?" Jason asked.

"Second Scientist Ambez," she said.

"My initial scan determined probably four entities. All four left the room, headed down the hallway and made a right turn. I found only one returned," Jason said.

"How did you determine that they left and where they went?" Amber asked. She immediately pointed her device down at the ground and started sweeping.

"He made it up," Wilmon muttered, under his breath.

Jason struggled not to launch Wilmon into a wall when a voice called out, "Because he isn't an idiot and he looked up."

It was Dod and Bull walking toward them. Three guards cautiously followed. Bull was larger than usual and stood as tall as the guards.

Dod walked over, grabbed the female scientist's hand with the device and pointed it to the ceiling. The machine started flashing signs on its display. Dod turned to Wilmon, "If you had said that to me, I would have removed both of your arms and fed you to my friend here," she warned, pointing to Bull who bared his fangs.

The scientist's face went white as a ghost and he dropped the device he was holding, "My apologies. It was very bad manners on my part."

Dod glared at the man then turned back to Jason. "We followed the trail back to here. From what I saw, three went to the room where the attack occurred and the fourth stayed close by. My guess is that when things went wrong, the last one bailed, and came back this way and into that room. What's in there?"

"It's a linen closet but you will find something very interesting in there. What you find, keep to yourself," Jason said staring directly into Dod's eyes. "I have kept everyone out except for the two that initially found it. I have told these three they can go in after you go in." Jason pointed to the three scientists.

"Well Bull, let's go see what's so interesting in the room," Dod said.

I believe I already know what we will find but I may be wrong, Bull said.

Nexon unlocked the door and Dod opened it. She stood for several minutes just looking into the room. She slowly stepped in, followed by Bull. When one of the scientists tried to enter, Bull growled and bared his teeth. The scientist quickly retreated.

"This is unfair. You told me we could enter also," Wilmon demanded.

"That was before your comment but don't worry you'll get your chance. Just be patient," Jason said, trying not to be smug.

Dod slowly circled the room. Bull simply stared at the burnt mark in the floor.

After ten minutes, "Okay, I'm done, you three can come in." Dod said and walked out of the room. Bull paused for a moment and followed her.

"What did you find?" Jason asked, intrigued.

"Pretty much nothing you didn't already know. It looks like four intruders came out of that portal, went directly out the door, and crawled along the hallway ceiling to where you were attacked. Besides the circle in that room, the thing that interests me most is not here, but back where the attack occurred," Dod said.

"And that is?" Jason asked.

"I don't think they originally meant to attack you in the hall. It looks like they were making their way toward where the Eminent met you but then backed up just before you came out, Dod said. "I would like to go see the bodies of the attackers again."

"We can do that in a minute, but I want to hear from Bull first," Jason said.

From what I can smell I believe I know the attackers. They are highly paid assassins, but usually use poison or some other much more subtle way to kill their victims. Armed combat is not their strength. Either one of them made a fatal mistake or failure to kill the Eminent was not an option, Bull said.

"My guess is that when they thought they had been discovered they went with plan B. Which didn't work out for them," Jason said.

I am more concerned with the portal that was used.

"Agreed."

This realm is heavily protected, most cannot simply portal here without prior consent by the Glassoners. But the portal that was used went through the Glassoner security blocks. Not unusual as no one has found a way to block a God's portal. But it takes considerable amount of money and resources to create a portal like that. Whomever created it, spent not only a lot of money on the assassins but on the portal itself. I can only imagine that the remaining assassin has gone into hiding after their customer paid that much money and failed.

"Any idea on why the Meathonians would try to attack us here?" Jason asked, hopeful for any information.

I am not sure you and Mistress Nelson were the targets of the attack.

"I agree. This attack feels well organized and was probably meticulously mapped out," Dod said. "How far in advance did you plan this trip?"

"This was a last-minute decision. We didn't know we were coming until yesterday." Jason considered the situation. "So, the Eminent was probably the target and our arrival somehow upset their plans. If that is the case, it would be good to know why the Meathonians wanted to kill the Eminent."

I doubt the Glassoners will tell you unless somehow it concerns warlocks in general.

"Well, we can try. One more thing, if this was a planned attack then either someone from the inside fed them information or the assassins have been here before. Nexon, can you display the map again?" Jason asked.

Nexon tapped his device and the map appeared again.

Dod reviewed it, turning the map in the air to get a better look. "Very impressive. From this location you have multiple paths to and from the Eminent's office. If I were to guess, I would say they knew the area well. This probably wasn't their first trip here."

"Nexon, any reports of a burned circle like the one in the linen room?" Jason asked.

"Not to my knowledge, sir."

Is there any construction going on or recently finished?

"Yes, a closet at the far end of this hallway was recently repaired. Some cleaning materials were spilled and caught on fire, heavily damaging the room."

"My guess is the fire was used to cover up the assassins first trip here. Did anyone scan for magic?" Jason asked.

"Not to my knowledge as it was ruled an accident."

"Take us to it, please."

The Arm's Guard led them for about five minutes before stopping and opening a door.

"The fire was in here," Nexon said.

I can sense the residual of a portal.

"I can feel it to," Dod added. "The assassins came through here to scout out the place. Not wanting anyone to know they were here they caused a fire to cover up their portal. If the construction crew hasn't already destroyed what they took out of there, we will probably find the same burned material."

"Time to go question the Eminent and give him an update," Jason said.

"Yes, well," Nexon paused. "He is with their Excellencies. Your orders are to report your findings to them when you are ready. Sir." Nexon saluted then ordered his guards into formation.

Jason's jaw almost dropped to the floor and he now wished he had taken up the Eminent's offer for a second drink. Jason looked to Bull and Dod.

"Why do I get the feeling this isn't a good thing," Dod said, looking between Jason and Bull.

Glassoners are strict on their social etiquette. It is very easy to offend them and the consequences of doing so can be severe.

"Nothing we can do about it," Jason said, looking around desperate to find something to delay their report. "Dod, only speak unless spoken to and keep your answers short."

"Is this how they treat women here? I'm not sure I can do that," Dod said, her cheeks flushed.

Jason was tired and his patience were fried. "No, it's not how they treat women here but until you know how to interact with the Glassoners, it is what you will do. You are a member of my team and if you screw up and insult the Glassoners, it's me that pays the price."

Dod's look of shock made it clear his message had hit home. He turned on his heels. "Arm's Guard. Let's go, now. I need to get this over with."

Nexon yelled and the guards fell in line and started marching down the corridor. Jason followed with Dod and Bull behind him. He could feel Dod trying to bore holes in his back with her eyes, but he was beyond caring for the moment.

As they followed the parade of guards, Bull sped up and walked next to him.

You know Dod was just being Dod. There was no disrespect intended, Bull said breaking the silence between them.

Yes, I know. But this could go very badly and now is not the time for Dod to try and make a point. I will make amends with her soon.

Jason tried taking several deep breaths to relax but it didn't work. They turned a corner and entered a large hallway lined with guards. At the end, he could see two large doors with guards standing in front of them.

As they approached the doors. *Any last advice?* Jason asked Bull.

They do value the truth over everything. Be honest and you may do better than you think. Good luck.

The Arm's Guard announced their arrival, and the doors were opened.

Just before they entered the room, he turned to Dod. "I am going to try something. Follow my lead," just before he was about to turn back, he added, "Please."

Dod smiled. "I always have your back, even when you're an ass."

Jason smirked and stepped into a grand hall. Expensive looking decorations and artwork hung everywhere. Down the center of the room a purple rug with gold trim ran to the end of the room where two large chairs and desks sat. They looked like a combination of an executive's desk and a monarch's throne. About halfway down, a man and a woman stood, wearing glass-like crowns, and dressed in flowing robes. Looking like the two in the portrait above the Eminent's desk, he assumed they were the Excellencies. A few people stood around them, but all cleared when Jason and his team were announced. Guards lined the sides of the rug with a fair number of people standing behind on both sides.

Jason spotted Mistress Nelson near the Excellencies, holding the Eminent's arm. The man was standing but seemed to sway in place. He could sense Mistress Nelson sending energy to the Eminent, probably to help sober the man.

They walked until the Arm's Guards stopped and kneeled. "Your Excellencies. I have brought Senior Canin and his team for report."

The woman with the crown replied, "Very good."

Nexon stood and stepped to the side.

It was now their turn. Jason, Bull, and Dod stepped forward. Jason sent a message to Bull through their link. *Here goes nothing.*

Bull replied with a, *Good luck.*

The three kneeled and waited.

"Bull, a special thank you to the Laciter nation for your efforts to help us," his Excellency said.

It is my honor, your Excellencies, Bull said, he stood and walked to the side.

"Senior Jason, rise and report," His Excellency commanded.

Jason looked up to the Excellency but did not rise.

"Is there a problem Senior Canin?" His Excellency asked.

"I hope not your Excellency, but I need to state something before we report," Jason said.

His Excellency looked around the room then back to Jason, "Go on."

From the corner of his eye, he could see Mistress Nelson staring wide-eyed at Jason.

"Your Excellencies, this was a last-minute trip and I only had a short briefing to prepare me to work with the Eminent per your customs. I have had no training to properly address your Excellencies. My teammates have had no training at all. I fear we may unintentionally offend you or someone of your staff. I wanted to make my concerns known to you before I cause an incident," Jason said. It was a last-ditch attempt to try and keep him and Dod from creating an incident.

Jason dared another look to Mistress Nelson who now stood smiling. The Excellencies looked at each other with a bit of a smile. "Please rise," His Excellency said.

When he did, His Excellency went on. "We appreciate your candor and concern. It means a lot. Mistress Nelson has informed us of your ability to attract trouble wherever you go. But she has explained it has always been for the best."

"Considering that you helped save the lives of the Eminent, Captain Welxs, and a guard, we think we can overlook any minor transgression," Her Excellency said. "Although in doing so we may break your reputation."

"Thank you, your Excellencies. To not cause a scene would be a feather in my cap," Jason said. As soon as he said it, he wished he hadn't.

The Excellencies eyes immediately went to the top of his head. Mistress Nelson held a complete look of horror on her face.

"Funny, I don't see a cap on his head," Her Excellency said.

"Maybe it is hidden. I hear warlocks are very good at that," His Excellency added.

Jason could feel every eye in the room on his head. He heard his wand chuckle, and he could feel Bull fighting to keep from laughing. Dod smothered a snicker.

His Excellency turned, "Mistress Nelson, do you have one also?"

Mistress Nelson now held a deer-in-the-headlight look as every eye turned to her. She quickly recovered, now with a bit of a twinkle in her eye. It was clear she was planning on toying with Jason. "No, but very good observation, your Excellencies. Only Seniors carry them. It is a test to see how well they can camouflage. If anyone spots it before the test is over, he will fail. Also, he doesn't have to wear it on his head. He just needs to carry it on his person."

All eyes reverted to Jason. He was starting to get used to everyone staring at his head when someone in the back whispered loudly, "I think I see it on a belt loop near his butt." Jason could now feel every eye behind him fixated on his butt, fighting the urge to shake it at them. His wand was now laughing hysterically, and he could feel Bull desperately trying not to laugh. Behind him, Dod broke into a coughing fit to hide her laughter.

"What an excellent idea," His Excellency said. "General, maybe we could do something similar for your spies in training?"

"That is a great idea, your Excellency. We will start at once," the General said.

"In respect to Senior Canin, we will not attempt to reveal where his cap is hidden. Is that understood?" His Excellency said. All around him nodded but one person behind Jason said, "I am sure I see it on his butt."

When his Excellency was certain all had agreed, he continued, "Now, Senior Canin. Please report your findings."

"I will, your Excellencies, but before I begin, I need to know if the Eminent is usually in his office at the time we arrived?" Jason asked, not sure his request would be granted.

Her Excellency turned to the Eminent. "Fair question. Eminent Clayton?"

Eminent Clayton looked steadier now. "No, I usually am not in that office until much later. It was only because I was meeting you that I was there early."

Jason nodded. "Thank you, Eminent. That makes sense and is in line with our findings. We believe four Belchenick assassins were hired to kill the Eminent via poison or some other subtle method. Our arrival, along with the actions of Captain Welxs and his guards, spoiled their attack."

Jason let the news settle in before continuing. "From what we can determine, the four assassins used a portal and landed in a linen room. They were making their way to his office when we interrupted them. When it was clear we had detected them, three decided to make a last-ditch attempt to kill him. It obviously failed. The fourth did not engage and returned to the linen closet and escaped."

"Why a linen closet?" Her Excellency asked.

"It is out of the way and has multiple paths to the Eminent's office. We believe they recently portaled to a Utility room. They then surveyed the area and picked the linen closet as the best landing spot to launch their attack. Then set a fire in the Utility room to cover their tracks."

"The Utility room fire was caused by assassins?" His Excellency spun on his heels to confront his general. "Why are we just finding this out now?"

"Your Excellencies, we asked the Royal Science Academy to send someone to scan the area for magic. The junior scientist that was sent said it was nothing but an accident," the General said, looking to Scientist Wilmon.

"Scientist Wilmon, can you shed some light on why a junior scientist was sent to deal with a matter of security?" Her Excellency asked.

Wilmon, who up until then, had been surrounded by a group of people, all looking to him with admiration, suddenly found himself alone as everyone around him quietly backed away. "I do not know, Your Excellency. But I will investigate and get to the bottom of this," Wilmon said, recovering quickly.

"Good. When you are ready you will make your full report directly to us," Her Excellency said. Clearly, she was used to dealing with people like Wilmon.

Returning his attention to Jason, His Excellency asked. "Do you know who hired the assassins?"

Jason had hoped to discuss this in a less open forum. "Yes, we do. Would you like to know now or later?"

"We are an open court, and we wish to know now," His Excellency said. "But we do appreciate your discretion."

"Not too long ago, the Meathonians opened a similar portal on earth and sent through some beings," Jason said. "We are not sure why they did it other than to try out the portal. We believe it was the Meathonians that hired the assassins to kill the Eminent."

"That is not good news," His Excellency said, looking to his wife then back to Jason.

"Can I ask if you know why the Meathonians would want to kill the Eminent?" Jason asked.

"Eminent, is this something you wish to discuss?" Her Excellency asked. Although it was a question, it was obvious that anything other than a yes would be a problem.

Mistress Nelson released her lock on the Eminent's arm and stepped back.

"Of course, your Excellency," the Eminent began. He looked much more in control of himself. "A small Meathonian delegation approached me about one of your earth's months ago. They offered us many things in exchange for the Glassoners to side with the Meathonians in a war with Zycros and possibly the Warlocks."

The Eminent glanced quickly at Mistress Nelson who had taken another step back and was watching the Eminent very closely. "I immediately declined their offer as both the Zycros and the Warlocks have been close friends and allies."

Mistress Nelson relaxed and smiled. "Thank you, Eminent. The feeling is quite mutual."

"The Eminent reported this to us directly," His Excellency said. "We fully supported his decision and immediately asked the Meathonian delegation to leave. Relations with them have become very frosty as to be expected."

"Thank you, that helps," Jason said.

"I would like to know how they managed to get through our security measures undetected?" His Excellency asked.

They used what many call the God's portal. Your Excellency, Bull answered.

His Excellency nodded with a grim look. "I was hoping you wouldn't say that. Tell me, has anyone found a way to block a God's portal?"

"Per Bull, there is no known way. As a Laciter, I respect his judgment," Jason said.

"I am a bit confused on one thing. Why didn't they just portal directly into the Eminent's office or to our chambers for that matter?" Her Excellency asked.

"We had the same question, but Trainee Dod worked out the answer." Jason turned to Dod. He was taking a chance but had confidence that Dod would handle herself appropriately.

"We noticed you have motion and heat sensors in all primary areas. Their portal would have caused those sensors to send an alert. With the amount of energy the portal gives off, they needed to be as far away from any sensor as possible," Dod said.

"Good find. Thank you, Trainee Dod," Her Excellency said.

"No problem. It was nothing," Dod said then caught herself. "I mean, you are welcome, your Excellency."

Dod then went to curtsey and realized that wasn't correct and then tried to nod, which she did a little too violently and sent her hair flying over her head.

Jason was doing his best not to laugh, and he could tell the Excellencies struggled also.

"Trainee Dod is one of the best at tracking and evasion. She has never failed me," Jason said, trying to help Dod out of an awkward position.

Dod took a step back and nodded to Jason, her face ruby-red.

"Your Excellencies, with your permission I would like to bring in my expert on detecting magic. He may be able to tell us more about this portal and how to better detect it, may be even how to block it. He would work with your scientists, of course." He looked to the three scientists now standing in a corner, trying to stay as far from the center of attention as possible. "I would be remiss in not commending their work. Their efforts were crucial to our findings." The look of surprise on Wilmon's face was almost worth it, Jason thought.

"Thank you, Senior Canin, for pointing that out," His Excellency nodded in the scientists' direction. His lack of a smile made clear he had not forgotten about their prior mistake. The three scientists bowed, avoiding eye contact.

"Mistress Nelson," Her Excellency said, turning to her. "We must commend you on your team and their efforts. You have saved several Glassoner lives and we owe a debt of gratitude to you."

"Your Excellencies, the warlocks highly regard our friendship with the Glassoners, and we are happy to have been of service," Mistress Nelson said with a bow.

"As for your request to have your team do further research, it is granted. Please coordinate with the Eminent on the matter." His

Excellency then extended his arm to his wife and the two walked to their thrones. Everyone in the room either kneeled or nodded their head in deference. Once the two dignitaries sat in their thrones and turned to the documents on their desks, the room relaxed, and a general buzz of conversation started.

Mistress Nelson approached, smiling. "Well done to all of you. That went well." She looked directly above Jason's head. "Well, not perfect but we can manage. I sent a message for Weston and a science master to come look at the portal to see if they can find anything we missed.

Jason was about to ask about Steven when Mistress Nelson cut him off. "No, Steven will not be coming. Until we have things settled with him, he is not to leave earth." She gave Jason and Dod a stern look, "Am I understood?"

"Yes, Mistress Nelson," Jason said.

"Bull, I would like you and Dod to review the Eminent's office to see if there is anything else that was missed. I will have them bring you lunch while you wait for Weston and the master." Mistress Nelson turned to Jason. "We have a couple of items to discuss."

Jason assumed their discussion would be around Nemal's wand. Bull and Dod nodded and walked off but not before Dod gave Jason a questioning look. Jason tilted his head toward the door hoping she would read it that he would update her later.

Five minutes later, they stood in the Eminent's study. The room had been cleared of everyone except for Jason and the Mistress. Guards were stationed at the door to make sure no one would enter uninvited. Mistress Nelson cast a shield that would not only block anyone from listening in on their conversation. It would also block any hidden cameras.

"There, that should do. No one will be eaves dropping on our conversation. The Glassoners are very good at using technology to bypass our magic. That is why we must continue to embrace technology," Mistress Nelson said.

Jason walked over to the bottle that the Eminent had poured for them earlier. He poured himself a drink and then held it up to Mistress Nelson with a questioning look.

"No, thank you. As it was, the Eminent and I did quite a bit of damage to that bottle earlier," the Mistress said.

Jason held up the bottle and examined it. The first time he had seen the bottle it was nearly full. It was now half empty. He gave Mistress Nelson an appreciative look. The woman could obviously hold her liquor.

Mistress Nelson blushed then pulled out Nemal's wand, but her hand started shaking.

"I can't do it. Can you try?" Mistress Nelson asked.

Jason quickly scooped up the wand before she dropped it. He took a deep breath and slowly let it out. *Can you help me talk to Nemal's wand?* Jason asked his own wand.

I can try. Talk to it and I will try to make sure the message is sent.

Concentrating on Nemal's wand, Jason started. *We have come to where you requested. Can you talk to me and tell me where Nemal is?* Jason stared at the wand for over a minute. He could feel his wand reaching out but with no luck. He was about to give up, fearing the wand was dead.

Yes. I can hear you. Thank you for taking me here and give Salis my thanks. Her emotions are too hard to overcome to talk with her, especially with me being so weak. But the longer I stay here, the stronger I will become. Nemal's wand responded, causing Jason to jump. He had not expected it to talk to him.

Mistress Nelson looked to Jason with hope. "Did it speak?"

"Yes," Jason said. "I am about to ask it if it knows where Nemal is."

Concentrating on Nemal's wand. *Do you know where Nemal is?*

Nemal is in the Diarhar realm but which planet I do not know as of yet. Give me a little more time and I might be able to narrow it down.

"The wand thinks Nemal is in the Diarhar realm," Jason said to Mistress Nelson. He had been studying other realms but had never heard of that one.

Mistress Nelson's face fell. "That is unfortunate."

"Why?" he asked.

"For many reasons. It is a very long trip. It could take up to a month to get there from the Castle. Also, while warlocks have some friends there, we also have many enemies there. It is not a good place for a warlock to be, especially one without a wand. We need to know what planet in that realm he is on," Mistress Nelson said. Clearly this wasn't the news she wanted to hear as a tear ran down her face.

I can hear Salis now. Tell her if I can stay here another day or two. I may be able to narrow down where he is. Also, by then, I should be able to communicate directly with her, the wand said.

"Nemal's wand says if it can stay a couple of days it may be able to narrow down Nemal's location. It should also be able to communicate with you. As it is, it can now hear you," Jason said as he handed the wand back to the Mistress.

"Two more days would be considered a proper stay in this type of situation. I will make arrangements to extend my stay. Unless Weston finds something else, you should plan on resting up and leave tomorrow with your team. If it is okay with you and Bull, I would like Bull to stay with me," Mistress Nelson requested.

"Why?" Jason asked, his curiosity piqued.

"The Glassoners would like to better their relationship with the Laciters. Giving them more time with Bull would be seen as a goodwill gesture."

"Considering how much we have done today; I think we are doing well with goodwill," Jason said.

"The Glassoners came to the aid of the warlocks during the great wars. It cost them dearly and we owe them much."

Jason nodded then dropped into a chair, relaxing into the thick cushions. He closed his eyes and rubbed his temple.

"I see your injuries are almost healed. But you need rest."

"Yes, I do but still have a few items to cover." His stomach rumbled, reminding him he hadn't eaten recently. "One question, why did the wand want to come here? What is so special about this place that it is now able to talk to us and restore its power?"

"It makes sense now that I know where Nemal is. We have put up many barriers to keep those from the Diahar realm away from earth and the Castle. Those barriers probably interfered with his wand's connection to him. This realm does have barriers, but they are different from ours and will not affect Nemal's wand and its connection to his."

A knock at the door startled Jason. He stood, quickly pulling his wand and energizing his shield. A quick scan told him it was the Eminent and several others.

"You might want to put your wand away before you open the door," Mistress Nelson offered.

"Yes, sorry. Just a bit jumpy." Jason dropped his shield and stowed his wand.

He waited for Mistress Nelson to remove her shield. Opening the door, he found the Eminent and several others who looked like chefs.

"Sorry to disturb you but I know how warlocks are very fond of food. I asked my chef to whip up a lunch for us." Eminent Clayton made a slight bow.

"Of course, Eminent. We would be honored to have lunch with you." Mistress Nelson walked over and took his hand in both of hers. "Senior Jason is still recovering from his wounds and wonderful Glassoner food would do much to help him heal."

"Then we should let my chef setup." The Eminent stepped aside with Jason and Mistress Nelson following suit. A very tall, thin man in a white suit started giving orders as three tables of food were wheeled in. The man kept his voice low but spoke with such authority that Jason almost jumped in to help. After a minute, everything was setup and the staff lined up against the wall. "Your Eminent, welcomed guests, your lunch is ready," the chef said with bow.

They were about to sit when Dod and Bull joined them. Two more chairs were placed, and all sat. Jason waited for whatever formality would come next but was surprised by the Eminent.

"I won't bore you with any long-winded speeches, please eat," the Eminent said.

The look of surprise on Mistress Nelson's face told Jason that this was not the norm, but he went with it and attempted to not stuff the entire meal into his mouth with one bite. After a quick taste, he was glad he hadn't as this was a meal that could hold its' own with any that the Castle could come up with. He tried to slow his eating to enjoy this wonderful meal.

After what he thought was only a few minutes, and a few refills of his plate, a slight nudge from Mistress Nelson caused him to look up. Everyone else had finished eating and were waiting for him to finish.

Putting down his fork. "My apologies. The food was magnificent, your Eminent."

From the corner of his eye, he could see the chef stand a little taller and a slight smile appeared briefly on his face.

"No apologies necessary. You were injured saving my life." The Eminent turned to the Chef, "Senior Canin is still recovering from his injuries. Would it be possible to have food available in his room as it will help his recovery?"

"It would be my honor, Eminent," the Chef said, bowing.

While this was going on, Jason felt Dod glare at him intently. Evidently, she had not heard he had been injured. Jason knew she would be upset but was too tired to worry about it.

"Can you tell me how Captain Welxs is doing?" Jason asked, trying to change the subject.

"He is doing well. The man is as tough as dragon scales. He will be in the infirmary for a few more days then will rest at home for a while," the Eminent replied.

"I'm sure he will be happy to get out of the infirmary and into his own bed," Jason said.

"I think the infirmary staff will be happy also. Evidently, he is not a pleasant patient to deal with," the Eminent said with a smile.

"I can easily believe that," Jason said with a chuckle. "I would like to thank you for your kind hospitality, but I need to request my leave. I need to catch up with my team and possibly rest for a short while."

"Of course. We have prepared rooms for you and your team. My aide will take you to them." The Eminent rose.

Everyone stood and Jason followed the Eminent's aide with Bull and Dod in tow. The three were silent until the aide entered a smaller hallway and stopped. "The red door is your room, Senior Canin. The blue door is for Bull. The green door is for you, miss," the aide said with a bow. He then stepped away so they could talk in private.

"So, when were you going to tell me you were injured?" Dod asked, brusquely.

"I'm sorry, Dod. I should have mentioned it earlier, but we haven't had a spare moment to talk. Not being one hundred percent meant I needed backup, hence the reason you are here." Jason leaned back against the door and closed his eyes for a moment.

"You need to get some rest. Bull and I will wait for Weston's arrival and let him start his work," Dod said, her voice softening.

"Thank you. If you happen to run across that last assassin..." Jason began.

"I will capture him, torture him, and then spread his body parts across this realm," Dod finished his sentence.

"I was hoping for a simple stop him, but do as you need. Do me a favor and please don't get any blood on their Excellencies," Jason joked.

Weston will be here soon, and I need to make a stop before I meet with him. They found the debris from the construction and I want to inspect it, Bull said.

"Then let's go," Dod said.

Before they left, the Eminent's aide approached with two men and a woman. "These three will be your valets if you would let them."

Dod opened her mouth to protest but Jason cut her off. "Thank the Eminent and their Excellencies for the valets service. We accept their services and are honored," Jason said as he cast a hard look at Dod.

"Thank you, Senior Canin. I must say, you are getting the hang of this," the aide bowed, then left.

Jason's valet opened the door to his room. Any other time he would have been overwhelmed by the splendor of the room, but he was exhausted. Still, he forced a few "This is wonderful" type statements out, no doubt his valet would be reporting back. A bath awaited him.

"My name is Beates and I have the honor of being your valet. Anything you need, just let me know. I understand that your uniform only comes off by magic?"

"That is true. How did you know?" Jason asked.

"As soon as we heard you might be staying with us, we sent a request to your Castle on how best to serve you. Included in the response was information about your uniform and how to clean it."

"Great. I will change behind the screen and leave my uniform on the rail. I can take it from there but if there is any chance to have some food ready for me when I awake, I would be appreciative," Jason said.

"The chef is making a special meal in your honor. I am not sure what you said to him, but he seems intent on making sure you and your team are well fed. I will make sure that food is ready for you when you wake up."

Jason went behind a changing screen, removed his uniform, and watched as it folded itself on a rail. His wand floated nearby and settled on a table. Climbing into a huge bathtub, Jason slowly lowered himself into it. His chest was almost healed except for a red area in the center and the water stung as it hit his chest. After a moment and a few choice words, the pain subsided. After a few minutes in the water, he climbed out and put-on the pajamas and a robe that had been set out for him. Made of a silk like material, they felt wonderful.

"I may need to see if I can buy these," Jason said to himself.

Walking to the bed, he found it to be the largest bed he had ever seen. Climbing to the center of it, took a few seconds of crawling. Once settled, he pulled up the covers. His head sank into the most luxurious pillow he had ever laid his head on. His wand floated nearby and settled on the edge of the bed.

"These Glassoners do know a thing or two about hospitality. I am going to nap for thirty minutes," Jason said to his wand.

His wand chuckled. *I will wake you in two hours.*

"Nope, thirty minutes is all I need. I will wake myself." Jason yawned.

Two hours later his wand woke him.

Thirty minutes? His wand chided him.

"I guess my body decided it needed a little more sleep," Jason said, stretching. "What has happened while I was out?"

Weston arrived with Master Juan. They reviewed both sites and the debris from the fire. They agree with our findings. They were unable to track where the attackers came from but believe they may be able to create a better way to detect when a God's portal is used.

"Good, being able to go anywhere undetected is concerning," Jason said.

In theory, assassins could even enter the Castle, Jason thought. He was about to express his concern to his wand, when he caught a whiff of something that smelled heavenly. Searching for the source, he found a table covered with plates of all sorts of food.

It took Jason a minute to extricate himself from the covers and crawl across the huge bed. Crossing the room in an instant, he surveyed the bountiful feast. "There's enough food here to feed, well, a very hungry warlock," Jason said. With the amount of magic he had used today, he was going to be eating a lot of food. An annoying, yet reasonable price for being able to use magic.

Next to the table was his dress uniform, cleaned and ready for him. He dressed in his uniform before indulging in the food, doing a fair amount of damage to the stacks of food. He would miss his cushy pajamas.

"Rested and fueled. Let's go see what everyone is up to," Jason said to his wand.

He opened his door to find his valet waiting for him.

"Did you get a chance to eat anything..." the valet started to say. He stared at the meager amount of food left on the table. "I see you did, and it must have been good."

"It was excellent. Please make sure to pass my compliments on to the chef."

"I will," Beates said looking astonished. "The rest of your team is in the Eminent's office having a snack. Do you think they will want dinner?"

"Absolutely, I can pretty much guarantee their appetite will return by dinner," Jason said, "as will mine."

"Then I will arrange for dinner. Mistress Nelson will not be joining you as she will be eating with the Eminent and another visiting dignitary," the valet said.

"Good. A quiet dinner would be nice," Jason said. "I can find my way,"

"Very good, sir."

Jason slowly made his way to the Eminent's office, admiring the sites along the way and doing an occasional scan with his senses. As he neared the Eminent's office, he saw two men wheeling tables away from the office.

"Those warlocks can sure eat," the first man said.

"Yeah. Did you see the female? Pretty, but thought she was going to cut my hand off when I tried to take her plate," the second man said.

Jason chuckled. Dod sure had a way of making an impression. He stepped back into a corner so the two men wouldn't see him as they walked by. If they knew he had heard them, it could cause an awkward moment. After they were gone, he continued on and entered the office finding Dod, Weston, and Bull.

"Where is Master Juan?" Jason asked.

"He just left. He wanted to run some tests on the samples we collected," Weston said.

"Did you find anything new?" Jason asked, taking a seat.

"In a way, yes. The magic that was used for the portal is unlike anything I have ever seen. I am bringing back some additional material to research later. Also, I would like Steven to look at it," Weston said.

"Any idea how to block the portal or at least detect it?"

"Block it, no. Detect it, maybe. The portal uses a tremendous amount of energy that we should be able to detect. I will know more once our tests are done," Weston said.

"Is there anything left to do?" Jason asked.

Related to the attack, no. But there is a nearby museum that the Glassoners highly cherish. Leaving without visiting it may be considered a slight against them, Bull said.

"Then I think we should go for a visit. Do you know the way?"

I do, Bull said. *Follow me.*

Bull led them to the museum, and they spent several hours just wandering through it. The museum was massive. It would easily take them two days to see everything if they hurried. Their visit attracted a fair amount of attention as many Glassoners stopped them to either thank them for saving the Eminent's life or just to introduce themselves. Jason was concerned about proper Glassoner etiquette, but it was a non-issue as every Glassoner offered their hand first to shake. The group quickly found if they complimented the museum, it inevitably induced a smile on the Glassoners followed by a quick history of the museum. Later in the day, they returned to the Eminent's office to find a huge meal waiting for them.

Jason was surprised to find the head chef also waiting. He had expected the chef to concentrate on the Eminent and his visiting dignitaries. His team slowly worked through the meal, polishing off most of the food. They made sure to make frequent compliments as they ate. By the time the desserts were gone, the head chef was beaming with pride. The table was cleared, and they were surprised when two bottles of what Jason assumed was wine, were placed in the center of the table.

"Compliments of the head chef," the waiter said, as he poured glasses for each. A crystal dish was placed in front of Bull and wine poured for him.

Jason raised his glass. "Then, I think it is only fair that I toast the chef and his staff for a wonderful meal." Taking a drink, he wasn't sure it was wine, but the taste was amazing.

The head chef nodded. "Thank you. I am glad you have enjoyed the meal and I hope you enjoy the Vensmar. It is similar to your earth's wine, but I think you will find it a little better. We will leave so you may have some peace. If you need anything, my two waiters will be outside the room with the guards."

The chef indicated to two women standing across the room. The waiters gave a slight bow then left the room followed by the rest of the staff then the chef.

They enjoyed their drinks for a minute before Dod broke the silence. "So why were you and Mistress Nelson here? And why weren't we invited before everything went south?"

Jason contemplated his answer for a minute. "The reason we came is a deeply personal one for Mistress Nelson. It's not my place to say."

"So, it's related to Nemal's wand?" Dod asked, surprising Jason.

"Yes, but how did you know?"

"Steven mentioned a strange wand that the Mistress had, and I asked her," Dod said. "Was she able to find where Nemal is?"

"Being here, the wand is able to recharge itself and could tell us that Nemal is in the Diahar realm. It wants to stay a couple of more days in hopes of narrowing down which planet in Diahar Nemal is on."

Diahar is very far away. It is also a very dangerous place, especially for a warlock without his wand, Bull said.

"How far?" Weston asked.

"Mistress says it could take a month to travel there," Jason replied.

That is about right. Laciters can make it there in about two weeks as we can recharge faster, Bull said.

"Are you going after Nemal?" Weston asked.

"Until this thing with Tess is settled, I don't think so. I believe Mistress Nelson is thinking the same thing. She has waited this long; she can wait a little longer," Jason said.

Jason stayed long enough to finish off the Vensmar then excused himself. "I am heading to bed. I will see if I can have some quick breakfast in my room and will leave early tomorrow. Please let me know when you have returned."

The next morning Jason awoke to the smell of breakfast. He quickly dressed then sat down to enjoy his food. While he was eating, he found a small note on the table.

It read, *If you need me, please pull the chamber cord near the door.*

After eating his fill, Jason found the chamber cord and pulled it.

A minute later his valet walked through a concealed side door. "Yes sir?"

"I am leaving but want to make sure I am following proper etiquette. It is our custom to leave a monetary gift for you and your staff, but I understand that would be an insult. But I do wish to thank everyone for their efforts and make sure you are recognized for your outstanding service. How may I do that?"

"You are correct that leaving money or any gift for us would be improper. But a handwritten note from you would be considered an honor. Paper and special envelopes are by the door. If you wish to leave a note, please put it in an envelope, seal it, and address it to the Eminent. You may place the envelope in the box on the wall. His Eminent's aides will pick up the envelope and deliver it." Beates added. "You are not required to leave a note and there would be no insult taken if you do not."

"Thank you, Valet Beates. Your help is much appreciated," Jason said, giving a slight bow.

Beates made a deep bow. With a "With your leave?" he left.

Jason wrote a note thanking the Glassoner staff for their excellent service. Jason signaled Weston and Dod, telling them to also leave notes. Before leaving, he surveyed his room. Jason could get used to living a lifestyle like this. Well maybe for a while he thought, but he would become bored quickly.

Are you ready? He asked his wand.

Yes, let's go home.

Jason opened a portal and started his journey home.

Chapter Nine

For the next few weeks, things were quiet. The work at the Data Center continued but progress was slow. There were no signs of Tess and every single failed warlock trainee they could find was tracked aggressively.

Mistress Nelson had returned from Glassoner and reported that the wand had found Nemal on a planet called Evanderal. According to her, this was probably the most warlock friendly planet in that realm and she had friends that lived there. She sent a message to them asking them to try to find Nemal. Due to the distance, it would take at least a week to hear anything back. For Jason, the search for Nemal was on hold while he prepared to deal with Tess.

While reviewing reports from the data center, Jason soon found he needed to be careful what he asked for from Katon's group. One of the reports he received was a statistical analysis of the number of toilet flushes in both attack areas along with comparisons to national averages. Various statistical methods were employed, and all pointed to no anomalies. He took several deep breaths before sending a message to Katon. "Very detailed work, please send my thanks to the team. I think we can move on from this."

A very embarrassed Katon sent a note to apologize.

Jason and his family continued to attend church on Sundays. Reverend Jim now made it a habit of greeting him when they entered. The man he now knew as Tyinth, continued to hover nearby but left him alone. Almost as if he were afraid of the reverend.

It was common for Gatron to sit near them, but she also left them alone. Bull had sent a warning to the Zycro's to leave Jason and his family alone and so far, there were no more attempts to follow him home.

Katrina was enduring the surgeries to restore her body back to normal. Gail reported they were making great progress, but the surgeries were painful. Jason wanted to visit but Katrina felt awkward with his presence and Gail asked that he only call. Reluctantly he agreed, calling every night.

Jason visited his forest as much as he could to see if his grandparents were making progress on the magical doll. Each visit, their ability to communicate improved. It was still limited to simple words, spoken slowly, but they were improving.

"Grandpa, I have a problem I need help with," Jason said.

Yes? came a response a few seconds later.

"It's Rita. When we are training, she seems to tire quickly and has to return to the Castle often to recharge. My concern is that if she gets stuck someplace, she may run out of energy and die. I need something like a back-up battery to keep her going in case of emergency. I have the device from Tess that can store energy, but I don't know where to get the energy to fill it. I read everything I can find, and it seems there is no information on this. Any thoughts?"

He could feel a whirl wind of energy as if his grandparents were arguing. After a minute, he got his response, *Ask wand*, he heard.

"Okay, I will," he replied.

Turning his attention to his wand, *Did you hear what I asked my grandfather?*

Yes, I did. I can help but this is not the place to discuss it. You will need to return to the Castle and visit the library. I will guide you from there, his wand responded.

Jason was a little confused but agreed. He said goodbye to his grandparents and returned to his house. Even with the area under surveillance by the Castle, he did not want to Step when he was out in the open. All it took was one mistake and things could get complicated.

Once back in his house, he Stepped back to his room in the Castle. He half expected Rita to be there with a plate of food or his bath ready. He stood reminiscing for a second then headed to the library. Once there, he found only a few masters and the usual librarians. The librarians eyed him nervously but said nothing. Mistress Nelson had given him authority to go or do as he needed to stop Tess and the librarians knew it.

Okay, we are in the library. Now what? he asked his wand.

The last time you were here, you sensed some unusual books in the back. Find them.

When Dod taught them how to use magic to sense others, it was in the library. During her training, he sensed some books with bright and dark magical light. Opening his senses, he quickly located the books and headed straight for them. Along the way, he passed through several magical barriers meant to keep unauthorized visitors out. Mistress Nelson's authorization let him pass through easily. Finally reaching the back wall, he found the books he was looking for.

Start with the books with bright white light. Pull some energy so you can read them quickly, his wand instructed.

Grabbing the first book, he sat down at a nearby table, pulled energy, and started reading. Even with the help of magic, it took him over an hour to read two white-light books and two dark-light books. As he read, his wand added comments and answered his questions. Eventually he understood the basics.

Magic was made of both dark and white energy. Neither energy was inherently good or evil. The concept that dark energy was evil was a misconception that most warlocks and others held. It came from the fact that dark energy was considerably denser than white energy. A pebble of dark energy held as much as a bowling-ball-sized rock of white energy.

When magical entities cast spells, they were really using energy that had been created by a fusion of white and dark energy. There were several theories of how to recreate the fusion process, but none of the books specified how. There were reports of realms where you could find white and dark energy, but the data was incomplete.

He now knew the basics on how to build a 'battery pack' to recharge Rita in case of emergency. He could fill the pack they recovered from Tess, if he could only find a source of white and dark energy. He hoped Steven and Weston could create a device to fuse the two energies.

Any idea on where I can find a source of dark and white energy or stones to make more packs?

No, but ask Bull. His people have existed for a very long time. If anyone would know, it would be his people, his wand replied.

This was an incredible find; it could mean creating a huge power source for the Castle. A thought came to Jason.

Speaking out loud, he asked. "Castle, did Tess ever come here and read these books?"

Yes, with permission of Master Jenkins, she studied these books, the Castle replied.

"Can you tell me if she spent more time with any particular book?"

152

Yes, the Castle replied. *The book titled "How to Harness All Energy" on the bottom shelf was her favorite. She tried to remove it from the library, but we would not allow it. We became suspicious of her and worried that she may do something rash. We eventually banned her from these books.*

He picked up the book. It was getting late, but he needed to know what was in it.

"Castle, I need to take this book home. Please authorize with Mistress Nelson."

After a moment. *You have been authorized and the librarians notified. We will keep a close watch on that book and will retrieve it if we believe it is in danger of falling into the wrong hands.*

He took the book home and read it. He was amazed that anyone other than possibly the head mistress would be allowed to read it. The information was much more dangerous than the books that had a strong magical presence. In a way, it was equivalent to a dummy's guide to building a magical weapon. Granted, you had to be quite powerful and well versed in magic, but the power you could create from the knowledge in that book was beyond imagination.

The next morning, he called an emergency meeting, inviting only Mistress Nelson, Weston, Bull, Dod, Kien, and Guilford. Gail was too busy healing Katrina to meet.

Mistress Nelson arrived first. "Guilford won't make the meeting. There is an issue in another realm he is dealing with. It may be related to Tess."

"I wondered where he had gone off to. I hope he is back soon," Jason said.

Once the others arrived, he began. "I think I know what Tess is up to and how she helped the Meathonians create their stones." He held up the book he'd borrowed from the library.

"You think you can link Tess to a deal with the Meathonians?" Mistress Nelson asked.

"When Tess was here, she studied books about white and dark energy. She also studied this book. It teaches you the theory of how to combine the two energies to create a powerful energy source. But what is missing is the material that allows you to store the energies together without causing a chain reaction that could easily wipe out a small city. I'm guessing the Meathonians have that material," he said, looking to Bull.

Most Meathonians have no love for magic even though they are quite powerful. They feel that relying on magic is a crutch. Their realm is very different from most and it contains a material they call Stroth, that can be used to capture and host both white and dark energy. It is a rare material on their planet and highly treasured by them. But with it, you can probably create a device that can deliver a large amount of power if you know how to fuse the two energies together. As of now, they do not know how to do that, Bull said.

"And I believe that Tess does. My guess is that in exchange for creating the stones for the Meathonians to create a God's portal, she received Stroth in return," Jason said.

"But why are the Meathonians so interested in creating more stones?" Weston asked.

To prepare for war with the Zycros. This would give them a definite advantage as they could appear anywhere on earth. Possibly attacking the Zycros from their own base, Bull said.

"Which means, with you destroying six of their stones, the Meathonians traded more Stroth for more stones," Kien said.

"And Tess was probably happy to oblige," Jason added.

"They will probably trade for more soon," Weston stated. "Each time they use the God's portal it wears on the stones. They used the portal twice for the attack on the Glassoners and their stones are probably useless at this point. This means they will be trading again."

"Then we need to find their source of energy. If we can't find their source, then we need to get our own source of energy along with some Stroth," Jason said.

The Meathonians are not the only ones that have Stroth. The Zycros also have it, in a smaller abundance. As for white and dark energy, there are only a few places I know that you can get it. Most are heavily protected, and no one is allowed access. The Meathonians don't have a source but the Zycros do. They may help, Bull said.

"If the Meathonians don't have their own source, where is Tess getting hers?" Jason asked.

I am not sure. Someone must be allowing her access, or she has found her own source.

"At this point, it doesn't matter. We need to visit the Zycros and see if they will help," Jason said.

I will work on setting up a meeting with them. It may take some time and I will let you know when it is arranged.

"The sooner the better. Eventually Tess is going to make her big move."

While they waited to meet with the Zycros, preparations were in full force as they readied for Tess's next attack. If they wanted to stop Tess, they needed another approach to dealing with her. Full on frontal assaults were not going to work.

Weston created a spell that would neutralize the one being used to destroy the barrier walls. The problem was they needed to get close enough to the spell caster-to use it. While Jason had ordered that the information about the spell not be released, he still worried that Tess's spies would find out about it. He had to assume that Tess would adjust her strategy to protect whoever was attacking the realm boundary. As for a way to defeat Tess, Jason decided on going with an old standby and take a play out of a military handbook, aerial bombing.

The basic plan was for them to bomb the enemy enough to weaken any shield and cause enough disorder in their ranks to soften them up, then hit them with troops. Jason hoped it would be enough to get Weston in place to take out whoever would be trying to destroy the border wall.

Finally, an alert came in that another attack had begun. Jason met Weston in the Data Center Operations area and prepared. The rest of the team was in the Castle awaiting orders. Jason reviewed the monitor displaying where the attack was occurring and could see a dome shield protecting them.

Jason had expected this and made final adjustments on where the bombs would drop.

"This is it folks, ready the bombs," he yelled.

Several masters along with Gail, Dod, and their guides prepared. Each person would open a portal while another would throw aerial bombs through it, wait for the portal to close, then detonate the explosive.

"Now!" he ordered, and the team opened their portals and started dropping their bombs.

He watched on the monitor as the bombs started scoring direct hits on the shield. He could see panic among Tess's troops as one of the bombs got through a temporary hole and exploded. Tess was screaming for order among her troops.

Soon the shield was in tatters and Jason ordered his troops to attack. The plan was for twenty masters to attack followed by Dod, Gail, and their guides to give Weston cover to cast his spell.

Unfortunately, as soon as the masters engaged, explosions rocked his attack force. Tess had set up land mines around her forces and several masters were hit. The battle quickly disintegrated into a fire fight as the masters could not get close without tripping more landmines. There was no way Weston would get close enough.

Jason Stepped to where one of his commanders was positioned behind a dirt berm.

"Status," Jason yelled.

"Several masters down but no one seriously hurt. You warned us they may have a surprise and we had an extra shield up," the Commander said. Their position was taking fire and the commander returned fire. Jason joined in but it was easy to see they were at a stalemate. Jason had to do something quickly as his troops were too exposed.

"I have an idea. Be prepared to give me cover," Jason said.

"How will we know when?"

"Believe me, you will know it when you see it," Jason said, then Stepped back to Weston.

"Weston, do you trust me?" he asked.

Weston hesitated. "I know I am going to regret this, but yes."

"Just hold on and know I won't let you go," Jason said.

"What do you mean..." Weston began but Jason's next move cut him off.

Moving behind Weston, he grabbed him by his waist, and opened a portal beneath them. Before Weston could finish his sentence, Jason's portal put them several hundred feet above the battle zone. Instantly, they were sent hurtling down toward the battle. Wind rushed past and Jason had to yell for Weston to hear.

"When we get close, cast your spell and I will Step us somewhere safe," he yelled.

"You had better. If you don't, I am going to kill you," Weston yelled back.

Weston pulled his wand and held it close to him and Jason could feel him concentrating. While it was only a few seconds of freefall, it felt like an eternity. Looking down, they were in the perfect position and no one looked their way. He thought they were going to be okay until he saw

Tess look up. Before she could fire, he fired at her, forcing her to jump out of the way.

Jason's commander must have spotted them. His troops all started firing, sending a huge barrage at Tess and her troops.

Weston spotted the wizard casting the spell to destroy the barrier. He pointed his wand and yelled something Jason could not understand. A yellow beam flew from his wand and hit the wizard. This caused an explosion that wiped out the wizard and everyone near him. Those that weren't killed were sent hurtling by the explosion. Even some of Jason's troops were sent to the ground.

Jason opened a portal below Weston and himself then desperately tried to throw out an energy beam to slow them. Just as they entered the portal, the concussion wave from the explosion hit them and Jason lost control of his portal. He had planned on landing in his office but now his portal seemed to have a mind of its own. The portal view went from his office to a city, then to a waterfall. He clung onto Weston as he fought to regain control of the portal. He had always been able to adjust his portal landing, but now it was as if he were in a plane spiraling toward the ground.

He poured every bit of his energy into trying to control the portal. He could see flashes of what he assumed were other realms as he struggled to land. They were now heading straight for a small farmhouse when his wand yelled, *Help me turn!*

Jason pulled with all his might and between the two they turned at the last second. He hoped they were out of danger when there came a flash then a vast desert opened before them. This looked to be the best they could hope for and he tried to aim for it.

Jason yelled, "Prepare for a crash landing."

Weston had been screaming the entire time and Jason wasn't sure he had heard. A second later, they hit the top of a sand dune. Jason poured his remaining energy into his shield as they bounced several times like a rock skipping on water. He held onto Weston as hard as he could, trying not to lose him. Jason's shield was weakening, and he hoped they would stop soon. Just as his shield was about to collapse, they plowed to a stop.

Jason tried to breathe but got only a mouth full of sand. Pulling his head out of the sand he sputtered, trying to get the sand out of his mouth. He heard muffled screaming and found Weston stuck, headfirst, in the sand. He grabbed one of Weston's legs and tried to pull him out. It took several pulls but finally Weston was free.

They both rolled onto their backs, breathing hard. They sat in a large crater with the sand around them steaming. Jason could see a half-mile long streak across the desert where they had bounced.

"The next time you ask me if I trust you, expect a different answer," Weston sputtered, spitting sand out of his mouth.

Jason hesitated for a second then started giggling.

"What in the hell do you find so funny?" Weston growled.

Weston took a hand full of sand and threw it at Jason. This only caused Jason to giggle harder. Weston attempted to stand but as he did sand poured out of several parts of his uniform.

That was too much, and Jason started laughing. His wand quickly joined.

Weston let out a stream of expletives, which only made Jason laugh harder. Weston glared at Jason but soon joined in the laughter.

Jason stuck his wand into the sand, sending a message to Mistress Nelson telling her they had survived. He knew they weren't on earth and wasn't sure if the message would reach her, but he didn't have the energy to do anything else.

Within seconds Mistress Nelson, Dod, and Gail arrived, quickly checking Jason and Weston over for injuries. Gail nearly tackled Weston then held him for a minute. Weston closed his eyes and a smile crept over his face.

"Gail, I think Weston is fine," Mistress Nelson said after a minute of Gail holding Weston.

"Oh, sorry. Just sensing for injuries," Gail said as she stood, helping Weston up.

"Weston, what the heck was in that spell of yours?" Jason asked.

Weston frowned. "I watched as my spell hit the wizard. I could see the two spells combine. My spell should have simply disrupted the wizard's spell. Instead, the two reacted and exploded. From what I could see, the balance of dark and white magic was thrown off causing all spells to go out of control."

One of the border streams caused your portal to go out of control. The explosion Weston caused opened a small hole in the border stream and sent out a burst of energy which hit your portal. Much like a jetpack, it sent us flying into another realm, Jason's wand said.

"My wand says it was one of the border streams. A leak launched my portal, and we were lucky to land without killing either of us." Jason said.

"That makes sense. I am just glad the whole thing didn't break loose," Mistress Nelson said. "Who knows where you would have landed.

"What was the damage to our side from the battle?" Jason asked.

"Not as bad as Tess's people but still bad enough," Mistress Nelson began. "We have several masters in the infirmary who we are not sure will make it. Almost everyone on the ground was injured including Dod and Gail."

Jason looked to Dod and she favored one leg. Gail was holding her side. He had just enough energy to sense the two women. Both were bruised, and he could see Gail's ribs were still slightly fractured. The energy around an area of Dod's leg meant it was still healing a fracture. "You two should be in the infirmary," he said standing, "but thank you for coming to our rescue." He reviewed himself and Weston, except for some bruises and rashes they were fine.

He gave Dod a hug then put her arm around his shoulder to reduce the weight on her injured leg.

Looking up into the sky, he saw what looked like some form of a pterodactyl. This wasn't earth or at least present-day earth. He also noticed the sand had a green tint.

"Where are we?" he asked.

"I have never been here," Mistress Nelson started. From a distance, a wave of insects looked to be heading straight for them, "but I think it is time to leave."

She opened a portal and they all Stepped through. They landed in the infirmary with Jason and Weston helping the women to a bed. Jason grabbed another bed and napped while the two healed themselves.

Chapter Ten

J ason had locked himself in his office for the last few weeks trying to come up with a new battle plan for Tess. He occasionally left his office, grabbed his staff, and tried out new battle techniques. So far, he had only come up with interesting twists to things he had already tried. He was getting frustrated when he received a message from Gail asking him to meet her outside of the infirmary. He was concerned that something had gone wrong with Katrina's treatment and rushed there. As he approached the infirmary, he found Gail blocking the door.

"Gail. Is Katrina okay?" he asked, hoping nothing was wrong.

"Katrina is fine, actually the problem is you," she replied.

Jason went from worried to curious. "I'm the problem?"

"Well, not really a problem but you have some hang ups we need to address."

"Hang ups?" he asked. His curiosity was slowly turning to anger. He didn't like being toyed with and if there was something wrong with Katrina, he wanted to know. He folded his arms and remained silent.

"Oh, relax. This isn't that bad," she said putting her hand on his shoulder. "I'm trying to make sure you don't accidentally upset Katrina," she said. When he remained silent she sighed and continued. "I've known you for a while and I know where you come from. You're a bit old fashioned when it comes to women's bodies and you need to get over that before you see Katrina."

"I'm not old fashioned," he protested. "I have no issues with women's bodies."

"Oh yeah?" she waved her hand and the top part of her uniform floated off, leaving her bare-chested.

Jason immediately found himself averting his eyes and turning red. Not wanting to concede Gail's point, he tried staring into her eyes but kept finding them wandering.

"You're so red, you're lighting up the hallway," she said. "There is nothing magical about them, they're just breasts. So why are you turning red and boring holes through my head with your eyes?"

"Okay, so yes. I'm a bit old fashioned but see, I'm looking at them," he said. But as he did the room seemed to become even hotter and he had to turn away. "What is the point of all of this?"

"Like I said, I'm concerned about Katrina. She's not from earth and they do not have the same ideas about their bodies as you do. They have no issues about being naked in front of each other. They even openly discuss sex. The point is Katrina idolizes you and I don't want you to say or do anything that would hurt her. To her, you are a mentor, a leader, and someone she is attracted to. If it wasn't for Dod, she would be after you."

"What?" he asked, confused.

"Jason, she realizes you have Catie and if Catie were to break up with you then your attention would turn to Dod."

This conversation was becoming more and more uncomfortable for Jason.

"Okay, that probably wasn't fair bringing Dod into this, but it's obvious to everyone that you and Dod have chemistry. I'm going to let you into the infirmary. You do anything to hurt Katrina and I will make you pay," Gail stated. With a wave of her hand, she was fully dressed.

He nodded and stepped around Gail, but she called out to him. "Jason, um, do you think Weston would react the same way?" It was her turn for her face to turn red.

He stood stunned. Gail was one of the most perceptive people he knew, but somehow she missed the fact that Weston was smitten by her. Weston had a reputation of being steadfast in his work. Never made a mistake, never spilled, always followed protocol. Once, Gail visited Weston in his lab. She arrived in tight workout pants and shirt. It threw Weston off so badly that Jason had to make an excuse to get Gail out before Weston burned the lab down.

"Oh yes," he replied. "Ten times worse than me. If he found you topless with me, he would blow a gasket," he said. Her face lit up and she started humming as she opened the door to the infirmary for him.

Entering, there were nearly two dozen people in the infirmary, it looked like some sort of celebration was going on. He couldn't see Katrina but did see Le Anna.

"Katrina. Jason is here," Le Anna yelled.

Emerging from a small group, Katrina walked out wearing a robe.

"Jason. I'm so glad you are here. Look, I'm healed," she yelled then dropped her robe and ran up to hug him. She was completely naked.

It hit Jason instantly that Gail's warning was unnecessary. The pure joy in Katrina's face was more than enough to wash away any other feeling.

She pulled away from him and then slowly spun around. "Look, I am whole again. They did an excellent job and I feel like my old self!" Katrina looked at him expectantly.

"Katrina, you are absolutely beautiful. I can't tell you how happy I am that you are healed," he said with tears in his eyes and promptly hugged Katrina again. She hugged him back and began to sob.

"Thank you for this, I will never forget," she said between sobs.

Before he knew it, several people he did not know joined in the hug. Once he felt that Katrina had composed herself, he released her. Everyone else released.

"I guess I should introduce you to my family," she said.

"Honey, why don't you put your robe back on? People from earth are sometimes uncomfortable with naked bodies," a woman next to her said. Her eyes briefly flicked to a man in a nearby bed who was ogling Katrina. When he saw the woman and Jason looking at him, he turned red and looked away.

"That's my mom. Always worrying about others," Katrina said, slipping her robe back on.

Jason was introduced to what must have been Katrina's entire family. He met her mother, father, the dozen or so siblings, grandparents, aunts and uncles, and close family friends.

They all thanked him for what he had done. They also all felt quite free to discuss Katrina's healed body.

"Katrina has always had a very nice body, but she got her butt from her father's side of the family," her Grandmother told him.

Katrina nodded. "Yes Nana, but I like it. Not as good as Taskins, she has always had a beautiful butt." Taskin was her older sister who promptly turned around and shook her butt. This brought a round of applause from the group.

"Jason, see. Am I right?" Katrina asked with a huge smile on her face.

"I won't argue with you on that," he said. The conversation was heading in a direction that was making him uncomfortable. Gail's comment about him might have been a bit truer than he would like to admit.

"See Nana, he doesn't have all of the issues you said about earth men," Katrina said to her grandmother.

"Jason, are you married?" Katrina's grandmother asked.

"I was but she died. I have been dating a woman for over a year. Her name is Catie," he said hoping that would end the conversation. He was dead wrong.

"For a year and no marriage proposal? Did you know that Katrina is single? As you said a very beautiful girl and would make someone a wonderful wife," Nana said making no attempt to hide her intentions.

Katrina stood next to her grandmother and turned a deep shade of red. Dod, who had joined the group also turned red and walked away. His eyes following Dod as she walked away, Gail's comment fresh in his mind.

Nana met his eyes for a second. "Jason, can I borrow you for a moment?" She took his arm and walked him away from the group. "I can see you are a good man. My granddaughter has told me all about you and you seem to be an honorable man. But you need to make a decision soon." Nana stopped and faced him. "You have your Catie, but it is obvious you also have feelings for Dod, and she does for you too. Katrina is attracted to you, but she is smart enough to know you two were not meant to be."

He was about to argue with Nana but what she said was true. No matter how much he wanted to deny it. "I don't know how much you know about what is going on, but my supposedly dead wife Tess is not dead and if I don't stop her, she will end up killing everyone. If I were to propose to Catie, Tess will make Catie her number one person to kill. I admit I am totally confused by my feelings, but I can't deal with those now. Too many people are relying on me to stop Tess."

"I know about Tess and I have an idea of what you are going through. You are right, you must stop Tess but once that is done you have a decision to make." She got up on her toes and kissed his cheek then walked off.

Jason stood for a moment to collect his thoughts, then said goodbye to Katrina, and left.

Chapter Eleven

Jason came to work only to find his morning was clear. No meetings, no one needed his attention, a truly rare occurrence. He decided to take a walk with his team to enjoy the nice weather outside. They walked past shops to a point where a path through a nature preserve started. Since they had plenty of time, they decided a walk through the preserve would be nice.

The great part about being a warlock is that most nonmagical beings aren't really a threat individually. But collectively, humans were an extremely dangerous people. The rate at which they had developed advanced weapons scared many other realms causing them to regulate travel between earth's realm and theirs. Kien lectured them many times on always being on guard when it came to humans. Anonymity was the warlock's best friend, he always preached. Which meant avoiding situations that could accidentally reveal they were magical. If they did have to fight and use magic, the only appropriate outcomes were either to wipe out the human's memory or death.

That was why the Castle had secretly replaced the security staff in their building and surrounding area, including the preserve they were currently in, with members from the warlock security department.

As they walked along, they continued to sense for magical entities and except for the warlock security patrols there were none.

"It's hard to believe that something as beautiful as this is in the middle of a city," Dod said smelling a flower on the path.

"It's nice here, I like it," Steven agreed.

As they reached the farthest point and started to head back, Jason sensed a group of young men near them. Attempting to avoid a meeting, they changed their direction, but the men had spotted them and decided to block their path. This was not going to go well for them. He sensed for any cameras or recording devices and found none. The only thing he did find was one of the men carried a gun and the rest had knives. He sent a message to security.

"Excuse me gentlemen, we would like to pass," Jason said hoping this was nothing.

"Well, some guy paid us to deliver a message, but he didn't tell me there were some fine ladies involved. Maybe we should stay and visit," he smiled at the women and snickered. The rest of the group followed suit.

"I think you had better deliver the message and get out of here before you get hurt," Rita said. It was clear she had not taken a liking to the men.

"Shut up, old lady. I bet you haven't had a real man in a long time," the leader of the group said, trying to sound menacing.

Jason sensed the men were a little unnerved that no one in Jason's group seemed worried about them.

"Well, you are right about that. I would ask if you knew a real man but it's obvious you don't," Rita's comeback caused his group to laugh.

"Okay old lady, you're first," the leader said taking a step forward.

Before the leader knew what was happening, Dod had knocked his legs out from under him, pinned his arm and was squeezing his throat. His nose bled from an obviously broken nose.

"Apologize!" Dod ordered.

Jason could feel the anger radiating from her.

Another thug tried to pull his gun but found himself face down on the ground before he could. Gail now held his gun. Keeping his one arm pinned, she dismantled the gun and threw the parts into the bushes.

"I said, apologize," Dod repeated, this time barely above a whisper. She tightened her grip, her threat obvious. Either the man apologized, or he was about to be beat to a pulp.

"I'm sorry," the man said.

Just about then, several members of the warlock security team showed up. The lead was a behemoth of a man. "Ma'am, are these men bothering you?" he asked, with a bit of a smirk.

The rest of the hostile group shrank back.

"Are you kidding me, do you seeth me bleething down here?" the first thug on the ground tried to say through his broken nose. Dod released her grip.

The bear of a security guard grabbed the man and easily pulled him up with one hand.

"Now you gentleman said you had a message for me. I think now would be a really good time to give me that message," Jason said.

The group's leader nodded to one of the others. The man reached into his jacket and pulled out a paper crown. Jason took the paper crown and looked at it. Inside the words, "King Arthur's favorite food to not eat" were written. Jason could feel the blood leave his face. "Where did you meet the guy that gave this to you?"

"By the garage," the man that had given him the crown said.

"What did he look like?" Jason asked.

"I ain't no snitch."

Jason grabbed the man by the throat and lifted him up, using magic to keep the man from choking too badly. "If you want to see tomorrow, you will tell me now," Jason threatened.

The man shook his head and Jason released him. He took a few deep breaths. "Didn't see much, he was wearing a hoody and glasses. Body builder of some sort," the man said between gasps of air.

Dod eyed him. "Jason? Is something wrong?"

"Yes, this isn't good." Jason looked to the lead security guard. "Get these idiots out of here and alert your crew for possible computer hacks. Avoid using electronics." He turned to his group. "I have to go. Dod, alert the data center for a possible hack attempt and get everyone back to the office. Shut off all unnecessary computers and cut our tie to the internet," Jason ordered.

"Where are you going?" Dod asked.

"My hacker group is in town. I'm going to meet with them and before you ask. No, you can't come but you need to track me closely and be ready to step in if needed."

"Time for you gentlemen to go," the guard said.

"What about my bleeding noseth? I neeth medical attenthon."

It took everything Jason had to not laugh at the man's nasal lisp.

"Yeah, that looks bad. I would suggest the urgent care across town," the massive guard said, peering into his eyes.

The man blinked for a moment then nodded. "Leths go," he said to his group and they left with the security team right behind.

The note meant the hacker group was in town and they knew where he was. Jason had tried to communicate with them, but he didn't want them near his work. He couldn't risk Stepping to the meeting location, so he jogged to the parking garage. As he got near it, he quickly scanned the local area finding two security cameras pointed at him. Conjuring up a

166

dozen drones, he sent them to the devices with instructions to find out who was watching him.

He didn't think the drones would find the TRT members, but it would seriously distract them until he could meet with them. They needed to stay away from this area. Based upon the written message, he knew where he needed to go.

As he headed to his truck, he received a security alert that someone had tried to hack into his truck but failed. Just in case, he approached his truck carefully, making sure it was secure. Getting into his truck, he sensed the area. The TRT had hacked the video surveillance system in the parking garage and were watching him. As he pulled out, he flipped off one of the cameras.

Parking his truck in a nearby mall, he entered and made his way to the food court. He continued to scan the area. The mall's security system was ancient and there were plenty of areas where there was no coverage.

He ordered food from a stand that proclaimed world famous Italian food. To him, it was obvious that no one involved with the food stand had an idea of what Italian food really was. Adding lots of garlic to their food seemed to be their claim to fame. Paying for his food, he continued to scan until he found a man exiting an employee's only door. He had a lot of tech on him, some of which Jason did not recognize. Jason stared at the man until he nodded and went back in the door.

Jason walked to a table near the door, put his food down, and scanned the area behind the door. He found a long hallway with a man standing at the far end. There was a device by the door, plugged into the wall. It stored a fair amount of energy and he could sense it was waiting on a signal.

The device was an obvious one. On a signal, it would blast out an electrical charge to whomever was nearby. Most likely knocking them out. As he entered the door, he used magic to disable the device. He also checked again to make sure there was no other devices. Closing the door behind, Jason spotted the man standing at the far end wearing a hoodie and sunglasses.

He didn't fit the typical geek look. He stood about five foot six with broad shoulders and thick arms evident through his hoodie. The body builder comment earlier was right on. Jason could see brunette hair sticking out from the hoodie. His hands were in his pockets and Jason's senses told him that he held the remote for the device by the door. "Stay right there or you won't like the results," the man yelled.

"Lancelot?" Jason asked, ignoring his threat. The group was enamored with King Arthur and playing along with it was probably the best plan.

"Yes, fair king, it is I. We finally meet," the hooded man replied.

"We meet with a threat?" Jason asked, pointing toward the device.

"Things have become much more complicated, like the security systems on your truck and house. I have to admit that we are impressed but we are also concerned with who you are now working for."

Jason's scan of the man showed his pulse and blood pressure were high.

"To make it worse, you warn us of a major threat then you later reach out to us. This sounds like someone got to you."

Jason had sent out drones to scout out the area and they all started warning him of magical entities heading his way. "Lancelot. Did you bring others?" Jason asked quickly.

"No, it's just me. Why?"

"Because some people are coming and they're not with me," Jason yelled. Using his wand, he signaled that he needed back up. He magically sealed the door behind him and ran to Lancelot. Lancelot tried to activate the device but when he found it didn't work, he went for his knife.

"Lancelot, we don't have time for this, and your knife will be useless against these people," he said, grabbing him and pushing him through a door. On a whim, he reactivated Lancelot's device and left a drone to set it off if someone broke down the door.

"How did you know I had a knife?" Lancelot asked as they ran through the maze of hallways.

"Dod, I need a map of these hallways, now," Jason said, connecting his wand to his office.

"Here you go," Dod replied.

"Who are you talking..." Lancelot began but went quiet when an image of the mall and its hallways appeared in front of him.

"Adding the bad guy locations," Dod added.

"We're surrounded," he said. His options for a peaceful, non-magical ending were disappearing quickly.

"Security teams are in place. They can take them out, but it may get messy," Dod warned.

"No firefight in the open. Too easy for people to get killed and too many questions to answer. I am bringing Lancelot back to the office. Make sure to have someone there who can erase his memories."

Jason scanned Lancelot for any tracking devices and then before the man could say anything, he opened a portal and Stepped them back to his office.

Lancelot took one look at the office and fainted. Clearly, he was not used to that much excitement.

Back in his office, Jason started yelling commands. "Tell the security teams to capture their targets. But only if they can do it without involving outsiders." Looking down at the slumped hacker. "Someone help me get this idiot into a chair."

Dod grabbed one arm and he grabbed the other to hoist the hacker into a chair.

"Do we have someone that can wipe his memory, or do I have to do it?" Jason asked.

Kien came out of an office. "I'd better do this. We don't want to permanently disable him," Kien said, smirking.

"I could do it," Jason offered.

Kien only stared at him. "Oh, alright," Jason relented.

Kien's eyes turned blue as he put his hands on the hacker's head and drew energy. After a minute, the hacker moaned then started to wake. A quick splash of water to the face and he came to, albeit a little drowsy.

"What, what happened?" the hacker asked, shaking his head.

"We were being chased and you tripped and fell. We brought you back to our office," Jason said.

"I feel like I've been run over by a train," Lancelot said, rubbing his head.

"Okay, it's time for some straight talk. Are you ready?" When the hacker nodded, Jason started. "What I need to know is why did you try to contact me in person?"

The hacker rubbed his head for a moment. "Right after you sent out the warning, someone started coming after us. They tried to hack our old sites but got nothing. Pretty amateur stuff at first but they got better. When that got them nowhere, they tried to get information about us and even posted a reward for providing information. This is pretty standard stuff, so we ignored it," he took a breath. "Then a hacker that really wanted to join us, blogged that he knew where we were. He was a wannabe and was just trying to feel important. Three days later he was dead along with several others."

"How do you know they are dead?" Jason asked.

"We like to keep track of potential candidates and even try to hack their systems. If we can, we monitor them for a while. Two of those we tracked had video cameras in their rooms. Watching their recordings, we saw people literally appear out of nowhere. They tortured those two for thirty minutes and when they were sure they didn't know anything, they killed them," he shook his head and looked at Jason. "I know this is going to sound strange, but I think they were wizards. They had wands and did stuff no one should be able to do. At first, we thought we were being pranked but we checked the recordings. They were real."

"Do you have the recordings?" Weston asked.

"Yeah, I brought them along in case Jason turned out legit," he said and handed Weston a USB drive.

"Put it on a standalone machine with no network connections. Afterwards, destroy the machine," Jason said.

The hacker smiled. "We taught you well but there isn't anything on there that you should be worried about. Honest."

"I have been calling you Lancelot, what is your real name?" When the hacker remained quiet, Jason continued. "Believe me, the organization I belong to will find out. I'm just tired of playing games."

"My name is Brad. If you want more than that you will need to work for it," he smiled.

"That's enough for now."

"So what government are you working for?"

"All I can tell you is that I don't work for a government. But I will say if you leave us alone, we will leave you alone. That includes the hack attempts you've tried," Jason said.

"Yeah, you guys are a tough nut to crack. We had to stop when people started dying," Brad said, dropping his head. "Why is someone so interested in us?"

"It's because of your search for the holy grail," Jason said.

"You mean that woman we've been searching for is alive? How? No one could be that far off the grid."

"You would be surprised what she can do. She has a cult following and wouldn't hesitate to kill you if she can."

"Okay, got the video on the machine," Weston said.

They gathered around the machine and Weston clicked 'Play'.

The video started with a view of a young man at a keyboard, the camera must have been mounted on his monitor. They watched as he typed then three people, two men and a woman appeared out of thin air. The man started screaming and was quickly tied. They repeatedly asked him where the hackers were.

"I don't know," he answered. "I just said that to impress a girl," was all that came out before a flash of light from one of the attacker's wands sliced open part of his face. The man started to scream before being gagged. The rest of the recording was the same until the end where the lead attacker pointed a wand at the bound man and said something Jason could not hear. A flash from his wand, the bound hacker jerks, then goes limp. The man was dead. The second recording was of a woman who was similarly interrogated then killed.

"I want facial recognition on them along with voice recognition on all three of those…," Jason almost said wizards, as it was clear they were, "uh, attackers."

"We already did," Brad said. "We found images of them around the world and even tracked them a little. We believe they were trying to buy supplies from a couple of international companies. But when the others turned up dead and someone almost tracked us down, we stopped."

"That was actually us," Katan said, walking into the room. "We've learned a lot from you. We thought we had you, but you disappeared without a trace. I would love to learn how you did that."

Brad chuckled. "We were impressed when you found us, but sorry, trade secrets."

"Do you know the names of the suppliers?" Jason asked.

"They're on a file on the stick. We were also able to find a warehouse where some of the supplies were shipped to. That address is on the stick also."

Katan looked at the data stick as if it were the plague.

"Weston can bring the file up on the screen and we can write down the information," Jason said. "Meanwhile we need to get you out of here without being spotted. I'm pretty sure we're being watched. Do you have a safe place to go?"

"Yeah, an old warehouse off on the eastside," Brad replied.

"Okay, when you wake up you will be in an old car. No tech, take it where you need, then just leave it with the keys in the ignition. With any luck it will get stolen. If we get any information that they may be coming after you, I'll send another warning."

"Okay, but did you say, 'wake up'?" Brad asked.

Jason put his hand on the hacker, and he slumped in his chair.

"Get someone to take the Pinto out of the Bridge location and park it under the off ramp. Then dump him into it," Jason said. The Bridge location was one of his self-storage units in a rougher part of town. There were few cameras that actually worked in the area and the hacker group would not be able to track the car. "Also, send some drones to keep an eye on him so he doesn't get mugged," Jason said with a smirk. People were always trying to break into the facility, and they ended up hiring some local cops to park in the facility. Even then, people still tried to break in.

Jason turned to master Kien. "We need to check out that warehouse, see if it can tell us anything."

"Agreed, but just the two of us. I don't want any chance that Tess finds out we know about this place," Kien said.

This caught Jason off guard. He had fully expected Kien to order a whole contingent of masters. There was more going on here, but what it was he did not know. "Okay by me. Can we leave now?"

"Yes," Kien replied.

Jason walked over to Weston. "We'll be back in a little while. Keep an eye on our hacker friend and make sure he makes it back safe and sound."

"Will do. Where are you going?"

"Just stepping out with Kien to check on a couple of things," Jason said. He leaned in toward Weston. "Track me and if I am not back in an hour, send the team," he whispered.

Weston nodded. Jason walked back to Kien.

Kien opened a portal and Jason Stepped through followed by Kien.

Weston sent a drone through after them. Something wasn't right and Weston hoped he wouldn't have to send the team after Jason.

Jason and Kien Stepped to a warehouse district in New Orleans. Jason had visited New Orleans many times but had never been to this area. He followed Kien as he headed down an empty road lined with warehouses. They got about fifteen feet when something ran by on the other side of the road. Whatever it was, it wasn't human. It was followed by a man and a woman carrying what Jason thought were swords. Jason scanned them and was surprised when he found them quite powerful. Whatever they were, he didn't know.

"What the heck is going on over there?" Jason asked, eyeing the strangers as they ran down the street.

"Ignore them, we need to move quickly," Kien said, making sure the strangers continued on.

The unknown couple paused for a moment then ran after whatever they were chasing.

"You'll find a lot of strange things in New Orleans," Kien said as he made his way.

"Yeah, but definitely a lot of great food to be found. Not to mention bath salts," Jason added with a grin.

Kien gave him a pointed look and continued on. They made their way until Kien stopped in front of an older warehouse. The place looked like it was barely standing. The warehouse had a dark, ominous feeling about it, and Jason wouldn't have been surprised if it was haunted. Scanning it, he found the entire place covered in a magical shield. The shield looked strong but different from anything Jason had ever seen. Instead of a solid shield all the way around the building, it looked more like panels of shields connected together. While different, Jason didn't think they would get through it without tipping off whoever was inside.

"This is the address we got and based upon the shield; I think it's our place. Follow me," Kien said as he headed down an alley along the side of the warehouse.

Jason looked around, scanning the area. He detected a drone that must have been created by Weston. Weston always sent drones in the shape of moths.

"Keep close to me but as far from Kien as you can," Jason said to the drone. He wasn't sure it would understand but it was worth a try. Jason turned and walked down the alley after Kien.

Kien had stopped about twenty feet down and was probing the shield. "This type of shield has a flaw that if you know where to look, you can get by it."

Jason doubted they would get through but stood and waited while Kien slowly worked his way, feeling the shield until he stopped. "Found it." He announced with a hint of triumph in his voice.

Jason watched as Kien found an edge he could fit his finger into of one of the panels. Using a little energy, Kien pried open a larger opening, just large enough for them to get through. Kien went through followed by Jason.

"Remind me never to use this type of shield," Jason said, as he slipped through the opening. He moved slowly, giving the drone a chance to come through also.

Once through, they stood in front of a door. The building looked different, more modern and the sense of gloom he had experienced earlier was gone. Jason guessed that the shield had been augmented to help keep unwanted visitors away.

Jason expected Kien to unlock the door but instead he Stepped inside the building. Jason grabbed the drone and Stepped also, making sure to land a distance from Kien and then quickly releasing the drone. The place was completely dark, and Jason activated his night vision. He could feel Kien scan the area then send some energy and the warehouse lights came on.

Jason winced at the bright lights. "I thought we were trying to be stealthy."

"No one is here and it's a lot easier to check things out with the lights on."

The warehouse contained huge shelving units broken into three aisles. The shelves were full of boxes of assorted sizes. Kien started for the first aisle.

"I'll check this aisle and you check the far aisle. We'll meet up and come back down the middle," Kien said. He walked off before Jason could respond.

Jason stared after Kien. Kien had always preached that teams worked together in hostile search areas. Jason raised his shield and charged his wand. If something was about to happen, he would be ready. The familiar blue tint covered everything he saw.

The aisle seemed to be full of boxes and boxes of food. Jason stopped to open one, hoping to find something hidden inside. All he found were several cases of tomato paste. He scanned the boxes and found nothing magical about any of them. He could sense that several warlocks and wizards had been in the area, but it was a faint image, probably not recent.

He walked to the end and turned the corner, expecting to find Kien but he wasn't there. Jason waited a moment and was about to go down the aisle but Kien came running up.

"All I found were supplies. Probably enough to fuel a small army for quite some time," Kien said.

"Yeah, I found the same. Looks like no one's been here for at least a few hours," Jason said.

"I am going to do a quick inventory then head back. I need you to head back now and alert the Castle about what we found. I want this building watched and I want to know who is coming here."

Jason hesitated. "You don't want me to help you?"

"No, the Castle needs to know now, and I can get this inventoried quickly," Kien said. "Now get going so I can finish."

"Okay." Jason walked back to where he originally had Stepped. Weston's drone was still there.

He grabbed the drone then Stepped back to the opening in the shield. He slid through the opening and returned to the Castle.

Master Kien watched as Jason left. Once he was sure that Jason was gone. "You can come out now. He's gone."

From behind some boxes, Tess walked out. "Good, I only have a minute and we need to talk."

Chapter Twelve

J ason Stepped back to his office and immediately reported their findings to Mistress Nelson.

"Good find on the warehouse but I want to keep the knowledge of this to only those that need to know. If Tess finds out we know, she will destroy that facility," the Mistress said.

"Makes sense but," Jason hesitated. He wasn't sure he wanted to share his concern with her.

"But what?"

"It's just, the whole trip was weird. Only Kien and I went and when we did the search, he completely broke protocol. We should have brought an entire security squad with us, but we went alone."

"I understand but Kien wanted to keep this find quiet. We are also concerned about leaks in our security staff. We don't think they are spies but they may be sharing too much information in their off time. As for his breaking protocol, I wouldn't worry. He has immense trust in you and your abilities."

"If you are concerned with the security staff, why are they still at my house?"

"The staff at your house is fine, there are others we are worried about," Mistress Nelson replied.

Jason felt Mistress Nelson was hiding something. Maybe she thought he or someone in his group was a spy? Either way this conversation was getting him nowhere.

"Okay, anything else I should know?" Jason asked.

"Yes. Bull has arranged for a meeting with the Zycros' ambassador for midnight tonight. Please discuss the logistics with him," Mistress Nelson said then ended the call.

Jason shook his head. Things kept getting worse and worse.

****

That night, Jason stood in the middle of his church with Weston and Bull. Jason had asked for a meeting and this is where Ambassador Lysion of the Zycros, wanted to meet. Bull explained that since the Zycros felt this was holy ground, and they believed Jason felt the same, this was the safest place.

Jason's senses were on high and he could feel magic everywhere in the building. Most came from the Zycros he could tell, some he could not identify. Weston was wandering around like a kid in a candy store. He currently stared at a chair; the one Reverend Jim always sat in.

Jason felt a magical surge and a man he had never seen before walked in from a side room followed by Tyinth and Gatron.

Lysion, it is very good to see you, Bull said.

Lysion said nothing but hugged Bull. Jason could tell they were communicating mentally but he didn't try to intrude on their conversation. No sense starting off on a bad foot, he thought. When Lysion finally looked his way, Jason guessed it was his turn. Jason tensed, after Tyinth's and Gatron's less-than-warm meetings he was ready for a less-than-cordial greeting.

Lysion put out his hand. "Jason, it is an honor to meet you."

Jason was startled by the warm welcome but recovered quickly. "Thank you, Mr. Ambassador, it is an honor to meet you. Bull has spoken highly of you."

Lysion shot Bull a quick smile. "Bull," he said putting an emphasis on the word, "and I have been friends for a very long time. He has also spoken quite highly of you."

"I'm lucky to be able to call Bull my friend."

"In that you are correct. But I do believe that some of my staff may owe you an apology." Lysion gave Tyinth and Gatron a pointed look.

"We all have jobs to do and I hold no misgivings on what has happened. May be a fresh start is in order," Jason said before either of Lysion's staff could say anything. This was a chess game, and from what Bull had told him, he needed to get the upper hand quickly. A quick wink from Bull told him he had scored.

The Ambassador's laughter rang throughout the church. "I am sure we can all agree to a fresh start."

Lysion took Jason's arm and escorted him down the aisle. The pews magically moving out of their path. He stopped at the steps of the altar and motioned for Jason to sit. Weston had finally broken himself away from the baptismal urn and sat next to Jason. Bull sat facing them.

"Mr. Ambassador, may I introduce my friend and teammate Weston."

"Please, call me Lysion. Mr. Ambassador is too formal for this setting," Lysion said as he stood and shook Weston's hand. They held hands for several seconds as the two stared at each other. Finally, Lysion broke the silence. "You can see magic?" Lysion said, releasing Weston's hand.

"Yes, I can," Weston sputtered. "How did you know?"

Lysion gave another hearty laugh. "Well, your gazing at a chair like it was gold was my first clue."

Weston blushed.

"You are very special. You are only the second person I have met that can do that," Lysion said, turning to Jason. "Bull told me you had assembled a special team and it looks like he was right."

This meeting was not going anything like Jason expected. Instead of a tense standoff, it felt more like a reunion of friends. Bull warned that Lysion was smart and clever. Was Lysion's friendly demeanor real or part of the game?

"Thank you, I do work with some amazing people." Jason wanted to get to the real issue, but he needed Lysion to make the first move.

"Well then, I guess we should get to the reason for this meeting," Lysion said, quickly losing his friendly manner. "Bull says we may share a common problem and you might have a solution."

Lysion sat and folded his hands, looking expectantly. Bull had warned Jason to speak only the truth, but only tell just enough to communicate his problem. Information was gold and he needed to play his hand carefully.

"We believe the Meathonians have been trading with a rogue warlock. From their trades, the Meathonians have been receiving stones that allow them to create a 'Gods Portal' to travel anywhere they want. In exchange, the warlock has been receiving white and dark energy along with material to store it," Jason stated.

"We are aware that the Meathonians have been attempting to acquire more stones. We have been looking for whomever has been supplying them with the stones. Unfortunately, we haven't been able to track down your wife and prevent her from supplying more stones," Lysion said.

"Ex-wife, she stopped being my wife when she faked her death and abandoned her family," Jason said, just a little too strongly. He suspected

178

that the Zycros would know about his wife, but it was still a sore subject. "She's very good at keeping herself hidden."

"My apologies, ex-wife," Lysion said with a nod. "And you think if you can replicate what she is doing, you can stop her."

"Yes, she is determined to kill me and will keep trying until she completes her mission, or I stop her. The reason we are here is because I don't want to die," he stated as bluntly as he could.

"And why should your death be a concern of ours?" Lysion asked.

"Because I am the only one that can stop her. You have failed in your attempts to find her and you won't until it's too late. She thinks several moves ahead and will keep out of your grasp just long enough to arm the Meathonians. Then when your two armies have just about wiped each other out, she will make her move." Jason hoped he'd made his point.

Lysion's face went red and he sat still for a moment. "And what is her next move?"

"I'm not sure. But based upon the energy she has collected; I am guessing she will work to wipe out your remaining warriors on earth then turn her attention to replacing the warlock leadership with herself," Jason stated. It was the truth and a very logical plan. But Tess rarely went with the most logical option, so Jason doubted this was her plan.

"So, what is it you need from us?" Lysion asked.

"We need access to the same energy sources that she has had access to. With that, we hope to be able to track her, then neutralize her and her following."

Lysion sat for a minute staring at Jason, he turned and looked at Gatron. "I very much doubt she has been able to access the source we guard. There must be another source she is accessing. But since all white and dark energy are the same, we will let you use our source. You may take a small amount if you can prove you can handle the energies without killing everyone around you."

"Weston can create appropriate containers if you can give us enough Stroth," Jason said.

Gatron carried a heavy bag and placed it at Jason's feet. "We anticipated your request."

Weston lifted the bag and then looked inside. "This should do," Weston said. "I will need two days to process and have it ready."

"Then we shall meet at midnight, two nights from now," Lysion stood. He shook hands with Jason and Weston, bowed to Bull, and walked out of the church followed by his staff. Jason felt a surge of energy as they left the building.

"Well, that went better than I thought. Weston, it's up to you now," Jason said. Weston had turned his attention back to examining the chair again and hadn't heard Jason.

"Weston. We need to leave," Jason said, shaking his head. Sometimes Weston was intrigued with the most unusual things.

"What? Oh yeah. I will need Steven's help also. We need to leave now so I can start work," Weston said and walked out the door.

"What has got into Weston?" Jason asked Bull.

This place is much more interesting than you give it credit.

"I will take your word for it," Jason said, and walked out of the church followed by Bull.

Chapter Thirteen

As Weston entered the church to meet with the Zycros, he was immediately hit with the amount of residual energy in the church. Most of the energy was easily identifiable. He could see traces of where Jason, Jason's family, and Bull had been. When the Zycros walked in, Weston could see the energy emanating from them. Residue of their energy was all over the church.

He was fascinated by their energy until he looked at a chair on the altar. What he found there nearly floored him.

The energy on the chair was a pure bright white. Even faded, it was still amazingly pure. He tracked the energy between the chair and the pulpit. He could find other traces of the energy throughout the church. Based upon what he saw, it must have come from one of the ministers. Guessing it came from the ministers was easy as the chair was located where the ministers would sit, but which minister sat in that chair he had no idea. He would have to ask Jason.

Weston could only find one pattern of the energy and surmised that only one person had left the trace energy. Weston took out a small tube to collect a sample then hesitated. Would Jason or their new host appreciate what he was doing? Opening the collection tube, he quickly scooped some of the residual energy into the tube when no one was looking.

As he tried to pay attention to the conversation between Lysion and Jason, he pondered his find. The energy was definitely not from the Zycros. This meant Jason's church had another magical being in it. Worse, it was probably one of the ministers. He should tell Jason but hesitated. Jason had enough things on his mind dealing with Tess. He decided to work on researching the energy and then when he had more information, he would tell Jason.

As they drove away from the church, they saw a man walking down the road toward the church. Jason waved to the man and identified him as Reverend Jim.

"I wonder why he is taking such a late walk?" Jason asked.

Weston couldn't answer Jason's question, but he could detect the same unknown energy in Reverend Jim as he found in the church. Whatever the reverend was, he was not purely mortal.

Chapter Fourteen

Jason started the truck as Bull and Weston climbed it. Pulling out into the street, Jason gunned it to get home as quickly as possible, with the help of some of the magical options of the truck. He encountered only green lights all the way home and no police to stop him. When they arrived home, Catie and the kids were asleep, and they headed straight for Jason's office.

"I really need Steven in the lab for this. Do you think it's okay if he comes?" Weston asked.

"Hmm, I think I need to check with Mistress Nelson and the Castle," Jason said.

Weston gave him a questioning look and Jason realized how that sounded.

"The Castle is its own being. Exactly what it is, I don't know. That's all I really know." Jason then reached out to Mistress Nelson to ask about Steven.

Jason wasn't surprised when an image of Mistress Nelson appeared on the main screen. This had been an important meeting and she would want to know about the results.

"I can give a full report tomorrow but the Zycros have given us the Stroth we need and will allow us access to their energy source," Jason said. "Weston needs Steven at the Castle to help make the energy storage devices."

"I expected this and have already checked with the Castle and we are okay with it. There is one thing, Steven is special and gives us an edge in this battle only if Tess does not know about him. The less people that know about Steven the better," Mistress Nelson said, then ended communications.

Jason turned to Weston. "Mistress Nelson is right. You can take Steven to your lab, but only authorized warlocks should know about him. Go back to the office for meals and make sure he is back at the office by five p.m. so he can head home. Understood?"

"Yep, got it," Weston said. He checked the time, and it was now one-thirty in the morning. "I'm going to get a few hours of sleep then get Steven in the morning."

"Good idea," Jason watched as Weston Stepped back to the Castle. He snuck back to his room as quietly as he could, put on his pajamas, and slipped into bed.

"You would think they'd have taught you stealth at the Castle," Catie said, her voice groggy with sleep.

"Who said I was trying to sneak in?" Jason tried to pull her closer. The only response he received was light snoring. Guessing that sleep was his only option he closed his eyes.

It seemed he was only asleep for a second when his alarm, courtesy of his wand, went off. Catie was already up and showered. He showered, put on a uniform, and was out the door only minutes after Catie left.

Jason arrived at work at the same time as Steven and brought him to his office. Weston met them there.

"Steven, Weston has some research he needs help with at the Castle. Do you want to go?" Jason asked.

"Yes, I do. I really get to go to the Castle?" Steven asked, his smile was contagious, and you could see the excitement in his eyes.

"Yes, but we have to stay in the lab. Sometime in the future, I'll take you on a tour so you can see the entire Castle," Weston said.

"Let's go," Steven said excitedly.

Weston opened a portal and the two disappeared.

Chapter Fifteen

For the next two days, Weston and Steven worked on creating the containers. They both knew the basic principle but forming the containers and figuring out how to generate energy from the two was still trial and error.

First, they had to form the containers. They both expected to simply super-heat the material into a molten form, then pour that into the molds they had made. But the material never budged when heated.

"I have to wonder if two warlocks who can see magic are the best ones to be working with material that has no magic in it?" Weston pondered.

Steven smiled. "We will figure it out."

It took them a day to figure out that the material would take shape only if it was super cooled. After the third attempt at heating the material, Weston had decided to try something different. He asked Steven to put one of the containers of material into a refrigerator to cool it, accidentally putting it in a cooler which was set at zero degrees. Two hours later, when Weston opened the refrigerator door, he found the material in a semi-molten liquid. The two realized what had happened and turned the refrigerator temperature as low as it would go. Luck, for once, was with them and they now knew how to form the containers.

It would take a couple of hours for the temperature to fully drop and Weston turned his attention to the energy sample from the church.

"I don't recognize it," Steven said, as he stared at the sample.

"I don't either. A database of energy patterns would make things so much easier," Weston stated.

Steven simply shrugged.

"May be Katon can help," Weston said. He immediately gave Katon a call.

"Well, as it happens, we started a database of energy signatures. We are still documenting various species energy patterns but bring it by and we will give it a go," Katon said.

Ten minutes later, Weston and Katon stood in front of a small machine in a room off the data center. Steven had stayed in the lab to monitor the material.

Katon was reviewing how the system worked. "We put the sample inside the device, close the lid, and it will do its scan. The results will be sent to another system that will compare it with all known samples. Hopefully, we will get a hit," Katon said proudly.

"How long does it take?" Weston asked. This was some really cool technology and he hoped to utilize it more in the future.

"The scan only takes a few seconds. The search can take up to several hours."

"That works for me. Let's get the scan going, I need to get back to my work for Jason," Weston said.

Katon lifted the top of a small box attached to the device and Weston put the sample in. He sealed the box and hit a button labeled 'Start'. The box lit up then went dark.

"The scan is done, now we wait," Katon said.

Weston jumped when an alarm went off from the device. A monitor attached to the device started to flash a warning.

Weston looked to Katon. "What is it?"

"I don't know, I have never seen this before," Katon replied.

Before either could say anything else, Mistress Nelson's face appeared on the monitor.

"Katon, where did you get that sample?" Mistress Nelson demanded.

"I, uh, got it from Weston."

"Weston, where did you get it?" The mistress demanded again.

Weston froze, he always panicked around the headmistress. He would rather duel Jason and Dod at the same time then have a conversation with the woman. "I got it from a church we visited when we met with the Zycros," he managed to eke out.

"I need to see both of you in my office, immediately," Mistress Nelson said, then the screen went blank.

"What is this about?" Weston asked.

"I don't know but we better get to her office," Katon said.

Five minutes later, Katon and Weston stood nervously outside Mistress Nelson's office. Neither wanted to go in but both knew disobeying the Mistresses order would be worse than entering.

"Are you ready?" Katon asked.

"Yes, go ahead and knock."

Katon put his hand to the door then hesitated, "I can't, you knock."

Weston raised his hand to knock, then paused, "Why me? You're a Senior and the ranking warlock. You should knock."

The debate lasted another minute when the door opened by itself.

"I could grow old and die by the time you two figured out who would knock on my door," came Mistress Nelson's voice from her office. "Now get in here. I promise neither one of you are going to die by my hands," she paused, "at least not today."

Both men attempted to go through the door at the same time which resulted in a collision with both men temporarily stuck in the doorway.

"You first," Katon offered.

"I am not getting any younger in here. Weston first," she waited and when there was no movement, "Now!"

Weston almost jumped through the doorway followed by Katon. They approached the Mistress's desk as if it was a snake about to strike. When they determined they were safe they stood at attention. Stark still, their eyes laser focused on the wall behind the Mistress.

"And to think the fate of all warlocks may rest in your hands," Mistress Nelson said with her head in her hands. "Maybe I should retire now."

Weston sprang to life, "My father does retirement planning and can help if you do decide to retire."

Mistress Nelson sat, her mouth moved but no words came out. After a moment. "Maybe I was wrong about one of you dying by my hands today."

Weston immediately returned to looking straight forward. She waited to see if either man would dig themselves a deeper hole. When both remained quiet, she continued. "I want the sample destroyed, any record of the scan erased, and you two are never to speak of it again. To anybody. Am I clear?"

Weston opened his mouth to speak, he clearly wanted to know more but knew he already tread on thin ice.

"Look, I know you two like to solve problems and I promise that someday I will give you the rest of the story. But for today, you have to trust me," Mistress Nelson said.

Both men hesitated and then looked down.

"I will destroy the sample and never speak of it again," Weston said.

"I will erase the scan and never speak of it again, also," Katon said.

"Good. Thank you for your help. Dismissed."

She watched the two men file out of her office, both looking like they had been told to get rid of their favorite pet. An entity she recognized as the Castle formed next to her.

"Do you think they will keep their mouth shut?" the Castle asked.

"I give Weston about a minute before he caves and tells Jason when he sees him. Katon, about a day," Mistress Nelson said, with a slight smile.

"You really think Weston will last that long?" the Castle replied. When the Mistress didn't respond. "Are you sure about this? Why not just tell Jason?"

"Weston will tell Jason and yes, Jason does need to know but not right away. I want to watch how these two do. Eventually, Jason will need to resolve this issue but not before he takes care of Tess."

"You mean, kills Tess," the Castle said.

Mistress Nelson sat still for a moment. "Yes, he will kill her. It really is the only way he can save her."

The Castle image frowned. "I am not sure how killing her can save her. But for all our sakes, I hope you are right." It then disappeared.

Mistress Nelson looked to where the Castle had stood. "Oh, I am right. I just wish I wasn't".

Chapter Sixteen

Jason was in his home office reading about efforts to make sure that no more of Tess's spies remained at the Castle. From the looks of the reports, they were pretty much done but they still watched a few Castle employees they had concerns about. Out of the corner of his eye, he watched a monitor showing his maid slowly pulling into his driveway. She was followed by a string of contractor trucks that had got stuck behind her. Evidently, she drove as slow as she moved but he doubted anyone would complain. All of the workers stayed a fair distance from her but wouldn't tell Jason why.

Jason watched as the trucks pulled in then noticed something strange. Four men ran from the bushes near his driveway entrance and tried to follow the last truck in. Jason stood and headed toward the door and wasn't surprised when alarms went off warning of intruders. He energized his shield, and the familiar blue tint came over his eyes. He walked outside to find the four intruders behind a shield exchanging fire with the warlock security staff. Amazingly enough, their joint shield was taking solid hits but showed no signs of weakening. Jason was about to fire when he saw his maid drop her tray of cleaning supplies and then walk toward the intruders.

Jason was about to yell to her to get out of the way when she transformed into something he had never seen. It was a hideous creature in the shape of a ball with tentacles and spikes sticking out all around it. One of the attackers fired on the thing, which only seemed to make it mad.

The thing shrilled loudly then started rolling toward the intruders. Jason's security forces dove out of the way to keep from being run over. The creature took fire from all four intruders but did not slow. Slamming into the intruder's shield, it sent them flying and their shield disappeared. He saw a small box fly from one of the intruder's hand's and explode. The men tried to stand but the creature grabbed the nearest intruder with a tentacle and impaled him on one of its spikes. Another tentacle lashed out and grabbed another intruder who was promptly impaled.

Jason sprinted toward the thing. "Don't kill all of them," he yelled as he ran as fast as he could. He needed the last two alive.

The thing grabbed the two remaining attackers and impaled one and was about to impale the other, when Jason sent energy to grab the man and pull him away from the deadly spikes. "I need him alive to find out who sent him and why," Jason yelled again. He ran around the thing and stood next to the intruder still in the clutches of the angry ball. Jason was using a fair amount of power to keep the man alive when the thing released him.

One of the creature's tentacles started moving toward Jason. He pointed his wand at the thing while ramping up his power. Everything went silent as the thing's tentacle paused in mid-air. Jason waited, ready to fire. It let out another loud shrill and thrashed its tentacles against the ground. Clearly not happy with Jason's actions.

"You have a choice, disengage and go back to work or face me and my team," Jason said.

Several members of his security force now turned their wands toward the angry ball.

A mouth formed in the middle of the thing. A tentacle then removed one of the attackers impaled on its spikes, and then put him into its mouth. It started chewing on the dead man and Jason had to look away. Blood splattered across the yard and the sounds of bones crunching filled the air.

After a minute, the thing's tentacles and spikes retracted leaving the other two dead attackers to fall to the ground. Jason braced for an attack but instead the thing morphed back into his maid. For a second, the maid stared at him. Blood ran down her mouth and the maid took out a handkerchief to wipe it off. "Sorry," she said then let out a small burp. His maid turned around and slowly walked back to the house. Along the way, she picked up the tray she'd dropped.

Several security guards quickly bound the remaining attacker, putting him in the back of one of their trucks. They then threw tarps and tools over the two remaining bodies.

Jason picked up the wands of the four attackers. All four wands were the hybrid half-wizard, half-warlock wands. Approaching the remaining attacker, Jason saw the man was a mess. He was in tears and babbling on about the attack. Jason scanned him for any of the suicide packs that had killed the others they had captured but found none.

"It ate my friend," he screamed as Jason approached.

"And you are alive only because I think you are useful to me. Prove me wrong and that thing will come back and have you as a dessert," Jason said.

The man started screaming and thrashing around in the truck. "No, please, no! I will tell you everything."

"Start from the beginning and don't miss a detail."

The man started whimpering and tried to pull himself together. "Okay. I don't know much but I will tell you what I know. A couple of months back, some guy shows up at my door and tells me his name is Jenkins. Master or something, anyways he tells me I could be a warlock." The man took a couple of breaths, trying to calm himself. "But I failed the test. The wand he gave me would barely work. He said I couldn't be a warlock, but I could still be magical. He gave me a different wand that worked for me. He took me to a building where I met the other three."

"Where was this place?" Jason asked, interrupting the man.

"I don't know. There were only a few windows. I snuck a peek out of one of them and I have never seen anything like it. There were two moons, and everything had a weird yellow coloring."

"So, what happened next?" Jason asked.

"We trained together for a while, but Jenkins suddenly stopped checking in on us. One day, this woman shows up and says we report to her now and Jenkins is gone. She was really scary and very powerful. She brought us back to a warehouse where we worked. Things were going okay when yesterday some ugly ass dude shows up. The guy looked like a giant toad and had this really nasty creature with him. The thing looked like someone had melted a monster and put it on a leash. He told us that we were to sneak into this place and kill you. He gave me a special wand that we could use to travel here and back. He gave Anderson a special stick that the guy said would get us through the shields to get inside. He then gave us a box that he said would create a shield we could use if we got into a fight."

"What went wrong?" Jason asked.

"When we encountered a shield, Anderson was supposed to touch it with the stick, and it would get us through. It worked for the first couple of shields, but I guess it didn't work for the third one. That was when the alarms started going off. As soon as they went off, the wand to get us back disintegrated into dust along with Anderson's stick and Bellard put up the shield. When we got knocked over and the box exploded, I knew we were screwed. I could only watch as that thing started killing my friends," the man said, hanging his head.

"Considering you were sent to kill me I can't say I'm sorry for their deaths. But I would say you aren't out of the woods on this. Attempted murder of a warlock is punishable by death and we have things way worse than what you just encountered," Jason said, lying. He wasn't sure what the punishment was, but he wanted to make sure the man would continue to cooperate.

The man started crying and curled into a ball, his hands still magically tied behind his back.

"You sure have a way with people," Jason heard. Turning around he found Dod, Kien, and Bull.

"I have to admit. I'm impressed that you already have a prisoner in tears," Dod continued.

"After watching his friend get eaten by my maid it was pretty easy," Jason said.

Your maid is a Klakalian. They are very dangerous and unpredictable especially when angry, Bull said.

"I wish someone had told me that before. We could have captured all four alive if she hadn't started killing them," Jason said.

A police cruiser drove by slowly, Jason waved and smiled. The officer waved back but eyed the area closely.

"Your neighbor called the police about a disturbance," Kien said watching the cruiser drive by. "Has the prisoner said anything?"

"Basically, Jenkins recruited them, was training them in another realm, but then disappeared. I'm assuming that's when I killed Jenkins. Tess took over and had them working at a warehouse when, I believe, a Meathonian and a pet showed up yesterday and gave them orders to come here and kill me," Jason said.

"Tess didn't give the order?" Kien asked.

"According to him, no."

"I'll take him back and interrogate him and will have the remaining bodies autopsied. Maybe we can get some clues about where they came from," Kien said. Before anyone could respond, he walked over to the prisoner, put a hand on him, and they both disappeared.

The lead of the security detail assigned to his house jogged over. "Where the hell did Master Kien go with the prisoner? We should have been the ones to take him."

"I don't know," Jason replied.

"I'll check with Mistress Nelson. This isn't right," the security lead said and walked away.

He's right. Master Kien should not have taken the prisoner, Bull said.

Jason watched the security lead call Mistress Nelson and whatever she said did not go over well with the man.

Chapter Seventeen

Jason sat in his office waiting on Weston and Steven to report on their progress building the energy containers. Weston had hinted they had an idea on how to retrieve and store the energy. Lysion warned them they wouldn't be able to get within ten feet of the energy, lest their internal energy set off a chain reaction.

Initially, Weston had been optimistic about building the containers, but his last few updates had been cryptic. Jason tried to talk to Weston directly but kept getting told they were too busy.

Gail called Jason, worried about Weston. "What did you do to Weston? He is acting like a wet puppy and I can't get anything out of him."

"All I did was give him an assignment. It sounded like things were going well then suddenly he changed. Steven says they are almost done, so I don't know what the issue is," Jason responded, mentally reviewing what he had said to Weston. Had he said something to upset him?

"I don't know either but please fix whatever is wrong with him. I don't like seeing him like this," Gail hung up.

Weston had a major crush on Gail. If he was acting funny around her, something was really wrong. An hour later, Weston and Steven arrived at his office. Weston seemed both excited and depressed. "These containers are safer than the one's Tess created and will handle more energy than hers," Weston said excitely.

"Tell them about the stick," Steven urged.

"I almost forgot. We made an extendable pole that we can use to dip the containers into the energy pools. We didn't have enough Stroth to make the pole out of it. So, we manufactured a pole and covered it in

Stroth. Should work for what we need," Weston said, both men beamed with pride.

"Great news and congrats on your efforts." Jason waited a second, "Anything else you want to tell me?"

Steven replied with a 'No' then looked at Weston.

Weston averted his eyes. "No, nothing. Can we get going?"

Jason looked at his friend. Something was wrong and it had to be resolved before they went to retrieve the energy. Weston needed to concentrate on the upcoming task and Jason didn't think Weston could at the moment. When Weston was distracted, he was a danger to himself and anyone around him.

"Weston. Follow me. Steven, please wait here." Jason Stepped to the clearing he had once visited with Bull. He wasn't completely sure where it was, except he knew it was in another realm and very remote.

After a moment Weston arrived. He looked around but his usual curiosity was gone.

"We're friends, right?" Jason asked.

"Yes," Weston said, still not looking directly into Jason's eyes.

"Then you need to tell me what is bothering you. We can't go on this mission until we clear the air." Jason sat for a second. "If there is anything I've said or done that upset or hurt you, I'm really sorry. Just tell me what I did."

A look of surprise came over Weston's face. "You haven't done anything wrong."

"Then level with me." Jason put his hands on his hips and looked directly into Weston's eyes.

Weston considered the situation. He didn't want to disobey Mistress Nelson's order, but to betray a friend's trust was something completely different. Especially a friend who had saved his life at least once.

"When we were at your church, I spotted a strong energy residual that didn't match either warlocks, Bull, or the Zycros. I secretly took a sample. When Katon used a device to identify the energy pattern, Mistress Nelson stopped the process. She forced us to destroy the sample and any traces of the pattern. She also told us not to tell anyone."

"Do you know from whom in the church the energy came from?" Jason asked. He was pretty sure he knew the answer but wanted Weston to confirm his guess.

"Reverend Jim," Weston replied.

Jason considered what his friend just told him. There was another player in the mix. Someone able to keep himself hidden from both Jason and the Zycros. He considered the new piece of information but there was nothing to do about it until Reverend Jim decided to reveal himself. Since Mistress Nelson hadn't told him, it could only mean she didn't find the reverend to be a threat at the moment.

Weston was clearly worried about revealing his secret to Jason. Most likely Mistress Nelson knew Weston couldn't keep the secret. She probably gambled that Weston would spill his guts the first time he saw Jason.

"Thank you for telling me. I will tell Mistress Nelson I forced it out of you," Jason said. Weston's shoulders dropped and he breathed a sigh of relief. "Head back to the office, I need a moment."

Jason watched as Weston Stepped away.

"You two can come out now. Your stealth abilities need work," Jason called out.

Bull emerged from the bushes along with the Castle.

"Anything I need to know?" Jason asked.

"First, we accurately predicted it would take only a minute for Weston to tell you. Second, the reverend is not a threat at the moment," the Castle said. "He is, however, something in the future you will need to address."

All I can add is, concentrate on the task at hand. What Weston discovered is only a distraction, Bull said, then disappeared followed by the Castle.

"One of these days I am going to get a straight answer from one of you three," Jason said, knowing Mistress Nelson was listening. He then Stepped back to his office.

Watching from her office, Mistress Nelson smiled. Jason was learning. Her plans for him, while having taken some wild turns, were working out. In a hundred years, if he survived Tess, he might be ready. That was ahead of her original schedule, but those wild turns had sped her plans up.

Chapter Eighteen

Two days after the first meeting, Jason, Steven, Weston, and Bull arrived at the church just prior to midnight. Jason parked his truck a block away as to not raise suspicions. Lysion and his group were waiting as they entered the church.

"Are you ready?" Lysion asked.

"Yes, I think we are," Jason responded.

"Then we need to go."

Gatron motioned for Jason and his group to stand next to Lysion. They moved into position and waited.

"The place we are going is in a state of non-existence that lies between realms. I know what I say doesn't make sense, but it is the only way to describe it. Our people found it by accident, and we have protected it ever since. It's location changes on a regular basis but we are able to track it and can find it within minutes, most instances. Lately it has taken us a little longer," Lysion said, frowning. "Do you have everything you need?"

Jason nodded and waited. Everything went dark, just before a blinding flash. It took Jason's eyes a moment to adjust. They now stood in an open area about ten feet away from a large metal door. A mist surrounded the area, leaving a thirty-foot wide space for them. Just past the door was a small dirt berm planted with brush mixed with flowers. Most of the area was covered with some form of grass. The grass was a dark blue and made a slight crunching noise as he took a step. A roadrunner like bird stepped out of a bush, gave a mournful wail, and ran off into the mist.

His magical senses told him that there was nothing there. No door, no grass, no anything. He knelt and tried to pick a blade of grass, but it would not break. His fingers could feel the resistance of the grass, but he couldn't feel the grass blade itself. Almost as if it wasn't really there. Lysion's statement about this place existing between realms in a state of non-existence started to make sense.

They wandered around the area, inspecting everything. When Weston got close to the edge of the mist, Lysion spoke up. "I wouldn't get too close to the mist; it can be very dangerous."

Weston gave the mist a wary look and stepped away.

Jason inspected the door, at least he thought it was a door. It had the proportions of a door but had no doorknob. It stood ten feet tall and four feet wide. It was about a foot thick. He touched it and expected it to feel cold. Instead, he felt nothing. He could feel that there was something there but couldn't feel if it was warm or cold, smooth, or rough. It was as if his fingers had come against a barrier with no texture.

In the center of the door were drawings of three over lapping suns. Steven intently stared at the relief and smiling. "That is very pretty. I have never seen a purple sun before," Steven said, never taking his eyes off the door. The effect on Lysion and Gatron was amazing. Both wore a look of pure surprise and confusion. Gatron's mouth hung open and Lysion simply stared.

Jason smirked. "I told you, I have a special team."

Lysion slowly looked at Jason as if he were coming out of a dream. "Yes, you did." Lysion shook his head and recovered himself. "We must hurry, it is almost time for this place to move." He walked past Steven, giving him a wider berth than necessary and placed his hand on the door in the middle of the three suns. The door started to light up and he stepped back. He motioned that everyone should back away from the door, but they had already had. The mist moved allowing them even more space. A feeling of dread came over Jason and he backed as far away from the door as possible. They now stood thirty feet from the door and if Jason could have gotten farther away from it, he would have.

The door became brighter and brighter, giving off a purple light that was almost blinding. Jason put on his sunglasses, but they only helped a little.

The light in the door began to pulse, then small figures appeared in the door and shot about. The figures grew larger and before Jason could identify them, there was a bright flash. The figures were now spinning around the door like the electrons of an atom. The figures spun so fast it was hard to see what they were. Then the figures started to slow and with a flash it was over.

Now standing near the door were three creatures. To Jason, it was the most amazing thing he had ever seen. Creatures he had only read about in fantasy books now stood before him. A serpent like creature floated to his right, dripping water that vanished before it hit the ground. A three-headed dog stood to the left, growling. Its drool also disappearing as it hit the ground. In the center stood a creature that could only be one thing: a dragon. It roared, spewing flames into the air.

Jason was almost giddy with excitement. A dragon, a real dragon right in front of him. Despite the danger he stepped toward the dragon. This was THE magical creature he had always wanted to encounter.

"Very pretty, but not real," Steven said, breaking Jason's concentration on the dragon.

"What do you mean, Steven?" Jason looked from the dragon to Steven.

"What he means is that there are three entities standing before us. I am guessing that they somehow read our minds to see what creatures we fear. They then took the shape of those creatures," Weston said.

"Very good Weston and Steven. You are essentially correct," Lysion said. "One correction, they did not read your minds. Even for beings as advanced as they are, they cannot truly read your mind. When you saw the spinning orbs, your minds projected what it would expect to see and that is what they read. You must do a better job of shielding your thoughts."

Jason mentally kicked himself. Mistress Nelson had taught him, and eventually his team, how to shield their mind. The mistake he had made was that they only used it when they felt a presence attempt to enter their mind. He never thought that something could simply observe and learn his thoughts. He put up his mental shield to keep anymore secrets from escaping.

Even still, he was disappointed. He had always hoped to meet a dragon. He walked up to the phony dragon and stared at it. The dragon roared but when Jason just stared, it went quiet. Dejectedly, Jason turned and walked away.

"We must start your journey. This site will move soon, and you must be inside before it moves." Lysion slowly waved his hands. The three entities returned to their light form and flew into the door. The door swung to the side, revealing an entrance. Lysion motioned for them to enter and Jason led his team through.

Lysion did not enter nor did Gatron. "We cannot go in as we have only a minute before the door starts its journey to relocate itself. The energies inside are so volatile during its relocation period, our mere presence would set off a chain reaction. Return to this spot in an hour and the door will open. If we are not here when you return, simply wait. It usually takes us only a few minutes to find the door, but sometimes it takes longer."

"How much longer..." The door closed with a great crash before Jason could finish. With the portal closed, his team was cutoff.

"You trust Lysion?" Jason asked Bull.

With my life, Bull responded.

"Considering our current circumstances, that part was obvious." Jason gave Bull a quick look and walked off.

Jason started down the long corridor. Weston followed with his retrieval pole, twice hitting Jason with it.

Jason stopped and grabbed the pole and pointed it toward the ceiling.

"Sorry," Weston said, apologetically.

In the distance, Jason could see a bright light and he felt a light breeze with an occasional gust. The floor was hard pack soil with a top layer of loose dirt. Jason noted the few footprints he could see in the dirt. All were of those wearing shoes until he came upon a set completely different from the others. He stopped and knelt for a closer look. Whoever made the print was not wearing shoes and had rather large feet. From the divots in the front of the toes, the maker of the prints must have had some sort of claws.

"Bull, do you recognize these prints?"

They look familiar but I am unable to place them, Bull responded.

"Could they be from the Zycros?" Jason asked.

Bull thought for a moment. *No, I believe they came from a people that often work with the Meathonians but how they got here, I do not know,* Bull said.

They continued walking until they came to a small clearing. Standing in the middle of the clearing they were confronted by three tunnels. The center tunnel emitted a bright light. Stepping forward he looked into the tunnel to find a large chamber. Jason could see a pool of white liquid on one side, violently splashing about. On the other side was another pool with black liquid. It also splashed about. A wide path split the two pools, but it was not wide enough to keep the two liquids from splashing small amounts into each other. When the two liquids met, a small explosion would occur with a flash of light. This was their target.

Jason could feel the energy from the two pools, almost as if it were searching for his magic. A gust came through the tunnel and Jason could feel a surge of energy surround him. The energy almost felt alive and he struggled to keep his own energy from leaving him and joining the new entity.

He slowly backed away into the clearing. The heat coming from the room was stifling and Jason welcomed the cooler air. He was about to tell the rest what he saw when they heard the crash of the portal door closing. Someone else had come through the door. Jason signaled everyone to go into a side tunnel to hide.

Soon he could hear the padding of feet stop in the clearing. Cautiously, he poked his head out. He spotted two men, both about eight feet tall. They each looked like drawings he had seen of early cavemen except their hands were more like claws.

"What took Lysion so long to leave? He never takes that long," the first man asked.

"I don't know but we don't have much time. If we don't bring energy back, Mistress Tess will have our heads. Now, get your suit on and let's get this done," the second said.

Both men opened the bags they were carrying. Pulling out a full body suit, they quickly suited up. They each put on a hood and were completely covered. The suits were shiny gray and Jason recognized the color as the same as the magical containers Weston had made.

The suits had pockets that bulged. Each man took something out of one of their pockets and started walking into the cave.

"You do dark energy, and I will do white," the first said, his words muffled by the hood.

"Why do I always have to do dark? That stuff is dangerous," the second said.

"Each is dangerous. If either of us screws up, we will end up dead like the other team. Now concentrate."

They moved forward toward the pools.

Jason leaned over and signaled the others to move close, with the hoods the men were wearing and the noise from the chamber, they could whisper and not be heard.

"Are those suits made of Stroth?" Jason asked.

"From the color, I am guessing that they are. If so, they would be impervious to magical energy," Weston said.

The men are Jaanicos, a very non-magical people. They trade in anything they can, including slave trade, if it makes them money. They are a very disagreeable people and do a lot of business with the Meathonians. Being non-magical, they are impervious to the pull of the magic in the chamber, Bull said.

"I'm not sure how they got in, but we can't let them take back any of that energy. Also, I don't want them to know we were here," Jason said, watching the men, he considered the situation, "We might be able to track them back to Tess," Jason said. He laid out his plan. The plan was dangerous and could easily get the two Jaanicos, and them, killed.

Weston wasn't too sure about it.

Surprisingly, Steven didn't have an issue with the plan. "I will help," Steven simply said.

They watched as Tess's two men dipped containers similar to the ones Weston had made into the two pools. The men worked at a very slow pace, taking at least twenty minutes to fill their containers.

Jason could feel the heat from the room and knew the men must be suffering in their suits. When their containers were full, they sealed them, and returned to the clearing. After setting the containers down, both men pulled off their hoods.

"Not sure how much more I can take of this," the first man said, wiping sweat from his brow. His hair was soaked, and he panted hard.

"Just imagine what Mistress Tess will do to us if we fail." The second man pulled what looked like a watch from his pocket. "We need to get the second containers filled. We have only thirty minutes before the door relocates."

"We better get paid well..." the first man said as he put his hood on. Both men trudged back into the chamber, pulled another container out of their pockets, and resumed work.

This was the break Jason had been looking for. Jason and Weston crept forward and picked up the first two containers.

Once back in the shadows, Jason was ready to start the next phase of his plan. "Okay, time to start the fireworks," Jason said as he readied to send an energy burst into the chamber.

Weston reached over and lowered Jason's arm. "I think it would be better if I did this part," Weston said.

Agreed. Subtle is not your strong suit, Bull said.

"I can be subtle," Jason sputtered. Looking at his comrades, it was clear he was not going to win this argument. "Okay, you take this part."

Weston smiled. "Thank you." He crept forward and raised his wand, then sent several miniscule amounts of energy flying into the chamber.

"I could have done that," Jason murmured.

I'm sure you could have, Bull replied in a patronizing tone.

Jason ignored the snipe and watched as Weston's energy flew high above the Jaanicos head. Initially nothing happened, surprising Jason. He wanted to sense what Weston was doing but knew that would trip off the energy coming from the chamber.

Suddenly, the bits of energy changed color, causing the pools of energies to react violently. Both pools started boiling and small explosions went off in the room. Both men tried to roll away from the pools as the explosions continued. One dropped his container and it rolled dangerously near the other pool. Both men looked at each other and ran out of the room, right past Jason's hiding spot.

Both men continued running as a larger explosion went off, sending rocks and debris throughout the clearing. They stopped when they got to the portal door. The noise from the chamber reduced as Weston eased up his energy bits. Jason moved up to the edge of the clearing and tried to spot the two men. "We need to go back and get those containers," he heard one man say.

"We have to leave in two minutes, or we are stuck here. I am not sure which is worse, telling Mistress Tess we left the containers or what the Zycros will do to us if they find we have been raiding this tunnel," the second said.

"It sounds like things are calming down in there. We'll give it another thirty seconds and then, run back in grab what we can, and get the heck out of here." Both men started jogging back to the clearing. Jason scrambled back to where the rest were hiding.

"We need some more explosions in the chamber now," he whispered.

Weston raised his wand and sent more bits of energy into the chamber. The noise level started to rise, and Jason watched as the two intruders peeked their heads around the corner.

"It's getting worse in there, that container you dropped is probably leaking. If those two pools connect, it will wipe this place out," one said.

"Let's get out of here. We can come back on the next cycle."

Jason could hear them running back to the door and he moved forward to watch them. One pulled out the watch like device Jason had seen earlier. The other picked up a small stick. The men must have left it at the door when they came through. Both men had their backs to him, and Jason decided to gamble. He conjured two drones and made them as small as he could.

See, I could have done it, he said to himself, then sent the drones toward the men where they attached to their suits. The drones would only be able to signal their location and maybe send a picture or two back but that was all that he needed.

The man stared at the watch, then said, "Now."

The other touched the stick to the door and it shimmered and opened. Through the opening, Jason could see flashes of colors as if they were traveling through a vortex. The men stepped through the opening and then the door closed.

"They're gone," Jason said to the group. The other three came out of their hiding spots.

"I liked your drones," Steven said.

"Thank you, Steven," Jason said, proud of himself.

"I can show you how to make them better," Steven said.

"Thank you, Steven," Jason said, his ego deflated. He heard noises that sounded like laughter coming from Bull and Weston. Looking toward them, both broke into coughing fits. He frowned at them until they turned away. "Let's get the other two containers and get out of here. It's almost time for Lysion to return," Jason said.

Weston picked up his retrieval pole, extended it, and used it to pick up one of the containers the men had left in the chamber. He quickly sealed it and gave it to Jason. He did the same for the other that had been left. He then used the pole to fill the containers they had brought. Weston worked faster than the Jaanicos but did not seem worried.

Once Weston was done, Jason snapped the containers onto his belt.

"Are you sure that I shouldn't carry them?" Weston asked.

Before Jason could respond, Steven spoke up. "Let Jason carry them, if they leak, they will burn you up. Not Jason."

It was Jason's turn to start a coughing fit.

"Thank you, Steven," was all Weston could respond with.

"Now let's hope Lysion shows up so we can get out of here," Jason said.

They trudged back to the door and waited. After a few seconds, the door opened. They checked to see if the Jaanicos were still there, but they were gone. Jason's drones told him they were traveling.

Ten minutes later, Lysion and his team arrived.

"I see you were able to retrieve the energy but tell me how you managed to return with more containers than when you left," Lysion asked.

"We liberated them from a couple of visitors that we had while we were inside," Jason replied.

"Visitors? In the chamber? Impossible. I waited until the portal was ready to relocate, then left. No one was there," Lysion stated. The look on his face made it clear he did not believe them.

Lysion, it is true. Two Jaanicos were able to enter the portal right after you left and leave just prior to your arrival. I do not know how they were able to do it but, if you station a few warriors in the tunnel and capture the men when they return, I am sure you can convince them to tell you how they did it. Bull stated.

"Old friend, I will do as you say." He turned to Jason and his group, "I am sorry for my words. It's hard to admit that my best was not good enough to protect this site."

Jason understood all too well where Lysion was coming from. "I've been in your shoes before and I understand."

Lysion looked down at his shoes and then back at Jason with a look of bewilderment.

He means, he has been in your situation before and understands, Bull said.

"What an odd saying," Lysion commented.

Jason shook his head and let it go.

"It is time for us to return," Lysion said. With a quick wave of his arm, they were back in Jason's church.

"Lysion, one thing. When you capture those men, they must not be allowed to leave that place until I have taken care of Tess. If they leave, Tess will know her men were compromised," Jason said.

"We had no plans on those men ever leaving," Lysion said flatly.

Weston gave Jason a look but said nothing. The men they had seen would be dead soon and Jason felt nothing. It worried him that two beings were going to be captured, interrogated, and killed, and he was not upset. He wondered if becoming a warlock meant he was becoming less human.

Through a window, Jason could see the sun about to rise. "We need to get going. If the drones locate Tess's hideaway, we will need to move quickly." Jason and the others left by the back door taking care not to be seen and returned to his truck. As they drove away, they passed Reverend Jim out for another walk.

"That guy walks a lot," Jason said, as they drove past the reverend and waved.

"Someday I would like to meet Reverend Jim and ask him a few questions." Weston stared after the man.

Chapter Nineteen

They drove back to Jason's house and returned to the Castle via the mirror. While Weston was confident that the containers would safely contain the energies and block any outside magic from interacting with them, they still took precautions. Using the mirror seemed the safest way to return to the Castle.

Weston and Steven had created a mechanism that would fuse the two energies into a form that he could use. Without actual white and dark energy, they had never tested the device. Now that they had some, they ran it through several tests before stating it was ready for Jason to try out.

They stood in his Testing Room, connected to his room. Jason created an observation deck so those in his room could watch. The deck was crowded with his team, Mistress Nelson, and several medical staff. The form of the Castle floated in a corner conferring with the Mistress. Master Sophia stood next to Jason inspecting the device.

"We don't know if we have the mixture correct, so use as little as possible on your first try," Weston warned.

"Not exactly comforting," Jason replied.

"Maybe I should try it first," Master Sophia said, she looked worried.

Weston shook his head. "We calibrated it for Jason. It would take several hours to recalibrate for you."

"Jason should do it. He knows the magic in the containers," Steven said.

Jason had no idea what Steven was referring to, but he agreed, he had to do it. His drones had reported the two Jaanicos had traveled to a spot, waited a few hours, and were traveling again. Jason guessed that the men were told to go to one spot where Tess's staff would make sure that the men weren't followed, then transport them to her location. This meant they only had a few hours before Tess may become suspicious that Jason had found out about her energy source.

"Steven is right. I need to do this," he stated. "Let's clear the testing room and get this going."

Just as the last person left his testing chamber, Dod walked in. "Don't get yourself killed. I just got used to you being a Senior," she said, giving him a brief hug and left before he could respond.

He gazed after her, a little unnerved by her words.

"Okay, here we go. Please set the room's shields on maximum," he ordered. Shields went up all around him.

"Confirmed, shields are up and at maximum strength," Weston replied from the observation deck.

Jason set his own shield at maximum. It wouldn't protect him if something went wrong, but it would protect the Castle.

"Here goes nothing." He reached down and pressed a button on the device. He could feel an energy feed into him and strained to let in only a little. The device beeped, signaling that it had shut off the flow of energy. He kept the energy inside of him contained but was straining to do so and started to lose control. He allowed a little to escape to reduce the pressure. The energy bounced throughout his body and a sense of euphoria over came him. Jason laughed as more energy escaped and coursed through his body. His mind filled with ideas and it seemed that as fast as he could come up with a problem, his mind solved the issue.

"This is wonderful," he exclaimed and threw up his hands in victory. It was as if he was supercharged and everything suddenly became clear. Tess no longer worried him; he had a plan for her. In fact, he felt no worries in the world. He was now a super warlock and it dawned on him that he should now be the leader of the Castle. Mistress Nelson was capable but in his new state, he would be ten times the leader she was. He ran through issue after issue in his mind, solving each problem with ease.

He let out a laugh and fired his wand into the air, wiping out the Castle's shield. Debris rained down but he ignored it. Surprisingly, his wand stopped communicating with him. He would have to take care of that later as he couldn't have an insubordinate wand. Maybe a little more of the energy would make it easier to talk to his wand.

Before he could push the button, Gail entered. He expected her to bow to him. He was almost upset when she didn't but realized it would be a while before others would understand his change. Once they knew, they would bow.

"Jason, can you please drink this?" she asked.

He almost refused her request but what could it hurt? He tossed down the drink and was about to command her to get him some food, when the euphoria feeling left as fast as it came. The shock was almost too much for him and he dropped to his knees.

He could hear someone yelling, *Jason, can you hear me?* and realized it was his wand.

Yes, I can hear you. What just happened?"

The energy you absorbed took over. I didn't like the person you became, his wand said.

"Jason, are you okay?" Gail looked down at him with a look of concern. Others came in and all seemed worried.

His head pounded and he pressed his hands against his temples to help with the pain. Gail handed him another drink which he swallowed quickly. The pressure in his head slowly eased. She put her hand to his head and the rest of the pressure and pain disappeared.

Dod offered her hand and helped him up. He felt tired and a shiver ran through him. He checked his internal reserves, and they were low. He could feel his internal energy raging war on the last of the energy he'd received from the device. His body quickly cleared, and he felt better.

"Are you okay?" Dod asked. "I thought I was going to have to come in here and knock some sense into you."

Jason looked around and the damage to his testing chamber was immense. Did he do that?

"What happened? I took just a little bit of energy and I felt like I drank a thousand cups of coffee," he said, trying to comprehend the damage he had done.

"You started screaming non-sense. You seemed to think you had all the power in the world and knew the answers to every problem," Dod said.

"It felt like I did have an answer for every problem. Even stored them away."

Jason reached out with his mind to the memory structure he'd built. While he marveled at the structure, most of his answers were rubbish. To the problem of Tess, his plan stored away was simply to 'Kill her.' Not exactly helpful.

"It started out well," he said. "I built a memory structure to store issues and answers. Unfortunately, most of my answers are useless. Except," he stopped as he came across one answer that looked promising. "I think I have a better way to use the energy and it may explain something we saw during the last attack."

"Steven and I were monitoring you. We had the foresight to include sensors in the device. As soon as we saw your energy interact with the energy from the device, we knew our ratio was wrong. Too much dark energy. Luckily, we also built a safety switch into the device to shut down if it detected too much energy being used," Weston said.

"Is the device still usable?" Jason asked.

"Yes, even with the revised ratio I don't think you should try again today," Weston said, a worried look on his face.

"I agree. You are recovering but you need some rest before trying to use that energy again," Mistress Nelson said firmly.

"On that part, you're right. I'm not ready to try that part again. But I think I have an idea now how Tess is using the energy and I need to test that out."

"I really think you need some time," Mistress Nelson argued.

"Probably, but we need this working. We need something to level the playing field and we don't have a lot of time. Once the Zycros capture Tess's men stealing the energy, it won't be long before Tess knows about it."

Mistress Nelson frowned, but after a minute. "Okay, but at the first sign of trouble we are shutting this down."

"Good, but I need one thing. Weston, I need to be able to adjust the ratio as I am using it," Jason said.

"Easy, but we can't fix that here," Steven said.

"Steven's right, we need to take it back to the lab. It will only take a few minutes, but we need some of the lab's equipment." Weston grabbed the device and headed out the door with Steven right behind.

Thirty minutes later, Jason stood in his testing chamber while Weston showed him how to adjust the energy ratio.

"Good luck," Weston said and left the room, closing the door behind him.

"Here goes nothing," Jason muttered to himself, then activated the device. He felt energy flowing from the device and a giddy feeling started to come over him.

"Adjusting the ratio," he called to the group. He kept reducing the amount of dark energy until he could feel the energy wasn't affecting him. The energy now felt foreign, cold, but it worked. His own energy refused to mix with it no matter what he tried. He fired a burst to see how it worked but it was clear that the two energies wouldn't merge, even when fired from his wand.

I am unable to merge the energies as before. I can fire bursts like that and they will be very powerful, but it takes a lot more effort on my part. I will not be able to fire many bursts, his wand told him.

Okay, let's try something different, he told his wand.

Following the idea in his memory structure, he created a shield but kept it a foot away from his body. He pressed the button on the device and felt the energy start to flow. He caught it and redirected it to his shield. Once the energy from his device hit the shield, it became rigid. The shield looked impregnable. He walked around the room and the shield moved effortlessly with him. It took a little effort to concentrate the energy into his shield, but he wasn't worried about that.

This is much easier than firing but it is still work for me, his wand said.

Jason tried maintaining the shield without his wand's help and it took most of his concentration to maintain it. Eventually he found a balance of him maintaining the shield leaving his wand for firing.

"How are you doing in there?" Weston's voice echoed through the chamber.

"I'm doing well and so far, my experiment is working but I need to test the shield. Castle, please start with an easy shot then increase intensity," he said, not taking his eyes off his shield.

"Understood, first shot when you are ready," the Castle said.

"Ready."

An energy burst hit the shield having no effect. Jason could feel a little push from his shield.

"Again, but stronger."

In response, another burst hit his shield. The shield was unaffected but once again he felt a push.

"Again, but stronger," he called out.

Another burst hit, pushing Jason back a step. His shield wavered as he almost lost his concentration. After a second, it was ready to go.

"One more. Needs to be a really strong shot," he said and prepared for what he knew was coming.

A burst came slamming into his shield. The resulting jolt knocked him over. His shield wavered then disappeared as the jolt broke his concentration. He had his answer.

"Enough, I'm shutting this down. I have what I need," he said as he turned off the shield and the energy device. From the gauge on the device, he'd already used a fourth of the energy.

Weston and several others entered, including Master Kien. Kien had taken over tracking the drones attached to the Jaanicos. His presence meant that either he found Tess's hiding spot, or his drones had been discovered.

"I'm hoping you have some good news for me, Master Kien." He paused, "Good news that doesn't include bath salts."

Kien gave him a quick smile. "As for the bath salts, someday you will learn. As for everything else, we will discuss later."

Jason nodded. "Thanks. I look forward to our discussion." He turned to Mistress Nelson. "I think my experiment went well. I know the basics of what Tess is doing."

"It was a very strong shield. That last blast should have destroyed the shield and hit you. It destroyed the shield, but you look fine," Mistress Nelson said, impressed.

"Actually, it didn't harm the shield. Had I been able to keep my concentration on feeding the energy into the shield, it would have been fine," Jason said. "The shield created by the energy is rock solid. The problem is that it is not flexible, and it takes a lot of concentration to maintain. Even with my wand helping, it would be hard to maintain the shield and fight."

"Then the key is to break someone's concentration when battling an opponent with such a device," Kien said.

"Correct, the impact from the blast caused me to lose my footing and break my concentration. I think this is what happened to Tess during our battle. When I fired and hit her shield, she stumbled and fell. That broke her connection to the shield. I'm betting she probably hit her head when she fell."

"The shield is like being in a steel box. You can't dent it, but you can knock the person inside around by slamming into it," Dod mused.

"Correct. That is what happened during the attack at my house. One of the attackers was dedicated to maintaining the shield. When my maid slammed into their shield it knocked him over and he lost his concentration," Jason said.

"I saw that you weren't able to mix your energy with the energy from the device," Weston said.

"I was hoping to use the energy to augment mine, but it didn't work. I could use my energy to guide the energy from the device but not mix it," Jason said. "I tried several different approaches, but nothing worked."

"We might be able to help on that. Now that Steven and I have seen how you use the energy, we may be able to improve how it is delivered to you," Weston said as he removed the device from Jason's waist.

The device wasn't heavy, but Jason felt relieved when it was gone. He hadn't realized how tired he was, but now that the adrenaline effect of the testing was wearing off, fatigue set in. He could feel the same from his wand. "I need to sit down and get something to eat."

"Everyone, back to my office. I will have food brought in and we can hear what Master Kien has found," Mistress Nelson announced.

A brief time later, they were sitting in Mistress Nelson's office. Jason wanted to hear what Kien had found but as soon as the food was brought into the room, he knew the news would have to wait. As he ate, several discussions started but he wasn't in the mood to talk and took the time to enjoy the Mistress' office. Hers was a truly magical office and he was like a kid in a candy shop, watching things disappear and reappear. His eyes darted around the room trying to take in everything that he could.

After finishing his last bite, he rejoined the conversation.

"Master Kien, what did you find?" Jason asked, and the group went quiet.

"I'm not sure this is the right place to discuss this," Kien replied.

He was tired of all of the secrecy; it was time to put things out in the open. "We need to start trusting one another," Jason said.

Kien looked to Mistress Nelson who nodded. "Okay. Your drones found Tess's location. They reported where the Jaanicos landed and immediately detected sensors in the area. Before they could be discovered, they executed their self-destruct sequence and stopped reporting. A little while later, we sent one of our best operatives to the location. He did some searching and found what we believe to be is her Castle."

"Tell me about her Castle," Jason asked.

"The operative got only a quick view and had to leave before he was detected. He said he saw high walls and a heavily guarded entrance," Kien said.

"Was the Castle white with gold trim?" Jason asked.

"It was. How did you know?"

"Tess always loved Castles, she joked that when she had her own, it would be white with gold towers," Jason said, smiling.

Jason could remember Tess saying those words, a big smile on her face. It was one of the happiest times in his life. Jason's smile turned to a frown as he remembered what he had to do. Tess was dead, the woman he was battling was someone else.

"Based upon the information received, I'm not sure a full-frontal attack would be wise. A lot of people would die," Kien said.

"No, Tess will have thought through the most obvious attacks and built contingencies for them," Jason said. He pondered the situation. He glanced at Steven as an idea formed. "We have to come at Tess from a completely different direction and I think I know how to do that, if Steven will help."

Steven looked around the room. "I want to help."

"Good, I need a few things and we will meet back here in two hours to go over the plan," Jason said.

He stood and started to walk out of the room when he received a warning that there were two magical entities at the backdoor of his house. He quickly Stepped back to the hallway that led to his backdoor.

How they got through his house's defenses he didn't know, but he was worried. He powered up his shield and prepared for battle, the now familiar blue tint covering everything he saw.

"Not sure what is out there but time to find out," he said to himself. Redirecting his senses, he determined that the two intruders were simply waiting at the door. His senses scanned the two and they were familiar. He was even more surprised when one rang the doorbell.

"I guess it's time to welcome my visitors," Jason mused, and walked to the back door.

As soon as he saw the two through the window of the door, he lowered his wand and quickly opened the door. "Grandpa. Grandma.

You're here!" Jason said, as his heart leapt. He quickly hugged his grandparents as he fought back the tears. He was surprised when they felt real. He almost expected his arms to pass through them.

"Easy tiger, we are still getting used to these forms," his grandfather said.

"Grandpa Wes, is it really you? You're actually here?" Jason asked excitedly.

"Yes, well mostly here," his Grandfather replied. "If you could give us an energy boost it would speed things along."

Jason reached over and gave each some of his energy. They didn't require a lot.

"You are coming along nicely in your power. In another couple hundred years, you could challenge Salis, I mean Mistress Nelson," his grandmother said. Jason raised an eyebrow. "I knew her before she became Head Mistress. I have some stories of when her and I would raid the Castle wine cellar," she said, giggling.

"I would love to hear them sometime. But first, tell me, what would she say if she saw you here now?" he asked.

"That I am not sure of. The Castle will know soon, if it doesn't know already."

"We can cross that bridge when we get to it. For now, can you come in the house? I would love for Catie and the kids to meet you," he said. His grandparents were back, and he couldn't contain his excitement.

"Sorry, we will have to return to the forest in a couple of minutes. We are still learning how to maintain our form and it will take a while. Until we can, it would be best to keep this a secret. Eventually the Castle will send someone to check out the situation and I want to be prepared," his grandfather said, trying to pat Jason's back but his hand went partially through his back.

Jason was disappointed. He very much wanted his family to meet his grandparents. "Before you return, what can you tell me about when you repaired the realm barrier?"

"Power, immense power is what I remember the most about it," he paused. "We didn't repair the barrier as much as we just redirected the power back to itself," his grandfather said.

"Redirected it?" Jason asked.

"Yes, the barriers are really huge streams of energy interwoven to create a barrier. The attack freed a couple of streams and they were flying around like firehoses. With my wand's help, we redirected them back into place. Touch and go for a while but my wand," he paused looking sadly at the wand on Jason's belt, "figured out how to manipulate the streams."

A nervous look came over his grandfather. "The amount of energy in the barriers is beyond imagination. A dozen streams could wipe out a city the size of New York in a matter of seconds. We saw hundreds, if not thousands."

"How did they loosen the streams?" Jason asked, intently. Something told him this was important and related to Tess.

"Well, they were firing continuously at the barrier with no effect. They had an interesting spell they thought would bore through the barrier. It was like spraying a garden hose at Niagara Falls and had no effect. We didn't know it and fired a counter spell at the same time as someone detonated a bunch of explosives. The two spells combined and exploded, that combined with the explosives loosened two energy streams. The streams killed nearly everyone nearby and many of those that survived the explosions were wiped out as the streams started flailing about. Luckily, Salis and I were far enough away from the initial blast, but our shields were wiped out. She went to mop up the rest of the enemy and I attempted to fix the barrier. It took us nearly an hour to reattach the streams. By the time we were done, everything within a half-mile around us was wiped out."

This was making sense and he now had an idea of what Tess was trying to accomplish.

"Grandpa, could you redirect a stream to harness the energy?" he asked.

"Once a thread is in place, they are extremely stable. Loosen one and they are uncontrollable. Firehoses out of control are dangerous but imagine a firehose twenty feet wide and spewing pure energy. Even if you could redirect a stream, I'm not sure what you could redirect it to that could handle that much energy. Not even the Castle could handle that much energy," he said.

Jason was missing something, and this was related to Tess somehow. An idea came to him, "Could you tap into one of the threads? Bleed off the energy you need?"

"Hmm, I hadn't thought of that. It may be possible, but I will have to think about it. Sorry, but we must return to our energy form. We will come back tomorrow, and we can talk more about this. Hopefully, I will have more information for you."

Jason hugged his grandparents and watched them return to their orb form. Other orbs appeared and started swirling around. He would have to ask who they were the next time he talked to his Grandparents.

To answer your question, yes, it is possible to tap into one of the energy streams, his wand said to him.

Jason almost jumped as it was rare that his wand spoke without him asking it a question.

Is it easy?

It is dangerous. You would have to loosen a thread first. When you reattach it, you must keep a connection. Only a wand could do it and it would be stuck, possibly forever. But the warlock could then harness as much energy as he or she could handle, the wand said.

How do you know this? Jason asked.

Reconnecting the streams was a battle. The streams were whipping around spewing energy. There was no spell we threw at them that made a difference. At one point, a stream was about to hit us, and we jumped, landing on the backside of the stream. To reattach, I connected to the stream and maneuvered it back into place. When I attached to the thread, I could feel the power trying to go through me to your grandfather. I wasn't sure that if I let it, he would be able to resist the power, so I prevented it. As we were reconnecting the stream, I almost became stuck in it. I would have become a permanent power source for your grandfather. We did the same for the second stream, but I made sure to barely connect to the stream, even still it almost killed me. I hibernated for a week afterwards, his wand said.

How powerful would my grandpa have become?

He would have been able to wipe out the Castle in minutes. Twenty Lion's Hunters would have had no chance against him, his wand said grimly.

We better make sure that Tess does not discover this, Jason said.

When your grandfather wrote up his report, he left out most of the details about redirecting the streams. The Headmaster at the time had all information about the event destroyed. Many asked your grandfather about it, but he never talked about it, his wand said.

Chapter Twenty

Mistress Nelson called a leadership meeting to discuss their next steps. Through several sources, they confirmed that the white castle they'd tracked the Jaanicos to was where Tess hid. So far, they had told no one the true location. Instead, they had leaked the location as being on a nearby realm on a desolate planet.

It was clear to Jason that the Mistress was still worried about spies in the Castle. She even refused to tell Jason where the additional information that confirmed Tess's location came from. The fact that she withheld information from him meant she either suspected him or someone near him. Jason couldn't blame her. There was a lot at stake.

Before the meeting, she filled Jason and Kien in on her thoughts. "I am afraid there is evidence we still have a spy in our midst." She looked around her office as if the spy could be in the room. "During the meeting, we are not to divulge the true location or the real attack plan. We will give them a plausible version that is in-line with the real attack. We can't tip off Tess that we know her true location."

"We expected something like this and have an alternate plan that should satisfy everyone in the room," Jason said.

"And when we find out who the spy is, I will enjoy extracting as much information and pain as I can," Kien added.

"You will need to get in line behind me and I doubt very much there will be anything left of the spy once I am done," Mistress Nelson said.

"Hmm. That could be a problem," Kien said. "Please excuse us as Jason and I want to run through our plan one more time."

Two hours later, Jason and Kien returned and stood in Mistress Nelson's office watching the invited masters file into the room. He looked over each one, trying to figure out if they were the spy. It was a fruitless effort but one glance at Kien and it was clear he was doing the same. Several rows of chairs had been set out in front of Mistress Nelson's desk. Her office now looked much larger compared to his previous visits. Jason assumed she must have used magic to enlarge it for the meeting.

Mistress Nelson stood at her desk with Kien on one side and Jason on the other. Once everyone was in and settled, she began.

"Dax, Solis, secure the room," Mistress Nelson ordered.

Her huge guards bolted the door shut and cast a shield over the room. She then used her wand to cast several other spells to further secure the room. Jason had never seen anything like the precautions she was using. Several of the attendees marveled at the shields and whispered to their seatmates. Jason's senses were ready, and he heard all the comments. Generally, they were about how impressive her shields were or wondering about why there was that much security being implemented. One master glanced at the shield but said nothing. His nonchalant attitude seemed out of place amongst the group and Jason decided to keep an eye on him. He couldn't place it but something about the man felt wrong. He didn't dare scan him, but his gut told him to be careful of him.

"Thank you for coming as we have some very serious items to discuss. Before we start, I need to warn everyone here that what we are about to discuss is top secret. You are to tell absolutely no one unless specifically authorized. That includes spouses, families, and friends. Your very life may depend on this."

"Is there a specific reason for this? I thought we'd found all of the spies," a master asked, the one Jason was watching.

"You are right. We have caught all the spies, but Tess is a very resourceful person and does know the Castle well. We are concerned that either she, or one of her spies, left listening devices in the Castle that we haven't detected."

Jason was impressed. She was very convincing in her response.

She waited a moment to see if there were any more questions. "Now to business. We have found where Tess and her followers are located. We will attack her hide out and end this business once and for all."

Mistress Nelson stepped away from her desk and waved her hand. An image of an old Castle covered in moss was displayed. The Castle was set into an old forest with a small moat. Various beings, some human, most not, patrolled the area. Jason almost laughed when he saw the image. Tess wouldn't have been caught dead in that Castle unless it was a last resort. Something that old and dingy wouldn't be something she would live in. Only those who had been close to her would know this.

"As you can see it is heavily guarded on the outside. Mostly by non-humans. Inside is where Tess's personal guards are located. They are less powerful, but they do have one thing on their side."

Mistress Nelson waved her hand and the image changed to the scene from the battle at his house. The image zoomed in on the four attackers behind their shield, their shield taking multiple hits.

"They have developed a shield that can protect several people at the same time and is hard to get through. As you can see in the video, it takes one person to maintain the shield, but it can protect several others. Luckily, one of our research teams has discovered a spell to disable the shield. Instructions on how to use the spell will be disseminated just prior to the attack," Mistress Nelson said.

The master Jason had been watching raised his hand. "Shouldn't we get that information now? I think we need to be better prepared."

"Master Keneg, I appreciate your concern, but the spell is not quite complete. The team is still working on improving the spell. Once it is ready, all teams will get plenty of time to practice."

"Then what is the plan of attack here?" another master asked.

"Jason, would you start?" Mistress Nelson asked.

"Yes. In a recent battle with Tess, we used aerial bombing which was initially very effective. We are working with an ally that has built a two-stage aerial bomb. The first part of the bomb explodes and can temporarily dissipate any magic in a small area. The second part of the bomb continues on and explodes on impact or if it detects strong magic. We will start with aerial bombing to disrupt their security on the ground. We will add smoke bombs to the mix to help confuse their soldiers and give us cover for the next phase."

He waved his hand and a new image appeared. It was an image of him in mid-air. "We will then use a similar technique where my team will Step above their shield then free-fall toward it. Once we get close, we will use a similar technique to temporarily dissipate any remaining shield, pass through, then either Step to a safe location or use magic to land. Dangerous, but we have been practicing and it should go smoothly. Here's a demonstration."

Jason waved his hand again and the image started moving as he dropped through the air, a bomb-like device fifteen feet below him. The device hit a shield, there was a flash of light, then a large hole appeared. Jason passed through the hole and Stepped away, disappearing from view. It had taken Kien and Jason an hour to make the video with over twenty jumps. He'd collided with the fake device several times and had bruises still healing from making the video.

The crowd of masters started talking, most saying, "better them than me."

Before anyone could ask a question, Jason continued. "Once inside and under the cover of smoke, we will open the main gates. We have information that the shield covering the entrance is disabled temporarily to allow the doors to open."

Kien took it from there. "Once in, my teams will break into groups. One will concentrate on capturing or killing Tess's troops. Other teams will have specific targets to cripple any defenses they may have setup. I will lead a select team that will pair with Jason's team and our mission will be to remove Tess."

"When will we receive our assignments?" Master Sophia asked.

"Our sources tell us Tess has a meeting of her direct reports at her Castle in three days. That is when we will attack. We will give final assignments the day before the attack," Kien replied.

"We want to start preparing for the attack. From the information we have, we have recreated her Castle on a remote realm. When you leave this meeting, you will be given the location of the training site. We want all teams to report to the site as soon as possible. Once you arrive, you will not be allowed to leave until the attack," Jason said.

"Our masters will be sequestered for several days. Is that wise?" another master asked.

"We understand that is a risk, but we have only one shot at taking Tess out and we need to get this right," Jason replied.

"Please meet with your teams and prepare them," Mistress Nelson ordered. "This will be a very deadly battle. Tess has proven to be a worthy adversary and we expect casualties. You are dismissed." She nodded to her guards and they unlocked the door while she removed her security shields.

The masters looked at each other and slowly stood to file out.

When they all had left. "Get them ready tomorrow and we will attack the next day," Mistress Nelson said.

"Will do," Kien replied. "Any idea who the spy is?"

"We will be monitoring everyone that attended, and we should know by tomorrow," Mistress Nelson replied. "Jason, can you stay a minute?"

"Of course."

"I guess that's my cue to leave," Kien said. He nodded to Jason and walked out.

"What did you want to talk to me about?" Jason asked, curious.

"I was wondering if we could meet at your house tonight. I would like to talk with your grandparents."

Jason stood for a minute considering the request. "We can, but I want to make sure that by doing so I am not putting them in danger."

"For now, there is no danger. But what they have done has caused alarm with the Castle and most likely the other leadership once they find out. This is uncharted territory. The decision to prolong lives such as Rita's was not a popular one," Mistress Nelson said.

"Why not?"

"There was a debate about life after death and what this would mean. It also didn't help that the first few that became extensions of the Castle either suddenly faded into oblivion or in one case, exploded almost killing two others. We have also seen some serious mental instability in many of the subjects."

"I can understand your concern but for this meeting I need your word that you and the Castle will not do anything. You're just there to talk," Jason demanded.

"You have my word," Mistress Nelson said.

"Then be at my house at eight p.m. and I will have my grandparents there," Jason said then left. He immediately returned to his house and went to his woods. To his surprise, his grandparents were holding hands and walking in his forest. He called to them, "Grandpa! Grandma!" He jogged to where they were and hugged them.

"So glad to see you. Your grandfather and I were going for a walk to enjoy the beautiful weather," his grandma said.

"Yes, it's a beautiful day," Jason said, taking in the sun and the colors of the trees.

"Why do I get the feeling you are here for something important," his grandfather said.

"Um, yes." Jason took a deep breath, "Mistress Nelson and the Castle know about you two and probably the others. She wants to meet tonight."

"While I would love to catch up with an old friend, I am not sure she wants to reminisce about the old days," his grandmother said.

"She has given me her word that tonight's meeting is only about getting together and discussing the situation. You will not be in any danger," Jason said.

"For now, but what about later?" his grandpa asked.

"I don't know. But we knew this day would come. Considering everything we have going on with Tess, I think the Castle has bigger issues to deal with right now. Can you be at the house at six? I would like you to spend some time with Catie and the kids. Mistress Nelson will be there at eight."

"We will see you then," his grandpa said.

Jason hugged both and returned to his office.

That night his grandparents arrived and spent two hours with Jason and his family. His kids quickly took to their great-grandparents and enjoyed spending time with them.

Just prior to Mistress Nelson's arrival time, Jason interrupted the conversation. "Sorry to bring business into the mix, but I need to know what happened at the house next to the forest."

"Dad, do you want us to leave?" John asked.

"No, I think you and your sister should hear this also."

His grandmother looked to his grandfather and began. "Your grandfather's sister, Angela, was also a warlock and she's in the forest. Now that we know the process works, we will bring her back next. Twenty years before she died, she married a non-magical human from earth. He eventually learned that she was a warlock and accepted it. Being around her, he picked up some power." His grandmother stopped and looked to her husband who continued.

"We left instructions for her on how to join us in the forest. We even left a note that said to memorize the instructions and then destroy them. Unfortunately, when Angela cast the spell to become part of the forest, she left the instructions on her desk. Josh found them."

"But he wasn't a warlock and from what little I know, you have to be fairly powerful to use the spell," Jason said.

"That's true but what we didn't expect was that my sister's wand decided to help him. When Josh picked up her wand, it spoke to him. The wand convinced him that it could help. In reality, her wand loved her deeply and couldn't understand why she left it. Her wand's real plan was to use Josh's power to help it join Angela in the forest. When the two cast the spell, Josh realized the wand was betraying him. They battled and we thought the two had died," Grandpa Wes said. He took a drink of water to compose himself.

Jason looked at his grandparents; both were distressed. Jason realized what had happened next, "They weren't dead, were they?"

His grandparents nodded in agreement. His grandfather continued. "It turns out they were stuck in the house, barely alive and hibernating. When you and Tess moved into the house, it caused a reaction in the forest. Power started coursing through it a little faster, mainly due to two potentially powerful warlocks nearby. When you took walks through the forest, it caused all sorts of disruptions. We suspect that they were feeding off that power, getting stronger," Grandpa Wes said.

"During our walks, why didn't you reach out to me?" Jason asked. All those years, they were there, and he didn't know.

"We tried but neither of you could see or hear us," Grandma Sue said. "As it was, there was little you could do for us until you became a warlock."

"Over the last several years, what was left of Josh and Angela's wand woke from hibernation as one. They went after anything with electricity, thinking it would power them. At first, it was harmless stuff but when you returned as a warlock, it caused a great stir in the forest. Magic flows through it now like it did when we were alive. Unfortunately, it also caused that thing to become more powerful. By then, they had become mentally unstable and insanity set in. They forgot who and what they were. If you hadn't stopped them, they would have eventually killed someone," Grandpa Wes said.

"Why didn't you warn me? I might have been able to do something," Jason said.

"We didn't know. Angela was trying desperately to help the two of them. She kept telling us that she was making progress and hid the truth. However, I think she was deluding herself."

Jason considered their words for a moment. The use of the spell to extend life continued to be a bad idea in his mind. He loved having his grandparents back, but he worried there was a price to be paid at some point. He tried to change the subject. "Grandma Sue, what happened to your wand?"

"Before I died, I explained to my wand what I was doing. It didn't like my plan and when I died, so did it," Grandma Sue said. "It was a good wand, and I respected its decision."

They went quiet for a moment and Jason gave his grandparents a minute to collect themselves. "I have one more question. Who else is in the forest?"

"There are only a few others besides Angela. They are ones that also figured out how to extend themselves, usually to help out someone or exact revenge. One has been in the forest for centuries. The problem is each used a version of the spell that was flawed. As long as they remain as an entity in the forest, they will live forever. If they become like us, they will go insane within days," Grandpa Wes said.

"They were amazing warlocks when they were alive and are quite knowledgeable. They can be of aid to you in the future. We can teach you how to talk with them," Grandma Sue said.

"Well, there is one thing I need to tell everyone before Mistress Nelson gets here," Jason announced. He took Catie's hand. "Catie and I are engaged and as soon as this thing with Tess is over, we are getting married."

"Congratulations!" his grandparents said in unison.

"We haven't told anyone because we were afraid that Tess would come after us if she found out. Until she is gone, we can't tell anyone," Jason said. "But I thought you should know."

All conversation ended when Jason was alerted that Mistress Nelson was asking permission to enter his home. He kissed Catie then went to his warlock office and received her as she stepped through the mirror.

"Welcome to my home, Mistress Nelson," Jason said with a slight bow.

"This was much overdue, and I am sorry that my first visit is because of business," she replied.

"I know Catie would love to have you over for dinner. Hopefully, we can make that happen," Jason said. "Follow me."

He led her back to where Catie and the others were. Along the way, they encountered Bull who gave a single bark.

"Nice to see you also, Bull," the mistress responded.

Walking into the living room, everyone stood as Jason made the introductions.

"Mistress Nelson, this is my girlfriend Catie, my son John, and my daughter Kira," he said, introducing each.

"Jason, you have a lovely family. You must be quite proud," Mistress Nelson said, beaming.

Jason smiled, "Yes I do. I'm a very lucky man."

"Please excuse us as I know you have some things to discuss and the kids have homework to complete," Catie said.

Catie and the kids left, and Mistress Nelson turned to his grandparents. "Wes. Sue. It is so good to see you."

"Salis, it is good to see you too," his grandmother said with tears in her eyes. She quickly crossed the room and hugged Mistress Nelson. His grandfather did the same. After a minute they all sat down.

Mistress Nelson finally broke the silence. "I was heartbroken when I thought I had lost you two. While I am happy to see you, I am also very concerned."

"Salis, why?" Jason's grandfather asked.

"After the spell to extend life was discovered, the Castle worried that it would get into the wrong hands. It only published an early version of the spell to deter its use. That version has severe side-effects. Most subjects lasted only a few weeks and dementia was a common issue. Several died a violent death."

"And you were worried that it would happen to us?" His grandmother asked.

"Yes."

"Then don't worry," his grandmother said. "I immediately saw the flaws in the spell and corrected them. There are still limitations to my version of the spell, and we have, at most, ten-to-fifteen years before we finally pass."

"Oh, thank goodness," Mistress Nelson said, starting to cry. "I was so worried."

Mistress Nelson and his grandmother held each other for a minute. Jason was fighting back his tears and his grandfather sobbed silently.

"I don't mean to interrupt, but you mentioned the Castle would be here tonight. I have to wonder how it will react to this," Jason said.

Almost as if on cue, he was notified of the Castle's request to enter his home. He granted permission and started to walk back to his office when the Castle appeared in front of him.

"Thank you, Jason, for allowing me into your home. I do apologize for not using the proper entrance," The Castle said.

Something about the way the Castle spoke irritated him. He wasn't sure why it did, but he needed to stay calm. When the Castle had first appeared in front of him, its image had slowly morphed between different forms. Jason noted the morphing was much quicker now. "Do we need to bring you up to speed on what was discussed?" Jason asked.

The Castle hesitated for a moment. "No, as you have surmised, I have heard the conversation."

Mistress Nelson stood. "Do you have any objections?"

"While I believe that Master Sue has addressed many of the issues of the original spell. We don't know if she was able to fix them all. That said, we are fine with the ten-year limitation."

"Good," Mistress Nelson said.

"But," the Castle started, "this needs to be kept quiet. If information gets out about the two of you, everyone will want to do this. Until we are sure there are no complications, we must hide your existence and no one else can use the spell. Also, if we see any early signs that the spell still has issues, we will not hesitate to end this experiment."

This was too much for Jason. "You will hesitate, and it will be discussed. You are not going to execute two people because you think you see a problem."

"I think this issue is too personal for you to make a proper judgement," the Castle said.

"And I would say the same about you," Jason said flatly.

"And how would you know?" The Castle asked, putting an emphasis on "you".

"Your appearance. It's obvious you are agitated and upset. I'm guessing that many of those that are part of you would have loved to have a few more healthy years. To say goodbye, make amends, right wrongs, and generally end their life in peace. I would say that jealousy is raging in you as we speak."

The image of the Castle was now continuously morphing. An image would just barely form before it started changing to someone else.

"I..." the Castle started to say then started frantically looking around. "I..."

"Stop!" the Castle yelled, and its image froze.

They all watched as the image took huge breaths. Its whole body moved in a desperate attempt to breathe. It grabbed onto the back of the sofa to steady itself.

"Are you alright?" Mistress Nelson asked with genuine concern on her face.

"Yes," the Castle said slowly. "Perhaps there was some truth in what Jason said." The Castle took one more large breath. "I apologize. I did not realize this subject would affect us so much."

"Apology accepted," Jason said. "If we are agreed on the terms."

The Castle looked to Jason's grandparents then to Mistress Nelson. Finally, the Castle looked back to Jason. "Agreed."

"Good," Mistress Nelson said. "May be now we can catch up?"

"I'm afraid I must leave," the Castle said and disappeared.

Mistress Nelson surprised Jason by casting a shield. "That should take care of anyone trying to eaves drop. I have to say that right now, I think we should be concerned about the mental stability of the Castle."

"Agreed," Jason replied.

Chapter Twenty-One

Two days later, Jason and his team found themselves in a thick jungle. Each quickly camouflaged themselves using a new spell that Steven and Weston had created. Jason signaled Dod to lead the way to Tess's location. She studied the locater and then slowly made her way through the jungle. Aware that there may be boobytraps, she made slow progress. Everyone behind her followed in her exact footsteps. It was slow going and it took them nearly an hour to come to the edge of the jungle.

Past the edge stood a large castle. To simply call it a castle did not do it justice. The walls around it were several stories high with the castle itself being at least ten stories. The stone walls looked to be white marble and the roofs of the buildings glittered gold. Every window held a gold tint preventing anyone from seeing inside. In the center, stood a tall cylindrical building with a large glass viewing area. The place was huge and must have covered at least twenty acres of land. Jason marveled at the structure. It was definitely beautiful and nowhere near the dark, foreboding fortress you would expect from a group trying to destroy the universe. A strong shield, unlike anything he had seen before, covered the castle.

A moat filled with some sort of black sludge surrounded the castle. The moat stood a good hundred feet wide and was nearly a two-hundred-foot plunge to the sludge. The only obvious way in was a drawbridge, wide enough for two buses to drive across. It was the only place where the shield did not block access. Soldiers with wands and several large creatures he recognized as Zaxens guarded it. The soldiers and Zaxens each kept to their own side of the drawbridge.

Zaxens were large creatures that walked up right but with heads like warthogs. They were extremely strong with very tough skin, fast but not very agile. They loved battle, having no issue with killing anyone, including their own kind. Zaxens traveled in small bands that avoided one another. Accidental encounters usually ended in blood baths. Jason wasn't sure of Tess's thought process for using the creatures as guards. A day without killing was a day wasted to them.

A steady stream of soldiers came and went into the castle. All arriving soldiers were searched thoroughly. When one started to complain his backpack was being destroyed, one of the Zaxens attempted to remove the soldier's head with an axe. The soldier ducked and fired on the creature, sending it over the edge and into the moat. The warthog-like creature screamed as it fell and when it hit the black sludge, it exploded into flames and was gone in an instant. Apparently, if the plunge didn't kill you, the sludge would. This caused a battle between the two groups, with the Zaxens almost happy to join the fight.

This was Jason's cue to send off their specially designed bots. The bots camouflaged themselves and flew down to the bridge. Crawling along the bottom of the drawbridge, they made their way into the castle. The bots were to get into the castle and infiltrate the security system.

"Enough!" came a commanding male's voice booming from the castle. Fighting stopped immediately. Whoever the voice belonged to was powerful enough to command the respect of both sides. Each side separated. Those too injured to continue vanished, presumably to an infirmary. Both groups resumed their patrols as if nothing had happened.

While they waited for the bots to get into place, Jason's team backed up and started setting up a landing spot for the troops they would need for the assault.

Weston placed additional spells that would hide them and the new arrivals. Gail sprayed some lotion over her uniform and then sprayed some in her mouth. She then handed another bottle to Jason.

"Those things have a good sense of smell. The potion in this bottle will hide our scent from just about any creature, even a Lion's Hunter," she said, obviously proud of herself.

He sprayed his uniform and took a squirt in his mouth. He almost vomited, "Beasts hell, that's awful," he said struggling to keep is breakfast down.

"Sorry, I must have forgot to put honey in that one," she said, laughing as she walked off to spray down the others.

During training, they'd learned to make a potion called Warlocks Remedy. He remembered to add honey to combat the awful taste only after Gail had drank hers. He hadn't realized that she still held a grudge and laughed it off.

Troops consisting of warlocks, wizards, and several other races started arriving. After fifty arrived, Weston warned that any more might be detected. His spell could only cover that many. Jason didn't think fifty would be enough, but he really had no clue how many of Tess's followers were in the castle. Once the battle started, then the rest of the troops could come in.

Soon the bots notified them they were in place. They could disable the alarm system but could not disable the castle's shield. That was where Steven came in and Jason led him back to the edge of the jungle.

"Steven, do you think you can get us through the shield?" he asked.

Steven stared at the shield then at Weston. "I like the spell you did, Weston, it is very nice."

"Thank you, Steven, that means a lot," Weston said. "Can you help us with this shield?"

"Yes, it is a very nice shield, very colorful. I can make a hole in it for a short time."

Jason decided they would send a scout team, disable the shield, and figure out where Tess was. Jason, Dod, Gail, Katrina, Rita, and Bull would go, along with four more Masters. It would be close if they could get that many through. Weston would stay behind to bring in more troops and get them ready.

"Our goal is to stay undetected until after we have disabled their shield. Do not engage unless absolutely necessary," he warned. Each of the team nodded that they were ready.

Jason checked to make sure he was ready. Several of his warlock energy packs, courtesy of Weston and Steven, sat on his belt along with several rock grenades. All fully charged and ready to go. He carried as much internal energy as he could hold.

He gave the signal and Steven opened a small hole in the shield. The group Stepped through, landing in an equipment room and immediately spread out.

"Check your camouflage to make sure it's in place," he ordered.

Inside the castle, it was easier to communicate with the bots which sent them a map of the castle. The bots were mining the enemy system for any and all useful information. They sent the castle's floor plan and Jason cast an image of it.

"Okay, here is the command center." He pointed to a spot that coincided with the viewing area they observed earlier. "Here is the computer center which looks like it controls everything. We need to knock that out. This looks to be their power generation center; we need to take that out also."

Rita looked over the map and frowned. "Usually, power centers are in the basement and this is right in the middle of the castle. It's also right below some sort of large laboratory. Something doesn't look right here."

"Agreed, I will investigate the lab. Rita, you take Carlson and Jill and head to the power station, Bull is with me. The rest will take out the computer center, Dod will lead that group. Let me know when you are in place and ready," he said.

When everyone agreed. "Please be careful. We all need to go home alive and well."

With that, the groups left.

"Bull, you are with me, fully camouflaged. We don't engage unless we have to." He double-checked his camouflage and headed toward the lab. Something about the lab stuck with him. It was large and according to the data, gave off a fair amount of power. Intuition told him that the lab was maybe more important than the power station. They crept through the hallways, only encountering a small number of guards. It was slow going but they made good progress. The inside of the castle was as beautiful as the outside. Each painting on the wall looked spectacular. Suits of armor shined, and they found beautiful carvings everywhere. Tess must have spent a fortune, assuming she paid for them.

As they moved forward, something nagged at Jason. This was too easy. There were no cameras, few security sensors, and little foot traffic. The guards they encountered were weak and clueless, they could have been taken out with almost no effort.

But as they approached the lab, the level of security rose. They had to bypass a couple cameras and circumvent a pressure-sensitive floor. Guards with dogs patrolled the area. Whatever was in the lab must be valuable. Finally, they were close to the lab entrance. Two very large security guards stood on either side.

It will be difficult to get by them without tripping an alarm, Bull said, evaluating the situation.

I should be able to stay camouflaged while getting near them. I can take one out without magic. Taking two of them with no magic is not going to happen unless you can take out one, Jason responded.

I have an idea. Start your approach, when you get close wait for my signal, Bull said.

And what will be your signal? Jason asked.

You will know it when you see it, now get going! Bull ordered.

Jason took a breath and thought about the best way to approach. His camouflage had improved to the point that he could not be seen as long as he moved slowly. He watched as a pair of guards with dogs walked by. Gail's potion was working well as the dogs did not pick up his scent. On a hunch, he slid in a couple of feet behind them and followed them to near where the two guards stood. The guards with dogs turned down a corridor, leaving Jason about ten feet away from his target. Now all he could do was wait and see what Bull had thought of.

He stood wondering when a lone security dog without a guard came trotting up and barked at the guards.

"Another dog got loose. Shall I call it in?" one guard asked.

Before his partner could respond. the dog transformed into Bull's real form and half swallowed the guard. A sickening crunch came as Bull bit down. The muffled screams quickly silenced. The other guard stood dumb-founded but then reached for his wand. It was Jason's turn and his training kicked in. He pulled energy as Rita taught him and time slowed to almost a stop. Walking quickly, he grabbed the man from behind, putting the sharp edge of his wand up under his rib cage from the front. Pushing up, it collapsed his lung and cut his pulmonary artery. Collapsing the lung prevented the man from screaming. He would die soon due to the cut artery, but he snapped the man's neck to end it quickly. He had never been so brutal in his life and tried not to look at the man's lifeless body in his arms. This would hurt later. Releasing his energy, time resumed. Bull looked at the dead guard and then Jason.

You are learning, Bull said.

They pushed through the doors dragging what was left of the two guards. They hoped to not run into anyone. But luck was not going their way as they found two elderly men in lab coats standing wide-eyed. When Bull spit out the first guard, one of the men vomited.

"Make any move, try to set off any alarm, and you will be next," Jason warned quietly.

He pointed his wand at both men, waving to them to move away from the computer station they were manning. Bull, changing into his partial form, approached them with a slight growl. The man who had puked now sprouted a growing wet stain on his pants.

Both men scrambled to the back of the room as Jason stepped toward what they had been looking at.

"Holy sheep dip," was all he could manage. Chained in the middle of the room was a female Lion's Hunter and her cub. Both looked at him and the female growled. Jason approached slowly but stopped when he sensed an unusual shield around them. Whatever it was, it was draining their energy. He tried to sense it, but any energy that went near the shield was sucked in.

He turned back to the two captives. "What are you doing to them?" he yelled. The two creatures were suffering, and he couldn't take it, not even for a Lion's Hunter.

"We're not sure," the first captive said. Bull growled, baring his teeth. "Honest, we just run the machines until the sensors tell us to stop."

"Tell me how to turn it off now. Anything goes wrong and you will be an appetizer for my friend here," Jason said in a slow, deep voice.

"Just pull the two levers back slowly," squeaked the second captive.

As Jason pulled the levers back, he could see the two animals relax. He approached the female and cub slowly. The female growled. "Touch the cub and I swear you will die."

"I'm not here to hurt you. Actually, I'm going to release you as we are about to take this castle. But I need your word that when you are released you will not attack me or my soldiers."

"You have my word. We may even join you, but why should I trust you?" the huntress asked.

"You wouldn't be the first Lion's Hunter I have given my word to and kept," he said, hoping he could end this soon. They were running out of time.

"You have met another and survived?" she asked incredulously.

"Yes, he had a long scar on his face. It would be too long of a story to tell now. Just know that I keep my word and I may call him to help us," Jason said.

The lioness laughed. "I know that one. He is this one's sire." At that, the cub looked at his mother then back to Jason. "I gave him that scar and he deserves another, but if he comes, I may forgive him."

Jason sighed, the last thing he needed was family drama from a group of Lion's Hunters, but his thoughts were cutoff.

"Jason, we are in position. We only have a couple of minutes before we are found," Dod said via her wand.

At that moment, he heard voices outside their door wondering where the guards were.

"Dod, Rita, cut the shield and the power now," he yelled as the first of three guards burst through the door. The guard was promptly bit in half by Bull, returned to his full size. The lights went out for a second and Jason fired a blast that killed the other two guards.

He turned and fired blasts removing the chains from the Lion's Hunters. He could hear his troops flood into the castle and for the second time he made a call to his nemesis, the male Lion's Hunter. He sent an image of the female and the cub with the message they needed help.

"I sent a message to him to join us, time for you to either run or fight," he said to the Lioness.

The cub looked up. "We fight, I have a debt with these people. Just stay out of my way."

The Lioness smiled. "Just like his sire. Now we fight alongside the Laciter." She sprung as more guards tried to pour through the door. She landed on several, sliding through the door, taking part of the wall with her. The cub pounced on two more guards.

Jason almost felt sorry for the guards. Almost.

Bull bayed a war cry as he ran into the action. Jason's mental link with him almost broke. Bull was in full battle mode, the rage that poured out of him almost stifling. The three worked well together, shredding the enemy. Tess's warriors were in shambles and started running.

"Jason, our troops are in and we are destroying them. This should be over in no time," Dod yelled. He could feel the excitement in her voice.

"Jason, this is too easy. Tess is too smart and powerful to let this happen," Rita said.

Jason agreed but what was her plan? He turned to where the Hunters had been kept. Looking up he saw a metal disc about twenty feet wide. It was the device that had drained the energy from the captives.

"I need to see what the viewing area looks like where Tess is now," he yelled. Dod quickly sent an image. It was huge and at the top was several similar discs only much larger.

"Ah, crap," he yelled. Tess had laid a trap. He knew what her endgame was. He sent a message to his troops. "All, do not, I repeat, do not enter the main area where Tess is located. It's a trap. Get them sealed in that room then await further orders."

He headed to the viewing area. He knew how to stop Tess, but it could be a one-way trip for him and anyone that went with him. He encountered several of Tess's troops who tried to ambush him, and he took them out with ease. They had so little power they were almost not worth fighting. He tried his best not to kill any of them. They were being used as fodder to make it look like it was a battle. Something was wrong, Tess never threw away pawns in her plans needlessly. To let so many die was not her typical plan.

As he walked along there were many of Tess's troops on the ground. Most were dead, several severely injured. Several of his troops were injured but only one dead. He healed a couple of the more severely injured troops but stopped when his medics started coming through, led by Gail.

"Heal everyone just enough to get them back to the Castle. That includes the enemy. Most of these idiots don't even know what they were fighting for," she ordered.

She looked around at the carnage. "Jason this was a blood bath for Tess. They didn't stand a chance. By the time we knew they weren't very powerful we had killed a lot of them. Damn senseless." Gail looked mad and frustrated.

"I know what Tess's plan is but her troops being wiped out is not something Tess would do. Something or someone else is involved and I need to stop this. I will leave all of this to you," he said and ran off.

He arrived to find the entrance to the viewing area packed with his warriors. Some had minor scuffs, but all had plenty of energy, each amped up due to the battle. Unfortunately, that was exactly what Tess wanted.

Dod ran up and gave him a quick hug. "Thank god you're okay."

"Thanks, I'm glad to see that you are okay too. Where is Bull and the Lion's Hunters?"

"They're guarding the other entrance. Bull and the three Lion's Hunters quickly found the enemy unable to fight back and pulled back. Not sure where you found the lioness and the cub, but she's giving the other lion a dressing down even I could learn from. I think I almost like her," Dod said smiling. "Are we ready to attack? I don't think Tess will be as easy to take down as her troops."

"We are not going to attack, that is what Tess wants," Jason said, staring at the large double doors leading to where Tess waited. "I will have to enter first..."

"If you think you are going to do some stupid-martyr shit, forget it. I'm going with you," Dod said flatly.

"Okay but stay behind me." He put his hands up when Dod started to protest. "Not because you can't defend yourself. It's because when I spring my trap, you do not want to be in its way." He lowered his voice. "I don't want you dying also. I can't afford to lose you," he said, trying hard to not look her in the eyes.

Dod relaxed. "Okay, but at the first sign of trouble, I'm killing Tess," she said.

"I don't think you are going to get that chance. That's my job. But keep your eyes open. There is something else going on and I think I know what it is," he said, surveying his troops.

He needed to let his troops know what was about to happen. Addressing them. "I am going in and if everything goes as I think it will, there is about to be some large explosions and I expect this castle to be leveled. If this starts to happen, don't try to save me, get the hell out because that is what I will be doing. To be clear, if you don't get out, I'm not going back in to save you."

His troops looked shocked and worried, most simply nodded. Gail looked stunned and Weston put his arm around her.

"Is there anything we can do to help?" Weston asked.

"Oh yes, I said I was going in first, but I didn't say not to follow me. When you hear my cue, I need everyone to come in but stay to the walls. Don't go near the center of the room. Once the fireworks start, get the heck out. Until then, I'll need as much firepower to cover me as possible," Jason said.

Be careful. There is someone else in the room with Tess who is powerful. We are ready to help, Bull said, his mental link re-established.

He spread his thought to the Hunter's Lions. *Actually, it's you and the Lions she truly wants. The amount of power she can harvest from you, along with the knowledge my wand possesses, is her true goal. Everything and every person here are expendable to her except you four and me,* Jason said.

Jason had finally put it all together. Tess was never interested in the One Realm theory, but led her followers along because she needed an army to make her true plans happen. Power was her true motive. To get it, she laid down a trail for him to follow. Jason wasn't sure if the person that Bull detected was part of her plan or not. He was about to find out.

He opened the door and took a step into the room and quickly surveyed the situation. Trying not to be obvious, he scanned for the devices Tess would be using to harvest energy from anything magical that fell into her trap. He easily found multiple around the ceiling. One step more and he would be in range of those devices.

"Tess, show yourself." His voice boomed with magical enhancement. His voice echoed throughout the hall but there was no answer.

"You abandoned me and your family. The kids hate you now and so do I," he said, knowing she would not be able to control herself.

"No, they don't. They love me. I made all these sacrifices for them!" came Tess's voice from a far point in the room. Her voice lowered as she probably guessed that Jason was prodding her to do something stupid. "Soon they will be part of the most powerful family in all of the realms!" she yelled. She removed her camouflage and Jason located her standing on the other side of the room, just outside of her device's range.

Standing next to her was someone who could only be a Meathonian, his toad-like appearance giving him away. Tess suddenly relaxed and shook her head as if coming out of a stupor. Her image changed for a split second, but it was enough for Jason to realize what must have happened.

Jason stood shocked. Tess must have died and used the same spell as his grandparents to extend her life. Her image flickered again as her face went from being calm to angry then back. Her image kept flickering and she looked like she was fighting to regain control. Clearly, she must have used a flawed version of the spell.

After a moment, the flickering stopped and then Tess looked at him. She then did something that completely confused him. She gently tugged her right ear. That had always been the sign she used to use with Jason to tell him to play along with whatever she said. Usually, it was to get them out of an awkward social situation.

"Who's your bodyguard?" Jason asked, trying to compose himself.

"I am no bodyguard, and I am in charge," the Meathonian said. "My name is Neath and soon you will work for me or die."

Before Jason could respond, he felt a nudge and found Master Kien and Rita standing next to him.

"The only person that will die today is you," Kien warned.

Kien put his hand on Jason's shoulder and connected his energy with Jason.

Don't say anything. Tess is undercover, working for us. We need to kill Neath and get Tess out of here before it is too late, Jason heard in his head.

When this is over, you have a helluva lot of explaining to do, Jason replied, trying to control his emotions.

"This is your last chance. Join me and we will rule all the realms. Just walk to me, all will be forgiven," Neath said.

"I don't think so. Your plans don't include me or any warlock for that matter," Jason said. He was trying to delay long enough to come up with a new plan to get him and Tess out of there alive.

"I am interested in what you think my plans are but first I may need a little back-up, Keneg?" the Meathonian called.

"Here sir," Keneg responded, appearing a few feet from him.

"Ahh good. Now I have my two best pets with me," the Meathonian said. As he turned toward Tess, Jason saw Keneg also tug his ear.

Through his connection with Kien, he asked, *Keneg also?*

Yes, was the response from Kien.

"Now back to my question: What exactly are my plans?" Neath asked.

"My guess is that you stumbled upon the One Realm group and saw an opportunity. If you could harness the power of a realm border stream, you would be invincible. You would have the power to rule not only over the Meathonians, but just about anyone else. You only had to play along long enough until you had the tools necessary," Jason said.

"Right so far. Go on," Neath said, smiling as if he was quite pleased with himself.

"I suspect Tess recognized your plans early on and played along until her plans could complete."

"True, I severely underestimated her at first. She almost ruined my plans," Neath said, giving Tess a hateful look.

"Actually, she has already ruined your plans. You just don't know it yet," Jason said, smug at having figured out Neath's plans. "I know what you are up to and it won't work. It's time to stop this farce. Give yourself up. There is still time," he said. He knew Neath wouldn't stop but he had to try.

"How about to save Catie? Would you come to me for her?" Neath said.

Jason felt like a brick wall had hit him.

"What have you done to Catie?" he yelled. Once again, he was one step behind. Frustration built and Kien put his hand on Jason's chest to keep him from going after Neath.

"What are you talking about Neath? Our agreement was that we leave his family alone," Tess said, taking a step back.

"She is safe, but if you want her to remain that way you need to come to me," Neath said sounding very triumphant. Turning to Tess. "Our agreement has changed. You have been too soft on the warlock and I now realize you have probably been working for them. I am in charge now."

"I need to know that Catie is safe," Jason said, to buy more time until he could figure things out.

"As you wish. Harold, bring forth the prisoner," Neath ordered. The room went silent, no one moved. Neath looked around, a panicked expression on his face. "Where is Harold?"

Neath pointed his wand at a man standing near him. "Where is Harold and the prisoner? He was supposed to retrieve Catie." Neath was in full rage, the pure power coming from him caused everyone around him to back away.

Two men holding a third appeared next to him. The two men kneeled, then stood. When the third did not, they kicked his knees out. He collapsed to the ground. "We found him trying to escape," one of the men said.

"No, I wasn't. I would never do that." The captive man screamed, looking around nervously. It was obvious he was buying time until he could figure out how to escape.

"Just one question," Neath said slowly. "Where is the prisoner?"

"Well, sir, there was, uh, an unfortunate accident," the man squealed as one of the two guards put a wand to his neck.

"Last time, where is the prisoner? If she is not here in the next ten seconds, I will splatter your guts across this floor, while keeping you alive to see it happen," Neath said, completely red in the face.

The prisoner dropped his head. "She is dead."

"You killed Catie?" Jason yelled, his rage took over and everything turned blue. He could hear Bull trying to tell him something, but he was losing his link. All he could think about was Catie was dead.

"You fool. What happened? Where is she?" Neath yelled. He watched Jason from the corner of his eye, his confidence waning. He looked nervous and scared.

"When we went to get her, she thought we were attacking the kids. One of her kids knocked down one of my men and he lost his wand. Catie picked up the wand and started firing. She killed two of my men, but one of our soldiers panicked and fired on her. She died instantly. Before we could do anything, some wizards showed up and took her body. The kids disappeared with the warlock guards."

"Idiot!" Neath blasted the man. He exploded with bits of him going everywhere. The men holding him dove out of the way. Unfortunately, one of the men dove into the center of the room. His energy instantly pulled from him, dropping dead on the spot.

Jason fired on Neath, more to release excess energy. It flew through the chamber hitting Neath. The devices sucked most of the energy from the blast, but some still hit him. He wasn't seriously hurt and seemed more surprised and frightened that Jason could still hit him.

Tess and Keneg turned their wands on Neath at the same time as Neath turned his on Tess. All three fired and Neath and Tess went down.

"Tess," Jason yelled. Jason's world was upside down. Everything he had done had led to Catie's death. Worse, the woman he once loved and then vilified, was actually a hero.

"Jason, we got to get to them," Kien yelled.

"You're right but afterwards you need to tell me why I shouldn't kill you for what you did," Jason yelled.

Kien nodded then ran around the edge of the room to try to get to Tess. He stopped when he saw Neath rise.

Neath was bleeding heavily and looked shaky but had a firm grip on his wand.

Jason now had a chance to exact revenge. The blue tint around him turned dark as he took one of the energy devices from his belt, released the shield containing dark energy, and threw it into the center of the room. Neath's eyes went wide as the devices sucked up the dark energy.

Jason had seen too much death, too much hurt. Now that Catie and Tess were dead he knew it was time to end it all.

The discs above were now heavily loaded with dark energy. They started to spark and warp as the dark magic threw them out of balance. A chain reaction was imminent.

The first disc blew up taking out a side of the roof, raining rock and debris on everyone.

"No! Do you know what you just did? We are all dead," Neath yelled as the discs around the room started to overload, energy firing off in every direction. One hit one of Neath's followers, vaporizing her.

Raising his wand, Jason fired at Neath, the shot knocked him against the wall, and he slid to the ground. Before he could get up, Jason fired again but a wave of energy from the devices sent his shot off to the side killing one of Neath's minions.

Until then the troops of both sides had simply watched the exchange. The death of Neath's minion knocked both sides out of their stupor. Immediately both sides opened fire. But the discs were sending energy wave after energy wave, playing havoc with the battle. Most of the shots from both sides either dissipated, blew up, or were diverted. The remaining power devices causing havoc on anything magical. Another disc exploded taking out another wall. The place was about to collapse. Time to end things.

Jason yelled at his troops, "Get out and save yourself."

Weston yelled back, "You too."

"I need to get to Neath," Jason yelled. He tried to find a way across to Neath but between the energy waves and parts of the building falling, he couldn't move. Suddenly, an energy tunnel opened with a path across the floor, just wide enough for him. Jason looked back and saw Weston and Steven. Weston had thrown a shield over the two to protect them from errant energy and the collapsing wall. Steven was reaching out with his hands. Jason could feel Steven manipulating the magic all around him.

"Hurry," Weston called. "We can't hold for much longer."

Jason, followed by Kien and Rita, sprinted forward into the opening. On the other side he could see Neath and he started firing as fast as he could. Some hit Neath's shield but one went through his shield, knocking him down again. Neath returned fire, slamming into Jason's shield. The three cleared the tunnel and looked back just in time to see a huge section of the roof headed toward Weston and Steven. Just before it would hit them, Mistress Nelson stepped out of a portal, grabbed the two, and the three disappeared. With their disappearance, the tunnel collapsed.

"I'm going to have to get Steven a wand for that," Kien said.

"Agreed," Jason said.

Turning back, they saw Neath had crawled behind a large piece of the collapsed roof. With Steven's tunnel gone, the pulses from the remaining discs resumed slamming against their shields. Knowing what he had to do, he removed another energy storage unit on his belt and threw it toward the discs, releasing more dark energy. The discs eagerly consumed the energy and the waves subsided for a moment. It was time to end Neath and his plot.

Kien ran to Tess who was now transparent. He picked up her body and Stepped away.

Jason continued to fire at Neath, but he kept ducking behind cover. Several of Neath's soldiers arrived and started firing on him. Jason jumped behind a large chunk of the roof as his shield was weakening under their fire.

"Oh no you don't," Rita yelled as she started firing on the newcomers.

Jason watched as Neath kept peeking out to see where Rita was. He gathered everything he had and when Neath came up to fire, Jason fired, using everything he could and hit Neath dead on. Neath slammed against the wall and dropped to the ground. His wand clattered away from him.

From his view, Neath was dead, but Jason wanted to make sure. As he was about to fire a final shot, a man appeared and started to pick up Neath's body. Jason was in full rage but a shout from Rita pulled him partially back to his senses.

"You. I have been looking for you!" she yelled, firing on the new arrival with every bit of energy she could muster. Two guards tried to help the new arrival, but two shots from Rita and they went down quickly. She then turned her attention back to the man. He fired back, hitting Rita, but she kept firing. Whoever this was, Rita was willing to die to kill him.

Just then, one of the discs fell from the ceiling, forcing Jason and Rita to jump out of the way. The man opened a portal and Stepped carrying Neath.

"No!" Rita cried and dropped to the ground, translucent and fading fast. A final disc was still working, and it was pulling energy from Rita. Jason grabbed Rita and pulled her as far away from the energy fields as he could. He needed to get her energy, but his store was too low. He looked around for anyone to help but with the energy fields, no one could get to him. He decided to take a chance, either this would work, or Rita would die. Using his last energy device, he connected it to Rita. For a second nothing happened as the device drained into her. It was a tremendous amount of energy, but it didn't seem to be enough. Just as he was losing hope, her body solidified. She wasn't whole and she needed more energy, but Jason was out of energy devices. With what little energy he had left, he opened a portal and sent Rita back to the Castle.

From across the way he could hear Dod yelling for him. "Jason, get out of there!"

"I just need Neath's wand," Jason yelled and watched as Dod was nearly killed by another chunk of the roof. She Stepped just in time.

He wasn't sure why, but he knew that if he could get Neath's wand, it could help prevent the war between the Zycros and Meathonians. Searching, he saw it and leaped over a large piece of the ceiling. Jason grabbed Neath's wand, preparing to Step. But the final collection disc sent wave after wave of energy which pounded him. All around him the castle walls were buckling. All fighting had stopped as everyone was trying to get out and save themselves. The building was about to collapse, and he had only one hope. Timing the waves, he opened a portal to the Castle, then tried to Step between waves.

He could see Mistress Nelson through the portal beckoning him to come, but as he Stepped, he was hit by a huge wave of energy. The image of the Mistress disappeared, replaced with a chaotic view of different scenery, his portal was out of control.

As before, he tried everything he could to control the portal but with no luck. He seemed to be popping in and out of different realms. He could feel his wand trying to steer his portal and Jason poured as much energy as he had left into his wand to help it. Some of the most unusual images he had ever seen flew by. Dinosaur-like creatures flew by replaced by brightly colored fish with razor-sharp teeth. Barren landscapes with the bones of huge creatures appeared then disappeared, replaced by steaming oceans. Finally, the view solidified on a huge black mountain and he was heading straight for it.

Help me! His wand yelled. Jason pulled as hard as he could to turn and they bounced off the side of it several times, his shield saving them. The view changed to a snow-covered hillside and he found himself in a collision course with it. He tried to turn but had no energy left. He felt his wand go silent, it too had nothing left.

A sense of peace came over him. This was it, his death, and he released control of the portal. It didn't matter anymore, Tess and Catie were both gone. The hurt washed over him, and he just let go. It was time for the pain to stop. Time to stop being a warlock and just go home. His portal hit the top of the hillside and everything went black.

Chapter Twenty-Two

Jason found himself in a dark place, which surprisingly, didn't bother him. He could feel cold coming from somewhere, but he also felt a soft warm breeze blow over him. There was a distant buzzing, but he just ignored it.

He didn't know if he was dreaming or dead, but he didn't care. The darkness around him felt wonderful and he just wanted to slip into it and disappear. There was no pain, no pressure, just blissful sleep. He just needed to ignore everything else and all would be fine. He took a deep breath and settled into the darkness.

Tess is dead, he heard as a jolt shot through him.

Tess hadn't abandoned her family after all. She had gone undercover and sacrificed herself to save the realm. He cleared the thought from his mind. It didn't matter anymore, time to join her.

Once again, the darkness overtook him. All of the hurt and pain began to subside, but the annoying buzz got closer. Another warm breeze floated through and he just relaxed into it.

Peace. The darkness was taking him.

Catie is dead, another jolt went through him. Catie had fought hard thinking his kids were in trouble. She had killed two of Neath's soldiers but had been killed by another. She had predicted that Jason becoming a warlock would be the death of her. The pain from the thought was more than he could bare. He tried to ignore the thought. The women he loved were dead, he would join them, and hopefully they would forgive him.

The annoying buzz was now very close, and he recognized it as the pain currently flowing through his body. His body was repairing itself, but it wasn't complete.

"Why can't I have some peace? I just want to sleep," he cried. He tried to fight it, he just wanted to slip into the darkness. But thoughts of all that had happened kept coming back, the battle at the castle, Catie's death, and Rita nearly dying.

Another warm breeze floated through and he tried to relax into it. Sleep would come, it had too. There was nothing else left for him.

The buzzing grew louder then went silent. With the silence, the pain his body was enduring slammed into him like a freight train. It wasn't the worst pain he had ever dealt with. Killing Master Jenkins had seen to that. Still, the pain made sleep impossible.

With the return of his pain, so did his sense of hearing. To his surprise, he heard something very large breathing on him. Someone wanted him to live and he was about to make that someone very sorry.

He opened his eyes, but they would not focus. All he could make out was the blurry image of something huge directly in front of him. He knew he should be worried but wasn't. With any luck, whatever was in front of him would take his pain away for good.

The image backed away and he heard in his mind, *It's about time you woke. I have been keeping you warm all day and I do have much better things to do.*

Um, was Jason's only reply. How do you reply to something like that? Jason thought. He tried to shake his head; he couldn't even die right. The shaking sent streaks of pain through his body and he stopped. He waited while the pain slowly subsided and he could think again. Jason decided he needed to see what was talking to him and sent energy to his eyes to heal them.

After a minute, his vision cleared. He blinked several times, then the blurry image came into focus. In front of him was the head of a giant golden dragon. It backed away and reared, sending flames into the air as it roared.

The dragon lowered his head back down to Jason, *Welcome warlock to my planet. You may call me Darthe.*

ABOUT THE AUTHOR

Stone Keye lives in south Louisiana with his family and a menagerie of animals. He has spent most of his life in various roles in IT and continues to look for his next challenge. Meanwhile he enjoys spending time with his family, working his dogs and horses, and working on his house.

www.ingramcontent.com/pod-product-compliance
Lightning Source LLC
Chambersburg PA
CBHW022003170626
46808CB00001B/271